Lizzie doesn't know what she wants from life, but she's sure it's not the attention of her suffocating boyfriend, RJ. A chance encounter with a group of women on the day of the local Pride parade leads her to meet the wild, free-spirited Kerra. Lizzie begins to realise she's crazy about Kerra, but how can she come out in a small town where prejudice is rife and even her own mother thinks being a lesbian is wrong? Can Lizzie find herself without losing everything else in the process?

Published by
NineStar Press
PO Box 91792
Albuquerque, New Mexico, 87199
www.ninestarpress.com

Warning: This book contains sexually explicit content which is only suitable for mature readers.

Print ISBN #978-1-945952-16-6
Cover by Natasha Snow
Edited by Elizabeth Coldwell

FINDING LIZZIE

KARMA KINGSLEY

DEDICATION

Momma
An inspiration, even without trying

Brother Bear
My heart, my soul, the tether to my sanity

ACKNOWLEDGEMENTS

J-pop
I'd be dead without you. Literally. You constantly save me. In bars, in colleges, in life.

CHAPTER ONE

Tears streamed down her face as she threw a handful of clothes into a flimsy Hefty bag. The ruffling plastic seemed to echo in her ears as she shoved whatever was in reach inside. She pushed past her yelling boyfriend to the bathroom and knocked everything off the countertop into the bag in one fell swoop.

"Beth, you're being unreasonable. We've been together for four years. You can't just up and leave." He was making perfect sense, but she didn't care. She was done being convinced into her relationship.

"Watch me." She threw the Hefty bag over her shoulder and then headed toward the door, but he stood in front of it, blocking her path. "Move, RJ!" She attempted to push past him, but he had at least six inches on her.

"Listen to me, Beth. This is the best thing for us. This is our future, and it's a good one." He pleaded with her, his ever-logical tone pushing her closer and closer to the edge.

"Move, RJ." She was nearly screaming at him, as if volume could make her tiny frame more intimidating. She could just bet the upstairs neighbors were sitting with their ears pressed to the floor, judging her and laughing at her tantrum.

"Fine." He held his hands up in surrender and moved out of her way. "Take some time and think about what you're throwing away."

He had meant for the words to soothe her and encourage some bit of rationality, but they just infuriated her further. She shifted her weight beneath the overstuffed plastic bag and grabbed her keys off the end table. "I don't need to think. I'm done."

She barreled out of the door and to her car, throwing the ill-planned bag of random items into the backseat. Sliding behind the wheel of her savvy, environmentally conscious car, she willed herself not to burst into tears. *You're fine. You're doing the right thing. He doesn't make you happy.* She coaxed herself into believing that she was making the right choice, that she couldn't keep being railroaded into staying with a man simply because she'd invested so much time. When would her thoughts and feelings come first? She wasn't happy, and she hadn't been happy for almost as long as she could remember.

She straightened up behind the wheel of the car, feeling a bit more confident in her decision. She sucked in a deep breath, letting herself believe that all it took was the turn of a key to make the impending feeling of suffocation go away. *Just start the car, Elizabeth.*

She allowed herself one last look at the building in front of her before starting her car. Then she drove off down the road, leaving the last four years of her life in the rearview mirror.

She drove for nearly an hour, fighting every urge to turn back and second-guess herself before finally gathering the courage to whip out her phone and make the call. Letting out a regretful breath, she hit one on her speed dial and felt her heart pick up speed as she waited for an answer.

"Elizabeth Bridges, I know that you have not done what I think you have done." Her mother fussed in her ear, obviously having already talked to RJ.

"Mom—" She tried to explain, but the effort was futile. Her mother was a dog with a bone.

"Don't you *mom* me. Wherever you are right now, you turn right back around and go home, Beth." Even through the static of the phone, the condescension rang clear as a bell in Elizabeth's ears.

"Mom, you don't understand."

"Don't I? You left a perfectly good man. A doctor—"

"A resident," she corrected. She wasn't going to let her mother pull the doctor card. Not this time.

"A doctor-to-be, that treats you right. That loves you. That—"

"Accepts a job around the world and expects me to just pack my bags and serve at his feet?" she challenged. She had known her mother wouldn't understand. As much as she loved her, they lived in two different worlds. Her mother lived in a world of her own creation where

2

everyone who walked a righteous path was happy and found no fault with life, while Elizabeth lived in the real world. The real world, where her relationship made her feel suffocated and miserable.

"You're being dramatic, Beth. He's following his dreams, and as the woman who loves him, you should be supportive." Her mother's tone took on that belittling edge she never ceased to go a day without.

"Well, what about my dreams? What about me?" She pleaded with her mother, for once, to understand where she was coming from.

"Me, me, me, me, me. Could you be any more selfish? Do you even know what your dreams are? You've been switching majors for the last five years, Beth. It's clear that you have no idea what you want, and it blows my mind how you ended up with such a grounded man in the first place."

"Thanks, Mom, always nice to have your support." Elizabeth was quickly regretting making the phone call. She wasn't ready to hear the blunt criticism of her every failure. As expected, her mother had begun to make her feel small and regretful of leaving the one thing that made her significant. RJ may not have made her happy, but he made her some sort of second-generation hero in her mother's eyes.

"You have my support, honey, but I want better for you than I had, and a successful, grounded man like RJ is as good as it gets. I just don't want to see you throw it away because you're afraid of a little move." Her mother's sincerity touched her, almost making her forget her former irritation.

"I know, Mom, but it's not just that..." She hesitated, wondering if she could bring herself to say the words out loud. "RJ. He—he just doesn't make me happy." She felt the tears well in her eyes again as she said the words. She knew how ridiculous it sounded. Four years down the road and the perfect man doesn't make her happy. What more could she possibly want?

"You're just angry, Beth. Come over, sit down, and cool off, and you'll see how crazy this is."

It was true. If she went over to her mother's house and sat down and had a chance to think, she would almost certainly go running back into RJ's arms. But that's not what she wanted.

"No, Mom. I'm just going to drive for a while. I need to sort this out on my own."

"Fine, but be careful. They're having some sort of heathen festival in the city today, and you don't want to get caught up in any of that mess."

Elizabeth rolled her eyes. A heathen festival to her mother could mean anything from a few tattooed teenagers to a Satanist cult sacrificing virgins. Her mother had been born and raised a black Southern Baptist woman. In her eyes, everyone was a heathen. "Sure thing, Mom."

"I love you, honey."

"I love you too, Mom." She hung up the phone and continued to drive, never checking to see where she was or how far she'd gone. She wanted nothing more than to get as far away from her problems as she could.

She was so focused on her great escape, she hadn't taken the time to notice the blinking gas light on the dash until her car sputtered and spat and refused to move forward. She tried relentlessly to force the car to restart, but she'd killed it. Starved it to death.

"Damn." She climbed out of the car and kicked at the wheels. It was her own fault, but she'd still punish the car for letting her forget to fill the tank.

A quick look around reaffirmed her need to deliver another kick to the car. She recognized nothing. She clasped her phone in her hand and considered who to call. She wasn't sure where she was, and even if she had been sure, she didn't want to see her mother or RJ, but she didn't know anyone else. She let out a sigh as she contemplated her next move, debating who was the lesser of the two evils.

After a long moment of letting her thoughts fight it out, she decided on RJ. Even if she called her mother, it wasn't one hundred percent certain that she wouldn't call RJ and send him anyway in an effort to "fix" them.

She punched two on her speed dial and waited, trying her best not to feel sorry for herself and her lack of friendships.

"Babe?" She rolled her eyes. She hated when he called her that. It was so generic, just like him.

"Hey, I ran out of gas." She wanted to keep it short and simple. She knew he wanted to talk about them and their future, but she really only wanted to talk about getting gas in her car.

"Okay, I'll come and get you. Where are you?" She was almost saddened by the desperation in his voice. The feeling of guilt began its slow creep into the pit of her stomach.

She ignored the feeling and looked around for a sign. "I don't know. Somewhere outside the city. There's a Greensboro Burgers in front of me, whatever that is."

She could hear him clacking away at a keyboard as he searched for her.

"I found it. Okay. I'm on my way."

She let out another sigh and relaxed against her car. "Thanks."

The warm metal stung her arms as she slid down the length of the car to sit on the pavement. The instant need to sulk overtook her as she let herself obsess over her life choices, hating each and every one that had led her to the middle of who knows where, waiting for a man she didn't want to see.

She let herself wade in her misery, listening only to the sounds of her own sorrow. She didn't even hear the Jeep when it pulled up next to her.

"Hey hot-stuff, show us what you got!" a voice shouted from the backseat of the Jeep as someone tossed a necklace of rainbow beads at her. Elizabeth attempted to back away, her flight instincts kicking in almost immediately, but the two-ton car behind her blocked her path.

"Excuse me?" She squinted her eyes against the sunlight, searching the Jeep full of women for the culprit that was throwing plastic jewelry at her.

"Oh, are you not with the parade?" the woman behind the wheel asked her. She seemed genuinely confused as she scratched at the orange bandanna covering her forehead.

"Parade?" Elizabeth shook her head in apprehension.

A woman squashed in the middle of all the others stood up, grabbing hold of one of the bars connected to the roof of the Jeep.

"Excuse these crazy ladies. We thought you were part of Pride. We didn't mean to throw things at you for no reason."

The woman smiled at her, and Elizabeth felt her blood heat up. She was probably the most beautiful woman Elizabeth had ever seen and her smile made everything in Elizabeth's life seem a little less tragic.

"Are you okay, love?" Elizabeth realized she'd been staring at the woman for an abnormally long time without saying anything.

"Yeah. Um...my car broke down." Elizabeth pointed lamely at her car, as she fought against the dumbfounded stupor that smile had sent her into.

The woman jumped across all the ladies in the Jeep and landed in front of Elizabeth. It was the fastest, smoothest transaction of movement she'd ever seen, and she had to will herself not to gasp in awe.

"I'll take a look for you." She opened the front door to the car and stopped short. "I think you're just out of gas."

Elizabeth watched her every move, unable to tear her eyes away. "Oh, umm...yeah, I know. That's what I meant. My car umm...ran out of gas." She fidgeted uncontrollably as she babbled on like an idiot.

"You sure you're okay?" She took a step forward, and Elizabeth unconsciously took one backwards, keeping the distance between them.

"I think you make her nervous." One of the girls in the Jeep howled as the others erupted in giggles.

The woman looked back at the cackling group of her friends. She straightened her necktie as she took another step forward, the gesture seeming to make her even more attractive. Elizabeth swallowed hard, but she wouldn't allow herself to take another step away. "Is it true? Do I make you nervous?" The woman raised an eyebrow, making Elizabeth's heart beat double-time.

"N-no. I'm not gay." Elizabeth mentally scolded herself for her unorthodox reaction.

A smile spread across the woman's face. "Sure you aren't." She gave Elizabeth a wink before returning to her friends in the Jeep. "We're headed into the city to grab some drinks. You want to come along? We could grab some gas while we're out there."

Elizabeth looked down at her phone. "My boy..." She stopped,

6

rethinking what she was about to say. "I have someone coming to get me."

"Baby, it's Pride. It'll be hours before anyone makes it through the city to this side of town," the purple-and-orange-clad driver shouted at her.

"Yeah, come on, come with us," another voice from inside the Jeep called out to her.

"Come with us. Come with us," they all chanted at her, making her laugh as they continued in unison.

She held her hands up. "All right, all right. I could use a drink anyways." She considered her day so far and sighed at the truth in the statement. She could use several drinks.

She walked up to the Jeep and looked at it in horror. She wasn't particularly athletic, and there was no way she could climb in the way the woman before her did. As if on cue, the woman extended her hand. "I've got you, love."

Elizabeth gave her a trembling hand and let the woman pull her into the Jeep. She felt wild and free at the prospect of riding into the city in a car full of strangers. She'd never done anything so freeing in her life.

"I'm Kerra, by the way," the beautiful woman told her as she settled in next to her. She let her arm dangle around Elizabeth's shoulder. There was a casualness in the gesture that made Elizabeth smile at the sight of Kerra draped around her.

"I'm Elizabeth. My family calls me Beth though." She let herself relax against Kerra in the crowded Jeep.

"You don't seem like a Beth," Kerra told her through a smile.

"No? What do I seem like?"

"A Lizzie."

CHAPTER TWO

Swaying to the melodic sounds of the bar, Elizabeth leaned forward and almost toppled over. She was definitely feeling the effects of the alcohol, even though she'd had very little of it. She'd never really had friends who went out and drank in dive bars, pounding away the shots like they were the last drops of liquor on the planet. She shook her head at the thought, resisting the urge to dwell on the fact that she'd never really had friends at all, outside of RJ.

At first glance, she had been unsure of the tackily decorated bar with different shades of pastel-colored furniture sporadically placed around the tiny room, but after her first shot of sour liquor, she had decided the place was rather homey.

The warm feeling of intoxication spread through her as she crossed her legs in front of herself on the bright pink couch and listened while two of the women in her group argued over the perception of black women in society.

"They see us as aggressive and erratic. Always when you bring up the black woman, the front-running thought is attitude."

"Ashanti, I disagree." The second woman spoke up, straightening herself in her chair to voice her opinion. "I think black women are seen as strong and resilient and maybe occasionally aggressive, but who among us isn't?"

"Okay. Strong and resilient." Ashanti stood up from her chair, her eyes alight with the thrill of debate. "Do you see how limiting that is? An entire group of women expected to get over it, or in your words, 'be strong and resilient.' That's how society treats us, like rugs to be continually walked over but never to fall apart. God forbid those threads loosen and we come apart, then we're back to angry and aggressive. The age-old tale of the angry black woman, I know you've heard it."

The second woman smiled, rolling her eyes at the challenge. "All right fine, I may have heard that phrase once or twice in my life, but it doesn't mean that I feel that way."

"Maybe not, but it doesn't stop the perception from leaving us out of every discussion of progress. We're expected to be strong enough to get our own and resilient enough to recover if we don't."

Elizabeth nodded along in agreement as she listened to the sermon of honest thought. It was the first time she'd ever heard anyone speak so passionately about anything. Everyone in her life had their path carved for them, listening to the whispering voices of their parents as they told them who they were and what they would become. Everyone was made to think the same way where she was from. No one had a voice. But the woman in front of her had a voice, and she demanded to be heard. She was almost as intoxicating as the alcohol. Elizabeth had never considered how anyone perceived her or how it affected the plight of black women as a whole.

She kept her eyes on the woman as she continued on, wishing she felt even half of the strength and assuredness that Ashanti did. She didn't feel strong at all, or resilient. She felt weak and mindless and lost.

"Hey, Lizzie. You okay?" Kerra plopped down next to her with yet another drink in her hand. Elizabeth wondered how in the world she was still standing. She had nearly tripled Elizabeth's own drink count, and she was still going strong.

"Yeah. I'm fine. Why?" Elizabeth answered, only taking her eyes away from the preaching woman for a short moment, afraid to miss a single word.

"You're looking at Ashanti like she's going to take you to the Holy Grail." Kerra laughed at her fascination, obviously more accustomed to the free-thinking atmosphere than Elizabeth.

"Oh, sorry. I've just never heard anyone speak like her." Elizabeth flushed, embarrassed by her blatant naiveté.

Kerra cocked her head in confusion. "Speak like her? You mean, have an opinion?"

Elizabeth shrugged her shoulders. "Well, yeah."

"Where are you from, girl? The 1920s?" Kerra questioned as she took a sip from her drink.

A girl from their group handed them two more shots before taking a seat on top of a poorly painted wooden table across from them. Kerra effortlessly tossed hers back, but Elizabeth held on to hers, knowing that another shot would take her out. She wasn't known for her ability to hold her alcohol.

"I'm from Edenfield. Born, raised, and imprisoned." She shocked herself by admitting it to a stranger. She'd always felt like she didn't belong in her little town, but she'd never said it aloud.

"Oh, so basically the 1920s." Kerra laughed.

"Basically."

"I was born in Edenfield too, but I didn't turn out to be what I was supposed to, so they kicked me out. I was the misfit until I found my way to the city." She placed her drink onto the table, to focus her attention on Elizabeth.

Catching Kerra's gaze, Elizabeth lost herself in the crystal-blue eyes staring back at her. She was completely mesmerized, and the impulse to spill her secrets was overwhelming. "I guess I'm kind of a misfit too," she confessed, unable to stop herself.

Kerra smiled at her, that warming smile that turned her insides to jelly. She kept her eyes trained on Elizabeth, refusing to release her from the clutches of her stare. "So, it's kind of kismet that we found each other."

Kerra slid across the comfy couch, and Elizabeth felt her heart quicken with her proximity. Her chest rose and fell with abruptness as the intensity of the moment set in. She held her breath as she waited for some unknown phenomenon to take place. Her mind was a jumble of disconnected thoughts, and she scrambled to cling onto one of them. Any single thought to take away the ache coursing through her body from the unexplainable desire she had to lean in closer to the woman next to her.

The familiar tune of her phone sounded through the room, breaking through whatever moment she was sharing with Kerra. She let her gaze fall to the ground, embarrassed. By what, she wasn't sure. She had no reason to feel embarrassment, and yet her face heated in humiliation.

The letters that flashed across her phone reminded her that this was not her life; dive bars and outspoken women were not her reality.

"Oh, sorry. I have to take this." She climbed to her feet, leaving Kerra on the sofa staring after her.

"RJ?" She answered the phone, making a conscious effort to keep the sadness out of her voice. She was enjoying her time away from the world of Edenfield and the reminder that she didn't actually belong was unappreciated.

"Hey, babe. I'm here. Where are you? I see your car, but you're not here. I'm worried." RJ sounded frantic through the phone, and Elizabeth's annoyance was quickly replaced with guilt. She'd forgotten to tell him she was leaving. *Or maybe I didn't want to tell him.*

"Oh, I'm so sorry. I met some girls, and they invited me to have a drink with them, and I thought since I was waiting for you anyways..." She scrambled to explain herself. "I'm sorry."

She waited in silence for a reply.

"Okay, where are you now?" He seemed to accept her apology without much apprehension. It was the one good thing about his lack of passion. He was always easy to quell.

"At a bar in the city. I don't know the name. Hold on, I'll ask someone." She covered the phone with her hand and turned back to Kerra, who waited patiently on the couch for her to return.

"Hey, what's the name of this place?" she shouted over her shoulder.

"The Nipple Slip," Kerra shouted back without pause.

Elizabeth's eyes nearly popped out of their sockets as horror struck through her core. "Please, tell me you're kidding."

Kerra shook her head indifferently.

A sense of dread hit her like a ton of bricks at the thought of saying such a thing to RJ. She cleared her throat and put the phone back up to her ear, closing her eyes to steady her nerves. "I'm at the Nipple Slip downtown."

Silence filled the other end of the line, making her even more uncomfortable as she waited for him to respond.

"The what?" He said the words slowly, as if he was trying to decide if what she had told him was real or not.

"Please, don't make me say it again, RJ."

"Okay," he agreed, appearing to silently understand her. "I'll put it in the GPS and find you. Just...stay there. Okay?" His tone was back to concerned, brushing off the hint of judgment from the moment before.

"Okay," she agreed before hanging up the phone. She stood there for a moment, wondering what he must be thinking. It was completely out of character for her to forget to call him when her plans changed, and the thought of her in a place called the Nipple Slip must have completely perturbed him.

She turned back to Kerra, her mood taking on a sour edge. "My friend is coming to pick me up. I think I'll just go wait outside for him." She stared at her feet as she spoke, not wanting to get swept up in another stare-down.

Kerra stood up and nodded. "Okay, let's go."

"You don't have to wait with me. It's fine," Elizabeth assured her, finally looking up to meet her gaze.

"It's nighttime in the city. If you're going outside, I'm going outside," Kerra insisted, standing up a little straighter to look intimidating.

Elizabeth felt the bitterness in her mood lift. "Thank you, but you really don't have to. I'm pretty sure I can handle my own."

A slow smile spread across Kerra's lips as she let her eyes roll up Elizabeth's body, taking her in. "I'm sure you can, but you don't have to. You've got me. I'll protect you."

Elizabeth raised an eyebrow, examining the gangly, white woman before her.

"I'm stronger than I look," Kerra noted, guiding her toward the doors and leading her outside. She led her to a steel bench, conveniently placed in front of the bar, and took a seat next to her. They sat in silence, Kerra watching her with an intensity that made Elizabeth's stomach clench. It wasn't an uncomfortable silence; it was actually welcomed, peaceful. She'd have been completely at ease if her mind wasn't whirring beneath the concentrated gaze of the woman next to her.

She let out a sigh when she caught sight of RJ's car barreling around the corner. She couldn't decide if she was relieved or disappointed, but her shoulders slumped in exhaustion at the thought of trying to sort it out.

He jumped out of the car and ran to Elizabeth, wrapping her in an overly dramatic hug. "Are you okay?" He examined her from head to toe, as if he was picking her up from a brawl.

"I'm fine." She pulled away from him, agitated with his antics. His incessant need to treat her like a fragile child was becoming more and more tedious as their relationship dragged on.

RJ caught a glimpse of Kerra sitting on the bench behind her in the midst of his fit. He stared at her for a moment before a scowl made an appearance on his face.

Elizabeth considered how uncomfortable it must have been to see her sitting with someone like Kerra.

Kerra's choppy, black hair and boyish style of dress wasn't something you came across very often in Edenfield, and was something you avoided when you ventured outside it.

Kerra took his scowl in stride and climbed to her feet, extending a hand to him. "Hi, I'm Kerra. My friends and I found Lizzie distraught on the side of the road, so we filled her up with liquor to ease her woes."

Elizabeth giggled at Kerra's candor, but RJ kept scowling, staring down in disgust at the tattoo-covered hand extended to him.

"Get in the car. Let's go, Beth," he demanded as he pushed her forward, toward the car.

"Ouch, RJ. What's wrong with you?" He opened the door for her, and she climbed inside, too confused by him to argue.

She waved through the window at Kerra as he jerked the car forward and then set off down the road, moving as fast as he could to put distance between himself and the troubling atmosphere of the city.

Elizabeth turned in her seat, watching Kerra's figure get smaller and smaller as they drifted away. She was unnerved by the overwhelming sadness she felt over the idea that she would probably never see Kerra again.

CHAPTER THREE

Elizabeth stretched herself out across her bed, rolling over into the empty spot next to her with a sigh. She'd banished RJ to the sofa bed in the living room after fighting with him all night. He'd berated her for hours with questions and disgust directed toward the "despicable crowd" she'd run off with.

He was right in every point he'd made. It wasn't like her. It wasn't in her character at all to make a break for it with strangers, and the collection of women she'd taken to were everything contrary to Edenfield.

He'd asked her nearly a dozen times what had come over her, what she could have possibly been thinking, but the truth was she didn't know. There was something inexplicable about the way she'd been drawn to those women. To Kerra. There was something even more puzzling about the way she felt now, as if something had clicked into place inside her. She felt angry at RJ, disappointed in him for being so closed-minded. It was an unusual sensation for her. She was usually so passive in her feelings for everything, so accepting that small towns bred small minds and so at ease with the fact that her town was the smallest of them all. But now she felt alive, electric in her stance to get out, to experience something, anything other than Edenfield and RJ and her mother.

She rolled over in the bed again and let out a groan as she remembered the night, screaming and throwing things at him as he hurled insults at her about Kerra. What gave him the right to judge her? Kerra understood more about her in three hours of friendship than her entire family had managed to understand about her in a lifetime.

Her chest tightened as a vehement passion caught fire in her belly. Even the thought of Kerra awakened every one of her senses. It was the first time she'd felt any kind of drive, any kind of hunger for life, and she didn't want it to end.

The burning need to reconnect pulled her forward as she climbed off the bed and bounced over to her laptop, which sat on the small desk in the corner. She took a seat in the desk chair and opened the top of the computer, doing a quick sweep of the room as she went. She didn't want RJ sneaking up on her and seeing what she was up to. She didn't need his approval, but she also didn't want his judgment.

Her fingers clicked against the keys, typing out Kerra's name into the search bar. She felt herself begin to deflate at the realization that she didn't know Kerra's last name. She gave the screen a frown as it told her there were nearly a thousand Kerras located in the city.

Biting at her fingernails, she racked her brain for another way to find her. She wasn't ready to give up on that feeling of life and hope she'd experienced the night before. A ray of hope fluttered in her stomach as she remembered something, a seemingly insignificant detail that might narrow her field of options.

She took another glance around the room and typed into the search bar again. *Kerra from Edenfield.* She clenched her fists, her nerves tangling in knots as she watched the computer load her results.

A single photo popped up on her screen, and Elizabeth felt her heart flip. There she was. "Kerra Silvers." She said the name out loud without meaning to. It tickled her lips, provoking a smile to cross her face.

The sound of shuffling in the living room turned the corners of her mouth back down, as she slammed her computer shut in a panic.

"Beth? You okay?" RJ appeared in the bedroom doorway, rubbing at the back of his head and staring at her in sleepy concern.

"I'm fine," she huffed, still not in the mood to carry on a conversation with him. He'd acted like a complete jerk to Kerra, and she wasn't ready to forgive him. She wasn't sure she'd ever be ready to forgive him.

"Look, I don't want to fight anymore. Can we please just let this go and get back to being us?" he pleaded with her, taking a step into the bedroom.

She held up a hand to him, not wanting him any closer to her. She needed to say what she should have said before. "No, RJ. We can't. I told you, I don't want to be us anymore. I just need to be me. I need to figure out me and what I want." She stood up, holding her laptop to her chest. "The fact you can't understand that is just one more reason that we shouldn't be together." She moved toward the door, planning to push past him and head to her car, but he caught her arm.

He held her in the doorway, looking into her eyes, and she felt her heart shatter into a million pieces. She really did love him, but it was undeniable that there was something missing between them. She didn't want to hurt him, but she needed to do this for herself. If she didn't leave now, she'd run off with him and play the part of the compliant doctor's wife and hate every minute of it.

"Please," he begged her.

"If I stay, I'll only end up hating you." She released herself from his hold and headed for the door, letting the stray tear that escaped her eye drip onto her ruffled tank top.

She fought the urge to look back, knowing the sight of him would convince her to stay. As much as she wanted to leave, her will was weak. The longer she lingered, the less likely she would be to leave.

The walk to her car seemed endless as the weight of the sadness she was causing RJ settled on her shoulders. She felt responsible for his happiness and knowing that what she was doing hurt him somehow felt like a failure on her part. She slid inside the car and let herself sag against the steering wheel as sobs racked her body.

She cried for RJ and the life they had built together, knowing that this time she wouldn't go back. She was ready to leave him behind and move on to something different, to something she'd never even let herself consider.

She wiped her tears and sat up straight in her seat. Opening the laptop in her lap, she stared at the crystal-blue eyes that stared back at her. "Kerra Silvers." Something about saying the name aloud sent shivers through her body.

She opened another window on the screen and typed in a new search. *Kerra Silvers's address.*

Something about heartbreak made her bold. She watched the page load and wondered if she had the gumption to do anything with the address when and if she found it.

She bit at her nails and tugged at a braid of her hair as she waited.

Thirty results and only five in the city for Kerra Silvers stared back at her. She wrote each one down on a dirty napkin from the floor of her car, stopping several times to steady the nerves in her hand.

Clutching the napkin to her chest, she closed the laptop. What now? She drummed her fingers along the steering wheel and debated her next move. She knew she didn't have it in her to knock on five different doors looking for what was practically a stranger. The brazen move to look Kerra up was easy. She'd had the shield of a computer screen.

She glanced down at the napkin and thought about seeing Kerra. She felt that surge of passion and purpose flow through her again and knew she had to do something.

Letting out a sigh of frustration, she slipped the napkin into her pocket and started up her car. Without a second glance, she pulled out of the apartment complex housing her old life and headed toward the city.

She drove in circles for nearly two hours before she parked her car in front of the Nipple Slip. She had debated ferociously with herself as she passed by every address on the napkin before arriving at the conclusion that she wasn't as bold as she wished she was. The bar was the only other location she could think of to go to in search of Kerra's whereabouts.

She took the napkin out of her pocket and discarded it back onto the floor of her car in a huff. She hadn't even had the courage to park in front of the first address.

Climbing out of the car, Elizabeth attempted to amp herself up. *You got this, girl. You can do this.* Even with the vote of confidence, her hands trembled as she approached the door of the trendy dive bar.

She stepped inside and barely recognized the place. The atmosphere was much calmer than the first time she'd visited. It was the middle of the day, and without the thrill of Pride, not many people flaunted their day drinking.

Elizabeth approached the bar, seeing the familiar bartender wiping down the counter. Elizabeth would have recognized her anywhere. Even without her distinctive neck tattoos and frizzy red Mohawk, her eyes managed to captivate Elizabeth. Heterochromia. Elizabeth recalled the name of the birth irregularity that Kerra had told her the bartender had.

Elizabeth had found herself admiring the woman on more than one occasion for her utter confidence in her abnormality. She didn't hide herself from the world or cover her blue and black contrasting set of eyes but embraced it for what it was. She moved with the assuredness of a woman who knew who she was and what she wanted.

Even now, she looked Elizabeth straight in the eyes. "Can I help you, honey?"

Elizabeth stepped back, assaulted by nerves. She felt a sharp stab of jealousy, wishing she had even a fraction of the confidence the woman before her exuded. "Oh, umm... No... I mean, yes." Elizabeth tugged at one of her braids. "I'm looking for Kerra...Silvers."

The bartender rolled her eyes and went back to wiping down the counter. "Oh honey, I don't know what Kerra has told you, but stalking her won't make her follow through on her promises to run away together and start a big happy family."

Elizabeth shook her head at her assumption. "No, I'm not trying to—"

The bartender cut her off. "Honey, I get it. Trust me, I've climbed that tree a couple of times myself. The woman is a bombshell, but it's never going to go anywhere. Birds got to fly and all. Let it go, cut your losses, and find someone else." She reached out for Elizabeth's hand, patting it in a pitying show of support.

Elizabeth moved her hands into her lap as she felt another stab of jealousy shoot through her, but this time she wasn't sure why. "Look, I'm not trying to climb anyone's tree. Kerra helped me out, and I wanted to find her to say thank you," Elizabeth proclaimed, finding her nerve.

The bartender stopped her wiping and tossed her towel down onto the bar. "Well then." She raised an eyebrow, her multicolored eyes rolling up Elizabeth's body in slow motion, as she studied her.

Elizabeth shifted uncomfortably under her gaze. She'd never felt so completely bare beneath someone's stare before.

"Remind me of your name again, honey."

"Elizab...Lizzie. My name is Lizzie."

"Mm-hmm." The bartender gave her a skeptical look before pulling a phone out of the back pocket of tiny black shorts that left very little to the imagination. "Okay, Lizzie. We'll see what's what."

Elizabeth fidgeted, unable to keep herself still as she watched the bartender punch in numbers on the phone. She put the phone to her ear and waited, making Elizabeth's anticipation grow. "Hey Kerra, I've got a girl at the bar here for you. Says you did her a solid, and she wants to repay you."

Elizabeth couldn't hear what Kerra was saying on the other end of the line, but her stomach somersaulted at the possibility that she wouldn't remember her.

The bartender let out a laugh at whatever Kerra said. "Oh, I don't know if she's going to return the favor like that. She seems just a tiny bit shy." The bartender threw her a wink as she spoke.

Elizabeth wasn't sure how to react to that. She wasn't usually a shy person, as far as she knew, but she considered how very few new people she regularly encountered. Her small town wasn't really welcoming to outsiders. Even the students at her college seemed to all be people she had gone to high school with. And she had never in her life encountered a group of people as bold and outspoken as the women she had met in the last two days.

"Yeah, Lizzie. That's her... All right, well, I guess I'll keep her here then. Yeah... See ya." The bartender hung up the phone and smiled as she stared across the bar at Elizabeth.

"Well, it's your lucky day, Lizzie. It seems Kerra Silvers has taken an interest in you. She'll be here in an hour. Have a seat." She gestured for Elizabeth to sit in one of the stools. "You want a drink?"

Elizabeth suddenly felt overcome with anxiety. But this is what she wanted. Why was she so nervous? She took a seat and nodded at the bartender. Butterflies collected in her stomach, and her heart raced in her chest as she thought about what might happen in the next hour. She tried to calm herself, chastising her brain for making more out of things than they were. She was acting like she'd never made a new friend before.

She twisted at her braids with her fingers as the uncontrollable need to fidget overtook her. She thanked the bartender when she placed a colorful drink in front of her. She was going to need all the liquid courage she could get.

CHAPTER FOUR

Elizabeth nervously tapped her fingers up and down the length of her empty glass. The bartender had offered her another, but she had declined, not wanting to be intoxicated when she reencountered Kerra. She wiped her forehead, realizing that she was sweating. She mentally kicked herself for being so unreasonably on edge. She had convinced herself that she was only seeking out Kerra to say thank you for helping her, but there was something else beneath the surface that made her nerves stand on end. Her heart wanted to leap out of her chest at the thought of another encounter with the mysterious Kerra Silvers.

She forced herself to breathe, taking in long, slow breaths. The bar had no windows, and the glass door was so muddled with dirt it was nearly impossible to see through. She would have no warning when Kerra approached. She closed her eyes and kept breathing, feeling her head swim with the effects of the alcohol creeping into the darkness behind her eyelids. She'd only had the one drink, but the bartender was pretty heavy-handed on the liquor. There was definitely more vodka than juice filling her up.

Her eyes shot open, and she nearly tipped out of her chair as she heard the bar door swing open. Her breath caught in her throat, and she tried to force herself to swallow, but her mouth had gone completely dry at the sight of Kerra in the doorway, the sun illuminating her slim figure and casting a tall shadow across the bar. Elizabeth admired her jet-black hair, gelled back to hang loosely over her ears, highlighting the paleness of her skin. She had always been a fan of dark features, but they were usually paired with dark skin and the broad shoulders of a man.

Kerra spotted her on her stool at the bar and strolled over to her. She was effortless in her beauty. She carried herself with the confidence of a woman who knew she was attractive but the recklessness of a woman who didn't care. Elizabeth found herself swept up in the simplicity of her stroll. She forced herself to close her mouth before she started drooling.

"Lizzie, the not-so-lesbian. Not very often straight women come around the bar looking for me." Kerra flashed her a smile that made Elizabeth's knees go weak. "You are still straight, right?"

Elizabeth twirled at her braids, a nervous habit she was fighting to break. "Yes, I am. I just..."

Kerra leaned in with a raised eyebrow as she waited for Elizabeth to finish her sentence. "You just?"

Elizabeth let out an exasperated sigh. Kerra was obviously used to making women frazzled, and Elizabeth scolded herself for allowing her mind to get sucked in. "I'm straight," she finished matter-of-factly.

Kerra kept grinning. "If you say so." She shrugged, turning to the bartender. "Angela, can you get us two of whatever you feel like making?"

Angela seemed to be having the same reaction to Kerra as Elizabeth as she tripped over herself behind the bar, scrambling to make two drinks.

Elizabeth stood up, done with being the helpless, fawning female. She wasn't even attracted to Kerra. She was straight for crying out loud. She wanted to believe that, to believe her feelings for Kerra weren't attraction but just some latent nervousness about not having made friends in a long time, but the thought felt untrue. Kerra created a stirring in her that she wanted to embrace and run from all at the same time.

"Just one, Angela. I think I'm going to go." Elizabeth slid off her stool and started toward the door, uncomfortable with the feelings that she was having.

Kerra followed behind her. "Hey, Lizzie, wait. What's going on? Did I do something? Was it the gay stuff, because we can still chill. I solemnly swear not to hit on you anymore." Kerra held up a hand as she made her oath.

"No, it's not that. It's just—"

"Good, because you're gorgeous, and I don't think I could have kept that promise." Kerra reached out to grab Elizabeth's hand and brought it to her lips in a kiss of apology.

Elizabeth felt every part of her body heat up. She wasn't sure if her skin could blush, but if it could, she was certain she was blushing harder than any single person had ever blushed before. She pulled her hand back. "This wasn't a good idea," she declared. She suddenly wanted to scurry out of the bar and drive home to her mother. She wanted to convince herself that she was a regular little country girl, not meant for things outside her realm of understanding.

Is that what I want, though? Elizabeth considered how much courage it took for her to walk away from RJ. She was fighting like hell not to be sucked into the monotony of the life her mother wanted for her. Was she really going to tuck tail and run now?

Elizabeth stood frozen beneath Kerra's stare. Her icy-blue eyes made Elizabeth examine every part of herself. They seemed to plead with her to give into her whim to run off into the sunset alongside Kerra.

"How about a coffee?"

Elizabeth blinked her eyes at the question. Kerra had unconsciously just made her comb through her entire life with one look, and now she wanted to take her out for coffee. She let out a giggle before nodding her head. "Coffee sounds amazing."

She followed Kerra out of the bar. She knew that in the grand scheme of things, coffee with a stranger wasn't a big deal, but she walked a little taller, feeling triumphant over her own inhibitions. She was stepping off the leash that her upbringing had wrapped around her throat and opening herself up for all the possibilities that Kerra had to offer.

She stared at Kerra out of the corner of her eye, catching glimpses of excitement radiating off her as she talked about the coffee shop she was taking her to. Elizabeth nodded along in excitement as she listened to Kerra recount a story about the last time she was in the coffee shop. She threw her head back in laughter as she described a drunk girl named Sarah mooning a barista.

The sound of Kerra's carefree laughter drained Elizabeth's thoughts from her head. She wondered if Kerra was even aware of her calming powers. She felt at home walking alongside her.

The comfort was almost blinding. Without giving it thorough thought, she reached out and wrapped Kerra's forearm around herself, holding her as they walked down the street to the coffee shop. Kerra smiled down at her, staring with wide eyes, seemingly as shocked as Elizabeth was by her own behavior, but she didn't say anything. She placed a hand over Elizabeth's and kept moving forward, toward their destination. Elizabeth relished her touch, feeling at peace in the warmth of holding her, even if it was just her arm.

Kerra stopped in front of a quaint little building with "The Bean Spot" scribbled across the front in a cheap font. Elizabeth straightened herself, letting go of Kerra's arm as she opened the door for her. She took a deep breath before stepping inside. Whatever was coming next in her life, it was all going to start with a cup of coffee.

She took a cautious step inside the shop and took in the soothing smell of coffee beans and sweets. Kerra nodded distantly to the woman behind the counter as she led her to a table.

"I'll go get us something," Kerra told her without giving her the chance to object. Elizabeth watched her walk away, her head rattling with thoughts as she settled into the tiny green chair parked in front of a circular white table.

By the time Kerra returned with two large mugs of coffee in her hands, Elizabeth had managed to work herself up into a frenzy. *What am I doing here?* The thought continued to circle in her head.

"Lola makes a great cup of coffee." Kerra placed the mug in front of her with a grin and, just like that, Elizabeth felt her nerves settle. Everything about Kerra's smile comforted her, tranquilizing her nerves and allowing her to simply enjoy the company.

Kerra took a seat on the other side of the table and began to speak, telling her another story about the coffee shop and a girl named Lola's discovery of coffee beans. Elizabeth listened intently as Kerra shared memory after memory with her, through bouts of laughter. She found herself laughing along about women she'd never met and places she'd never been to. Kerra's life was so filled with wonders that Elizabeth had never even dreamed of. She giggled along with Kerra, admiring how full of stories she was. She was the most captivating woman Elizabeth had ever encountered, and she wanted to know everything about her. All her stories.

"So, how were you able to come and meet me in the middle of the day like this? Don't you work?" Elizabeth posed the question before she considered that Kerra could ask her the same thing.

She didn't, though. Kerra kept grinning as she placed her coffee cup down on the tiny round table separating them. "I do. Yes. But my job is a little more unconventional than what you're probably used to." Kerra rubbed at her eyebrow as she took a pause to explain her occupation. "I'm sort of a freelance artist."

"Sort of?" Elizabeth inquired, curious about the ambiguity of the response.

"Well, I freelance when I can, but I mostly work for a body painting company that specializes in nude art exhibitions." Kerra smiled at her, waiting for her reaction.

Elizabeth felt her face heat up again. "Oh."

Kerra let out a laugh at her visible discomfort. "Yeah. So how about you? What do you do?"

Elizabeth's face retained its heat as she realized she didn't have an answer to the question. "Oh, I, umm...go to school. My..." She stopped, realizing what she was about to say. "My ex-boyfriend used to take care of all of the bills." She felt stupid for having such a ridiculous answer to the question and even more stupid for having allowed RJ to stifle her as he did. She had no skills or real-life experience. She felt a tinge of jealousy at Kerra's life. She had the world on a string.

"Oh, that's cool. When did you guys break up?" Kerra asked before taking another sip from her oversized coffee mug.

"This morning."

Kerra spat her sip of coffee back into her cup. "Oh, my bad. I'm sorry, didn't meant to pour salt on the wound."

Elizabeth waved away her concerns. "No, it's fine. For the best, I guess."

"So what are you going to do now?" Kerra sat up in her chair as she asked the question.

Elizabeth shrugged in response. "I don't know. Get a job, I guess." She let out an awkward giggle. "Know anyone that's hiring?"

Kerra stared for a long time before speaking, contemplating her response. "Can you draw?"

Elizabeth shook her head, knowing that her collection of stick figures would barely pass for an acceptable kindergarten art project.

"Can you paint?"

She shook her head again.

"Can you pour coffee?" Kerra pointed behind her.

Elizabeth stared at her dumbfounded before turning around in her chair to see the big "help wanted" sign in the window. She let herself envision working in the tiny café, buzzing about the city in the afternoons like a carefree modern woman. She shook her head, shaking off the daydream as she turned back to Kerra. "I can't work here."

"Why not?"

"Because I don't live in the city."

"But you could," Kerra insisted, as if it were just that easy.

"Yeah, right, because every landlord is looking to hand out apartments to girls with no employment history and a job at a coffee shop." Elizabeth rolled her eyes at Kerra's naiveté.

"So, you'll stay with me."

She let out a laugh but cut it short when she caught a glimpse of Kerra's expression. "You're serious."

"Of course I am. Why wouldn't I be?"

Elizabeth was thunderstruck by the offer. "Because you hardly know me."

Kerra nodded. "True."

"I could be a crazy person, or a thief, or all of the above." Elizabeth threw her hands up in exasperation, but Kerra just kept nodding her head.

"Also, true."

Elizabeth stared at her openmouthed before she dropped her voice and leaned in. "Kerra, I'm still straight." She whispered the words as if it were a secret she didn't want anyone else to hear.

Kerra tapped her finger on the table. "A murky truth but a truth to you no less."

28

Elizabeth narrowed her eyes. "A truth."

"All right." Kerra put her hands up in defense as she halfheartedly agreed.

Elizabeth twirled her hair. "I can't stay with you, Kerra." She didn't want to give herself time to consider the offer.

"Why not?" Kerra leaned forward onto the table, and Elizabeth could feel the shift in her proximity.

"Because it's crazy."

Kerra gave her a shrug. "Crazier things have happened."

Elizabeth continued to twirl her braids as she bit down on her lip in thought. She really wanted to let herself believe that Kerra's proposition was a reality.

"Look, you don't have to stay with me. I'm just putting the offer on the table. Think it over and let me know." Kerra pulled her phone out of her pocket. "Give me your number."

Elizabeth reached into her bag and grabbed her phone with trembling fingers. The whole conversation was sending her nerves into a spiral, and giving Kerra her phone number felt like enough to send her free falling.

Kerra must have taken note of her shaking fingers. "How about I give you my number, and you call me when you have an answer."

Elizabeth silently thanked her for understanding without actually having to voice her terror. She pushed down the numbers Kerra called out to her and saved them into her phone.

She slid her phone back into her pocket, taking solace in the notion that she had a way to always reach out to her.

Kerra still leaned across the table, spinning her phone in circles as she watched her.

Elizabeth watched her back, refusing to flinch under her gaze. There was something so intimidating about being the object of Kerra's attention, Elizabeth wanted to shy away from it and keep it forever all at once.

Kerra's phone buzzed in her hand, but she didn't break her stare. She kept her eyes trained on Elizabeth until she broke.

Elizabeth shifted uncomfortably, reprimanding herself for not being able to handle Kerra's intensity. "Are you going to answer that?" Elizabeth asked as the phone continued to buzz.

Kerra flashed her an all-knowing grin as she put the phone to her ear. "What's up?"

Elizabeth rolled her eyes at the unorthodox method of phone answering.

"Yeah, all right... No, I know that Shelia is the owner...."

Elizabeth watched her as she talked on the phone. She took the brief moment that Kerra's attention was elsewhere to take in all of her without the embarrassment of her knowing she was doing it. Elizabeth's eyes scanned along her hands, long and delicate as one tapped against the table and the other wrapped around the phone to her ear. She let her gaze travel to Kerra's face, all sharp and dramatic angles that made her beauty intense and electrifying.

"All right... Yes, I know, I know..." Kerra kept talking into the phone, becoming further engrossed in her conversation.

Elizabeth stared at Kerra's neck, admiring the unblemished skin that ran down to dip beneath the collar of an androgynous button-up shirt.

Kerra caught her staring and arched an eyebrow.

Elizabeth froze in place, too embarrassed to move. She didn't know when her finger moved to her lips, but at some point she had begun to bite down on it as she was swept away in her trance of Kerra-admiration. Elizabeth straightened herself up in her chair, removing her hand from her mouth and then placing it in her lap.

Kerra smiled. She obviously loved making Elizabeth uncomfortable.

"Yeah, all right. Chill out. I'm on my way." Kerra hung up the phone and kept smiling at Elizabeth, who fidgeted in her chair as she waited for her to say something.

"I have to go." Kerra finally released her from the intensity of the silence.

Elizabeth stared at her in surprise. That wasn't what she had expected her to say, and Elizabeth hadn't anticipated feeling so overwhelmingly sad at hearing it.

"Oh." It was all she could think to say.

"Yeah, it's work. I…"

"Yeah, okay. Sure. I'll…call you." She tried to appear indifferent, but her chest tightened at the thought of watching Kerra walk away again.

Kerra nodded, and for a moment Elizabeth sensed that she wasn't ready to leave either.

She climbed to her feet to leave the table, giving Elizabeth an apologetic look as she went, but she stopped as she neared the exit of the coffee shop. "Do you…want to come with me, maybe?"

It was the first time Elizabeth sensed any inkling of uncertainty in Kerra, and her vulnerability made a warm tingle race through Elizabeth's body.

"To your job?" Elizabeth wanted to say yes without thinking, to just give in, but her inhibitions forever plagued her.

"Yes."

"To draw on naked people?" Elizabeth felt her face heat up just saying the words. She wasn't sure she could handle actually seeing the naked people she spoke of.

"Well, it's mostly paint, but yeah."

Elizabeth stared at her in horror, fighting against her desire to spend the day with Kerra and her fear of being surrounded by a sea of naked bodies. "Kerra, I—"

"Please, I'm asking you. Please come with me."

Elizabeth felt a lump in her throat at her sincerity. An earnest Kerra was an impossible thing to say no to.

She swallowed down the drowning wave of dread that washed through her at the thought of what she was about to agree to walk into. "Okay," she decided as she stood up and collected her bag.

She followed Kerra out of the coffee shop, her nerves standing on end at what she might see.

Kerra wrapped an arm around her shoulders. "Hey, nothing's going to happen to you when you're with me. You know that, right?" she told her, clearly sensing her uncertainty.

Elizabeth's nerves melted at the reassurance, even though logically she knew Kerra couldn't protect her from her own timidity. Having Kerra's arm draped across her made her feel safe from anything that may come her way, even her own inhibitions.

Elizabeth smiled up at her. "Yeah, I do."

CHAPTER FIVE

Kerra led Elizabeth through the doors of a lavishly decorated building. Even from the outside the place was eccentric, shaped like a dome with intricate engravings carved throughout the structure. Just standing in the entrance, Elizabeth immediately felt underdressed. She glanced down at her dirty, smudged Converse and tattered jeans and wished she had thought a little harder about her attire before bolting from her apartment. *RJ's apartment*, she corrected herself. She felt like it had been an eternity since she left him, and it seemed unreal that it had only been a day.

"Hey, don't worry about it. We're the artists. Nobody cares what we're wearing. They expect us to be a little scruffy and rebellious," Kerra assured her when she caught her eyeing her own attire.

Kerra placed a hand on her back to move her through the crowd of people that seemed to be standing around waiting for instruction. Kerra's reassuring touch kept her moving forward, pushing through the open floor plan as she admired the large space with high, rounded ceilings. She didn't know much about architecture, but it was obvious that the building was made to appeal to eclectic tastes.

A tiny woman in a tight black dress and heels that were probably taller than her entire body barreled toward them. She wore a headset over her ears that she screamed commands into as she stopped her aggressive stride in front of them. She gave Kerra a hard look as she continued to berate the voice on the other end of her headset.

"Shelia, this is—" Kerra moved to introduce her to the howling woman, but she held up a hand to stop her.

"I don't care, Kerra. Where the hell have you been?"

Elizabeth watched as Kerra rolled her eyes in agitation. "Does it matter, Shelia? I'm here now. Where do you need me?"

Shelia held up a finger to Kerra as she listened to someone on the other end of her headpiece. "Okay, yes. Sounds perfect," she said into the speakerphone. Her tone was finite and commanding, but there was something softer in the way that she spoke into her headset than the way she snapped at Kerra.

Kerra huffed in annoyance, and Elizabeth stifled a giggle. It was nice to see someone get under Kerra's skin.

Shelia finished her headset conversation and turned her attention back to Kerra. "Cathy is going to be doing some asshat rendition of *She is the World* on platform A. I need you to get the body work done for her. Showtime is at eight. I need her done by seven. Send her back to station when she's done." Shelia quickly rattled off all the information, never giving Kerra a moment to respond before she stomped off to yell at someone new.

Elizabeth looked at Kerra with concern. She couldn't remember any of the instructions that Shelia had given them, and she worried that Kerra might not either. Shelia didn't seem the type to enjoy repeating herself.

Kerra grumbled under her breath as she pressed Elizabeth forward. "So, that was Shelia. She's not my biggest fan."

Elizabeth moved her legs faster, struggling to match Kerra's long, quick strides. "Did you get all of that?" She sounded more shocked than she had meant to, but her brain was running at full speed just trying to keep up with the layout of the building. The thought of trying to interpret instructions through Shelia's multi-conversation tactics was more than she could handle.

"Of course I did. It's my job to get it," Kerra reassured her with a smile.

Kerra led her up a set of carpeted stairs that cascaded around the room in a neat circle. She was completely unaware of how impressive she was, and Elizabeth had a hard time understanding how anyone could not be a fan.

"Is she always like that? She seems like the type to hate everyone. Is it really just you?" Elizabeth asked breathlessly. She was nearly leaping up the stairs to keep pace with Kerra.

"A little of both. She's not an enthusiast of my 'alternative lifestyle.'" Kerra let out a groan at the comment.

"Alternative lifestyle?"

"Yeah."

Elizabeth's cheeks heated up as she realized what she meant. "Oh, I didn't know people in the city cared."

"People everywhere care, Lizzie."

Elizabeth nodded, even though she didn't completely understand what she meant, but she was too tired to press further. Her breaths were coming in sharp from climbing the long set of stairs, and her legs gave her a silent thank-you as she stopped at the top of the staircase, taking a moment to catch her breath. She let her eyes wash over the building once more, taking it in from a new height. It really was quite extravagant in its quaintness, and possibly the most beautiful place she'd ever been inside. She'd have been able to enjoy it if she could forget why she was there.

"Where are all of the naked people?" Elizabeth asked.

Kerra smirked, a knowing gesture that made her features seem wise and transcending. "Soon enough," she promised.

Elizabeth straightened up and let out a huff of air at her vagueness. She'd have been annoyed if she hadn't been so taken with that smirk.

"Ready?" Kerra had been waiting for her as she caught her breath.

Elizabeth nodded and moved forward behind Kerra as she led them down a series of decorated hallways to the back of the building. A heavy black curtain dangled from the ceiling, behind a tiny plastic sign with "painting stations" scribbled across the front.

Kerra pulled the split of the curtain open and led her through it without giving her a moment to prepare herself.

Elizabeth's breath caught in her throat, and every part of her body trembled in discomfort. At least fifteen people stood around the room, letting their nakedness be seen without shame. Some of them wore paint while others just paraded their bare bodies through the room. Everyone seemed to be oblivious to the fact that they were naked. They carried on conversations and drank out of to-go cups of coffee as if they were simply lounging around at a convention center.

Elizabeth spotted a few other artists in the room that wore clothes; some hovered over naked bodies spread across clothed tables, mapping out a landscape for their artwork while others worked their brushes across the delicate skin of a standing canvas.

Elizabeth tried to keep her breathing normal and appear as casual as everyone else in the room, but she couldn't seem to force her legs to move any farther inside.

"You okay?" Kerra placed a hand on her shoulder. "You can wait outside if you want."

Elizabeth shook her head against the offer. She had come so far, and she didn't want to shy away now. She took a deep breath and scanned the room again. *Picture everyone in a parka*, she told herself.

She moved awkwardly behind Kerra, following her inside the room and trying her best to keep her eyes trained on the floor, when a pair of bare feet invaded her line of sight.

She lifted her head and watched as a naked woman threw her arms around Kerra.

"Kerra, honey. Where have you been? It's so good to see you." The woman stepped back and narrowed her eyes. "You are late, late, late. I have two hours to be perfected and ready." She wagged her finger at Kerra.

"I know, Cathy. Two hours is enough time. I promise." Kerra placed her hands on Cathy's shoulders and looked into her eyes

Elizabeth watched as she melted beneath Kerra's stare. "Are you sure?" Cathy squeaked.

"Positive," Kerra reassured her as she kept her focus on her eyes.

"Because it has to be perfect. I've been working on this rendition for weeks." Cathy's argument waned as Kerra's eyes continued to bore into her.

"I promise, Cathy. As much as I'd love to take my time with you." Kerra's eyes rolled up the naked woman's body. "I can put a rush order on it."

Cathy stepped forward, meeting Kerra's boldness with her own brazen retort. "Well, maybe not too much of a rush." The woman leaned in and placed a kiss on Kerra's cheek. "Where do you want me?" She suggestively purred the words into Kerra's ear, making a grin appear on her face.

"Oh, any and everywhere, Cathy. But for now, let's get started in Block C."

Cathy turned on her heels and slowly walked toward a cloth-covered table surrounded by shelves of paint and materials beneath a big "C" hanging from the ceiling. Kerra watched her go, licking her lips as her eyes stayed trained on Cathy.

Elizabeth felt a white-hot stab of jealousy boil in her veins as she watched Kerra ogle Cathy's derriere. She had completely forgotten her discomfort with the nakedness in the room as she seethed with her hands on her hips, glaring in Kerra's direction.

Kerra tore her eyes away from Cathy to catch a glimpse of the miffed Elizabeth at her side. "What?" Kerra furrowed her eyebrows at her in confusion.

"Nothing," Elizabeth huffed. She attempted to calm herself. She had no reason to be jealous. She didn't have any feelings for Kerra, and she certainly had no claim to her. But even as she told herself that, she couldn't suppress the feeling of possessiveness that overcame her as Kerra started toward the naked Cathy, laid across the table.

Elizabeth followed, trying to wrangle her emotions. She took a seat on a small stool near the table and watched as Kerra grabbed and carefully mixed bottles of paint from the shelves surrounding her area. She gathered brushes and plates and tiny tools that Elizabeth had never seen before and couldn't name.

Kerra moved around the room with confidence, as if every movement was second nature. It was almost euphoric to watch her perform her symphony of artistic enchantment.

Kerra finally sat down with all her equipment and lorded over Cathy as she lay back on the table. She stared down at Cathy, examining every inch of her body and mapping out her work.

As uncomfortable as it made her, Elizabeth looked too, watching Cathy's chest rise and fall with a steady rhythm. She seemed so natural, so comfortable. Elizabeth envied her. No wonder Kerra was so attracted to her; she was stunning and confident and everything that Elizabeth was not.

Elizabeth shooed away the thought. *You shouldn't even care*, she reprimanded herself.

Kerra dipped a brush into a tiny pile of paint on a silver plate and began brushing strokes to Cathy's neck.

"Oh, do be careful when you get downstairs. My waxing lady was sick this morning and some amateur with a glue gun went absolutely crazy on my lady business. So just be gentle." Cathy managed to lay perfectly still as she spoke.

Kerra nodded. "Aren't I always?" She gave Cathy a wink before returning her focus to her brush strokes.

"And so modest too." Cathy giggled. "Are you ever going to introduce me to your friend or are you going to have her keep sitting in silence while you flirt with me?"

Kerra kept her eyes focused on her painting. "While I flirt with you? I was simply following your lead." Kerra stopped her brush strokes to stare at a startled Elizabeth. "Lizzie, this is Cathy. Cathy, Lizzie."

Elizabeth suddenly felt awkward. She had examined the woman's naked body without ever having been properly introduced.

"Nice to meet you, Lizzie. I'd shake your hand, but this one gets really pissy when I move." She rolled her eyes over to Kerra.

"Umm, nice to meet you too," Elizabeth choked out uneasily. She wasn't sure what else to say. Naked cordiality was a new wheelhouse for her.

"Is this your first show?" Cathy asked her.

Elizabeth nodded.

"I can tell. Don't worry, you get used to it, and before you know it, you'll hardly even notice that you're the only one wearing any clothes." Cathy giggled again, and Elizabeth tried to join her, but the sound came out choked and uncomfortable.

Elizabeth watched Kerra as she carefully stroked patterns across Cathy's body while she chattered away, asking Elizabeth question after question. Elizabeth considered that maybe this was the woman that coined the term "chatty Cathy."

She answered the questions, sometimes looking to Kerra for reassurance. Kerra always gave her a nod or a look that set her at ease.

Cathy's incessant yammering eventually made Elizabeth forget that she was naked, and watching Kerra make art of her body became a fascination. Elizabeth found herself unable to look away as the patterns began to weave together to create an incredible work of art. She didn't even look away when Kerra's brush stroked against Cathy in areas that would normally make her blush with embarrassment. She was utterly captivated and in awe of Kerra's talent.

Kerra stood up and disappeared behind a shelf of paints. She returned with a full-length rolling mirror and moved it in front of Cathy's table. "All done. What's the verdict?" Kerra announced as she held the mirror in front of Cathy.

Cathy stood in front of it to examine herself.

"She's beautiful." Elizabeth hadn't meant to interject, but the words flowed freely from her lips.

"Thank you, honey." Cathy turned to examine her backside in the mirror. "You're right. As always, Kerra's work is perfection." Cathy placed a kiss on Kerra's cheek. "Thanks, doll. Call me sometime, okay?"

Kerra nodded and watched as Cathy skipped her way out of the curtained-off room.

Kerra turned her attention to Elizabeth. "Help me clean?"

Elizabeth nodded her head as she climbed to her feet from the little stool. "What do you need me to do?"

"Reshelf the paints. I'll do the rest."

Elizabeth gathered a handful of the tiny bottles of paint and began putting them neatly back onto the shelves. She could see Kerra on the other side, collecting items off the back end of the shelf.

"Your work really was beautiful. I didn't expect you to be so talented." Elizabeth spoke absentmindedly as she shelved. Cathy had apparently put her in the mood to chat.

Kerra popped her head up from what she was doing. "Thanks?" She said it as more of a question than an actual thank-you.

Elizabeth considered what she had said. "No, I don't mean anything by it. It's just, you know, everyone thinks they're an artist, but you, you actually are."

Kerra walked back around to the front of the shelf to stare at

Elizabeth. "I'm glad you liked it, Lizzie."

Elizabeth felt herself begin to heat up again, and she looked away, returning her focus to putting the paints on the shelf.

Kerra let out a laugh at her avoidance as she moved to the table to remove the cloth covering.

Elizabeth grabbed the last of the paints and snuck a peak at Kerra out of the corner of her eye. She watched as Kerra carefully folded each end of the dark cloth, until the entire thing was a neat little square. Kerra set the square of cloth at the edge of the table and then made her way over to Lizzie. "Need help?" Kerra asked, gesturing at the bottles of paint.

Elizabeth shook her head. She only had two more bottles to put away, and if she hadn't kept letting Kerra distract her, she could have been done.

Elizabeth fumbled her last bottle of paint, and it fell through her fingers to the floor. "Dammit." She bent down to pick the bottle up and felt the hairband keeping her braids in place snap in half. "Dammit, twice."

She placed the runaway paint bottle on the shelf and ran a hand through her free-flowing hair, her braids cascading down her shoulders to dip at the center of her back. She rummaged around in her pockets for an extra hair band. She always carried two or three on her for just that reason. This wasn't her first dance with a broken scrunchie. She felt around in her front pockets, finding nothing but lint, and let out a grunt as she reached behind herself to check her back pockets. She caught Kerra's eye and was immediately flustered to find her standing there, staring like she'd never seen her before.

"What?" Elizabeth felt even more awkward than usual with Kerra staring at her like that.

Kerra shook her head and stepped closer to Elizabeth. "Nothing. It's just mesmerizing how beautiful you are."

Elizabeth rolled her eyes and fought her body's desire to blush. "I'd probably feel more complimented if you didn't think every woman was beautiful."

Kerra's eyebrows jumped in surprise. "Well, I do think every woman is beautiful, but I have a feeling you're hinting at something a little more specific."

Elizabeth swatted a piece of hair from her face before placing a hand on her hip, her indignation swelling in her chest. "You and Cathy. The flirting. Ring any bells?"

Kerra grinned, patronizing her aggressive demeanor. "Did it bother you that I was flirting with Cathy?"

"No." Elizabeth answered a little too quickly, dropping her hand from her hip. "It's just something I've noticed that you do."

"Flirt?"

"Yes. You flirt, you get what you want, and then you flirt with the next girl."

Kerra rubbed at the back of her neck, her smile fading as she thought it over. "Is that what you think I'm going to do to you?"

Elizabeth stayed silent for a moment as she considered the question. "No, I don't think you're going to do anything to me. I'm straight. Flirt with whomever you please."

Kerra nodded, slowly, taking in the suggestion. "I will."

Elizabeth shrugged her shoulders in indifference. "Good."

"Good."

The two of them stood in a stare-off, both refusing to speak before the other as they fumed. Elizabeth didn't even know why she was so upset. What difference did it make who Kerra decided to charm? It wasn't any of her business.

Kerra was the first to break as she let out a sigh. "Is that why you don't want to stay with me? Because you think my apartment runs like a whorehouse?"

Elizabeth tugged at her hair. "No. I actually hadn't considered that. I don't want to stay with you because I don't know you."

"So stay with me and get to know me."

"Kerra."

"Lizzie." Kerra took another step forward and reached out to tuck a wandering braid behind Elizabeth's ear. "I promise I'll make a better roommate than your ex-boyfriend."

Elizabeth couldn't help but laugh at that. "I bet." Elizabeth considered her limited options. She couldn't go back to RJ and she would prefer not to go back home to her mother. "I guess I don't really have a lot of options on the table."

Kerra cocked her head at her. "Is that a yes?"

"That's an I guess I have no choice."

"I'll take it."

CHAPTER SIX

Elizabeth followed Kerra in her car to a tiny apartment complex on the edge of the city. It wasn't lavish or expensive, but it wasn't as bohemian as she had expected either.

She took a quick glance around, taking in the area and trying to convince herself that what she was about to do wasn't completely insane. She had one bag of clothes in her car, the first surefire sign that she wasn't thinking her decisions through today. She hitched it over her shoulder as she climbed out of the car and headed to the front of the building. Kerra met her halfway to the stairs and took the bag from her, carrying it effortlessly with one hand. She was definitely stronger than she looked. "I can carry my own bag," Elizabeth informed her.

"It's cool, I got it. Host duties." Kerra moved forward before she could protest, leading Elizabeth up a flight of stairs to an apartment door that read "2A."

Elizabeth held her breath as she waited for Kerra to unlock the door and reveal what was on the other side. She began to panic. What had she gotten herself into? She had agreed to live with a perfect stranger in an apartment that she'd never seen before. Her nerves rattled in her belly in anticipation as she let herself imagine all kinds of horrific things hiding inside the apartment, waiting to teach her a lesson about being impulsive.

Kerra opened the door and stilled all her fears. The large, open apartment sent Elizabeth's mouth dropping down to her chest in shock. The outside of the apartment was a deceptive undersell for what it held inside.

Kerra held the door open for her, and she hurried inside, taking in the space. It was beautiful. The kitchen was spacious and carefully kept, while the adjoining living room was quietly festive. The decorations around the room spoke to who Kerra was. Simple and yet powerful.

Elizabeth wandered into the living room and gawked at the artwork displayed around the room. She ran her hands across a painting that took up nearly an entire wall. The picture featured a woman wrapped in rainbows and riding on a cloud. "It's beautiful." Elizabeth found herself entranced by the picture. There was something utterly absorbing about the woman; her eyes seemed to hold a level of depth that one wouldn't expect from an inanimate piece of artwork.

"It's a friend of mine," Kerra informed her as she stepped behind her to stare at the painting in unison.

Elizabeth let out a grunt as she came to a conclusion. Another one of Kerra's hypnotically beautiful friends.

"Not that kind of friend." Kerra must have heard her deduction in the grunt.

"Then why is she on your wall?" Elizabeth turned to face Kerra, accusations shooting from her eyes.

Kerra had taken a seat on the tan love seat that fit perfectly with the room. "Because she died." Kerra answered the question matter-of-factly, providing no extra detail.

Elizabeth immediately felt guilt wash through her. Before she was only being petty and insecure. Now she was also disrespecting the dead. "Oh, I'm sorry." She felt embarrassed by her behavior. Kerra seemed to make her into an emotional train wreck.

Kerra's expression clouded for a moment, and Elizabeth moved toward her. The drive to comfort Kerra overwhelmed her.

Elizabeth kneeled down to take Kerra's hand, holding it instinctively and hoping that the gesture chased away the clouds in her eyes. There was something about seeing a saddened Kerra that made her heart drop.

Kerra stared down at Elizabeth's hand cupping her own and entwined their fingers.

Elizabeth watched as her fingers laced with Kerra's, her heart picking up pace inside her chest. They both stared in silence at Elizabeth's dark skin interweaving a pattern across Kerra's paleness. There was something beautiful and haunting in the moment that kept

Elizabeth in place against all her impulses to pull away.

Kerra was the first to break the silence, clearing her throat and dropping Elizabeth's hand from her own.

Elizabeth felt a sadness overcome her at the loss of Kerra's touch. Kerra climbed to her feet, moving away from Elizabeth. "I should show you where you can put your things."

"Oh, okay." Elizabeth scrambled up from her kneeling position, muddled by the sudden change in atmosphere. She followed behind Kerra as she led her down the hallway to a bedroom decorated entirely with drawings and artwork Elizabeth could only assume were the work of Kerra. She had only seen very little of her art, but Elizabeth could already sense her style.

"You can stay in here. My room is across the hall. There's food in the fridge if you're hungry." Kerra lingered by the door, watching her take in the room.

Elizabeth turned around in circles, admiring the space. "How can you afford all this?" She knew it was an inappropriate question to ask someone, but a nice apartment in the city had to be costing Kerra an arm and a leg.

Kerra smiled at her as she appreciated the room. "Shelia may be a homophobic wench, but she pays well."

Elizabeth stopped spinning to stare at Kerra. She let out a giggle that quickly turned into hysterical laughter.

Kerra watched her with a grin turning up the corners of her lips.

"Sorry, I think I should eat. I get silly when I'm hungry," Elizabeth explained, wiping at tears that had collected in her eyes from her fit.

"Want me to make you something?" Kerra still smiled at her from the doorway as she propped herself against the frame.

"You cook?" Elizabeth hadn't pegged Kerra for the domesticated type.

"I dabble," Kerra offered with a shrug.

Elizabeth pursed her lips in thought before she nodded in agreement. She let Kerra lead the way to the kitchen and took a seat at the table as she watched her bustle around collecting food and adding spices to a simmering skillet.

She watched in silence as Kerra performed her dance of ingredients. When Kerra was finished, the plate that she set in front of Elizabeth was nothing short of perfection.

Elizabeth stared down in shock at the food before her. "Where in the world did you learn to cook like this?" She took a bite of her food and realized it didn't just look pretty but was also delicious.

Kerra shrugged as she ate directly out of the skillet, and Elizabeth couldn't help the eye roll that followed. Kerra had spent all that time on presentation to eat out of the skillet. Elizabeth smiled at her nonsensical behavior.

"You don't want to make a plate?" she suggested.

"Nope. I reserve my fancy for my roommates."

Elizabeth stared at her, startled by the word. "Huh, I've never had a roommate before."

"Honestly, me neither," Kerra admitted as she walked to a cabinet. She pulled out a bottle of wine and then reached up into a cupboard and pulled out two glasses. "Here's to hoping it works out," Kerra toasted as she poured wine into the glasses and handed one to Elizabeth. She raised her glass to cheers with Kerra before taking a sip.

"I'll call Krissy tomorrow and see about getting you that job at the Bean Spot," Kerra told her as she placed her glass onto the table.

"You know the owner of the coffee shop?" Elizabeth asked, surprised that she hadn't shared the information with her before.

Kerra nodded nonchalantly. "I know everybody."

Elizabeth pushed around food on her plate, feeling awestruck with how much Kerra was doing for her. "It's okay, you don't need to do that. I can manage on my own. I don't need any favors."

Kerra leaned in to catch her eye. "It's okay to let me help you, Lizzie. I don't expect anything from you in return."

Elizabeth set her silverware down and turned to fully face Kerra. "But why, Kerra? Why don't you expect anything in return?"

Kerra sat back in her chair, giving her an indifferent shrug. "I don't know. I just...don't."

"That's not normal, Kerra." Elizabeth crossed her arms across her chest. Kerra's kindness terrified her for reasons she could put together.

Kerra reached out for her wine glass. "I guess I'm just one of a kind." She gave Elizabeth an earnest grin.

Elizabeth let out a sigh, letting her arms fall from their guarding position across her chest. "I can't argue with that."

"Good. So I'll call Krissy then." Kerra took a triumphant sip from her glass.

Elizabeth watched her in her arrogance and couldn't stop herself from smiling. "Do you ever not get what you want?"

Elizabeth saw a tinge of something fog Kerra's eyes as the corners of her mouth relaxed down from her grin. "All of the time."

CHAPTER SEVEN

Elizabeth woke up in a panic, beads of sweat forming on her forehead as her unfamiliar surroundings befuddled her. After a fleeting moment of worry, she remembered where she was, and a smile crept across her face as she recalled the night. Her heart slowed down as she relived the hours she'd spent talking to Kerra and drinking wine until she just couldn't keep her eyes open any longer. Even now, her first waking thoughts drifted to Kerra and if she was awake and thinking about her too.

Elizabeth climbed out of the comfortable bed and stumbled across the room to check herself out in the mirror. She was quite the sight. Her braids ran wild on her head and fell in heaps down her back, and her makeup-free face looked dull and lifeless in the bright sunlight that beamed into the room.

She tried to fix herself up before heading into the hallway to find the bathroom, but it was futile. She needed a shower and longtime mirror session to fix up the first-awakening face she was wearing.

She stumbled out of her room and made her way to the end of the hallway where she found the bathroom, along with a towel neatly laid across the sink and waiting for her. Kerra was determined to make her feel welcome.

Elizabeth jumped into the shower and let herself bask in the warmth of the water. It had never felt so good to be clean. She considered that the last shower she'd had was in RJ's arms, in the apartment that they shared, and she felt a sadness tug at the edge of her excitement. The new life she was embarking on was thrilling and adventurous, but she was leaving a lot behind. A life that had been comfortable and safe. She let herself cry beneath the steady stream of water, letting herself miss RJ, even if only for a moment.

When she was done, she gathered her emotions, turning off the water and promising herself that this would be the last time she let herself be consumed by things she so desperately wanted to leave behind.

She was on her own now, the freedom to make her own choices dancing at her fingertips. Was she really going to let RJ take her joy and continue to control her? Was the safety of routine really what she wanted for herself?

Elizabeth wrapped the waiting towel around her body, letting the wet tips of her braids continue to drip onto her shoulders.

She started down the hall and nearly jumped out of her skin when Kerra appeared in the doorway of her room. Kerra jumped back in surprise too, probably having forgotten that Elizabeth was even there.

"Oh, hey. Good morning," Elizabeth stammered as she tried to catch her breath.

Kerra silently nodded, her eyes still wide with the shock of seeing Elizabeth. There was something else in her features that Elizabeth couldn't quite discern.

"Hey, do you have any eye liner that I can borrow?" Elizabeth dabbed at the end of her braids with a section of her towel.

"I'm not really a makeup kind of girl," Kerra informed her, dropping her eyes to the ground.

"Not even eye liner?" Elizabeth was mystified at how Kerra managed to be so flawlessly beautiful without any help.

"I have a Sharpie you can borrow."

Elizabeth let out a giggle. "I'll pass."

Kerra gave her another nod, keeping her eyes to the floor.

Elizabeth furrowed her eyebrows at Kerra's strange behavior. "Are you okay?"

Kerra cleared her throat before answering as she fidgeted in her doorway. "I'm fine. It's just, you in a towel is a little...distracting."

Elizabeth heated up in embarrassment. She had been so comfortable she had nearly forgotten that she wasn't wearing any clothes. She wasn't usually so bold. She had dated RJ for nearly two years before he even caught a glimpse of her naked body.

"Oh, umm...I'll go get dressed." Elizabeth fumbled the words out as she scurried back to her room to dress herself.

She quickly pulled on a pair of clothes, settling on another tattered pair of jeans and a tank top. It was a simple and careless outfit, but it was exactly who she wanted to be.

She eyed herself in the mirror, pleased with her appearance, even without the help of a little liner to make her look alive. She was feeling so brazen that she even decided to leave her hair down, big and wild and free to dance in the wind.

She left her room to hunt down Kerra and apologize for the awkward scene.

She found Kerra leaning across the sink brushing her teeth. Even foaming at the mouth with toothpaste, her beauty drew Elizabeth in. "Oh, hey. The Queen is clothed." Kerra spat into the sink and wiped her mouth with a towel.

"Yeah, sorry about that. I wasn't even thinking." Elizabeth swatted at a braid that had fallen into her face.

"No need to apologize. I thoroughly enjoyed the thoughtlessness." Kerra flashed her that smile that made her knees go weak.

Elizabeth dropped her gaze to the ground and fidgeted uncomfortably.

"Sorry, I forget how uncomfortable you are with your beauty," Kerra apologized as she watched Elizabeth squirm.

Elizabeth swatted at more hair as it fell into her face. "I'm not uncomfortable with my beauty," she protested.

Kerra cocked her head at her.

"I'm not. I just..." Elizabeth let out a sigh and walked past Kerra to take a seat on the lid of the toilet. "Can I be real with you for a minute, Kerra?"

Kerra settled down into a crouch to match her eye level and took Elizabeth's hand. "Always."

Elizabeth met her eyes, pausing for a moment to explore them. "You make me feel..." She searched for the word as Kerra's eyes continued to absorb her in their pool of blue. "Weird," she finally settled on, though the word did none of her feelings justice.

"Weird?" Kerra started to pull her hand away, but Elizabeth caught it, loving the feel of her touch.

"Not weird, bad. Just, different. Like I'm not myself." She tried to explain, hoping that Kerra could understand.

"Maybe you're just not who you think you are."

Elizabeth nodded. "Maybe." She swatted at another strand of hair. "Ugh, I thought I could wear this stuff down, but I'm over it." She released Kerra's hand to dig in her jeans for a hair tie.

Kerra rose to her feet and watched her fumble in her pockets before pulling out a black ring of elastic.

Elizabeth struggled with her hair, fighting against the thickness of it to collect it into a bundle.

"Here, let me." Kerra moved behind her, taking the hair tie into her hands and beginning her own tussle with Elizabeth's braids.

She moved with the clumsiness of a woman that hadn't dealt with much hair in her lifetime. Elizabeth let out a giggle as she felt her trying to collect the ponytail one strand of hair at a time.

"Hey, don't laugh at me. I'm a sensitive beautician," Kerra called over her head as she continued to bemuse Elizabeth with her method of ponytailing.

"Okay, done." After five minutes of struggling, Kerra finally called it.

Elizabeth rocked her head from side to side, feeling the uneven weight of a poorly crafted ponytail. She stood up and walked over to the mirror and burst into laughter at the sight of herself. The mass of hair recklessly collected in a lopsided pile shot off at an awkward angle from the side of her head. "Wow, Kerra. Just wow."

Kerra rubbed at the back of her neck as she examined her work. "All right, so maybe the ponytail is not my forte."

Elizabeth tapped at the tangle of hair on her head. "You think?"

"Here, I'll take it down." Kerra moved toward her to take down the mess, but Elizabeth stepped out of her grasp.

"No, I think I'm going to wear it like this. It's your first ponytail; it deserves to see the world."

Kerra stared at her for a moment before responding. "Yeah, you're right. Plus, Krissy will probably think you're artsy and eccentric. She'll love it."

Krissy. Elizabeth had nearly forgotten about going to meet the woman at her potential new job. She suddenly felt very nervous about agreeing to rock Kerra's messy ponytail.

Kerra must have sensed her panic. "Don't worry about it. Krissy is a longtime friend. You've all but got the job."

Elizabeth's sense of uneasiness resumed. "What if she doesn't like me? How can you possibly know that she'll just hand me the job?"

"She'll love you. Have I ever lied to you?"

Elizabeth considered the question. In the short time that she'd known Kerra, she'd never been untruthful with her. Unlike the rest of the people in her life, Kerra treated her as an adult, able to make decisions and handle the realness that life had to offer. "No, you haven't." She nodded, about to leave the bathroom to let Kerra get herself dressed. "All right, let's do this. I'm ready to pour coffee like I've been doing it my whole life," she joked. She turned around to add something witty to the end of her statement, but she caught sight of Kerra as she removed her shirt, and the words stuck in her throat. She swallowed hard, yanking her vision away from the sight.

Her breaths came in hard, fast intervals, and she struggled to regain control of herself. Was this what Kerra was feeling seeing her in a towel? She pushed away the thought, refusing to let herself believe that she was experiencing any semblance of the sexual attraction that Kerra may be feeling. *I like men.* Yet she couldn't deny the heat that pulsed through her body at the image of a topless Kerra that lodged in her brain.

CHAPTER EIGHT

Elizabeth sat in silence in the passenger seat of Kerra's car as they drove down the road. Kerra had insisted on driving her to keep her nerves steady as she went off to meet the owner of the Bean Spot. Elizabeth hadn't put up much of a fight, not wanting to change Kerra's mind. The truth of it was that she needed Kerra there. As illogical as it might be, something about having Kerra by her side made her feel like she could conquer any foe, even her own demons.

Elizabeth stole glances of Kerra as she drove. She still couldn't get the image of her body out of her brain. And against all her determination, she couldn't help but want to see it again, to study her and trace her fingertips along Kerra's skin. Elizabeth cleared her throat, making herself awkward with her own thoughts.

"You okay?" Kerra asked her, taking her eyes off of the road for a brief moment to look her over.

"Mm-hmm." Elizabeth nodded, keeping her eyes trained on her feet. She knew if she looked at Kerra, she'd spill every thought she'd had since the morning. Kerra had a way of making her want to share everything with her. Kerra had that effect on most women. *She's a freaking siren*, Elizabeth thought, stealing another glance at Kerra as she returned her eyes to the road.

"So, who are you avoiding?"

"Huh?" Elizabeth had been lost in her own head, debating the possibility of Kerra being a mythological creature.

"Your phone. It's been going off all morning. I can only assume that you're either deaf or there's someone that wants to speak to you and you don't return the sentiment."

Elizabeth let out a sigh as she heard her phone buzz in her bag. "It's my mother."

55

"Oh. Afraid you're going to get grounded?" Kerra let out a laugh, but Elizabeth kept silent.

"Actually, yeah. Kind of. If I call her back, she's just going to demand that I come home—or worse, convince me to go back to RJ." There she went again, spilling all her secrets.

Kerra was silent for a long time, and Elizabeth waited. She listened to the steady click of the turn signal as they weaved around a corner.

"Are you going to say anything?" Elizabeth had grown impatient for a response.

Kerra shook her head. "I don't think I should."

"Why not?" Elizabeth huffed. Kerra's thoughts and opinions had grown increasingly more important to her.

"Because it's not my place." Kerra wore a thoughtful expression as she kept her eyes forward.

"Yes, it is. You're my roommate and my friend, and I want to know what you think," Elizabeth insisted, desperate to know what thoughts had brewed in her mind.

"I think..." Kerra took a long pause, choosing her words carefully before she spoke again. "I think that you're a grown woman, Lizzie. Nobody can make your decisions for you. Not your mother, not your ex, and certainly not me. You have to do what Lizzie wants to do because, ultimately, you're the only one who has to live with those decisions."

Elizabeth sat back in her seat, mulling over her words. Kerra nervously drummed her fingers along the steering wheel as she waited for a reaction. "I'm sorry, I didn't mean to—" She started to apologize, but Elizabeth waved her off.

"No, it's okay. You're right. I am responsible for me. I've lived my whole life trying to keep my mom's approval. I've kind of just given the reins to my life over to her. And this—moving to the city, leaving RJ, and working in a coffee shop—it's going to disappoint her, and that's terrifying to me." Elizabeth glanced down at her bag as it buzzed again.

"As the product of two disappointed parents and an angry brother, I can tell you it's not going to be as bad as you think. You get used to it, and you realize that you have to make you happy, and if they really love you, they'll come around."

Elizabeth twirled her thumbs in her lap. "Did your family come around?"

Kerra rubbed at her neck as she considered her response. "I'm still waiting."

Elizabeth rested her head against the window, looking out onto the sights of the city. There were a hundred different people wandering around with a hundred different styles, coming in and out of a hundred different buildings. She imagined herself amongst them, living a life that was hers. A life that she could fill with anything she wanted.

She glanced across the car, thinking about how much she wanted to fill her life with Kerra. As a friend, of course, she reminded herself.

She reached into her bag and pulled out her phone, starting at the fifteen missed calls from her mother. Maybe she could make her understand. There was no denying how much her mother loved her; it had always been just the two of them. Before RJ came along, they were all each other had. Maybe now that he was out of the picture they could get back to that. She wanted so desperately for her mother to understand her.

She let her finger hover over the return call button, feeling her will strengthen. *If she loves me, she'll support me.*

Elizabeth hit the call button as Kerra pulled up in front of the Bean Spot. She hung up the phone before putting it to her ear, not wanting to delay her meet and greet for an uncomfortable call with her mother.

"Ready?" Kerra put the car in park and turned to look at her.

Elizabeth gave her a nod even though butterflies collected in her stomach at an alarming rate.

"It's going to be fine," Kerra reassured her before she climbed out of the car.

Elizabeth opened her door and stood on shaky feet as she moved toward the shop behind Kerra. She unconsciously reached out for her, clutching onto Kerra's wrist for comfort as she led her inside.

As soon as they were through the door they were bombarded with hugs. A tall, shapely woman moved quickly to Kerra, sweeping her up into an embrace that took her off her feet. Elizabeth lost her grip on Kerra's wrist, but before her panic set in, she was being grabbed around her shoulders by a dainty woman in a quilt-pattern sundress. "Oh my, you must be Lizzie," the woman said into her hair as she squeezed her. "She's even more beautiful than you told us, Kerra."

The woman changed positions, and Elizabeth felt herself being pulled off the floor into an aggressive hug by the plump girl in front of her. "Oh, wow." Elizabeth let out a shocked response to the breathtaking introduction. This was not how she had expected the interviewing process to go.

"It's so good to see you, Kerra. How are you holding up? The city has been treating you good, in my absence? You look fantastic as always." The slender woman placed a kiss on Kerra's cheeks in between rattling off her questions.

Elizabeth watched the two of them. Kerra was right; her crooked ponytail was probably impressive to the woman standing in front of her. The woman's own hair sat like a crow's nest on top of her head, and neither of the shoes she wore matched the other. She was definitely eccentric.

"I'm good. The city is good. Things are—"

"Let me guess. Good?" The tiny woman cut Kerra off.

Kerra grinned at her as she nodded in agreement.

Elizabeth found herself smiling at the exchange as well. Something about the way they interacted with one another was touching. Like something more than friendship. The woman hovered over Kerra protectively, as if on the instincts of a mother.

"Oh my, how rude of me. I've held you in my arms, and you don't even know who I am." The woman caught Elizabeth staring at the two of them. "I'm Krissy, and this is my daughter, Lola."

Elizabeth looked at the plump woman that had embraced her. Lola looked nothing like Krissy. She was shapely and pale in sharp contrast to Krissy's light brown skin tone and slim figure.

"I'm adopted...sort of," Lola told Elizabeth as she caught her puzzled expression.

"Oh, sorry, I didn't mean—"

"Nonsense. We're an odd pair. It's perfectly natural to be curious," Krissy assured her. She led them to a table and gestured for Kerra and

Elizabeth to take a seat. Without prompting, Lola disappeared behind the counter, fiddling with machines and mugs to make them drinks.

"So, tell me about yourself, Lizzie. I've gotten nothing but vague details about who you are from this one. Getting her to share is like pulling teeth." Krissy placed her hand over Kerra's, casually placed on the table. There was so much affection in the gesture that it made Elizabeth's heart ache.

"Oh, I umm..." Elizabeth wasn't sure what to say. All the things she knew about herself didn't make her qualify for the job. Her heart began to thump hard enough that it echoed through her temples. "I-I... Uh..."

Krissy let out a laugh. "Conversation skills, not your strong suit, apparently."

Elizabeth swallowed back a nervous choke. She was bombing this interview hard.

"Honey, don't worry about it. I trust this one with my life. If she says you can do this job, then I believe her. You're hired. Relax."

Elizabeth let out a sigh of relief as Lola returned and set three coffee cups in front of them. "Welcome to the team." She gave Elizabeth's shoulder a squeeze before returning to her work back behind the counter.

"Thank you," Elizabeth whispered after her. She felt like she was in the twilight zone. Why would anyone hire her to do anything? She was practically a mute today.

"I'll only be in the city for another couple of days. Can you start tomorrow? I'd love to train you myself before I leave you to Lola."

Elizabeth nodded, still not trusting herself to speak.

"Great. Then I can get to know you a bit; see what it is about you that's gotten my Ker-Bear here so smitten."

Kerra shot up in her chair. "Krissy."

Elizabeth felt herself blushing at Krissy's frankness. Something about the thought of Kerra speaking affectionately of her to someone she obviously cared about made Elizabeth's chest swell with excitement.

Krissy watched her carefully as a smile crept onto her face. "Clearly, she's not the only one."

"All right, Krissy. Thank you for sufficiently freaking out my roommate. You met her, you embarrassed me, we hugged. Can we go now?" Kerra stood up, fidgeting uncomfortably. Whoever Krissy was to Kerra, she made her into a twiddling child.

Krissy let out a sigh mixed with a laugh. "Fine, go. But don't you forget to call me tomorrow. Even if only to check on your girl here." Krissy stood up to embrace Kerra, and the two of them shared a lingering hug. "I love you, Ker-Bear," Krissy said into her ear and stroked the top of her hair.

"I love you too, Krissy."

Elizabeth stared in amazement. It was the first time she'd seen Kerra be affectionate in a way that wasn't sexually motivated, and Elizabeth had to admit that it made her yearn for Kerra. It made her crave to be the object of Kerra's affection that didn't linger on physical attraction. There was something majestic in Kerra's love. In the two minutes of seeing her with Krissy, there was an unspoken trust and understanding between the two of them. There was no doubt in Elizabeth's mind that they would go to hell and back for the sake of the other. Elizabeth desperately wanted that in her life. The security of knowing someone was always in her corner, unconditionally.

Elizabeth was ripped from her daze by Kerra staring at her impatiently. "Come on," Kerra urged her. She had completely morphed before her eyes. The cool and confident Kerra had turned into an impatient and whiny twelve-year-old in the blink of an eye.

Elizabeth found herself smiling at the transformation. Kerra was the most endearingly adorable twelve-year-old in all the world.

Elizabeth followed her back out of the Bean Spot to the car. "Krissy seems nice. I wish I hadn't been such a fumbling idiot in front of her," she told her as she started the car.

"Trust me, I was a lot worse the first time she met me."

"How did you meet her? You said she was a friend but…it seems like there's more there than that."

Kerra didn't answer her. She kept driving in silence as she mulled over the question. "Krissy is my family. Lola too. It's kind of a long story."

"I don't start working until tomorrow." Elizabeth was curious. Kerra knew so much about her already, and she knew very little about Kerra.

Kerra ran a hand through her hair. "It's not really a story I'm ready to share yet." Kerra took her eyes off the road to glance at Elizabeth, her eyes begging for understanding.

Elizabeth nodded. "Okay. Well, when you're ready, I'll be here."

"Will you? I mean, you still haven't talked to your mom yet."

Elizabeth smiled. "I will. You were right. I'm a grown-up, and I have to make choices for me. And this will make me happy."

"This?"

"Yeah, living in the city, working at the Bean Spot…you."

"Me?" Kerra jerked her head around to stare at her.

"Yes, you. I've never had a real friend before."

"Oh." There was some sort of disappointment in her tone as she said the word.

They drove in silence, both taking in Elizabeth's proclamation of happiness. Kerra pulled up in front of her apartment, tapping her fingers nervously against the dashboard.

"Are you going to turn the car off?" Elizabeth watched her, curious about her behavior. She seemed to be deep in thought about something Elizabeth was unaware of. "Kerra?" Elizabeth opened the door to the car, hoping the sudden movement would break Kerra out of her trance.

"Lizzie?"

"Yeah?" Elizabeth closed the car door again, wanting no interference for whatever Kerra was about to say.

She turned in her seat to stare at Elizabeth, her eyes boring into her. Elizabeth felt her heart pick up speed, and her mouth went dry beneath Kerra's gaze. She felt full and consumed beneath the clear blue pools of hope and desire that observed her. Her breath caught in her throat as Kerra parted her lips to speak. "You make me happy too."

CHAPTER NINE

Sitting on the edge of her bed, Elizabeth stared down at her phone. She had been pacing the floor of her room since they had gotten back to Kerra's apartment, trying repeatedly to call her mother and losing her nerve. Kerra popped in on her occasionally, repeating the same question each time she strolled by: "Did you call her yet?" Each time she was met by a flying pillow to her face.

Elizabeth was growing impatient and frustrated with herself. Why couldn't she just do this? She remembered the hug she watched Kerra and Krissy share. Their love came so easily, so absolutely; Elizabeth wanted that with her mother. But she knew the terms of her mother's love were not unconditional. There was an invisible line that Elizabeth was never allowed to cross, and her whole life she had been so careful to keep teetering on the tightrope.

A wave of anger washed through her. She'd been blaming RJ and her mother for her unhappiness for so long, when it was really her own fault. If only she had been more like Kerra, free thinking and unafraid to strike out on her own, to live in a way that made her proud of herself. She envied Kerra; everything seemed to come so easy to her.

Putting the phone to her ear again, for the tenth time, she pressed the call button. *Breathe, you can do this. Just tell her what you want.*

Elizabeth's nerves jumped at the sound of ringing through the phone, and she pulled it away from her head again, ready to hang up and hope that the eleventh time was a charm, when she caught a glimpse of Kerra standing her doorway giving her a thumbs-up. She was so busy wishing she could be like Kerra, she hadn't realized it could be as simple as just making this call.

She nodded at Kerra, thankful for her presence and somehow feeling Kerra's strength radiate off her body to boost her own.

Her heartbeat intensified with every ring on the other end of the phone. *Keep breathing*, she reminded herself as her chest tightened and stilled.

"Elizabeth, honey, where are you? I've been calling you for days. Are you okay?" Her mother sounded frantic, and Elizabeth felt guilt swell in her throat. She had been so consumed in what it was she was feeling she had neglected to consider her mother.

"I'm fine, Mom. I just—"

"Because RJ told me what happened. He said you left and haven't been back and then I don't hear from you and..." She finally paused to take a breath. "Elizabeth, what is going on?"

The guilt in the pit of her stomach grew as she felt her mother's concern. She was touched by how much she cared, but the feeling was short-lived.

"Elizabeth, are you on drugs? Is that what's been going on? Because I raised you better than that, and I won't have—"

"Mom, I'm not on drugs, I just needed some time to get myself together." Elizabeth let out a sigh and looked back to her door, hoping to see Kerra's encouraging face. But she had disappeared, giving her privacy to talk.

"I called Lindsey," her mother continued on as if she hadn't heard her. "I thought that's where you might be, and she said she hadn't seen you either."

"Mom, I don't even like Lindsey."

"Oh, yes you do. Don't say that. The Cantells are wonderful people." Her mother brushed aside her protests and continued to chastise her for her behavior. "Why would you leave and run off into the night without telling someone where you were going? It's so very irresponsible, Elizabeth. I know you didn't tell Lindsey because she wouldn't lie to me. RJ had no idea where you were, and every time I called, I just got your answering machine..."

Elizabeth let out a groan of frustration as she listened to her mother continue to prattle on about how poorly she had handled her situation. She shook her head, feeling herself grow more and more distant from her mother. She had wanted to call and be strong and tell her what she wanted, and instead she was being chewed out, debating the morals of the Cantells. *Is this really how you want to live your life? Never being heard?* Elizabeth felt a fury build in her chest that she had never felt before. It was now or never. If she didn't put her foot down and demand that her mother hear her and treat her like a human being, she would forever be victim to her whimsy.

She might as well take her bag of clothes and run off to marry RJ.

"Mom, stop. Just stop it! I'm done listening to you criticize me and tick off one by one all the things that are wrong with me."

"Excuse me?" Her mother's appalled tone would have normally been enough to stop her in her tracks, but she was too far gone, too far in. She'd tasted what it was like to be unleashed from the constant pressure of living up to her mother's expectations, and she wasn't about to let it go.

"I get it. I'm a constant disappointment in your eyes who has to go running to you, or RJ, or Lindsey to take care of me. You don't think that I'm smart enough or capable of being on my own and..." Elizabeth's voice broke as a sob escaped her throat. "And that's fine, Mom, but I am. I can be on my own. I will be on my own." Tears streamed down her face and clouded her vision, and she listened as silence enveloped the other end of the line.

"Elizabeth." Her mother's strained voice cut through the silence. "Do you remember two years ago, when you told me you were moving in with RJ? What did I say to you?"

Elizabeth let out another shaky sob. "You pitched a fit about morals and marriage and told me to remember how you raised me."

"And then what did I say?" she urged her.

The memory of the day she packed her bags to move in with RJ came rushing to the front of her mind. Her mother had yelled and screamed at her for days up until the move, Elizabeth determined to have her way, and her mother determined to have hers. Her mother was an immovable object, and Elizabeth an unstoppable force. It was the first time she'd ever gone against her mother, and she had been nearly ready to back down when her mother had come to her, tears filling her eyes, and told her she trusted her. She had told her that she was strong and smart, and although she didn't agree, she trusted her and she trusted RJ. Elizabeth's heart ached at the memory. She had demonized her mother and blamed her unhappiness on everyone around her, when the blame lay inward.

"You told me you trusted me. You told me that I was smart and strong," she answered, suddenly feeling ashamed for having lashed out.

Her mother sniffled through the phone. "Honey, you are not a disappointment. I only want what is best for you. You're my little girl, and I want to protect you and keep you on the path that God has paved for you. Does that really make me so horrible? Do I not deserve to want what's best for you?"

The sadness in her voice broke Elizabeth's heart. Deep down she knew her mother only wanted what was best for her. And shielding her and tying her down to RJ was what her mother thought was best. Elizabeth had to admit RJ had a bright future and blaming her mother for wanting her to be a part of it wasn't fair.

"I'm sorry, Mom. I don't think that you're horrible, and I should have called. I just…I needed to figure things out."

"And you didn't think I could help?"

"I didn't think you'd understand."

"I don't understand, but that doesn't mean that I don't want to try."

Elizabeth took a deep breath, trying to steady her voice. The conversation had taken a more emotional turn than she had anticipated. "I want to move to the city. I've already found a job and a place to stay."

Her mother fell silent, and Elizabeth could almost hear the wheels in her head turning, scraping for a way to talk her out of it.

"Mom, I need this." She was pleading with her to understand. The fire to defy her mother had left her, and all she wanted now was her support.

"Where are you living? Are you safe?"

Elizabeth nodded, even though she could not see her. "Yes, I'm safe. The apartment I'm staying in is very nice, and my roommate is the one that helped me find a job."

"I'd like to meet her."

"My roommate?"

"Yes. If you're going to be living with someone, I would like to meet them. Just for peace of mind."

Elizabeth swallowed hard. Her mother was certainly being more cooperative than usual, but she wasn't sure how she would react to Kerra. "Umm...I'll have to see about her schedule, Mom. She's very busy."

"How about Friday? I'll cook dinner. She eats dinner, doesn't she?" Her mother was clearly not taking no for an answer.

"Yes, she eats dinner." She let out a sigh. "Fine, Mom. I'll see if she can do Friday."

"Great. I'll see you on Friday." Her mother sounded chipper again, as if their conversation had never happened.

"I'll see you Friday," Elizabeth offered, not sure how she felt about the change in tone. It felt like she was right back where she started, bending to the will of her mother.

"I love you, honey."

"I love you too, Mom." She hung up the phone, biting her lip as she mulled over what had just happened. She had gotten her mother's blessing to live in the city, or had she? She wasn't sure where she stood, but she didn't feel in control. She had expected to feel free and powerful after she called her mother and demanded respect, but she really only felt confused and manipulated.

Elizabeth stood up, hoping that the shift in weight would help to clear her head. She caught sight of Kerra in her doorway, staring at her with concern. "You all right?" She posed the question gently.

Giving her what she hoped was a convincing nod, Elizabeth sat back down on the bed, realizing that standing only made her exhausted.

Kerra crossed the room to her, moving carefully as if she was afraid she might spook her. She took a seat next to her on the soft mattress and held out her hand.

Staring at the hand in skepticism, Elizabeth debated if she should take it. She yearned for the feel of Kerra's fingers entwined with hers, but the thought of her mother pinged around in her head, warning her of the slippery slope she was sliding down.

"I just want to be here for you, Lizzie. That's all." It was as if Kerra

67

could read her thoughts and feel her skepticism.

Elizabeth smiled, taking the hand held out for her and lacing her fingers through it. Kerra had been in her corner since the moment she met her and never asked for anything in return. There was a spark in Kerra that Elizabeth had never encountered in anyone else; maybe her mother would see that. Once she got past the tattoos and the boyish way of dress, maybe her mother would see the amazing person who lay beneath. Elizabeth clutched Kerra's hand tighter as she let her gaze travel to meet Kerra's eyes, the pools of blue radiating support and adoration. Elizabeth didn't want to hide her. If her mother was going to support her new life, she was going to support Kerra too.

Elizabeth breathed in deep before asking the question. "What are you doing on Friday?"

CHAPTER TEN

Elizabeth moved deftly across the café with a confidence she never expected from herself. She'd entered the Bean Spot that morning terrified of what the day would bring, and yearning for Kerra to be by her side. But Krissy had provided her flawless guidance with a kind and gentle touch that made Elizabeth want to impress her.

Six hours into her shift she was gliding across the café like a professional. She'd nearly burned her fingertips off from touching the wrong part of the coffee machine so many times, but she barely even felt the raw skin aching in her appendages as she cascaded through a maze of tables delivering orders.

She could feel Krissy's eyes on her as she moved. She knew the stare. It was the gaze of a proud mama bear as she watched her cub succeed. Krissy had given her the same stare every time she accomplished something, even the most menial of tasks, and Elizabeth relished it. There was something so utterly inviting about Krissy that the instant you met her, you craved her approval. She was a hell of a woman. It was no wonder Kerra seemed to care for her so much.

Sliding a crumpled bill that had been left as a tip in her pocket, Elizabeth made her way back to the counter. She slipped behind it, grabbing up a tray of empty coffee mugs as she went. She set the tray in the wash bin, as she'd done a hundred times in the last few hours, and went to cleaning the coffee maker.

"You are a natural, Lizzie." Krissy complimented her as she watched her take apart the machine.

Heat crept around Elizabeth's neck at the compliment. "Thank you."

"No, I mean it. You're as sharp as Kerra insisted. I certainly hope you stay with us for a while."

Elizabeth could feel her blush intensifying at the mention of Kerra.

Krissy leaned herself against the counter to watch her. The hustle and bustle of the café was dying down as they neared their closing hour. The few customers left straggling sipped their coffee without much need of service.

"Can I ask you something? And don't think that your answer in any way affects your employment." Krissy slipped her hands into the pockets on her apron, waiting for Elizabeth's permission to proceed.

Elizabeth put down the pieces of the machine to turn and watch Krissy, suddenly curious.

"Okay." Elizabeth let the answer out slowly, suspicious of what she might be walking into.

"What exactly are your intentions for my Ker-Bear?" Krissy asked the question casually.

"My intentions?" Elizabeth stared at Krissy in surprise.

"Yes." Krissy answered her in a matter-of-fact tone, as if the question were a simple one with a simple answer.

"Well..." Elizabeth mulled over her reply. "She's my roommate."

Krissy gave her a nod. "Yes, and?"

"And my friend."

"And?" Krissy pressed her forward, but she had nothing left.

"And, that's it. She's helping me find my way, and I appreciate her for that." Elizabeth returned to her task of cleaning the coffee machine.

Krissy moved forward to stop her. She closed her hand over Elizabeth's. "I've known Kerra for a very long time. I know her better than she knows herself, and I know that she is very taken with you, Lizzie. Very taken. And if your intent is to be friends and roommates, make it clear. Don't blur those lines because she's not as unbreakable as she seems."

Krissy caught her eye and held it, boring into her and pressing her to come face-to-face with her own emotions. Elizabeth's heart picked up speed, and she nearly gasped at the words that spilled from her mouth. "But what if the lines are blurred for me?" She hadn't meant to say it, and she barely even knew she felt it, but Krissy stared at her in understanding, as if she had known all along her feelings.

Elizabeth hadn't realized her eyes had watered over until Krissy wiped at a tear flowing down her cheek. Krissy pulled her into a hug and stroked her head. "Oh, honey. Then you follow your heart."

Pulling out of Krissy's grasp, Elizabeth wiped her cheeks, embarrassed by her behavior. Krissy had worked some sort of magic spell on her, making her crumble in tears on her first day of work. Elizabeth turned back to her work, attempting for the third time to finish cleaning the machine in front of her.

She worked in silence, putting the pieces of the machine back together. She could feel the burn of Krissy's stare as she watched her. "It's not strange, you know?"

Elizabeth sniffed as she wiped the counter where coffee grounds and milk littered the pale-yellow countertop. "What's not strange?" She didn't want to talk to Krissy any longer. Krissy made her too comfortable, too honest; she made her face things she wasn't ready to face yet. But she couldn't stop herself.

"That she's falling for you."

Stopping in her tracks, Elizabeth turned to stare at Krissy. "What?"

"You're clever, you're kind, and you're enduringly innocent. Why wouldn't she be smitten?" Krissy gave her a smile as she listed off her positive traits. "Speak of the devil." Krissy sailed past her as Elizabeth stood frozen by her declaration that Kerra was "falling" for her.

Elizabeth could hear Kerra's voice as she and Krissy greeted one another behind her, but she couldn't force her body to move. What if Kerra really was falling for her and she wasn't just some girl in a catalog of flirtations? Could she really handle that?

"So, how's the first day? Krissy giving you a hard time?"

Forcing herself to turn around at the sound of Kerra's voice, Elizabeth was struck with a warm sensation cascading through her body at the sight of her. She let the sensation fill her as she continued to adore Kerra's presence.

"You all right?" Kerra stared at her in concern, and Elizabeth realized she'd been silent for an abnormally long time.

"Yeah, sorry. I'm fine. First day was fine. Coffee Queen." Elizabeth offered in response, giving a halfhearted, dramatic bow.

Kerra gave her a half smile that lit her insides on fire.

Elizabeth considered Krissy's advice. Could her heart really lie with Kerra? She always felt electric in Kerra's presence, strong and invincible. But maybe she was infatuated with the lifestyle and appreciative of Kerra's help.

Her emotions felt like they were ripping her in half. Everything she thought she knew about herself seemed to be crashing down around her. The last thing she wanted to do was hurt Kerra because she didn't know what she wanted. She had to figure herself out. She had to figure out her heart and unblur the lines before she made mistakes that she could not come back from. She wanted some alone time with Kerra, to figure out where friendship ended and sexual chemistry began, but her nerves bundled in her throat.

"Kerra?" She choked out the word, hoping Kerra wouldn't notice how overwhelmingly flustered she was.

"Yeah?" Kerra stared at her from the other side of the counter.

"Would you like to have dinner with me tonight?"

☆☆☆

Elizabeth nervously flittered around her room, rifling through her three available outfits for something suitable to put together. Kerra had gone to get ingredients for dinner, even after Elizabeth had insisted she let her pay for them to go out. Although Elizabeth was definitely low on funds, she figured finding out if she had the hots for her female roommate was worth the expense. But Kerra had her head wrapped around making them dinner, and Elizabeth had a hard time refusing Kerra the things she wanted.

Maybe I just want to please her. It wasn't a far-off thought. Elizabeth was a people pleaser. It was in her nature to make her wants coincide with the people who surrounded her. She couldn't ever really be sure if what she wanted was actually what she wanted or if it was just what everyone else wanted.

She let out a sigh as her mind once again began to rally against her. How could she even be considering this? She was with RJ for nearly half a decade; she obviously liked men. But Kerra. Even the thought of her filled her with something. Respect? Adoration? Love? She didn't know.

But Krissy was right. She had to decide one way or another because if Kerra really did feel something for her, she didn't deserve to be jerked around.

The sound of the front door opening yanked her from her daydreams and made the panic in her gut intensify. She still hadn't sorted the details of her ensemble. Creaking the door of her bedroom open, she poked her head out to catch a glimpse of Kerra.

Kerra's tight black tank top, wrapped graciously around her body, sent a wave of heat through Elizabeth. There was definitely something stirring within her for Kerra.

"I'm going to start cooking," Kerra informed her as she noticed her head peeking out into the hallway.

Elizabeth nodded before a realization struck her. "Wait, you're not going to change?" She had suspected when Kerra offered to cook that her intentions for the night to be a date were unclear, but she was too nervous to clarify. Seeing Kerra, prepared to spend the night in ripped black jeans and a matching tank, solidified that Kerra was definitely not aware of the weight of the night.

"Nah, I'm good," Kerra assured her.

Elizabeth felt herself deflate. She had so vehemently been looking forward to seeing Kerra don a slick button-up shirt and one of her ties that made Elizabeth's head swim, her jet-black hair ever so slightly gelled back, so that the tips dangled above her eyes. Even the not-so-shallow part of Elizabeth that didn't just yearn for Kerra's snazzy appearance wanted to scream to Kerra that she had asked her on a date. There was something important about the distinction. Even though Elizabeth wasn't sure how she felt, and she certainly wasn't sure she would want a second date, she wanted the acknowledgement that it was in fact a date.

Letting out a sigh, Elizabeth attempted to convince herself that maybe it was better Kerra didn't know. Maybe it would take some of the pressure off and give her the opportunity to know Kerra when her charm was turned off.

She pushed her outfit choices to the side, realizing that the mood was set to casual for the afternoon. Tying her hair up into a neat bun, she took a deep breath. *It's just a casual dinner.* Her nerves were beginning to set in. She had felt so confident and sure of herself when she made the decision to determine her feelings, but as the moments crept by, her mind began to shout at her that it was a bad idea to open the door to the possibility of feeling something more than friendship for Kerra.

Elizabeth pushed down the nerves that clawed inside her and headed to the kitchen where she found Kerra moving around with the expertise that she always seemed to possess in everything she did. Kerra's eyes found her where she stood in the doorway, and she gave her a grin. "Hey, you look nice."

Elizabeth had forgotten that she had applied her makeup before she realized how un-date-like her date night was going to be. "Oh, thank you."

"Want to help?" Kerra asked her the question without ever looking up from her station at the stove.

"Oh, I can't cook."

Kerra waved off her response. "Psh, everyone can cook. Come here, I'm about to do the best part."

Elizabeth made her way into the kitchen and stood awkwardly as she waited for instruction.

Kerra rolled her eyes. "No, come here. As in, to me," she demanded as she gestured at the tiny space between herself and the stove.

Elizabeth moved closer, hesitant about filling the small space and being so close to Kerra. She was suddenly grateful for Kerra's misinterpretation of her intentions. There was no way she'd be able to focus on her heart with a gussied-up Kerra standing so near.

"Here. So you grab the handle." Kerra closed the small bit of distance between them and wrapped her body around Elizabeth's to guide her. She moved her hand to the handle of the pot filled with colorful vegetables sizzling on the stove top. "Just move the pot back and forth over the eye," Kerra instructed her as she closed her hand over Elizabeth's to direct her movements.

Even through the smell of the sizzling vegetables, Elizabeth caught wafts of Kerra's scent, making her thoughts dance away from the notion of food. She pushed away the thoughts of Kerra's body pressed neatly against her back and tried to focus on her task. She was grateful that Kerra moved her arm for her because all her muscles had gone weak.

"All right, here comes the flip," Kerra whispered into her ear, making a shiver travel down the back of her neck. Her hairs were standing on end, and she wondered if Kerra had any idea of the effect that she was having on her.

"The what?" Elizabeth asked the question breathlessly.

"Just flick your wrist," Kerra told her as she moved Elizabeth's hand to flip the vegetables. Elizabeth watched in awe as all the contents of the skillet traveled seamlessly into the air to rainbow back into the pot.

"Wow, that was fun." Elizabeth echoed Kerra's earlier comment.

"Ready to fly solo?" Kerra let go of her hand and moved away from her. Elizabeth frowned at the cold spot that attacked her back as Kerra moved away with her warmth. She focused on flipping the vegetables again and moved her hands to mimic the movements that Kerra had just shown her, but her vegetable flick was unsuccessful. The beautiful rainbow that Kerra had created bore no semblance to rainstorm of vegetables that she sent flying into the air. Elizabeth let out a squeal as food rained down onto the floor and counter.

She whirled around as she heard hysterical laughter being released behind her.

"Are you laughing at me?" Elizabeth accused Kerra.

Kerra attempted to bite back a laugh as she shook her head innocently.

"I told you I can't cook," Elizabeth huffed as she set the skillet back onto the stove.

Kerra let out another series of chuckles before she composed herself. "It's okay. We'll clean up and order takeout."

Elizabeth crossed her arms and pouted. She wasn't too pleased with being made of.

Kerra sighed at her pout and reached out to place her hands on Elizabeth's shoulders. "I'm sorry I laughed at you...but you screamed at flying vegetables."

Elizabeth fought the urge to laugh. She didn't want to let Kerra off that easy.

"All right, I'll clean up, while you order takeout," Kerra offered in apology.

Elizabeth finally let herself wear the smile she'd been fighting, accepting the idea of shucking the cleanup duties. "Sounds good to me." Elizabeth uncrossed her arms and headed out of the kitchen to retrieve her phone.

She made it back to the kitchen to find Kerra sweeping up her mess. "Want help?" She felt guilty about leaving her with the cleanup.

"No, a deal's a deal." Kerra stopped her sweeping to stare at Elizabeth. "Though you did hustle me into it."

"Hustle you? No way." Elizabeth knew the move was to deny, deny, deny.

Kerra propped the broom against the counter and rounded the stove to move closer to Elizabeth. She stopped in front of Elizabeth and narrowed her eyes. "Really?"

Elizabeth let out a giggle. "Maybe a little."

"I knew it." Kerra leaned back against the counter. "I let you, you know."

Elizabeth took a step closer to Kerra, closing the gap between them to near inches. "You let me hustle you?"

"Yep." Kerra flashed her a wide grin.

"Why would you do something like that?" Elizabeth was unconvinced.

Kerra gave her a shrug in response. "I just did."

Elizabeth took another step forward, noting that there was no longer any space between them. Her heart raced as she realized what she was doing, but she couldn't stop herself as she leaned in and placed her lips against Kerra's.

The touch of their lips sent volts of electricity through Elizabeth, and she felt the sudden need for more. She pushed herself forward, wanting to kiss Kerra more deeply, to let her hands explore, but Kerra pulled away from her, nearly moving across the room to put distance between them.

Elizabeth stared after her, dumbfounded by Kerra's sudden repulsion to her. "What's wrong?" She hadn't meant for it to sound as accusatory as it came out, but she needed to know what caused the sudden shift in atmosphere. Elizabeth had taken a monumental leap of faith, and she could feel the tears stinging at the backs of her eyes from being rejected.

Kerra ran a hand through her hair as she moved from side to side, unable to stand still. "What are you doing, Lizzie?"

"What do you mean, what am I doing? Wasn't it obvious?" Elizabeth was barely hanging on to the urge not to burst into tears.

"I mean, what are you doing with me? What do you want from me, Lizzie?"

"I don't know. I was trying to see if I...I don't know." Elizabeth swiped at a tear.

"Do you want to be with me?" Kerra stopped fidgeting and stared at her, an emotion glinting in her eyes that Elizabeth couldn't interpret.

"I don't know," she offered weakly, as she took a step forward.

Kerra matched her movements, taking a step back to keep the distance between them. "I can't be your coming-out project, Lizzie. I really like you, and I can handle being just your roommate, but I can't be your in-between. If we go there, you have to know, and you don't and I...I just can't." Kerra let out a sigh. "I'll finish cleaning later. I need a walk." Kerra turned to leave the apartment without giving Elizabeth a chance to stop her.

Elizabeth watched after her, feeling every tear she'd tried to hold back burst from the dam. Her legs no longer carried the will to hold her up as she collapsed to the floor in sobs. She hoped Kerra's walk lasted a while because she wasn't sure her tears would ever stop.

CHAPTER ELEVEN

Elizabeth climbed out of her bed, her eyelids heavy from the weight of crying through the night. She wanted to kick herself for being so stupid, but seeing as she couldn't get her foot to bend that way, she settled for all-night tears.

She'd known the moment Kerra walked out of the door that she wanted to be with her. Against every ingrained instinct in her body, Elizabeth wanted Kerra. She wanted to hold her and feel that electricity she felt when their lips touched, but she had second-guessed herself. She'd let Kerra believe that she was unsure. That her actions were some flaky experiment to toy with Kerra's emotions and then leave her in the dust.

Wiping at another escaped tear, Elizabeth tried to clear her head. She wasn't sure what to do next. Along with feeling embarrassed, she felt like she might have ruined the only stable friendship she had—or at the very least altered it to an unbearable level of awkwardness.

She wished she could have found the strength to leave her room when she heard Kerra return home in the dead of the night, but she was too busy feeling sorry for herself and moping in her pity puddle.

Staring at herself in the mirror, she examined her puffy face and skewed hair. Maybe she didn't deserve Kerra. If she couldn't muster up the courage to tell her how she felt, what made her think she was strong enough to carry on a relationship with a woman so phenomenally fierce? She let out a sigh as she realized she was back in the cycle of her pity parade. *Stop it!* she commanded herself. *If you want her then just go get her.* Elizabeth felt the familiar hit of confidence and self-assuredness that she'd been getting in waves since she first set foot in the city. She wiped at the puffiness under her eyes and took a deep breath before heading out into the hallway, to Kerra's door.

"Kerra?" She tapped twice against the wood, her heart beginning to jump so fast, it skipped beats. *Just tell her what you want,* Elizabeth encouraged herself.

"Yeah?" There was an abundance of noise on the other side of Kerra's door as she shuffled to answer her call. Kerra's voice sounded strained, and Elizabeth felt her confidence beginning to slip away. Kerra was probably still not too pleased with her actions the night before.

"Can I talk to you, please?" Her voice was meek, and she sounded like a child begging for a toy.

"Uh, yeah. Just a second."

Elizabeth waited on the other side of the door, listening through the wood as Kerra trudged around behind it. She froze in place as she heard a giggle travel through the door. A familiar giggle that she couldn't quite place, but she knew it wasn't Kerra's. Her chest tightened at the realization of what was happening. She positioned herself to run back to her room, but Kerra's door began to open.

"Hey," Kerra greeted her as she slid out of her door and into the hallway, careful to hide the contents of her room from Elizabeth's view.

"Hey." Elizabeth felt a swell of emotions build inside her, and she wasn't sure which to address first.

Kerra ran a hand through her hair that stood straight up on top of her head. "I uh—"

"Sorry, about last night." Elizabeth blurted the words out before she had time to think about them.

"Oh, uh, yeah. Me too. Lizzie, I—"

"No, it's fine. Too much pregaming beforehand made me a little crazy." Elizabeth cut her off. She didn't want to hear Kerra explain anything to her. Her heart twinged in pain at the thought of what was behind her door. Some other woman cuddled up in her sheets, giggling at what a fool she was making of herself. She'd been so wrapped up in not wanting to hurt Kerra, she'd forgotten how easily Kerra could hurt her.

"Lizzie."

"No, you're busy. We'll talk later." Elizabeth turned to scurry back to the safety of her room. She hoped Krissy had made good on her word and left the city to go back home. She wouldn't be able to take the interrogation that was sure to follow the second Krissy set eyes on her. She'd see right through Elizabeth and know something was up. Krissy would force her to face the heartache she felt, and that was something Elizabeth wasn't ready to admit.

"Lizzie." Kerra caught her arm and held her in place. Elizabeth let out a sigh as she turned to face her. There was something pleading in Kerra's eyes, but Elizabeth kept her stare hard, refusing to let her in.

Kerra let go of her, seeing no breaks in Elizabeth's armor. "Are we still going to your mom's tonight?"

Elizabeth's heart dropped. She didn't know what she expected Kerra to say, but bringing up her mother's dinner wasn't it. She gave Kerra a nod. She was still angry, but in the event that they could repair the friendship, her mother would still demand to meet her.

Kerra stared at her for a while longer, and Elizabeth began to think she would say something more, but instead she dropped her eyes and headed back into her room to the giggling woman.

Elizabeth dragged her feet as she made her way back into her room, her heart feeling like it had just gone ten rounds in the ring. She gazed at herself in the mirror again before slipping on her work uniform. At least now she wouldn't have to avoid her mother's stare at dinner. Maybe it was for the best that their relationship remained a friendship. There was no way she would be able to explain her feelings to her mother. This way she didn't have to lie or feel guilty. *But the feelings are still there, just not reciprocated.* Elizabeth waved the thought away. If she dwelled on it too long she'd be a crying heap on her bed again.

"No. The feelings are gone." She gave herself a hard stare in the mirror and dared to take it even further. "The feelings were never even there."

☆☆☆

Elizabeth busied herself around her room, cleaning things that didn't need to be cleaned while she waited for six o'clock, for Kerra to come home and drive them to her mother's. Her shoulders ached with the strain of a busy day pouring coffee, but she was thankful for the painful distraction.

Krissy had made good on her promise to return home, and Lola wasn't nearly as intuitive as her mother. She took care to be gentle with Elizabeth on her first day flying solo, but she didn't seem able to sense anything was wrong. Elizabeth had initially been thankful for Krissy's absence, but toward the end of her shift she felt sadness engulf her. She needed someone to take the weight off her chest that threatened to make her suffocate. She wanted to face what she was feeling, but she was too afraid to face it alone.

Elizabeth jumped at the sound of the front door swinging open. She could hear Kerra moving down the hallway to her bedroom. The image of Kerra in a paint-spattered T-shirt and oversized jeans filled Elizabeth's mind. The image made her cheeks warm and her heart ache all at the same time.

"Lizzie." The sound of her name ringing through the hallway made her jump again. She shuffled out of her room and across the hall to find Kerra spread out across her bed.

"Yeah?" Elizabeth stared at Kerra in curiosity.

"What am I supposed to wear?" Kerra propped herself up on her elbows to stare at her.

Elizabeth gave her a shrug in response. "Wear whatever you want."

Kerra sat up, pursing her lips together in thought. "You have to know it's not that simple."

"What do you mean?" Elizabeth furrowed her eyebrows, unsure of how it could be more complicated.

Kerra let out a sigh. "I mean, I saw the way your ex looked at me the first time he met me, and I know Edenfield. Your mother probably won't be all that accommodating to..." Kerra gestured at herself. "This."

Elizabeth moved forward to take a seat next to Kerra on her bed. "Kerra..." She took a moment to find Kerra's eyes, making sure to meet her gaze as she said the words that burned inside her. "You are an amazing woman. You're talented, and kind, and accepting, and inspirational all at the same time. It doesn't matter what the surface is, once my mother sees all of that she'll love you as much as I do."

Kerra sat up straight, never taking her eyes off Elizabeth. "I...uh...thank you." Kerra seemed taken aback by Elizabeth's admiration of her.

Elizabeth sat uncomfortably under Kerra's silent, openmouthed expression. "You can borrow something of mine if you want." She said it just to break the silence, but as Elizabeth tried to imagine Kerra dressed in her clothes, a laugh spilled from her throat. Aside from the drastic difference in style, Kerra's slim frame would drown in her full-figured clothing.

"What's so funny?" Kerra frowned.

"The thought of you in a flower-patterned dress and tights." Elizabeth's laughter continued.

"Hey, I wear dresses."

Elizabeth narrowed her eyes, cocking her head in curiosity. "Do you?"

"No, but I would if it would make tonight easier." Kerra reached out for Elizabeth's hand but stopped herself in midair. She let out a sigh as she stared at Elizabeth. "Lizzie, I think we should talk about—"

Elizabeth cut her off, knowing what she wanted to say and not being ready to hear it. "No, it's fine. We don't need to. You should get ready anyways. My mother will pitch a fit if we're late." Elizabeth hurried herself out of the room, not giving Kerra a moment to protest. She closed the door behind herself and let out a shaky breath. Having a conversation with Kerra about their kiss terrified her. She hoped Kerra wouldn't press the situation and just let the two of them fade back into their routine.

Elizabeth wandered into the kitchen, fiddling with items she didn't know how to use while she waited for Kerra to ready herself. She was so sure her mother would love Kerra, and she had no idea why. If history had proven anything to her it was that Kerra was right; the Edenfield born and bred weren't all too keen on Kerra's type.

Kerra's type? Elizabeth kicked herself at the thought. Kerra wasn't a *type;* she was a wonderful woman with all the attributes that her mother always encouraged her to befriend.

"You ready?" Elizabeth was pulled from her loop of thoughts by Kerra's voice.

Kerra stood at the end of the hallway in her usual button up shirt with jeans. She had forgone gelling her hair back and let it sit in a mess of spiked black madness atop her head. Elizabeth wanted to run her fingers through the chaos, and she chastised herself for the urge. *The feelings were never there,* she reminded herself.

Elizabeth nodded and headed for the door, hearing Kerra twirl her keys behind her.

The two of them walked in silence to the car, and for the first time Elizabeth could feel Kerra's edginess. She hadn't ever expected that Kerra could get nervous, but once they got to the car Kerra managed to fiddle with everything inside before starting it up. Elizabeth watched her and couldn't stop thinking about how adorable she found Kerra's nerves to be. She knew she shouldn't touch her; she knew it was too early after "the incident," that they were still in such an awkward place, but Elizabeth couldn't help herself. She reached out for Kerra's hand and held it. She was surprised that Kerra let her without commentary.

Elizabeth held her hand for the entire drive. The two of them riding in silence, as Elizabeth relished her touch. She was thankful for Kerra's ability to drive one-handed because she couldn't fathom letting go. Even as they parked in front of her mother's house Elizabeth continued to hold Kerra. She'd have been content to blow off the dinner entirely and spend the rest of her life in the car just clutching her hand.

Kerra must have felt it too because she made no attempts to turn the car off, knowing that she would need her hand to take the key out of the ignition.

"We should probably get in there before we're late," Kerra suggested, without moving.

Elizabeth nodded but kept in her place. She caught Kerra's eye and held it without reprieve. There was something there, something pulling her forward. She could almost taste the tingle of Kerra's lips as she moved in closer across her seat, yearning for that electric shock the two of them shared with every touch. Kerra moved forward in time with her, and Elizabeth's heart quickened. Her thoughts fixated on the touch of Kerra's lips to hers, but she was abruptly pulled from the notion by a knock on the car window.

Elizabeth jumped back, letting go of Kerra's hand in the process. She nearly banged her head on the window with the force of moving away.

"Hey, what are you doing? Your mom's waiting for you guys."

Elizabeth stared at the figure hovering outside the window and climbed out of the car in a huff. "What are you doing here, RJ?"

Elizabeth heard the car die down as Kerra finally turned off the ignition and climbed out after her.

"Your mom invited me. She told me it was a family dinner." RJ reached out for her, but she shied away from his grasp.

She let out a grunt. "A *family* dinner, RJ. You're not family."

"I'm more family than *she* is." RJ spit the words with disgust, and his face turned up at Kerra as she loomed behind Elizabeth.

Kerra rubbed at her neck, obviously feeling uncomfortable at the shift in mood.

"I can't believe you brought her here. Have you completely lost your mind? Don't you have any respect?"

Elizabeth felt anger swell in the pit of her stomach as her vision went red. She felt a protective instinct overwhelm her. "You *will not* make Kerra feel unwelcome here, RJ. Especially considering that *you're* the guest I don't want here." There was venom in every word, and she hoped it bit at him. How dare he? He didn't know Kerra, and he didn't know her mother. Four years with him and it took Kerra to show her what a monster he was.

Elizabeth walked to Kerra's side and gave her shoulder a reassuring squeeze. "Just be yourself My mother will love you. RJ's an ass. Don't let him shake you." Elizabeth moved her toward the house to meet her mother, shoving RJ out of her way as he tried to block her path.

She was grateful for the moment to see him for what he was. All the doubts she'd had about the changes she was making seemed to melt away, and she suddenly felt confident and assured in every decision she'd made in the last two weeks. She felt powerful as she walked to the door of her mother's house, and she knew beyond whatever awkwardness that might be between them at the moment, she and Kerra would persevere because Kerra was her strength. The new clarity in her vision could all be attributed to one source and, at the moment, it stood beside her, nervously fidgeting in the doorway of her mother's house.

Elizabeth rasped her knuckles across the wood and waited, keeping her jitters steady so as not to further spook Kerra.

After only a moment her mother opened the door to welcome them inside and froze at the sight of Kerra. It was to be expected. Kerra wasn't the normal sight around Edenfield. Elizabeth moved to ease the tension. "Mom, this is Kerra, my roommate. Kerra, this is my mother, Cynthia Bridges."

"Nice to meet you, Ms. Bridges." Kerra extended a hand to Elizabeth's mother.

Elizabeth held her breath as she waited for a reaction. She was pleasantly surprised when her mother took Kerra's hand. "Nice to meet you as well. Come inside, wash up. Dinner is on the table."

Her mother ushered them inside. Elizabeth caught the look of dismay written on RJ's face, and her heart did a happy dance of triumph as they all entered the house.

RJ shot Kerra looks of repugnance all through dinner as he avoided Elizabeth's threatening glare. She couldn't believe he was acting that way toward a guest in her mother's home. She knew he was closed-minded, but in all her years with him she'd never suspected that he was hateful.

"So, what do you do, Kerra?" Her mother had been doing a splendid job at idle chitchat for the duration of the meal, and now she was ready to pry.

Elizabeth bit her bottom lip, forgetting about how dicey Kerra's occupation was.

"I'm a painter for an art gallery." Kerra answered with confidence, aware of which parts of her life to share and which to keep between the two of them.

Elizabeth gave her a smile as her eyes lingered just a bit too long on Kerra.

RJ cleared his throat. "Did you go to school for that? Art doesn't seem like much of a major."

Elizabeth glared at him. He was being an unbelievable ass, and she had just about had enough, but Kerra seemed to take him in stride. "No, actually. I wasn't able to go to school. Life of the nonprivileged, I guess."

Seeing RJ's astounded response forced Elizabeth to bite back a smile. She beamed with pride over Kerra's elasticity. She was brilliant and unshakable, and Elizabeth couldn't help but be proud to be by her side.

"Oh, well where are you from?" her mother pried.

"I'm from Edenfield, but things didn't quite work out, so I left to make it on my own." Kerra's voice began to lose some of its boisterousness, and Elizabeth took her cue to intervene.

"Mom." She shot her mother a pleading look.

"Sorry, I'm just curious about a woman that would take in a complete stranger." Her mother's tone held something in it that Elizabeth couldn't quite place. A part of her felt contemptuousness in her voice, but since her mother had been so pleasant all evening she knew she must be mistaken.

"I'm curious as well. You obviously couldn't make things work with your own family, so are you just attempting to build a new one?" RJ snarled at her as he spoke the words.

Kerra dropped her silverware without a response and pushed herself away from the table. "I think maybe we should go." Kerra whispered the words to Elizabeth, but she barely heard them. Her eyes were on fire with rage.

"Maybe you should shut the hell up, RJ." It was all Elizabeth could say to keep herself from lunging across the table at him.

"Elizabeth!" There was a warning in her mother's voice. "You will not be rude to our guest."

"He's not my guest. And *he's* the one being rude to the one and only person who was invited here."

Kerra put a hand on her arm as she attempted to climb to her feet. "Lizzie, it's fine. I'll just go wait in the car while you say good-bye to your mother."

"Kerra, no. You don't have to—"

"It's fine." Kerra assured her as she stood up from the table. "It was very nice to meet you, Ms. Bridges."

Elizabeth watched as Kerra disappeared from the dining room. She listened as the front door opened and shut with Kerra's exit.

"I can't believe you, RJ." Elizabeth turned on him, ready to give him a piece of her mind, when her mother climbed to her feet.

"And I can't believe you, Elizabeth Bridges. How dare you bring that woman into my house?"

Elizabeth stared at her mother in shock. "Wh-what?"

"Beth, whatever it is you're going through, it has to stop before you get in too deep." RJ reached out for her hand, but she jerked it away.

"Why the hell are you still here?" Elizabeth snapped at him.

"He's here because I asked him to be here. I thought the two of you could reconcile. I had no idea..." Her mother breathed a shaky breath to fight back tears.

"Mom." Elizabeth moved around the table to put a hand on her mother's shoulder. "Mom, I don't understand. I thought you liked Kerra." Guilt dug a pit in her stomach as she watched a tear slide down her mother's cheek.

"Beth honey, I've tried so hard with you. I've tried to be understanding, I've tried to keep you on the right path. Your life is set up to perfection, Beth. Why do you insist on hurting me? What have I done to deserve this kind of treatment?"

RJ moved to put a hand on her other shoulder, and her mother leaned in to embrace him, shirking away Elizabeth's hand.

"Beth, it's not too late to fix this. We only want to the best for you. We love you." It was as if RJ spoke for her mother as she cried into him, nodding in agreement.

Elizabeth stood, baffled by the scene in front of her. "I don't understand what's happening."

Her mother lifted her head, wiping at her tears. "I raised you better than this. I taught you values, and I taught you to see things through the eyes of the Lord. And then you bring in that girl. That girl with no morals or value, and you want me to accept that. To watch you on the path to hell and support you in it." Her mother sniffed. "I won't do it, Beth. You need to pack your things and find your way back home and back on the path to the Lord."

"Mom, I'm not on the path to hell. Kerra is a good person and—"

"Elizabeth, I've said my piece. You can leave the devil behind, and I will be here for you to reclaim your soul, or you can continue to dig your own grave, but I will not be a part of it. I won't let you shake my faith. I love you dearly, honey, but I won't stand for this."

Elizabeth stared openmouthed at her mother. The evening had taken a sharp turn into territory she hadn't expected, and she hadn't a clue how to respond. Her mother was offering her an ultimatum. Forcing her to choose between her own happiness and the love of her only family.

"Mom, please." Her own tears began to collect in her eyes. She could deal with her mother being upset and disappointed in her, but to propose completely disowning her cut into her like a razor blade. Her chest tightened with emotion, and her mind kept begging her to wake from the nightmare she was having. But it wasn't a nightmare. Her mother really wanted nothing to do with her if she pursued her friendship with Kerra.

"Get out, Beth. Collect your things and I hope to see you in the morning, ready to start anew."

Elizabeth let the tears flow freely down her cheeks as she backed out of the house. Her legs felt heavier with each step, and her mind lost the ability to process thought. Everything felt surreal as she walked down the path leading back to Kerra's parked car.

"You okay?" Kerra stepped out of the car upon seeing her tear streaked face. She reached out for Elizabeth and held her in her arms.

Elizabeth let out a sob into her hair and wrapped her arms around Kerra's gangly frame. "Kerra...I..." She let out another series of sobs. "I don't think we can be friends anymore."

CHAPTER TWELVE

Kerra sat quietly behind the wheel as Elizabeth worked at composing herself. She'd expected some sort of reaction from her; screaming, yelling, crying, something. But Kerra had no response to her throwing away their friendship. It was almost as if she had expected it.

Elizabeth watched her as she drove them back to Kerra's, the place that she had been so ready and willing to call her own home. She wiped at the lingering tears on her face as she felt a wave of misplaced anger wash through her. Kerra's indifference was usually something she found endearing, but in that moment she needed something, anything. She didn't know what she would do if Kerra begged her to stay, but a part of her felt angry that she'd never get to find out.

"Don't you have anything to say?" Elizabeth nudged her, hoping for an inkling of emotion from her.

"No." Kerra kept her eyes on the road, offering Elizabeth nothing.

Elizabeth let out a huff as she sank down into her seat. "Kerra the enigma."

She felt herself fly into the door with the abrupt movement of the car as Kerra whipped onto the shoulder of the road. She unbuckled her seat belt and turned toward the pouting Elizabeth. "I'm not a puzzle, Lizzie. My feelings have always been clear. *You* are the enigma. You had to have known this is what it would come to. The choice to be who you want to be or to continue to live under your mother's thumb doing as you're told. You want me to say something? Well, then tell me why. Why move in with me, just to turn tail and run at the first sign of disapproval?"

The shadows of Kerra's sharp angles danced across the car as other vehicles passed them on the road. Her gaze bored into Elizabeth as she waited for an answer.

"I…" Elizabeth started, but she didn't have an answer, not a good one anyway. "I'm weak. Twenty-four years, I've always fallen in line, and I thought I was ready to go against the grain. I thought that I could be you, but I can't. My mom is all I know, and she's going to walk away from me if I choose this life, and I don't know where I go from there." Elizabeth gave up wiping at the tears that fell; they had become an endless stream and trying to cover them was futile.

Kerra resumed her silence as she stared at her, her eyes giving away none of what she was thinking. "You don't have to be me to make choices that make you happy."

Elizabeth nodded her head, looking away from her to cast her glance out of the window. "Yes, I do."

Kerra reached across her to open the dashboard and then handed her a tissue. She let out a sigh as she turned her eyes toward the road again, putting the car back into drive. "Maybe it's for the best, anyways. My life has never been kind to the people closest to me."

Elizabeth stared at her in curiosity. There was a sharpness in the comment that she wanted to ask about, but she knew Kerra well enough to know she wouldn't get an explanation. It didn't matter anyway; she was one foot out the door, and chances were once she was back in her mother's clutches she'd never see Kerra again. She felt a pain go through her at the thought. She hadn't known Kerra for long, but somehow it was hard to imagine a life without her.

Elizabeth stewed in her thoughts, feeling a sinking pit build in the base of her belly as they pulled up in front of Kerra's apartment building.

"Come out with me tonight." Kerra blurted the words out after turning off the ignition.

"What?" Elizabeth reacted, shocked by the invitation. She expected Kerra to be angry with her, to be pleased by the thought of never having to see her weakling face again.

"Come out with me tonight. We can go by the bar and have a few drinks. Give you a proper send-off."

"You don't hate me?" It was such an insecure question to ask, but Elizabeth felt like she was past the point of pretending she wasn't an emotional train wreck.

Kerra let out a laugh. "Of course not." Her face turned serious as she reached out for her hand. "I understand where you're at, Lizzie. More than you know. And I'll never give you an ultimatum. If you want to go, go. I'll still be here for you." She gave her hand a squeeze. "I promise."

Elizabeth let out a sob as she squeezed Kerra's hand back. Kerra had a way of always saying exactly what she needed to hear. "Yes, let's go out tonight. Drinks sound like exactly what I need."

✩✩✩

Kerra pulled up in front of the Nipple Slip and Elizabeth felt an overwhelming nostalgia for the first time they met consume her. Kerra had come into her life exactly when she needed her to.

Elizabeth reached out for her as she turned the car off. "Hey." She clutched her hand and caught her eye, struggling to find the words that she wanted to say. "Thanks." She frowned at herself. She'd wanted to say so much more, and *thanks* felt like a lame substitute for what she felt for Kerra.

Kerra smiled. "Always."

Elizabeth couldn't help the grin that spread across her face. She was always elated by Kerra's ability to know what she was thinking.

"Shall we?" Kerra gestured to the building.

Nodding, Elizabeth let go of her as they climbed out of the car. She took in a deep breath of stale city air. There was a sadness that hung around her, but she was hoping the liquor would fill the pit in her stomach.

As Kerra led her through the door of the bar, Elizabeth soaked in the familiarity. She was beginning to regret their night out. The longer she waited to move out, the harder it was going to be to walk away.

Kerra directed her through the tiny crowd to a comfy, tattered couch in the corner. "Here, you sit, and I'll go get the drinks."

Elizabeth nodded in agreement, plopping herself down onto the sofa. She watched Kerra make her way back through the crowd toward the bar for a moment before she let her eyes scan the room. Her eyes fell to a woman across the bar with a long frame and soft eyes who watched her back with intensity. Elizabeth nearly gasped from the fire in her eyes

93

as she gazed at her, taking every part of her in and making her squirm beneath the examination. The woman was gorgeous. Unbelievably so, and Elizabeth couldn't fathom why her eyes regarded her with so much hunger.

"Hey, you okay?" Kerra broke the intensity of the moment, pulling Elizabeth's gaze away from the mysterious woman.

"Yeah." Elizabeth nodded, but she couldn't help her eyes from returning to the spot where the woman still sat. Still watching her.

"You sure?" Kerra pulled her focus again. Elizabeth stared at her as she took a seat on the couch, meeting Kerra's eyes as she peered at her in concern.

Elizabeth hadn't realized how rattled she'd let the mystery woman make her until she found the worry in Kerra's expression.

"It's fine. It's..." Elizabeth let out a sigh. "Nothing. It's nothing."

Kerra set two drinks down on the tiny table next to the sofa. "It's clearly *something*."

Elizabeth fought against the urge to look back at the woman across the bar. "No. It's not." She lost the battle against her urges and turned her head once again to meet the woman's stare.

The woman winked at her as she took a sip from a glass full of dark liquid.

Kerra followed her gaze. "Oh, I see."

Elizabeth whipped her head around stare daggers at Kerra. "You see? You see what?"

Kerra raised an eyebrow. "I see the same thing that you see. Sierra."

"Sierra." Elizabeth whispered the name, feeling the exotic tingle of the syllables leave her lips.

Kerra let out a giggle at her obvious infatuation.

"What?" Elizabeth asked defensively.

"Nothing. I just didn't take you for the easily taken in by the shiny and beautiful."

"Excuse me?" Elizabeth stared openmouthed at Kerra's statement.

"She's beautiful, but she's a predator. Tread carefully." Kerra picked up the drinks from the table and handed her one.

"I don't need to tread carefully because I'm not *taken in*. She just kept staring at me, and I stared back," Elizabeth said defensively.

"Of course she's staring. She's a predator, and you're fresh meat," Kerra told her flatly as she took a long swig of her drink.

Elizabeth found herself intrigued by the judgment in Kerra's tone. "So, what does that make you?"

"What do you mean?" Kerra stared at her questioningly.

Elizabeth tasted her drink, noticing Angela behind the bar and knowing she should sip in moderation. "I mean, if Sierra is a predator for staring, what does that make you? Wasn't I just your slice of fresh meat?"

Kerra's face took on a serious edge. "I'm not a predator, Lizzie."

Elizabeth took another sip from her drink, this time being less cautious about how much she took in. "Interesting because I hear you're no stranger to...well, anyone." Elizabeth could feel herself growing bold. Her festering hurt from Kerra's quick departure into another woman's arms after their kiss was starting to rear its ugly head.

Kerra sat back, putting distance between them. "Promiscuous and predator are not the same thing."

"Then what's the difference?" Elizabeth challenged.

"The difference is that I saw that you needed a friend and not a coming-out one-nighter." Kerra gritted her teeth before letting out a sigh. "You want to tell me why you're angry with me or should I guess?"

"I'm not angry with you."

"Then why are you attacking me?"

"I'm not. It was just a conversation, Kerra." Elizabeth shrugged the conversation off with nonchalance. She wanted to kick herself for not being able to say how she really felt. She didn't want to leave things broken and buried with Kerra. If she was going to move back to her mother's she wanted to be honest, to tell her how she really felt and how much it had hurt her to hear the giggles of another woman behind Kerra's bedroom door.

Elizabeth tipped the rim of her glass to her lips and threw caution to the wind as she finished off her drink. It was time to stop being a child. She needed to be an adult and own up to her emotions, regardless of how terrifying they may be.

"Kerra, I—"

"Lizzie! Kerra." Angela interrupted her train of thought as she made her way toward them, moving in the elegant way she had. She carried a round tray of drinks with her, balancing it on the palm of her hand, and the crowd parted for her. She handed a drink to both of them and then took their empty glasses and placed them on the tray before taking the last full glass of alcohol for herself.

"Thank you." Elizabeth nodded at her as she placed her tray on the table.

"No problem, honey," Angela purred before taking a casual seat across Kerra's lap.

Elizabeth stared wide-eyed at the scene in front of her as Angela gently placed a hand on Kerra's cheek before enveloping her into a kiss. Elizabeth could feel her face heating up as they carried on as if she weren't even there. Kerra's hands moved to grip Angela's tiny waist as she pulled her deeper into the kiss.

Elizabeth's heart quickened, thudding loudly in her ears as she continued to watch, unable to tear her eyes from the happenings before her. She cleared her throat a little more loudly than she had intended to get their attention.

"Oh sorry, Lizzie. It's just so hard for me to keep my hands off of this one sometimes." Angela placed one last kiss on Kerra's cheek before she climbed to her feet and took her tray from the table. "I get off at two. Shall we pick up where we left off last night?" Angela offered shamelessly.

Kerra wore a big, seductively distracting grin as she stared up at Angela. "It's actually Lizzie's last night out. Rain check?"

"Sure, sweetheart." Angela bent down to give Kerra one last kiss before turning to Elizabeth. "Bye, Lizzie," she offered with a delicate wave of her fingertips.

Elizabeth watched her make her way back behind the bar. Her ears were burning with embarrassment. *Or is it jealousy?*

Elizabeth turned to Kerra to find her still watching Angela. "Not a predator, huh?" Elizabeth spit the words out. Whatever she was feeling it had quickly given way to anger.

Kerra turned on her. "Angela and I have known each other a long time. We have an understanding."

Elizabeth let out a snort before she downed her new drink.

Kerra watched her for a moment before speaking. "Are you jealous of Angela?"

Elizabeth coughed, nearly choking on the last bit of her drink. "No."

"Because I asked you if you wanted to be with me, and you said no."

"I didn't say no."

"You might as well have." Kerra sank back into her seat.

Elizabeth put her glass down to lean in; her gaze meeting Kerra's with ferocity. "Fine. If you want to have this conversation, then let's have it. You asked me if I wanted to be with you, and I said I didn't know, and twenty minutes later you had Angela in your bed."

"So you are jealous of Angela."

"Don't patronize me, Kerra." Elizabeth had finally found her will to vomit out all her feelings, and she didn't want to play a game of semantics.

"I'm not, but Lizzie, you're mad at me because you told me you didn't want me, and I didn't sit around waiting for you to change your mind."

"I never said I didn't want you." Elizabeth said the words much louder than she had meant to, and she felt the embarrassment creep back into her cheeks as a few heads turned to stare at them.

Kerra didn't seem to notice the eyes watching them. She leaned in toward Elizabeth. "Fine, I'll ask again. Do you want to be with me, Lizzie?"

Elizabeth chewed at her lip. She hated that she was hesitating. She had promised herself if she got the chance again she would jump at being with Kerra, but things were more complicated than that. "What does it matter, Kerra? I'm moving back home."

"So don't." Kerra took her hand, and Elizabeth felt that immediate electric shock run through her that always accompanied Kerra's touch. "Stay and give us a chance. Say that you want this, Lizzie, and I'll fight like hell to make it work."

"Kerra, I can't. I-I don't know..."

Kerra released her hand. "And that's the problem. You don't know what you want. I do, and it's you, but I won't sit around waiting for you."

Kerra climbed to her feet and dug around in her pocket. She pulled out a handful of bills and set them in front of Elizabeth. "Listen, I've got to get out of here and get my head right, and I can't do that around you. I'll have Angela call you a cab."

Kerra turned and walked away from her before she had a chance to respond. Elizabeth wanted to go after her, but she knew she still didn't have the answers that Kerra wanted. That Kerra deserved. Elizabeth stared down at the empty glass in her hand for a moment before she felt the tears come.

☆☆☆

Elizabeth wiped at the tear stains on her cheeks as she gazed at herself in the spotted bathroom mirror of the bar. What was wrong with her? She'd lived her entire life without knowing Kerra. Why was she letting the thought of losing her rattle her so much? She'd spent four years with RJ, and they were good years. He always treated her wonderfully and loved her with all his heart. So why was she dreading returning to her old life?

The sound of the bathroom door swinging open made her jump, and she abruptly turned away from her reflection in the mirror.

"Oh, hello." She strolled through the door of the restroom.

"Hi." Elizabeth tapped the edge of the sink, suddenly feeling awkward. It was one thing to fall apart in a bar bathroom. It was another to have someone watch.

"You okay, sugar?" Sierra took a step toward her and cocked her head in concern.

"Yeah, I'm fine. Just a hard night, I guess." Elizabeth sniffed and held back the tears that wanted to escape just thinking about it.

"Oh, I understand. That Kerra can be quite the heartbreaker." Sierra took another step forward, closing the space between them.

Elizabeth winced at the sound of her name. "No. Kerra didn't—"

"Shh, it's okay, sugar. I'll take care of you." Sierra wrapped her arms around her and stroked her head. It was meant to be a comforting gesture, but it made Elizabeth wildly uncomfortable. She squirmed her way out of Sierra's grasp and moved for the door.

"I should go." Elizabeth reached for the handle on the door, aching to put as much distance between the two of them as she could. There was something unsettling about Sierra's presence. She was gorgeous, and it seemed she was only trying to appease her, but Elizabeth couldn't help but feel as if she was being manipulated. Seduced instead of comforted.

Sierra pulled a card out of the tight blue jeans that hugged and accented her body in all the right places. "You call me when you change your mind, all right, sugar." She slipped the card into the palm of Elizabeth's hand.

"Umm, okay. Thank you." Elizabeth wasn't sure what else she was supposed to say. She avoided eye contact as she scrambled out of the door and back into the crowded bar.

She breathed a sigh of relief, feeling better being out from under the peering gaze of Sierra. But it was short-lived as the three back-to-back glasses of the Angela Special hit her with a vengeance. Elizabeth reached out for the wall, to steady herself as warmth engulfed her body and dulled her senses.

"Oh no." She felt her knees buckling under the weight of her body and dreaded the impact of the dirty bar floor as she went down. Elizabeth stared in shock at the two arms that locked around her, holding her up through sheer force of will as the dainty body underneath her struggled to keep her upright.

"Hey, hey, it's okay. I got you, sweetness." Angela's body trembled with the exertion of holding her up. "I called a cab for you; it's on the way. Come on, let's get you outside."

Elizabeth found her feet and lazily shrugged Angela away. "No, thank you. I don't need your help." Her words were jumbled, and she could hear the drunken contradiction in them as she used Angela's shoulder for balance.

"Sure, you don't, but just in case, I'm going to see you out anyways, okay?" Angela's voice maintained its willfulness.

Elizabeth nodded, letting Angela carry her out of the bar to a bench on the curb. "Thank you, I can take it from here." Elizabeth focused to keep her head up straight as she spoke the words, but it was a futile effort as her head bobbed and weaved back and forth.

"That's okay. I can use a break anyways. I'll wait with you until the cab gets here. I promised Kerra I'd see you off safely."

Elizabeth let out a grunt at Kerra's name, and Angela giggled at her. "I take it you two are on the outs?" Angela arched an eyebrow.

Elizabeth let out an exasperated sigh. "I guess. I think she's making me crazy." She could feel some of the drunken fog beginning to clear. She knew she should thank Angela for bringing her out into the fresh air, but the cattiness in her still slinked below the surface.

"Yeah, that's kind of her thing. The bewitcher of women. She makes us all crazy." Angela stared at her for a moment before speaking again. "Can I tell you a secret that you probably won't remember in the morning?"

Elizabeth nodded, leaning in closer to her.

"I'm a little jealous of you."

Elizabeth's eyes widened in disbelief. "*You're* jealous of *me*? Why?" She stared at the beautiful and confident bartender in front of her and couldn't wrap her head around what she could possibly be jealous of.

"Isn't it obvious?"

Elizabeth stared at her, letting her know it was very much not obvious.

Angela giggled again. "It took me a long time to come to terms with what Kerra and I are, and for a while I convinced myself that it was just who she is. A free bird, not willing to be grounded by anyone or anything, but then you came along and..." Angela let out a breath. "Well, you've bewitched the bewitcher, and I'm jealous."

Elizabeth let her words soak in. "I don't know what I'm supposed to do," she confessed. She felt a tinge of disappointment as her cab pulled up in front of them. She was enjoying talking to Angela, and she knew she'd never have the gumption to be honest with her in sobriety.

Angela helped her up and put her into the cab. "It's none of my business, but if it were me, there's nothing in this world that could make me turn away Kerra's affection," Angela told her before she closed the cab door and left her alone with her thoughts.

Elizabeth watched her wave from the curb as the cab driver pulled away from the Nipple Slip. Her heart was beating a million miles a minute as she thought about the options in front of her. What was really waiting for her back at her mother's house? A bigot of a boyfriend and a mother that she was afraid would stop loving her if she made a wrong move. Is that really what she wanted? And then there was Kerra and the way that Kerra made her feel. *The bewitcher*. She laughed to herself as she thought about Angela's nickname. It was beyond accurate. Kerra had completely warped her mind, and she reveled in every crazy moment of it.

Elizabeth gazed out of the window, willing the cab driver to move faster before her resolve melted away. She felt brave and bold. She wanted to make the decision that was best for her, to give in to every urge that she'd been fighting since the moment she left RJ.

Her body was nearly vibrating with determination by the time the cab driver pulled up in front of Kerra's apartment building. She threw all the bills she had at him before jumping clumsily out of the cab. Her head was clearer, but standing reminded her of just how much alcohol was in her system.

She stumbled her way up the stairs, cursing each one for existing as she went, before she finally reached the door to Kerra's apartment. To *their* apartment. She fumbled with her keys, managing to stick each one into the door incorrectly before it swung open to a confused Kerra standing in the doorway.

"What are you doing?"

Elizabeth drunkenly waved off the question. "Stupid keys wouldn't work. I tried them all and nope. Nothing."

"You're drunk," Kerra stated.

She shook her head as Kerra helped her inside, wrapping an arm around her waist to pull her forward. "No, I was, but I'm not anymore," Elizabeth assured her.

"Uh-huh," Kerra agreed without much enthusiasm.

"No, really." Elizabeth straightened up and removed Kerra's hand from her waist. "See, all good," she exclaimed, standing up straight on her own.

"Uh-huh." Kerra crossed her arms to stare at her.

"Okay, so listen. I want to stay, if you'll still have me." Elizabeth focused all her energy on not swaying as she spoke.

Kerra uncrossed her arms and reached out to take Elizabeth's hand. "Of course you can stay, Lizzie. I never put you out. But I think maybe you should sleep it off before you make that call."

Elizabeth stared down at Kerra's hand over her own and followed her instinct without hesitation. She leaned forward and placed a soft kiss to Kerra's lips. Even in the numbness of her intoxication, she felt the electrical pulse of kissing her.

Kerra let go of her and took a flustered step backwards. "What are you doing?"

"I don't want to go home, and I don't want to be your roommate. I want you, and I'm sure. I've always been sure, just scared and confused. But I'm not scared anymore." Elizabeth moved forward to close the distance between them and placed another kiss on Kerra, this time with more ferocity. Her heart thudded in her chest as Kerra returned her kiss, placing a hand at the small of her back to bring her in closer.

Elizabeth let out a gasp as Kerra's lips moved against hers, the rhythm of her mouth blocking out everything around them. Elizabeth hadn't even realized they were moving toward the couch until she felt her back fall against it. She was in a wonderland of euphoria, and she never wanted it to stop. She pulled Kerra down to her, wanting to feel to touch of her body on top of her. She let her hands wrap around Kerra's neck as she absorbed her in another mind-melting kiss.

She was stunned by a cold gust of air that hit her as Kerra pulled away, stumbling backwards as she ripped herself from Elizabeth. She ran a shaking hand through her hair before putting it to her face in frustration.

"What's wrong?" Elizabeth was still in a cloud of intoxication and lust, and she couldn't figure out where they went awry. The unnerved vision of Kerra in front of her was a sharp contrast to where she thought the night was going. "I thought...don't you want me?"

Kerra kneeled down beside the sofa. "Of course I do. God, Lizzie, I *really* do, but you're still drunk."

"But I'm not drunk." Elizabeth moved to kneel down next to her but stumbled over her own feet in the process. "Okay, maybe I'm a little drunk, but I meant what I said."

"Then you'll still mean it in the morning." Kerra wasn't compromising. "If this is going to happen, it's going to happen right. And sober." Kerra wrapped her arm around her to help her up. "Come on, I'll help you to your bed."

Kerra helped her down the hallway. "My bed." Elizabeth repeated the words. "I like the sound of that."

Kerra let out a laugh as she maneuvered her into her bed. "It's yours as long as you want it to be."

"Thank you, Kerra." Elizabeth tapped the spot next to her. "You're welcome to stay here in *my* bed with me." There was an undeniable seduction in the offer, and Elizabeth felt herself flush at her own boldness.

Kerra smiled at her, making Elizabeth's ache for her even more intense. "Maybe tomorrow, if you still want me to."

She watched in disappointment as Kerra left the room. "I will," she assured herself. "I will."

CHAPTER THIRTEEN

Elizabeth opened her eyes to the bright light of day shining into her room. "Ouch." The headache pulsing through her body didn't appreciate the morning sunshine. She stared up at the ceiling as the rush of the night's memories came flooding back. She was suddenly thankful that all she had was a headache. She'd had much worse hangovers from drinking a lot less.

"How are you feeling?" Elizabeth shot up in her bed at the sound of Kerra's voice and immediately regretted the abruptness of the motion. The sharp pain that ran through her head seemed to course through her entire body.

"Ugh, like I should learn to hold my liquor better." Elizabeth put a hand to her head to steady the room that had suddenly started spinning.

"Here." Kerra crossed the room to her and handed her a glass of water and two green pills. "Take them now and thank me later."

Elizabeth didn't hesitate before downing the water with the pills. She'd have taken anything to quell the screaming headache. "God, I hope these work fast or work is going to suck today."

"Work?" Kerra asked, raising an eyebrow at her.

"Yeah. I mean, you didn't call Krissy already and tell her I was leaving, did you?" Elizabeth was beginning to feel all the weight of her flip-flop decisions crash down on her.

Kerra shook her head. "No, I was going to call this morning."

Elizabeth breathed a sigh of relief. "Good."

Kerra took a seat at the edge of her bed, rubbing at her chin as she debated what she wanted to say. "So, you really are staying then?"

"Yes, I said that I was." Elizabeth watched her carefully, waiting for a reaction to indicate what Kerra may be feeling about that.

"You said a lot of things last night," Kerra whispered, not meeting her eyes.

Elizabeth pulled her legs into her chest. "Yeah, I'm sorry about that. Last night, I mean."

A flash of disappointment clouded Kerra's face.

"No, no. I'm not sorry about *that*," Elizabeth corrected herself, realizing what Kerra thought she was apologizing for. "I meant, I'm sorry about comparing you to Sierra. I had a pretty close encounter with her last night and...well, I know what you meant by predator now."

"What did she do?" Kerra's disappointment turned to concern.

"Nothing. She may have actually been trying to help, but there was something...wrong about her. I can't explain it."

"You don't have to. I know Sierra, and I'm certain she wasn't trying to help."

Elizabeth pulled her legs in tighter as the awkwardness of the moment set in. There was a lot she wanted to say, but she had made her move. The ball was in Kerra's court.

As if sensing her thoughts, Kerra moved in closer to catch her eye. "So, umm...the other stuff, last night. About you and me..."

Elizabeth couldn't stifle the grin that her spread across her face. Seeing Kerra frazzled didn't happen very often, but when it did she couldn't help but be smitten by it. "I told you, I wasn't that drunk."

A grin of Kerra's own tugged at the corners of her mouth as she reached out to lace her fingers with Elizabeth's. "So, what now?"

Elizabeth admired their entwined fingers before she spoke. "Now, I need to ask you the question that you asked me. Are you sure that you want to do this?"

"Of course I'm sure." Kerra answered her without pause.

"No, Kerra. Really think about it. I'm putting everything on the line here, and I don't want to have a fight and come home to find you in bed with Angela."

Kerra winced at the words. "Do you really think I'm capable of that?" She moved to pull her hand away from Elizabeth's, but Elizabeth clutched her tighter, unwilling to let her go.

"I think that monogamy isn't in your wheelhouse," Elizabeth explained.

Kerra sat in silence, her expression giving away none of what she was thinking. "Lizzie, if you're sure, then so am I. I want to be in this, rain or shine."

Elizabeth's smile returned as she rested her chin on her knees to stare at Kerra. Her heart raced as Kerra stared back at her. "I really want to kiss you right now, but every time I move, my head feels like it's going to explode."

Kerra let out a laugh before she placed a kiss on her cheek. "So, kiss me. Tonight. On our date."

"Our date?" Elizabeth leaned forward, to keep Kerra's hand in her clutches as she stood to leave. The movement rocked her body, sending another regrettable wave of pain through her.

Kerra tried to hide her smile at Elizabeth's visible pain. "Ten more minutes and the pills should kick in," she promised.

"God, I hope so." Elizabeth had forgotten her mission to keep holding Kerra, and her hands shot to her temples, trying to rub away the pain.

"If you want, we can postpone the date," Kerra offered.

"No. Ten minutes, I'll be fine. I'm going to work, and we're going on our date." Elizabeth kept her eyes shut as she declared the day's festivities.

"Okay, I'll meet you here after work."

Elizabeth listened as Kerra left the room. Her body warmed at the thought of a date with Kerra. She let herself fantasize about the afternoon alone with her, holding her hand and stealing kisses, and her heart fluttered. She hated that she'd waited so long to choose Kerra. The joy that surged through her was one she hadn't felt since she was a child. *How could I ever have fought this?*

Elizabeth could feel the pain of her headache subsiding. She knew the credit belonged with Kerra's mystery pills, but a part of her believed her headache relief could be contributed to the weight of her indecision being lifted off her shoulders. She finally felt indescribably right with herself. She was finally living on her own accord.

She made tiny movements to climb out of her bed, afraid of the possibility of a return headache. Making her way slowly to her messy pile of clothing, she couldn't stop herself from giggling with glee. She shuffled around for her work uniform, smiling at it once she found it. Her life had dawned a new day, and she was overwhelmingly happy with it.

☆☆☆

Elizabeth arrived at the Bean Spot with her morning smile still plastered on her face. The hangover was fluctuating in intensity, but it couldn't chase away her excitement. She practically skipped through the front door of the tiny coffee shop and made her way behind the counter.

"Well, you're certainly in a good mood."

Elizabeth turned to the voice that called out to her and was surprised to see Krissy standing at the coffee maker.

"Krissy? What are you doing here? I thought you went home." Elizabeth closed the space between them and then embraced her. Krissy's hugger mentality must have rubbed off on her.

"I did. I am. I just popped in for a client that needed me last night."

"A client? For coffee?" Elizabeth knew coffee could be addicting, but the circumstances seemed extreme.

Krissy let out a laugh. "No, no. I moonlight as a juvenile drug counselor...or I used to, but since Kerra and Lola, I mostly just pop in when old patients need a little extra support." Krissy poured herself a cup of coffee. "Would you like one?"

Elizabeth nodded. "Yes, please." She watched as Krissy poured her a mug full of coffee before the words sunk in. "Wait, Kerra does drugs?"

Krissy handed her the coffee, but she was suddenly uninterested in it.

"No, of course she doesn't," Krissy assured her as she offered her the coffee again.

"But she used to." She was remembering how little she actually knew about Kerra.

"That's not..." Krissy put the mug down once she realized Elizabeth wasn't going to take it. "I think this is a conversation better had with Kerra."

"Yeah, you're right." Elizabeth took the mug from the table. She was suddenly overcome with doubts. She had been so ready to put everything on the line for Kerra, and she barely knew her.

Krissy must have sensed her change in mood. "Kerra is exactly who you think she is, Lizzie. She's a human being, and she's made some mistakes in her life, but she has never lied about who she is."

Elizabeth gave her a smile. "Thank you." It was exactly what she needed to hear. The gentle reminder of why she wanted to dive in headfirst. Kerra was genuine, and whatever was in her past didn't change the way Elizabeth felt around her. "We're going on a date tonight." Krissy hadn't even pried her for the information, but she was bursting to tell someone.

"I thought you were straight."

Elizabeth jumped at the sound of Lola behind her. "Oh, umm...I am." Elizabeth realized how ridiculous the proclamation sounded after announcing her evening plans with Kerra.

Lola furrowed her eyebrows, reiterating the absurdity of her claim.

"I mean...well, I guess I'm not but—"

"She's a human being, interested in another human being. Don't be a labelist, Lola. I raised you better." Krissy came to her defense.

Lola gave them both an eye roll as she opened up the register for the morning money check. "Whatever you are, know that Kerra is like a sister to me." Lola closed the drawer to turn on Elizabeth. "Don't play games. I'm not as understanding as my mother."

Elizabeth stared after Lola in shock as she walked away to finish her morning opening routine.

"Sorry, Lola's still a work in progress." Krissy placed a hand on her shoulder.

Elizabeth nodded and let out a sigh. "That's okay. I think I am too."

☆☆☆

Elizabeth finished putting the finishing touches to her outfit and gave herself yet another mirror check. She didn't know why she was suddenly so self-conscious. Kerra knew what she looked like. Even on her worst days.

She patted the neatly laid bun tied to the back of her head and jumped at the sound of Kerra opening the door to the apartment. She gave herself another once-over, debating on changing her outfit again for the ninth time and deciding against it. She'd never be ready on time if she did. Kerra could always manage to look twice as stunning as her in half the time.

She smoothed down the sides of her carefully selected orange sundress and took a deep breath, closing her eyes to convince herself once more that orange was definitely her color. She let herself take one last peek at her intricate updo and placed three extra bobby pins in the artwork for good measure. "Okay, I'm ready," she assured herself, knowing that the words had about a hundred different layers to them.

"All right, I'm ready when you are." She called out the words as she exited her bedroom, hoping that she wasn't leaving anything behind. She made her way down the hallway, hoping to grab a snack before they left, and was stopped in her tracks by the sight in the living room. She consciously reminded herself not to drool. "Oh, you're ready. How is that even possible? You just got here." Elizabeth was feeling all her self-consciousness rush back in. Orange may have been her color, but Kerra was a vision in a silk black button-up shirt and pinstriped slacks. Elizabeth's hands went unconsciously to her hair to twirl it around her fingers, but she grabbed at air instead. She silently cursed herself for tying all her hair up.

"I work in a body painting studio. Showers are a dime a dozen, so I got ready at work." Kerra crossed the room to take her hand. "You look beautiful, by the way."

"Thank you. So do you." Elizabeth fought the urge to reach for her phantom hair again. She was suddenly more nervous than she'd ever been in her entire life.

"Should we go?" Kerra gave her a smile and nodded toward the door.

Her smile was enough to light Elizabeth up from head to toe. In the span of two minutes, Kerra managed to wipe away every second thought she had.

"We should," Elizabeth agreed, taking a step forward, ready for the night to come.

She led the way to Kerra's car, excitement bubbling in her chest with every step. "So, where are we going?" She asked the question not really caring what the answer was. Kerra could be taking her to the depths of hell, and it wouldn't have mattered as long as they were seated side by side.

"It's a surprise." Kerra flashed her another quick smile as she slid behind the wheel of the car.

The thrill of being on a date with Kerra was getting to her. She was nearly flush with anticipation, and she thought she might pass out if her heart rate increased anymore. She tapped her fingers along the dashboard, unable to sit still as Kerra strapped on her seat belt.

"Kerra." She called out her name with nothing to say after it, but her instincts led her forward. Leaning across her seat, she placed a kiss on Kerra's lips, taking in the soft touch of them as they kissed her back. Warmth shot through her, burning her cheeks as she lost herself in the kiss. She placed her hand on the side of Kerra's cheek and let her lips dance to their own rhythm.

Elizabeth struggled to catch her breath as they broke their kiss, staring at each other in silence for what seemed like an eternal stretch of time. She could have lived in Kerra's gaze forever.

"You know you'll never get a proper date if you keep giving me kisses like that for free." Kerra gave her a grin as she laced their fingers.

"Ah, right. I should save my lips for when you impress me." Elizabeth leaned back into her seat as Kerra started up the car. She licked her lips, never wanting to get the taste of Kerra out.

Elizabeth spent the twenty-minute drive to the middle of nowhere staring at Kerra as she drove, taking in every part of her and loving their date. It had barely even begun, and she was already happier than she'd been in years.

Kerra put the car in park, and Elizabeth forced herself to tear her eyes away from her. "Umm... Where are we?" Her eyes scanned the deserted field of nothingness. "Is the surprise that you're going to kill me?" Elizabeth climbed out of the car to get a better view of the poorly lit sight in front of her.

She watched as Kerra lugged a large square light out of the trunk. "Follow me. I promise, I don't plan to kill you." Kerra gave her a wink as she started toward the abandoned space in front of them.

"'Things a killer would say for five hundred'," Elizabeth mocked as she followed behind her.

Kerra led her through a sea of forgotten trash and uncut grass to a leaning metal fence that seemed to be on its last legs. The small traces of lighting disappeared beyond the fence and utter darkness engulfed her.

"Kerra, I can't see anything." As soon as she called out the words she felt Kerra's hand embrace her, moving her forward.

"It's just through here," Kerra assured her as she guided her through the opening in the fence.

Elizabeth took five more steps before Kerra abruptly stopped her in her tracks. "Okay, here. Turn to your left."

Elizabeth moved her body to face left. "Oh good, darkness in a different direction." She was ecstatic to be on a date with Kerra, but she had assumed their first date would be less about hiking to her death and more about romancing one another.

"Just one more second." Elizabeth could hear Kerra behind her, wrestling with the big light in her hand.

Spots appeared at the edges of her vision as the light turned on, spewing a wave of bright whiteness on to the wall in front of them. Elizabeth could only make out the edges of the wall as her eyes adjusted to the sudden flare of light. She let out a gasp as her eyes focused on what was in front of her.

Her own eyes stared back at her, but there was sadness and confusion in them. The girl in front of her looked like her, but she wasn't somehow. The car behind the girl was unmistakable. That was definitely her car.

"It's the first day that I met you. I couldn't get you out of my head and so—"

"You painted me." Elizabeth whispered the words, still in disbelief at the picture in front of her.

"Yeah." Kerra set the light down and moved to her side. "It's not finished. I still have some shading to do and—"

The words were lost as Elizabeth wrapped her arms around her, devouring her in a kiss. The passion inside her burned from both ends. Elizabeth's lips were no longer gentle as she caressed Kerra's. There was a hunger in the kiss that demanded to be fed. Kerra could obviously feel it too. Her chest rose and fell with speed as she tried to catch her breath. "So, I take it you like it?" Kerra asked as she broke the kiss.

"Very impressive." Elizabeth pressed forward to kiss her again, but Kerra stopped her.

"There's more date, and if you kiss me like that again, we won't see any of it." Kerra lingered in front of her for a moment, her uncertainty over whether or not she wanted to kiss her or continue their date evident on her face. Elizabeth too was uncertain. A part of her wanted to get to know Kerra, but a larger part of her just *wanted* Kerra.

Kerra let out a breath, having made up her mind. "Come on. We should go." She grabbed Elizabeth's hand and led them out of the gate, following the bouncing glow of the floodlight as they went.

Elizabeth's nerves danced on end. Her hormones were going haywire, and she couldn't remember anything that happened on a date outside of sex. She stopped walking, pulling at Kerra's hand to bring her in closer to her. She let her hands find the sides of Kerra's face as she narrowed the distance between them, hoping that Kerra's promise was true as she readied her lips to communicate all her desires. "We can date later."

☆☆☆

Elizabeth stumbled over her own feet as she pushed Kerra forward. Both of them fumbled to make their way to the car, but neither wanted to release the other from their passionate embrace. She knew she should let go of Kerra and pay attention to where she was going, but every second their lips weren't pressed together felt like a second wasted. She felt her feet slip out from underneath her for the last time as she went toppling to the ground, taking Kerra down with her.

The hard impact of the dirt and cement knocked the wind out of her long enough to gather her thoughts. Kerra let out a sound that was a mix of coughing and laughter as she came crashing to down next to her. Elizabeth joined her in breathless cackles as she relived the moment. "We should probably at least make it to the car," Kerra suggested.

Elizabeth nodded in agreement even though Kerra probably couldn't see it in the dim lighting. She climbed to her feet, dusting at the dirt and grass that had certainly left an imprint on her dress. "Ugh, all that time picking out this dress, and now it's ruined."

Kerra followed her lead, picking herself off the ground and dusting at her pants. "Nah, you're a vision in grass stains."

"You can barely even see me." The smile that spread across her face gave away her appreciation of the compliment.

"I don't need to be able to see you to know you're still beautiful."

The calm that had settled over her evaporated as another flare of passion sparked. Elizabeth felt that all-consuming need to kiss Kerra again, and she gave into it. Wrapping her arm around Kerra's neck, she brought her into another passionate kiss. A slow and deep kiss that set her whole body on fire.

"Hey!" An uninvited voice invaded their moment, but Elizabeth barely noticed. She was content to kiss Kerra all night in front of whoever wanted to loiter. But Kerra must have felt differently as she pulled her lips away, abruptly looking over her shoulder for the source of the call.

Two young men strolled toward them, laughing at some whispered joke. Elizabeth couldn't tell with the bad lighting, but they seemed to be around her age. The apparent leader of the two spoke again, calling out to them as they approached. "Hey, ladies. How are you doing tonight?" There was a malicious edge to his tone that made her take an unconscious step back.

Kerra had the opposite reaction, turning around and taking a protective step in front of Elizabeth. "We're fine." Kerra's tone was curt and abrupt. It was a tone Elizabeth had never heard from her before.

Elizabeth stepped forward to stand beside her, but Kerra wouldn't allow it. She kept her body positioned slightly in front of Elizabeth as some sort of impenetrable protective shield.

A feeling of uneasiness washed through her as Kerra's gaze

narrowed on the men. She reached out to lace her fingers through Kerra's balled fists, needing the comfort of her touch as a nausea washed through her.

The tension in Kerra's body relaxed as she gave Elizabeth's hand a squeeze, but the moment was short-lived as the men let out a laugh. A sharp, vicious sound that was more antagonizing than gleeful. "Why don't you ladies let me and my boy here take you out for a good time?" The leader took another step closer to them as he spoke, and Kerra's shoulders tensed again.

Her eyes gave him a benevolent warning not to take another step closer. "No, thank you. Like I said, we're fine." Kerra's voice kept its edge as her eyes stayed trained on the two men.

Elizabeth's eyes danced back and forth between the three of them. She knew she should do something but her instinct gave her nothing. Her mind was blank, and her only impulse was to keep holding onto to Kerra. Their hands laced together seemed to be the only thing tethering her to world.

"Come on, ladies. If you were fine you wouldn't be out here dyking it up. Let us show you what real loving feels like, and *then* you'll know what fine is." The leader gave Elizabeth a wink, sending a wave of disgust through her body. Everything about the two men in front of her repulsed her to no end. She clutched Kerra's hand tighter, needing more grounding.

"If you were half as good as you think you are, then you wouldn't be out trying to pick up lesbians." Kerra spat the words at him, making her own repulsion evident for them to see.

"Kerra." She whispered her name to caution her. The men weren't particularly robust, but Elizabeth couldn't see herself taking either one of them down if it came to a fight.

"Yeah, *Kerra*. Listen to your friend here. You don't want to be rude now, do you?" The leader took another step forward, putting a condescending finger to Kerra's cheek as he antagonized her.

An unexpected rage shot through Elizabeth at the sight of his hands caressing Kerra, her previously void instincts suddenly commanding her to charge. She moved forward, readying her fist to swing into his jaw, but Kerra beat her there. The hard thud of Kerra's knuckles making contact with the leader's face rang in Elizabeth's ears as she watched his head fling to the side. Kerra let go of her hand and reached into her back pocket. She pulled out a blade and pointed it at the second young man. A flash of debate ran across his face as he deliberated his next move.

"You crazy bitch." The leader stood hunched over with a hand to his face as he spat out a mouthful of blood with the words.

"Exactly. Walk away before I do more than break your jaw."

The leader's second-in-command moved forward to his buddy and backed him away from the threatening Kerra. "You dykes aren't even worth it," he proclaimed as he dragged his friend backwards.

Elizabeth watched them disappear into the darkness before she turned to stare at Kerra, who still stood poised and ready with her knife.

"Let's go," Kerra ordered without moving her eyes away from the direction that the men disappeared into.

"Kerra?" Her mind was racing a million miles a minute, and her emotions seemed out of control.

"Let's go," Kerra repeated, gesturing for her to move toward the car.

Elizabeth moved forward, obeying her command, too frazzled to argue. She made it all the way to the car before she looked back to see that Kerra followed. "Kerra."

"Inside of the car." Kerra's tone left no room for debate.

Elizabeth slid into the passenger seat of the car and strapped herself in before she spoke again. "Kerra. What—"

"I just need a minute, Lizzie. We can talk about it when we get home."

Elizabeth eyed her, searching for some indication that she was just as frazzled, but she found nothing. The only emotion she could feel from her was anger. An enormous amount of anger that Elizabeth couldn't interpret. She was feeling a lot of things, but anger wasn't one of them.

Elizabeth drummed her fingers along the window as Kerra drove them home. She hated the silence between them. Her head was all over the place, and all she wanted was to say something, to talk about what had just happened, but Kerra had made her wishes clear. She didn't want to speak to her. Elizabeth bit down on her lip, fighting back the urge to cry as the quiet lingered. She was afraid of the silence, terrified that the longer it lasted, the less she felt like she knew the woman sitting next to her.

CHAPTER FOURTEEN

Kerra parked in front of their apartment and climbed out of the car without a word or a glance back. Elizabeth hesitated before following after her. Having worked up all the most monstrous thoughts in her head, she wasn't sure where she wanted to start a conversation with Kerra. She made it up the stairs and through the door of the apartment before she couldn't bear the silence any longer. "Kerra, I—"

"I'm sorry, Lizzie. I just want to go to bed." Kerra waved her off as she headed to her room, the exhaustion written across her face.

Elizabeth followed her down the hallway, feeling a flick of her own anger at being put off. She'd been reeling the entire car ride, and she wasn't pleased to be so casually dismissed. "So you're not even going to tell me why you're angry with me?"

Kerra turned on her, her shoulders sagging with the weight of the day. "I'm not." Her face contorted in confusion at the question.

"Are you sure, because you seem angry." She didn't want to sound as accusatory as she did, but even if Kerra wasn't angry with her, she was still being a pill.

"Lizzie, I *am* angry. I'm angry with the way that this world works. I'm angry with those guys. I'm angry with my homophobic boss. But I'm not angry with you." Kerra reached out for the handle on her door and winced in pain as her fingers wrapped around it. "I just don't want to talk right now."

Elizabeth let out a sigh as she turned on her heels and headed for the kitchen. She grabbed a towel off the counter and filled it with ice before returning to the hallway where she found that Kerra had disappeared into her room. She pushed herself forward, hesitating in the doorway as she stared at Kerra lying across her bed, staring aimlessly at the ceiling. She had never been inside Kerra's room before, and it felt wrong to be there when Kerra was in such a sour mood. But her fingers began to numb as the coldness of her makeshift ice pack seeped through the fabric.

"I brought you ice." She announced herself as she entered the room, but Kerra didn't look at her. She kept her eyes dancing along the patterns in the roof.

Elizabeth ignored being ignored and moved to sit next to her on the bed, placing the bag of ice on her knuckles as she sat down.

"Thanks." The word was barely audible as it came from Kerra's lips, but it was unmistakable.

"So if you're not angry at me, why won't you talk to me?" Elizabeth wasn't done pressing the matter.

Kerra sat up, but she kept her eyes on the ceiling, avoiding Elizabeth's gaze. "Because I really wanted us to work."

"And now we can't?" Elizabeth reached out for her, cupping the side of her face in her hands to meet Kerra's cool-blue eyes.

"No." Kerra whispered the word as she pulled out of Elizabeth's grasp, climbing to her feet. "There's more to this than dive bars and art shows, Lizzie. My life is dangerous because of who I am. Do you know how many assaults are made on openly gay women? I should have never asked you to do this. I let myself get caught up, and I forgot..." She ran a hand through her hair as she let her words fade into the air.

Elizabeth climbed to her feet and moved toward her. Everything Kerra was telling her were thoughts that she'd already gone over in her head a hundred times, and none of it seemed to matter. For every doubt she conjured up, she had double the reasons to stay. "Kerra, you didn't ask me to do anything. I chose this. I chose you, and if that means a little danger, then so be it. I'm not running away anymore."

"Choosing not to risk your life isn't running away, Lizzie."

Elizabeth reached for her hand. "Please don't try to convince me out of this. I've made up my mind. I'm done making the choices that everyone else wants me to. And that includes you."

Kerra stared at her in surprise. Elizabeth couldn't blame her. Her new resolve was shocking, even to herself, but she wasn't backing down. It had taken twenty-four years, but she was ready to fight for her right to be happy, and she wasn't going to let anyone take that from her. Her head had been all over the place all night, but that thought had been a constant. To fight for her happiness. "Kerra, when I decided to stay and be with you, I decided to take on everything that comes with that. All of you." Elizabeth let out a chuckle. "Even the terrifying, knife-wielding badass that I just met a moment ago."

Her heart jumped as Kerra smiled, the sharp edges of her anger seeming to dull. "I just want to protect you."

"I'm a big girl. I can protect myself. All I need from you—" She paused as she laced her hand with Kerra's "—is this." She gestured at their entwined fingers.

Kerra nodded, bringing their clasped hands to her lips and delivering a kiss to her knuckles. "Done."

Elizabeth caught her gaze, and a familiar fire ignited inside her at the pull of Kerra's crystal blues. But it was a different kind of fire. A fire unweighted by the fickleness of indecision. There was nothing holding her back anymore; she was ready to let it all go. To let herself be with Kerra, uninhibited. "I love you." She hadn't expected the words to spill from her lips. She knew she felt it. She knew that it was true, but she hadn't expected it to be so easy to say. The fear of the night had liberated her, giving her a freedom she never thought was possible. And at the base of that freedom was all the happiness that Kerra brought into her life. "I love you." She repeated the words again to Kerra's startled expression before pressing her lips against her.

Elizabeth's heart raced as her their mouths met in a familiar dance of tongues and lips. She couldn't be sure if it was the rush of confessing her love or the thrill of the touch of Kerra's lips on hers, but her body was on fire with desire. The feel of Kerra's hands finding their way to her waist and pulling her in closer nearly made her knees buckle. Elizabeth could feel herself moving backwards as Kerra guided her to the bed, her body seeming to float effortlessly in Kerra's grasp.

"Lizzie." Kerra whispered her name against her lips, sending a chill down her body.

"Mmm-hmm." It was less of a response, so much as a guttural sound, but it was all she could manage as she let her forehead rest against Kerra's.

Kerra placed another soft kiss on her lips as she traced a finger down the side of her face, making Elizabeth's hairs stand on end as it grazed down the crook of her neck, to her shoulders, and then down the length of her arm. "I love you too."

Elizabeth smiled against Kerra's lips as the words rang in her ears. *I love you too.* It was the simplest combination of syllables, and yet it made her heart soar with joy. She let her fingers trace along the edge of Kerra's hair before running them through the jet-black waves. Kerra watched her intently as she moved, her eyes glowing with the heat of hunger.

Kerra let her fingers run up and down Elizabeth's arms as she continued to dote on her hair.

Elizabeth leaned forward, letting her lips graze along Kerra's jaw before they found the lobe of her ear. She felt scandalous and seductive as she let her tongue toy at Kerra's ear.

"Lizzie, are you sure you want to—?"

"Yes." A breathless answer to a breathless question. Her heart was beating ten times its normal rate, and she was concerned that she wouldn't survive the amount of passion building inside her. The tingle of the soft caress of Kerra's fingers across her collarbone made her not care one way or the other. She'd die smiling.

She let out a sigh as Kerra's lips met her shoulder with light kisses that traveled to her neck. The straps of her dress slid down her arms beneath the push of Kerra's fingers. Elizabeth shuddered as Kerra's hand met the bare small of her back as she guided her down to the soft mattress, letting her lips travel down Elizabeth's body from her chest to her stomach. She let out a giggle as Kerra's kisses reached her inner thigh, followed by a gasp as her kisses trailed closer to her more delicate areas.

"Wait." Elizabeth propped herself up on her elbows to stare down at her. "I don't really want to...umm...do *that*. I mean, I don't want you to do that to me." She closed her eyes as she tried to gather her thoughts in less rambling idiot form.

Kerra cocked her head in confusion as she stared up at her, trying to piece together what she was saying. "You don't want me to go down on you?"

"Yeah. I mean no. I mean yes. No, I don't want you to go down on me. It's just not really my thing. I've tried it a few times and...I'm just not a fan."

Kerra let out an exasperated breath as she rolled over onto her back. "I don't understand, Lizzie. I thought you wanted to have sex."

"I do."

Kerra sat up, her eyebrows furrowed in confusion and frustration. "How?"

"With stuff."

"Stuff?" Kerra arched an eyebrow.

"Yeah, you know. *Stuff.*" Elizabeth widened her eyes, urging Kerra to understand.

Kerra let out a laugh at her bashfulness. "You mean sex toys?"

Elizabeth gave her an obvious nod.

"Okay. Well, I don't have any of those."

"What?" Elizabeth's shock radiated in her tone.

"I don't live in a lesbian porno, Lizzie. I don't have some secret sex dungeon filled with chains and dildos."

Elizabeth rolled her eyes at her patronizing tone. "You don't need an assortment of them. Just the one would do."

Kerra bit her lip, holding back more laughter. "Well, I don't have the one either."

"Oh." Elizabeth brought her knees into her chest, suddenly very aware of the fact that she was in her underwear as the awkward silence set in.

"What is sex to you, Lizzie?" Kerra turned to her, finally breaking through the quiet.

Elizabeth shrugged. "I don't know. Just sex, I guess. What is it supposed to be?"

"Well, for me sex is connection. It's the most intimate physical thing you can do with another person. It's a personal, pleasurable connection that you get to have with that person, and once it's done it can't be undone or changed. Sex is an infinite link between two people." Kerra reached out for her hand. "I want to connect with you, Lizzie. I want an infinite link with *you*. Not a plastic toy."

"Wow." It was all she could think to say. She'd never had any sort of introspective thoughts on sex. It had always just been a task that she felt she was supposed to complete. "I want that with you, Kerra, but I—"

"Is it possible that the problem wasn't you?"

"What? RJ? No, RJ had been with a lot of women before we got together. He had experience. It was definitely me."

"I play a lot of Scrabble, but that doesn't mean I'm any good at it." Kerra let out a laugh, and Elizabeth fought the urge to join her.

Kerra had a point. Elizabeth had never let herself consider that her likes and dislikes in bed were a symptom of who she was sleeping with.

Kerra must have seen the flash of indecision on her face and took the opportunity to propose a solution. "How about you give me five seconds from the moment that my lips touch you, and if you want me to stop then I will, and we'll just live a hopelessly boring, sexless life together."

Elizabeth cringed at the thought. "That sounds horribly depressing."

Kerra gave her a self-assured smirk. "I don't think we'll have to worry about it."

"Oh, well somebody's confident."

Kerra gave her a shrug. "I know my strengths."

Elizabeth let out a giggle. "Okay. Five seconds?"

"I could probably make you want it in three, but I like to give myself a safety net."

Elizabeth gave her an eye roll, but she couldn't deny that every bit of her wanted Kerra in almost every way. She had vehemently begun to hope that it really was a shortcoming on RJ's part. Her desire intensified as Kerra moved to position herself in front of her, spreading her legs apart as she leaned in to place a kiss on her lips. The taste of Kerra always electrified her, and the electricity intensified as the kisses traveled back down her body. Elizabeth smiled despite herself at the special attention that Kerra paid to each part of her body, taking her time to rebuild the sensuality of the moment. She let out a moan as Kerra's hands found their way to her panties, toying at the fabric and teasing her with the promise of a velvet touch to her waiting wetness.

The foreplay already had her on edge, and Kerra's clock hadn't even begun. She was suddenly wholly confident in Kerra's ability to make her crave her southern kisses.

Elizabeth let out a groan as Kerra continued to toy with her, placing kisses down the crease of her thighs and the tip of her pelvis as she continued to tease the cloth of her underwear against her center. She almost breathed a sigh of relief as Kerra slipped her panties down the length of her legs. She tossed them over her shoulder as she positioned herself between Elizabeth's legs.

Elizabeth was nearly shaking with anticipation, desperate for Kerra's mouth to move against her. But Kerra continued to withhold, blowing against the mound of her sensitivity as she arched in eagerness for Kerra's touch.

"Kerra." There was yearning in her tone as she begged for her promises of pleasure.

Kerra smiled up at her, a smug aura surrounding her that somehow made her even more desirable. The simple sight of her between her legs nearly brought Elizabeth to orgasm without even the first touch.

Kerra leaned in, letting her lips graze against her as she vibrated with excitement. Elizabeth let her hand travel down between her legs to tangle in Kerra's hair as her body tightened with the wave of impending ecstasy. Kerra's tongue moved against her in ways that made her body shiver unrelentingly in pleasure. Elizabeth let out a yelp as Kerra's fingers dug into her thigh, and she pushed her mouth farther into her center. "Oh, my..." Elizabeth couldn't stop the screams that poured from her lips as her fingers tightened in Kerra's hair.

Kerra pulled her lips away and stared up to meet her eyes. She unwrapped her fingers from Elizabeth's thigh as she wiped her lips with the back of her hand. "My five seconds are up," Kerra teased, a cockiness in her voice that sent Elizabeth reeling.

"Kerra, please." She begged her to stop her teasing, but there was a warning in her tone. A demand that she hadn't purposely intended.

Kerra smiled at her. Elizabeth let out a squeal as she returned to the work between her legs. Elizabeth could feel Kerra's mouth smiling against her, and she bit down on her lip as it brought her to the edge of explosion. Her mind went blank as her body rode out the waves of her orgasm. She rocked against the work of Kerra's tongue, attempting to put distance between them for just a moment to recover and collect herself from the dizzying euphoria, but Kerra held her in place, moving her mouth against her and slipping her fingers to work inside her. Elizabeth's eyes rolled to the back of her head, and she thought she might faint against the pleasure as another barrier of the dam broke, releasing the flood from her orgasm.

Elizabeth closed her eyes, trying to catch her breath as her body shook with the aftershocks of her desire. Kerra let her go, placing a kiss on her stomach as she let her recover.

Elizabeth's body was spent. In a matter of minutes, she felt as if she'd run a marathon. She looked down to find Kerra staring up at her, her chin resting on her belly, and Elizabeth was hit with a craving to reciprocate. The overwhelming need to taste Kerra and feel her body tighten against her in satisfaction hit her like a ton of bricks.

She licked her lips and pulled at the sleeves of Kerra's shirt to bring her up to her. Then she delivered a kiss to her lips. A long, slow kiss that allowed her to taste the mingling of Kerra with the sweetness of her own sex.

She rolled Kerra onto her back, positioning herself on top of her as she kissed along her jaw. She loved Kerra's jaw. The sharp, strong angle of it elated her every time she saw it. She delivered one final kiss to Kerra's chin as her fingers fumbled with the buttons of Kerra's shirt. She fought the desire to just rip the whole thing off her and send every button soaring through the air. Elizabeth wanted to sample every part of her, to run her tongue along every inch of her body, and the shirt seemed like a time-consuming hindrance.

She finished her dance with the buttons on Kerra's shirt and slipped it down her shoulders, placing kisses across her collarbone as she did.

"Lizzie, you don't need to—"

"Shh." Elizabeth quieted her, wanting to focus on her mission. She wanted to remember the feel of Kerra's skin beneath her fingertips and sound of her heavy breathing as Elizabeth's fingers trailed down her torso.

Elizabeth felt a wetness collect between her legs again as Kerra let out a shaky breath when Elizabeth's lips found her nipple. On instinct, Elizabeth brought the tiny pink rosebud into her mouth, toying at it with her tongue as her lips danced around the edge.

"Lizzie." The sound of her name on Kerra's lips made her suddenly understand why Kerra teased her. It was erotically stirring to feel the heat of anticipation radiating off Kerra.

Elizabeth let her lips graze down Kerra's stomach, stopping along the way to taste the skin above her belly button, swirling her tongue in sensual circles to lick at the salty-sweet midsection before letting her lips continue their path south.

She slipped Kerra's underwear down her body, and her heartbeat quickened at the sight before her. She wanted to give Kerra the same pleasure that she had, but she was painfully aware of her own inexperience. She leaned forward, walking her fingers across Kerra's inner thigh and hoping that her instincts would guide her through as she let her tongue play at the heat of Kerra's sex. Kerra's shudder in response made Elizabeth move with more confidence, flicking her tongue and moving her lips in a rhythm that kept Kerra squirming beneath her before she felt her unconscious bucking, signaling that she was on the edge. Elizabeth moved her fingers to slide inside her and bring her down the slippery slope of orgasm. The tightening feel of Kerra's insides against her fingers brought her to her own wave of pleasure, and she moaned against Kerra as she felt her release with her.

She rolled onto her back next to Kerra, exhausted and satisfied as she licked her lips, tasting the flavor of Kerra on them. Her salty, sweet tang had quickly become Elizabeth's favorite meal.

Elizabeth smiled as she listened to the sound of Kerra catching her breath, a sense of accomplishment building in her. She rolled over to place her head on Kerra's chest, listening to her heartbeat as it began to slow back down. Kerra wrapped an arm around her and kissed the top of her head, making her smile at the feeling of her embrace.

"I love you, Lizzie."

"I love you too." Elizabeth filled with warmth. She had never felt more perfectly satisfied in her life. "Kerra."

"Hmm?"

Elizabeth looked up to see that Kerra had closed her eyes, probably halfway to sleep. She smiled even harder at the sight of her peaceful expression. "It was *definitely* RJ."

CHAPTER FIFTEEN

Elizabeth woke with a smile on her face that quickly disappeared as she rolled over to an empty spot next to her. She had been hoping to wake up early enough to cuddle up to Kerra for an extra hour before she had to go to work, but the smell of pancakes in the air told her that she had overslept. She climbed out of Kerra's bed, hoping that she hadn't already left, and then headed for the door, stopping short when she realized she was naked.

Even though Kerra had already been intimately acquainted with everything she had to offer, she still wasn't the type to parade around the house with no clothes on. She quickly pulled the sheet off of the bed and wrapped it around herself before continuing her rush to the kitchen.

"Good morning." Kerra called out to her, wearing a smile as Elizabeth made her way down the hall.

"Good morning." Elizabeth practically skipped to the table, intending to take a seat next to Kerra, but instead her legs carried her to Kerra's lap, where she wrapped herself around her and delivered her a welcoming morning kiss.

"A very good morning," Kerra acknowledged with a smile as she caught her breath from Elizabeth's morning passion.

Elizabeth returned her grin tenfold, excited to get her morning cuddle in even if it was only for a minute.

"Nice outfit." Kerra's eyes traveled down the sheet wrapped around her.

"Thank you. I think I'll call it morning-after chic."

Kerra let out a laugh, and Elizabeth joined her, basking in the perfection of a morning with Kerra.

"I should get going to work, but I made you breakfast," Kerra announced, deflating Elizabeth's mood as she stood up, sliding

Elizabeth off her lap and onto the chair alone.

Elizabeth pouted at the end of her morning bliss with Kerra. "Great. Just what I wanted with my breakfast. A reminder that my girlfriend will be painting beautiful naked women all day. Most of which, she's probably—"

Kerra cut her off with a soft kiss to her lips. "None of whom I've ever let call me their girlfriend," she reassured her.

Elizabeth puffed up at the comment, feeling a bit of her morning joy return.

"I'll see you tonight." Kerra made her way to the door.

"I'll be here," Elizabeth called back as she pulled a plate of pancakes across the table toward herself. She frowned down at the food as the door shut behind Kerra. She missed her already. She hoped she wasn't so dumbly smitten at work for the day. She already had multiple burn wounds for her shifts where her head was in the game. The last thing she needed was to daydream over a hot coffee machine.

Elizabeth nearly jumped out of her skin as the front door swung open, startling her enough that she nearly knocked the plate of pancakes to the floor. Elizabeth stared wide-eyed at Kerra as she lingered in the doorway, peeking her head into the apartment.

"Umm, I love you," Kerra told her awkwardly as she drummed her fingers along the side of the door.

A smile tugged at the corners of Elizabeth's lips as she watched her. "I love you too."

Kerra straightened up in the doorway, her eyes lighting up at Elizabeth's response. "Okay. Bye."

Elizabeth giggled as Kerra disappeared through the door again. She stared down at the pancakes, knowing she wouldn't be able to stop grinning long enough to eat them. She let out a happy sigh as she mentally said good-bye to her fingertips. There was no way she wasn't getting burned at work today.

☆☆☆

Elizabeth closed her eyes at the sound of shattering glass as she dropped her fourth coffee mug of the day. "Shoot. Lola, watch your step,

I've got to clean up a spill back here."

Lola gave her a nod and an eye roll from across the counter as she headed to deliver an order to a customer.

Elizabeth headed for the back room for the broom that had practically been attached to her arm all day. She was a goofy, clumsy ball of joy and in a place of business where all the drinks are served in glass containers she was the ultimate destructive force. Lola made no efforts to hide her annoyance with every broken glass.

Elizabeth had been immensely disappointed to see that Krissy wasn't at the café when she arrived at work. She had no doubts that Krissy would have been more accommodating to her lovesick blunders.

Her mind wandered once again to thoughts of Kerra as she swept up the chipped shards of coffee mug.

"That's like six today." Lola made her way back behind the counter to the register.

"It's actually only four," she corrected.

Lola shot her a murderous glare that made her recant. "But I see your point," Elizabeth assured her.

Lola let out a grunt as she punched in buttons on the register. "So let me guess. The date went well, and Kerra sexed the sense right out of you."

Elizabeth's eyes widened in shock at the crass nature of her tone. As right as she may have been, it wasn't any of her business. Elizabeth was entitled to an off day every now and again. "Umm, that seems like kind of a personal detail."

Lola closed the register and turned around to face her. "But the date went well?"

Elizabeth was surprised at the concern on her face. "Yes, the date went well." She couldn't help the grin that spread from ear to ear.

Lola pursed her lips in thought and tapped her chin. "Good."

"Is it?" Lola had made it painfully obvious that she wasn't her biggest fan. It surprised her that her reaction to a positive outcome of her date with Kerra would be something she found *good*.

"It is. I love Kerra, and I want her to be happy. You seem to make her happy, so I'm glad it went well."

Elizabeth's forehead creased in suspicion as she examined Lola for sarcasm, but she found only sincerity in the words. "Thank you."

"You seem surprised." Lola took note of her hesitation to accept the compliment.

"Well I am, a little. I just didn't think that you liked me very much."

Lola let out a sigh as she moved across the tiny space behind the counter to the coffee maker. "I like you just fine, Lizzie. I just don't trust you."

"Well tell me how you really feel," Elizabeth muttered, more to herself than to Lola.

Lola poured coffee into two mugs on the counter. "I'm sure you're a nice person, but Kerra just got her life back together, and I don't trust that you're not going to rip it back to shreds."

"Lola, I love Kerra. I'm not going hurt her."

"And I want to believe that, but three weeks ago you were a straight woman. You're not really the pinnacle of reliance."

Elizabeth sucked in a breath. Lola had a point; she hadn't been the most consistent person in the world, but that didn't stop Elizabeth from wanting to shove her face into the coffee machine. "Lola, I assure you, I only have the best intentions for Kerra." She spoke slowly and deliberately, feeling at her wits' end for Lola's candor.

"Well, you know what they say about the road to hell." Lola grabbed her coffee mugs by the handle and headed out toward a table to deliver their order.

Elizabeth stared after her with her teeth gritted against the harsh words swirling in her head. She could almost hear her mother's voice in her ears telling her to turn the other cheek and watch her tongue. She rolled her eyes at the nagging thought of her mother; even when she was out of Elizabeth's life, she was still in her head. *You can take the girl out of the country, but you can't take the country out of the girl.* She smiled to herself. As much as she didn't want to go back home, she was glad to know that a piece of her would always be the product of her mother's upbringing.

She let out a sigh. Her nostalgia came crashing down around her as she remembered why she was on the outskirts with her mother. A part of her hated her mother for throwing their relationship away. She hated that she could never go home again. Even if her mother came around about Kerra, she would never accept her for who she was now. Elizabeth jumped as another shattering sound hit her ear. She hadn't realized she was still holding the largest pieces of the mug she'd broken before until they slipped from her hands again.

She stared down at the glass and mentally kicked herself. She really needed to get her head in the game. She looked up from the broken pile of glass to find Lola staring at her in annoyance. "You've got to be kidding me."

CHAPTER SIXTEEN

Elizabeth let out a groan as she put her car in park on the busy street's shoulder. The flashing blue lights taunted her as they reflected off her rearview mirror. She squinted her eyes against them as she gazed in the mirror, waiting for the officer to emerge and present her with a speeding ticket that she couldn't afford.

She sank her head into the headrest and let herself sulk. She had been about ten miles too excited to make it back home to Kerra, and she hadn't even seen the cop behind her as she flew down the road, passing a truck that clearly didn't have a smoking-hot girlfriend waiting at home for them.

Resentment streamlined in her belly as multiple cars raced past them, seeing the green light to speed since the authorities had met their quota with her. She sucked in a breath and forgot her sulking for a moment as the officer climbed out of his patrol car, straightening his belt and toting a clipboard.

He was the picture of attraction as he moved toward her car. His broad shoulders moved with the confidence of authority, and he carried the swagger of a man who knew just how attractive he was.

Her heart raced as he approached the side of her car, eyeballing the vehicle as he went and speaking into the walkie-talkie clipped to his shirt. She rolled down her window and focused on her breathing. She might have been less nervous if he had just been a good-looking man in a bar, but the aura of his control complex and the badge on his chest backing him up made her nerves jump into her throat.

"Hello, Officer." She greeted him in the most respectful tone that she could manage.

"Hi, sweetheart. Do you know why I'm pulling you over?" His accent was thick with the fine-tuned tongue of the country. It wasn't Edenfield, but Elizabeth could sense that it wasn't too far off either.

"Umm, I was probably going a little faster than I should have," she confessed, embellishing her own Edenfield drawl.

The officer smiled, undoubtedly a smile that won him the affections of any it shined on. "You're not from around here, are you?" He tucked his clipboard under his arm, throwing away whatever intention he had to write something on it.

"No, not really. What gave me away?" She was shocked by her own tone with him. *Are you flirting?* She waved off the voice in her head, telling her that she was falling victim to the man in a uniform with a bright smile. The ultimate cliché.

"Your honesty. The people from these parts wouldn't so quickly admit to their own wrongdoing. City people like to always think they're right." He leaned in to rest himself against her open window.

She gave him a grin, letting him linger closer to her than was appropriate for a routine stop.

"Well, I've learned the only way to get past your wrongdoing is to just confess and accept the punishment. My mother always found me out anyways. It always made for easier consequences if I just told the truth."

He gave her a nod and a laugh. "Yep, same here." He tucked his pen away into the pocket of his shirt, abandoning the original ticket writing intentions he had for it. "I tell you what, in honor of our mothers, how about I let you off with a warning and then maybe instead of writing a check to the State, you'll have some extra free time to get dinner with me."

She reached out to place a hand on his arm that rested casually in the frame of her window. His relaxed demeanor reminded her of his confidence. He'd probably never received a rejection before, and it didn't make Elizabeth beam with excitement to be the first. "You're sweet, but I don't think my girlfriend would appreciate it if we went to dinner."

He straightened up, moving his arm out of her grasp. "Your girlfriend? Like, you're..."

"In a relationship with a woman. Yes." Elizabeth kept her smile on her face even though his had melted into a frown.

He took a step away from her window, the temperament of his mood changing to one much more aggressive than when he first approached her. He took his pen back out of his shirt pocket and repositioned himself with his clipboard as he muttered under his breath.

Elizabeth stared at him disbelief as she caught the end of one of the words. The *faggot* rang in her ears, as if he'd screamed it at her. "Excuse me?" Her indignation was written across her face as she challenged him to say the word aloud to her.

The officer ignored her confrontation. "I'm going to need to see your license and registration," he told her flatly. His new demeanor was calm and steady as if the two of them hadn't just been laughing and flirting a moment ago.

"Because I won't have dinner with you?"

He caught her eye. "No, because you were going ten miles over the speed limit and it's standard procedure."

She stared at him in disbelief, her mind racing a million miles a minute, toiling over her next move. After a moment of pause, she reached into her glove compartment and practically threw her papers at him. The feeling of helplessness that she had no other options but to comply made tears well in her eyes.

Her mind managed to block out the next twenty minutes as she waited for him to issue her a ticket. She could barely steady her hands against the wheel on her drive home as her body shook with anger and sadness.

She'd been at ends with discrimination before. Being a black girl in Edenfield had toughened her skin against every racial slur under the sun, but this was something different. It cut deeper somehow.

Racial prejudice was blatant. There was never any guesswork in it, but this... She had let him flirt with her, and she had flirted back. She wiped at a tear that slid down her cheek as she recalled the situation. She hated herself for showing him even a moment of kindness.

She sat in the parking lot of her apartment building, willing herself not to sulk. She didn't want to give him anymore of her time, but the thought of him nagged at her. She wanted to take action, to do something to make him understand that his actions were unacceptable.

She stormed up the stairs to her apartment and swung the door open on the warpath to make the officer from hell pay. The smell of tomatoes and rosemary hit her as she stepped through the door, reminding her that her actions weren't hers alone.

Kerra stared at her from the table, her brow furrowed in concern. "What's wrong?"

Elizabeth wiped at the remaining tear streaks down her face, knowing that she must have looked a sight as she barreled through the door like a madwoman. "Nothing. I'm fine. You made dinner?" She moved to the dinner table, taking in the elaborate spread of breads and sauces that Kerra had put together. "It looks amazing."

Kerra stood up, meeting her at the middle of the table. "Yeah, I'm a great cook. But that can wait. Tell me what's going on." She reached out for her, clutching her hand in comfort.

"I got a speeding ticket this afternoon."

"That's what has upset you?" Kerra stared at her in inquisitiveness.

"Yes."

"Were you speeding?" She cocked an eyebrow at her.

"Yes."

"Well, love. That's kind of how speeding tickets work. Want me to help you pay it?"

Elizabeth shook her head. "No, it's not that. I got a speeding ticket because I'm gay."

Kerra's eyes widened as she stood frozen by the words. "What are you talking about?"

"I mean, we were talking, and everything was fine. He was going to give me a warning if I went to dinner with him, but I told him no, because I have a girlfriend and—"

Kerra dropped her hand and took a step back. "Wait, you told a cop that you were gay. Alone?"

Elizabeth didn't answer, assuming the question was rhetorical.

Kerra put her fingers to her temples. "Lizzie, you can't do that. Do you know what he could have done to you?"

Elizabeth threw her hand in the air. "Yeah, give me a ticket. Which he did, and I can't even contest it because I actually was speeding..." She noticed that Kerra was no longer listening.

She clutched at the ends of her hair as she closed her eyes against Elizabeth's rambling.

"Lizzie, this could have turned out so much worse than it did. You can't just go around and be..."

"Gay?" She huffed the word as she brought her hand to her hip in irritation. "You do."

"It's not the same, Lizzie."

"How is it not the same?" Elizabeth challenged, her annoyance with Kerra's reaction growing.

"Because I'm not going to cry when they don't accept me."

Elizabeth dropped her hands to her sides, feeling the sharp sting of Kerra's words ring through her body. Tears welled in her eyes despite her best efforts not to prove her right.

Regret immediately flashed across Kerra's face. She stepped forward to reach out for Elizabeth, but she pulled away. "I didn't mean that." Kerra let out a sigh. "I just meant that I expect it from people, so I'm better suited to handle it when it happens."

A tear slid down Elizabeth's cheek, and she swiped at it, no longer wanting to let Kerra see her cry. "There's nothing wrong with caring, Kerra."

"No, there isn't." Kerra moved closer to her, cautiously reaching out for her. "I'm sorry that I said that. I shouldn't have."

Elizabeth stood still, letting Kerra wrap her arms around her. The touch of Kerra's arms around her diminished her will to hold back her tears. "I love you, and I think that you're amazing, and I can't tell people that? It's not fair." Elizabeth sobbed into her shoulder as she brought her arms around Kerra to return her embrace. "It's not fair, and I hate it. You can't tell me I'm not allowed to be hurt by that."

Kerra stroked the back of her head, holding her tighter as she cried. "I know. I know. I'm sorry. I just..." She leaned back, crouching down to meet Elizabeth's eyes. "If something happens to you out there because of me, I don't think I'll be able to handle it."

Elizabeth scrunched her forehead in confusion. "Kerra, this didn't happen because of *you*. This happened because some backwards cop went on a power trip."

"Yeah, but—"

"No. No buts. You are not to blame. I am not to blame. This was him and *his* issues. If something happens to me, it's not your fault. It's theirs."

Kerra placed a hand to her face, wiping at the stray tears running wild down her cheeks and placed a kiss on her lips. "I love you."

"I love you too."

Kerra placed another kiss on her. Elizabeth felt her smile against her lips as she let out a chuckle. "What? What's funny?" Elizabeth asked, breaking their kiss.

"Nothing. It's just, I've never seen you so fired up before. You're usually so..." She searched for the right word. "Compliant."

Elizabeth stepped forward, giving her a playful push backwards. "I am not." She bit back a smile. "Okay, maybe I am a little." She reached out for Kerra, and laced their fingers together. "You make me fierce and strong and completely uncompromised. You make me a better woman than I ever thought I'd be."

Kerra moved closer to her, letting her lips linger over Elizabeth's. "That's pretty sexy."

"Oh yeah?" Elizabeth teased.

Kerra nodded as she brought her lips down to part against Elizabeth's. A deep kiss that made her delirious. Elizabeth pulled her in tighter, craving the closeness of her before a thought snuck its way into the back of her mind.

"You always expect it from people. So that's why you carry the knife?" Elizabeth felt Kerra's fingers loosen their grip on her hand.

She let out a sigh as her lips set in a straight line. "I knew we'd have to talk about this eventually. Go ahead. Ask your questions." She dropped her hand and turned to take a seat at the table.

Elizabeth joined her, taking the seat next to her. "Do you carry it all of the time?"

Kerra nodded. "Better to have it and not need it than the other way around."

Elizabeth gave herself a moment to process that before she asked her next question. "How many times have you had to use it?"

"Three times. Four, if you count the other night."

"And all of those times...were they like last night? Where just the threat was enough?" She asked the question, but she was afraid of the answer. Afraid for the heartache that Kerra must have lived through. She watched as Kerra's eyes clouded over, and she shook her head.

"No." The answer was hardly above a whisper.

"Have you killed anyone?" Elizabeth matched her whispered tone with her last question.

Kerra shook her head again. "No." She met Elizabeth's eyes. "But that doesn't mean that I wouldn't. If it came down to protecting someone I loved, I wouldn't hesitate."

Elizabeth kept her gaze, catching sight of the sincerity in Kerra's eyes.

"Does that scare you?" Kerra's stare pierced through her, begging her for an honest answer.

"Yes. But I understand it."

"You do?" Kerra stared at her in surprise.

"Yes. If you hadn't swung first, I probably would have. Seeing that guy touch you the other night. I don't know. It made me insane. Maybe I should get a knife too."

Kerra laughed as she moved closer to her. "I don't think so. You're kind of clumsy."

Elizabeth rolled her eyes. "Clumsy, compliant, any more thoughts on my character?"

Kerra leaned forward to place a kiss on her cheek. "You forgot sexy." She whispered the words into her ear, sending a shiver down Elizabeth's spine before trailing her lips down the outline of her jaw. "We should go to bed."

"But what about dinner?" She asked the question, but the touch of Kerra's lips tickling the side of her face made her unconcerned with the answer.

Kerra mirrored her feelings. "I already know what I want to eat, and it's not on the table."

CHAPTER SEVENTEEN

Elizabeth woke with Kerra's arms around her and smiled at the sensation of her breath tickling her spine. There was nothing quite as euphoric as waking up in Kerra's arms. Elizabeth considered their activity during the night. *Almost nothing as euphoric*, she corrected herself with a grin.

She could have lain there all day, sleeping and waking up for an eternity as long as it all took place in her current position. But the sneaking suspicion that her alarm was about to sound kept her awake, and eventually she gave into the urge to check her phone to see how long she had before she had to drag herself out of bed. *Five minutes*. She groaned against the confirmation that her time to sleep had come to an end.

"Hmm?" Kerra responded sleepily to her sounds of frustration.

"Nothing. Go back to sleep. I have to get ready for work."

Kerra nuzzled herself against Elizabeth's back. "No. Skip it."

Elizabeth smiled, a warm feeling spreading through her at the notion that Kerra wanted to keep in their current position as much as she did. "I can't skip it. It's my job. My fairly new job, might I remind you."

Kerra grumbled in protest but loosened her grip around Elizabeth's waist.

Elizabeth squirmed her way out of bed, sighing at the loss of Kerra's warmth against her as she went.

The fairy tale was over. It was time to get in gear to make a living. Elizabeth made her way lazily to the shower, griping silently to herself as she went. She perked up at the thought that Krissy was supposed to be at the café for the day. She wasn't sure she was in the mindset to deal with Lola's cold indifference toward her. A part of her was still reeling from her recent encounter with the corrupt ideals of the law, and she wasn't sure she wouldn't project her cop anger onto Lola in the heat of another one of their passive-aggressive moments.

Elizabeth made her way out of the apartment, delivering a kiss to the forehead of a sleeping Kerra before she left.

Kerra deserved her days off, but it didn't stop Elizabeth from feeling a tinge of envy that she didn't have to work on weekends. She let out a grunt of jealousy as she slid her way out of the door.

☆☆☆

Elizabeth glided across the café with confidence, feeling almost giddy as she worked. Even with the hiccups that came with her new life, she found herself experiencing almost dizzying bouts of happiness. Kerra made her every nerve come alive, even when she wasn't present.

"Girl, you couldn't smile any harder if you tried." Krissy teased her from across the counter as she balanced a tray of coffee mugs.

Elizabeth gave her a shrug. "What can I say? I'm a happy person."

"Mhmm. So, I hear," Krissy muttered knowingly.

Elizabeth was certain that she knew nearly every detail of her love life. She could see it in their first meeting that Kerra and Krissy had a tight-knit bond. Normally, it would have bothered her to know that someone else was privy to the private details of her romantic escapades, but with Krissy it somehow comforted her. As if by extension, she was confiding in someone as well. It helped her deal with the severed ties of her own relationship with her family. Her mother was never her confidante, but she was always there, and in a way that was all she really needed—someone to be there.

She was suddenly overwhelmed with a feeling of sadness and self-pity at the thought of her mother. She missed her. Despite all evidence to the contrary that she shouldn't, she did. The most constant person in her life had dismissed her, and it hurt like hell.

Elizabeth swiped at a tear collecting in the corner of her eye.

"You okay, dear?" Krissy never seemed to miss anything, no matter how subtle.

"Yeah, I'm fine. Just thinking too hard, I guess."

144

Krissy nodded. "It happens to the best of us," she agreed without pressing her for more information.

Just as Elizabeth was allowing herself to let in the negative thoughts she'd been forcing herself not to think about, Kerra strolled through the door, lightening her mood and returning that almost hideously big smile to her face.

"Hey, what are you doing here?" Elizabeth put down the coffee mugs in her hands with just a little too much eagerness. She cringed at the loud clank of the glasses as they hit the counter and waited to see if she was going to add to her growing tally of broken mugs. She let out a sigh of relief as the mugs stayed whole and then made her way to Kerra and wrapped her arms around her.

Kerra returned her embrace and placed a soft kiss on her cheek before she was bombarded with another hug. "Hey, what are you doing here?" Krissy echoed her sentiments as she wrapped her arms around Kerra.

Elizabeth stepped to the side as Krissy commandeered Kerra's arms.

"I was out painting, and I thought I'd stop by for a little inspiration." Kerra gave Elizabeth a wink over Krissy's shoulder, and her heart fluttered.

Krissy stepped back and narrowed her eyes at Kerra. "I'm assuming I'm not the inspiration you came for," Krissy teased, patting Kerra's cheek with her fingertips.

Kerra rolled her eyes. "Aww, come on, Krissy. You know I love you."

Krissy waved away her comments with dramatic flair. "Yes, yes but alas, you are in love, and I have been replaced."

Elizabeth's cheeks heated up at Krissy's proclamation of their love. She didn't think she'd ever stop feeling a tingle run through her at the notion that Kerra loved her.

Kerra bit back a smile, keeping her lips pressed into an unamused straight line. "Krissy Jackson in her performance of *All the World's a Stage*, ladies and gentlemen," she taunted, giving Krissy a patronizing round of applause. "All right, are we done?"

Krissy placed a hand to her chest in a theatrical gesture. "You raise them with love and kindness, and as soon as a beautiful, charming woman comes along, it's all for naught. One swift kick out of the door for Krissy."

Elizabeth giggled at Krissy's show, amused by the way it made Kerra squirm.

"Fine, Kris. Would you like to come to lunch with me?" Kerra asked. She was somewhere between annoyed and entertained, and it forced her face to contort into a combined expression of the two.

Krissy waved her off. "No, thank you. I have plans." Krissy turned on her heels, giving the bottom of her dress a melodramatic swirl for effect as she headed back behind the counter.

Kerra let out an exasperated sigh after her. "Ten years later and I'm still surprised by Krissy's crazy." Kerra stepped toward her. She placed an arm around her shoulders as she stared after Krissy.

"Yeah but I kind of love her." Elizabeth recalled how excited she was every time she saw Krissy buzz around the café.

"Me too," Kerra agreed, placing a kiss to the top of her head. "So, are you going to come to lunch with me?" Kerra slid behind her, pulling at the strings of her apron to slide her uniform off.

"Well, I guess I don't have a choice if you're just going to undress me here in the middle of the shop." Elizabeth blushed at Kerra's fingers on the back of her neck as she untied the top half of her uniform.

"I was just taking off the apron." Kerra bent down to whisper in her ear. "I'd take you to the back before I took off the rest."

Elizabeth's body heated up as the whispered words tickled her ear. "I'll tell Krissy I'm headed out for lunch."

Elizabeth could feel Kerra's eyes watching her as she moved quickly to the counter to tell Krissy she was leaving, and the feel of her stare excited her to no end.

Krissy caught sight of her coming and waved her off before she had a chance to speak. "Go. I'll see you in an hour."

"Thanks, Krissy." Elizabeth uttered the words gratefully as she turned and left, grabbing Kerra's hand as she went, overly eager for her touch.

Kerra followed her through the door, throwing a wave back to Krissy as they exited the café.

"Where are we going to eat?" Elizabeth asked as she skipped down the sidewalk toward Kerra's car.

"Wherever you want," Kerra offered as she opened the car door for her.

Elizabeth thought it over for a moment. "Well, I don't know what I want. What do you want?"

"Whatever you want is fine by me," Kerra insisted.

Elizabeth narrowed her eyes. "So, this conversation happens no matter what gender you date."

Kerra gave a smirk and a shrug in response.

"Fine, I want something spicy," Elizabeth volunteered as she slid inside the car.

"Okay. Spicy. I think I know a place." Kerra closed her door and wandered around to the driver's side. She climbed inside and then started up the car, easing away from the curb as she checked for traffic.

"Kerra?"

"Yeah?" Kerra glanced at her as she pulled up to a stoplight.

"What are you and Krissy?" She shook her head at herself, realizing how insanely insecure the question sounded. "I mean, I see you with her, and it's just the way you two are together... I just..." She had no real way to ask the question that she wanted to ask.

"Do you mean what kind of drugs did she counsel me for?" Kerra arched an eyebrow.

Elizabeth let out a grunt. It was almost annoying the way that Kerra could always read her. "No... Well, yeah. Maybe."

"It's okay, Lizzie. You can ask me about stuff. You have every right to know," Kerra assured her.

Elizabeth reached for her hand. "It doesn't matter what it is. The past is the past. I just...I don't know."

Kerra met her eyes. "You want to know. It's fine. You don't have to explain it." She tore her gaze away as a blaring horn behind them let her know the light was green.

"Maybe we should talk about it later," Elizabeth offered, acknowledging her poor timing.

Kerra shook her head at the idea, her dark hair waving from side to side with the motion. She'd neglected to gel it back that morning, and Elizabeth was just realizing how much she preferred Kerra's hair in a wild nest about her head. "It's better if I tell you while I multitask anyways." Kerra gripped the steering wheel tighter as she took a deep breath.

"The truth is by the time I found Krissy, I'm not sure what I was on. I was taking anything I could get my hands on, and when I was sixteen, I got arrested. They dried me out, and juvenile courts sentenced me to therapy and drug counseling. It changed everything for me. Krissy took me in and, long story short, we've been a family ever since." Kerra kept her eyes on the road, avoiding Elizabeth's gaze as they pulled up to another stoplight.

Elizabeth's mind was reeling. She had a thousand questions and no tactful way to ask them. "What's the long story, Kerra?" Elizabeth pressed her. She didn't know why, but it suddenly seemed important. It was as if Kerra's past was the last piece of the puzzle to make her real, to make *them* real.

Kerra stayed silent, the whites of her knuckles washing out as she gripped the wheel even tighter. "After I left home, I checked myself into The Center for Abused Children." Kerra paused, letting her take in the information.

Elizabeth had known Kerra's parents didn't accept her, as most Edenfield natives wouldn't, but she had never known to what extent Kerra's family rejected her. The new insight made her heartache for Kerra. She reached out to run her fingers through her hair, the need to touch her seeming nearly overwhelming.

The gesture seemed to steady Kerra in a way, and she took a deep breath to continue. "While I was there I met Jackelyn. The woman from the painting." Kerra glanced over at her, clearly waiting for the pieces to click into place.

"The one that died." Elizabeth practically whispered the words, her heart racing as she realized how much pain Kerra had dealt with in such a short lifetime. Her eyes burned with tears as understanding flooded through her.

"Yeah. Jackelyn was the first real friend that I ever had. She was just like me, trapped in Edenfield with people that thought she was a freak."

"She was gay too?" Elizabeth asked. It was a needless question. It was obvious that the two of them had bonded through a mutual sexuality, but Elizabeth had stared at that painting so many times, and there was something else hidden in Jackelyn's eyes.

Kerra shook her head. "Jackelyn was born as Jackson."

"Oh." She felt embarrassed at the surprise that escaped her. "Sorry," Elizabeth offered meekly in apology.

"It's okay. 'Oh' was a pretty common reaction to Jackie." Kerra laughed at some distant memory. "We ran away together; two senseless teenagers kicking ass and taking names. We lived nowhere and everywhere all at the same time. We probably tagged every wall from Edenfield to Havestat." Kerra's face lit up at the memory, and the smile that climbed her lips sent Elizabeth's heart soaring.

"I wish I could have met her." Elizabeth let her hand rest on the nape of Kerra's neck. There was nothing in the world that could have made her take her hands off Kerra in that moment.

"You two would have liked each other," Kerra assured her with a smile.

The light in Kerra's eye faded as her expression clouded. "Jackie used to swear the walls talked to her. That they told her what they wanted painted on them. I thought she was crazy at first, but she had such an eye for things, at some point I started to believe it was true." Kerra sniffed as she wiped at the corner of her eye with the back of her hand. "We-we were painting one of Jackie's visions one day, and we ran out of red paint. Jackie went to steal some from a shop down the street, and some guys caught her in the alleyway. She wasn't what she was supposed to be, so they..." Kerra stopped talking, unable to bring herself to speak the words. She pulled the car to the curb as she closed her eyes, taking in deep breaths to compose herself.

"Kerra." Elizabeth moved to place her arms around her. She was beginning to hate herself for making Kerra relive a pain better left in the past.

Kerra opened her eyes, returning her embrace. "I'm fine," she assured her. "I just...I beat myself up for a long time for Jackie. She was two minutes away from me, and I couldn't save her. She was my only friend, and I wasn't by her side."

Elizabeth loosened her embrace to stroke Kerra's cheek, wiping away the first tear that she'd ever seen her cry. "There was nothing you could have done," she assured her.

Kerra smiled at her. "If only you had been around back then." Kerra placed a soft kiss on her lips, the clouds in her eyes seeming to part a little. "Everyone I had left after Jackie hated me. I had no one, and I felt like it wouldn't be long before they killed me too for what I was. I'd have done anything to dull that pain...and I did."

Kerra searched her eyes, checking for judgment or repulsion, but she found none. Elizabeth had nothing but love and empathy for Kerra. There was nothing in her past that could turn off the way Elizabeth felt for her. Kerra must have seen that in her eyes. She smiled at Elizabeth, placing another kiss to her cheek before she continued. "If it hadn't been for Krissy and Lola, I probably wouldn't be alive right now. I still have no idea what Krissy could have possibly seen in me."

Elizabeth kept her gaze on Kerra, a sea of a thousand different emotions washing over her. "I do."

CHAPTER EIGHTEEN

Kerra pulled up in front of the Bean Spot, but neither of them made a move to get out of the car. They never made it to restaurant, but Elizabeth still felt like it was the best lunch she'd ever had. She was emotionally spent from all that Kerra had shared with her, but she felt undeniably closer to her, as if the two of them were somehow engraved on each other now.

She reached out to entwine her fingers with Kerra's. She would never stop loving the way that their hands fit into each other's. "Thank you."

Kerra lifted an eyebrow. "Thank you? You mean for the lunch date where I didn't actually feed you?"

"Yeah, actually." Elizabeth turned to face Kerra, leaning in to place a kiss to her lips. "And thank you for going through everything you've been through and coming out on the other end. You're amazing, you know."

Kerra gave her a half smile that turned her insides to jelly. "It wasn't me, really. Krissy did all of the work."

Elizabeth shook her head. "No. Krissy may have played her part, but the rest was all you."

Kerra chuckled at her observation. "I think you see me through rose-colored glasses."

"And I think that you should kiss me, right now."

Kerra didn't waste a moment, leaning in to oblige her commands. Every part of Elizabeth's body inflamed as their lips danced to their familiar rhythm. As Kerra's lips parted hers she wondered how late was too late to make it back to work.

Elizabeth unfastened her seat belt, maneuvering herself across the seat to straddle Kerra. Her senses went wild as Kerra's hands enveloped her waist, pulling her in closer.

She moved to cup Kerra's face, but her hands stopped in midair as a knock on the window nearly startled her out of her skin.

"Lola?" Elizabeth's tone was a mixture of surprise and annoyance. She met Kerra's eyes to see the sentiment mirrored.

Kerra let go of her grip on Elizabeth's waist and hit a button on the door. Elizabeth stared daggers at Lola as the window rolled down to reveal her expectant face. She seemed unfazed by the fact that she was interrupting an intimate moment. Lola barely even batted an eyelash as she peered into the car where Elizabeth sat straddling Kerra with a scowl on her face.

"What's up, Lola? You all right?" Kerra asked gently, through the window.

"Yeah, I'm fine. Krissy needs final plans for the trip." Lola gave Elizabeth a nod, as if it were a completely casual encounter for the three of them. "Hi, Lizzie."

Elizabeth cocked her head at her. "Hey, Lola." She returned the greeting out of the sheer pressure of the awkwardness that she was feeling. "Wait. Trip?" Elizabeth turned her glare away from Lola to stare questioningly at Kerra.

"A yearly trip to our cabin. It's a family thing," Kerra explained before turning her gaze back to Lola. "The trip isn't until next week. Can we maybe talk about this later? I'm kind of in the middle of something." Kerra nodded her head to gesture at Elizabeth still perched on top of her.

"Yes, sex in your car. How very romantic. But the trip is next week, and Krissy wants the plan *today*," Lola informed her with a roll of her eyes.

"Lola." There was a warning in Kerra's voice as she growled her name, and Lola pursed her lips in a pout. Elizabeth could see that she was ready to concede, but the moment had passed.

"It's fine. Plan away. I should get back inside, anyways." Elizabeth rolled off Kerra back into the passenger seat. "Thanks again for lunch." She gave Kerra a quick kiss before climbing out of the car. She made a conscious effort not to bulldoze Lola over as she made her way past her into the café.

"How was lunch?" Krissy's smiling face greeted her as she stepped behind the counter.

"It was really good." Elizabeth smiled to herself as she recalled her food-free lunch hour.

Krissy caught her smile and returned it with a grin of her own as she stared knowingly at her.

"What?" Elizabeth questioned as she caught her stare.

Krissy shook her head and pretended to busy herself with a task.

"What? Come on, Krissy. I can see that you have something to say. You're not the only one that can read people."

Krissy stopped fiddling with things on the counter and turned to meet her gaze. Krissy, having nearly a foot of height on her, beamed down at her. "It's nothing. I just haven't seen Kerra so taken with anyone before. It's refreshing to see her care about someone besides me and Lola."

Elizabeth's cheeks began to ache with the widening of her grin. She had always admired Krissy—her quirky, off-beat aura had always been alluring to Elizabeth—but now she saw her in an entirely new light. She was Elizabeth's own modern-day hero, and her approval meant the world.

"Thanks," Elizabeth squeaked as she stared adoringly at Krissy. She cleared her throat, realizing that she was staring at her like a child meeting Mickey Mouse. "Any tips on how to get Lola to share that sentiment?" she asked, shaking off her stupor.

Krissy let out a chuckle at the question. "Lola is my tricky one. It'll be a while before she comes around. I know it's hard but try to be patient with her. Lola's been through a lot, and sometimes she forgets that not everyone in the world is a horrible person. Give her time to see that you're one of the good ones."

Elizabeth's heart warmed at the compliment. Krissy thought she was "one of the good ones." Her day couldn't get any better if it tried. "Thank you, Krissy."

"Anytime." Krissy gave her a wink as she headed out from behind the counter to deliver an order.

Elizabeth busied herself cleaning the counter, trying not to think about the grumbling in her belly. She appreciated her moment with Kerra, but she was beginning to realize she really should have insisted on a drive-thru meal, at least.

She took in the unchaotic moment of the café and decided that Krissy could handle the only two customers in the place while she snuck a muffin.

"Didn't you just get back from lunch?" Krissy called out to her, moving uncharacteristically quickly back to the register.

"Oh, sorry." Elizabeth apologized around a mouthful of bread.

"No, it's fine. Eat as many as you like." Krissy gave her a warming smile. "I take it you didn't enjoy the restaurant?"

Elizabeth swallowed. "We actually never made it to any food," she informed her as she took another bite of her muffin.

Krissy smirked, wiggling her eyebrows in mischief as she did. "Oh, I see. No need to elaborate. I think I know what that means."

Elizabeth nearly choked on the food in her mouth. "No, not like that. I mean..." Her face flushed as she scrambled in embarrassment. "We just talked."

"Talked?" Krissy narrowed her eyes in suspicion.

"Yeah, umm...about you, actually."

"About me?" Krissy eyes widened.

"Yeah, about how you first met Kerra and stuff." Elizabeth stared down at the ground as she spilled the contents of her conversation with Kerra. She suddenly felt awkward about knowing so much about the woman who was supposed to be her boss.

"Oh. So, a big talk then." Krissy put her hands in the pocket of her apron and tapped her foot in thought.

"Yeah. A really big talk," Elizabeth agreed, fidgeting as she waited for a reaction.

"So, I have an idea." Krissy broke through the awkward moment, taking her hands out of her pockets and moving toward Elizabeth. "Why don't you take the rest of the day off. It's a slow day, and Lola is around here somewhere. We're overstaffed."

Elizabeth smiled at her in surprise. "Really?"

"Yes, I insist on it. Take your muffins and go." Krissy made a show of shooing her to the other side of the counter.

"Thanks, Krissy." She thanked Krissy as she untied her apron, excited about spending the rest of the day with Kerra.

"Oh, wait." Krissy stopped her as she made her way to the door.

Elizabeth turned slowly on her heels, hoping that she didn't change her mind.

Krissy ran to the register and pulled an envelope out of it and handed it to her. "Payday," Krissy informed her with a smile.

Elizabeth took the envelope and thanked Krissy again, this time feeling even more excited. She'd nearly forgotten why she was working. She had let herself become complacent in Kerra taking care of her, and she'd forgotten her entire reasoning for working at the coffee shop in the first place. It felt good to be reminded and to have money in her hands.

By the time Elizabeth made it to her car, the grin on her face was irremovable She was giddy with happiness, and she couldn't wait to make it home to share some of that joy with Kerra.

She drove home in her blissful daze, hardly taking notice of anything but her speed. She didn't want another arrogant cop pulling her over and killing her mood.

Elizabeth pulled into the parking lot of her apartment complex, her blood still fizzing with glee. She tried not to think about it as she counted out enough money from her envelope to pay her speeding ticket. She forced herself not to dwell on the potential mood dampener as she separated the money into her wallet so that she wouldn't forget it when she went to pay her fine.

Elizabeth grunted at the lightened envelope as she slipped it into her back pocket and then climbed out of the car. She practically skipped her way up the stairs to the apartment door, fumbling with her keys to unlock it.

"Hey, what are you doing home so early?" Kerra called out from the kitchen.

"Krissy let me off early because I'm such a phenomenal employee." Elizabeth tossed her apron across the couch and made her way to the kitchen.

"But if you were a phenomenal employee, wouldn't she want you to stay?" Kerra teased from behind a skillet of vegetables. Elizabeth made her way to the stove to wrap her arms around her.

"Hey, don't pull at the threads of my fantasy." Elizabeth placed a soft kiss on her lips. "What's this?" She gestured at the pot sizzling on the stove.

"I figured I owed you a meal." Kerra turned down the heat on the pot and then turned in Elizabeth's arms to face her.

"Mmm, food. I was going to bring you home half a muffin."

"But?" Kerra wrapped her arms around Elizabeth's waist, pulling her in closer.

Elizabeth frowned, shaking her head in mock sorrow. "The muffin didn't make it."

Kerra let out a chuckle as she brought her lips to Elizabeth's.

Elizabeth reveled in the sweetness of the kiss, floating away in their own stolen moment in time. She closed her eyes against the sensation of Kerra's lips, feeling a heat build inside her as her kiss became hungrier. She pushed her lips more aggressively into Kerra's, as her hands began to roam.

Elizabeth let out a moan as Kerra's grip slipped from her waist, to cup at the crease of her bottom.

"What's that?" Kerra asked breathlessly against her lips.

Elizabeth was lost in her own lust-filled frenzy, oblivious to what she was asking. "Huh?"

"In your pocket?" Kerra giggled at her stupor.

"Oh." Elizabeth reached into her pocket to pull out the bulging envelope. She took a step back, slipping out of Kerra's grasp to regain her focus. "This is for you, actually," Elizabeth announced, handing her the envelope.

"All right." Kerra took it and examined the contents. "What is it?"

Elizabeth rolled her eyes. "What do you mean what is it? What does it look like?"

Kerra glanced down at the envelope again. "It looks like an envelope full of money. Why are you giving me an envelope full of money?" There was something accusatory in her tone that baffled Elizabeth.

"For rent," Elizabeth answered cautiously, sensing an unexpected aggression from Kerra. "I mean, I know it doesn't quite cover my half, but Krissy's pretty flexible about my hours. I was thinking I could get a second job until I go back to school and—"

"My rent's already paid for." Kerra cut her off, still staring down at the money with hostility.

"Yeah, but mine isn't." Elizabeth could feel her own bit of irritation collecting.

"Lizzie, I don't need your money." Kerra extended the envelope to her, but Elizabeth pushed it back.

"Yeah, that's why it's not for you. You give it to a landlord or a bill collector." Elizabeth let out a sigh of annoyance. "How is this confusing?" She threw her arms up in exasperation.

"It's not. I just don't need help paying my bills. Keep the money. Use it for something fun." Kerra re-extended the money to her.

"Okay, well, they're *our* bills, and I don't want to keep the money. I want to pay rent." Elizabeth pushed the money back again.

"Well, you have sex with me. So consider rent paid in full." Kerra held the envelope out again.

"And if I were a prostitute maybe that would acceptable, but since I'm not, I'd rather deal in cash." Elizabeth huffed, pushing the money away again.

"Why are you making a big deal out of this?" Elizabeth could hear the frustration in Kerra's tone, which only served to trigger her own.

"Why are *you* making a big deal out of this?" Elizabeth perched her hands on her hips in agitation.

"Ugh, Lizzie. Just keep the money. The bills are paid. We're fine." Kerra left the kitchen, placing the money on the counter as she made her way down the hallway to her room.

Elizabeth gritted her teeth, ready to explode as she stormed down the hallway after her. "Are *you* really angry with *me*, right now? Because you're the one making this a thing."

Kerra whirled on her, pulling at the ends of her own hair. "No, Lizzie. I'm not angry with you. I'm just... Why does this even matter to you?"

"Because I've been here before, Kerra. I've let someone take care of

157

me, and I gave them all of the power to control me." Elizabeth shook her head, taking a step back from Kerra. "I don't want to do that again."

"I'm not trying to control you, Lizzie." Kerra took a step forward, closing the distance that she had just created. "I just want to take care of you. That's all." She reached out for Elizabeth's hand, clutching it without resolve. "Since the first moment I saw you, sitting helplessly in front of your car, I've just wanted to take care of you."

"Kerra..." Elizabeth started, wanting to protest but not having the words.

"Just let me take care of you. Please, Lizzie." Kerra moved her hand to her waist, bringing her in closer and making her lose her will to argue over it.

"Fine." She squeaked the word out, somehow feeling breathless in Kerra's grasp. "But I'm buying the groceries," she announced, feeling like that somehow made her the winner in their tiff.

"Okay, but you don't know what I cook with." Kerra moved in closer, letting her lips hover over Elizabeth's.

"Well, then make a list because I'm buying the damn groceries." Elizabeth made her voice sound forceful, but she knew if Kerra pressed her on it, she'd fold.

"Yes, ma'am. I'll make a list tonight." Kerra gave in to her, letting her feel as if she'd won.

"Good."

"Good."

Elizabeth's breath quickened as Kerra continued to linger over her, her hands steady at the small of her back as she swayed their bodies.

"Can we make up now?" Kerra placed a soft kiss at the corner of her mouth, and her knees nearly buckled.

"Yes, please."

CHAPTER NINETEEN

Elizabeth woke before Kerra, smiling to herself at the warmth that spread through her from Kerra's leg protectively draped across her torso. She wanted nothing more than to wake up next to her for the rest of her life. She let out a sigh of happiness as she basked in the thought.

"Good morning." Kerra greeted her sleepily as she nuzzled against her arm.

Elizabeth stared at her in surprise. "How do you always do that?"

"Do what?" Kerra responded without opening her eyes. If Elizabeth hadn't heard her speak, she may have thought she was still sleeping.

"Know that I'm awake. I didn't even say anything."

"You don't have to. Your breathing changes." Kerra answered her without making any definitive moves declaring that she was awake.

"You can hear my breathing in your sleep?" Elizabeth was completely mystified by the concept. She was dead to the world when she fell asleep. "Are you a ninja?"

Kerra finally opened her eyes, staring up at Elizabeth and chuckling at the seriousness of the question. "No, but life on the streets has made me a very light sleeper."

"I guess that makes more sense." Elizabeth wasn't sure if it was the fuzziness of just waking up, but a part of her really needed to be convinced that the woman next to her wasn't living a double life as a high-powered assassin. She stared at Kerra, watching her face for any signs of a tell.

Kerra stared back at her in confusion. "What's that?"

"What's what?" Elizabeth inquired back, still searching Kerra's eyes.

"The look that you're giving me."

"I'm trying to decide if I believe you," Elizabeth answered honestly.

Kerra continued to laugh, releasing her grip on Elizabeth and then sitting up in the bed. "If you believe that I'm not a ninja? Would it change things if I was?" she asked with a smile.

Elizabeth narrowed her eyes. "Is this you admitting that you are?"

"No. Just wondering."

Elizabeth mulled over the question. "Well, *if* you were, no. It wouldn't change things.... Though, I would probably start keeping a list of people I want you to ax off."

Kerra cocked an eyebrow. "Oh, so I'm a killer ninja?"

Elizabeth gave her a nod. "Obviously, is there any other kind?"

"Can't I be a crime-fighting ninja?"

Elizabeth shook her head. "No, you're definitely a killer ninja." She met Kerra's eyes and buckled under the ridiculous nature of the conversation as she burst into laughter. Kerra joined her in her own fit of giggles.

Elizabeth wiped at the corner of her eye, her laughing spell interrupted by the grumble of her belly. Kerra must have heard it too. "Shall I cook us breakfast?" she offered with an exaggerated bow.

"Maybe *I* should cook us breakfast," Elizabeth suggested.

Kerra cringed at the thought. "No offense, love, but I don't think I trust you in the kitchen alone."

Elizabeth opened her mouth to protest but closed it after taking further thought. "That might be a good judgment call," she agreed with a chuckle.

Kerra leaned in to place a kiss on her forehead before climbing out of bed. Elizabeth couldn't help but smile to herself as she admired the view of Kerra's backside as she slid into a pair of oversized shorts and a tank top.

"Any special requests?" Kerra stopped in the doorway to wait for her answer.

Elizabeth shook her head in response and watched as Kerra disappeared into the hallway. She could still feel the smile on her lips at the image of Kerra. Her smile widened as her phone vibrated on the nightstand next to her. "Are you texting me from the kitchen?" she called out to Kerra, knowingly. There were no other reasons for her phone to be going off at seven a.m. on a Sunday.

Elizabeth leaned over to grab her phone and was surprised as it continued to vibrate in her hand. "Are you calling me?" she asked under her breath, too quietly for Kerra to have heard her. She flipped the phone over in her hand, and her breath caught in her throat as her mother's number flashed across the screen. She watched wide-eyed as the number continued to dance across the screen, and the phone shook in her hand.

She climbed out of bed, halfheartedly dragging the sheet along with her as she walked in a daze down the hallway. The phone stopped buzzing in her palm, and she stopped moving. She stood and stared at it, frozen in place.

"You okay?" Kerra eyed her from behind the kitchen counter, as she chopped an assortment of vegetables.

"My mom just called me." Her own voice sounded a million miles away to her.

Kerra dropped the knife she was holding and started toward her, stopping at the end of the counter. "What did she say?" There was an expression on Kerra's face that Elizabeth couldn't quite read.

"Nothing. I didn't answer." Elizabeth stepped forward, attempting to close some of the distance between them. "Should I call her back?"

Kerra shook her head as she moved back to her cutting station. "I can't answer that for you, Lizzie."

Elizabeth jumped as her phone began to buzz again. "It's her again."

Kerra stared at her, her expression taking on its usual stoic concealment. Elizabeth was growing increasingly envious of Kerra's ability to read her mind. She wished she would tell her what to do or at least how she felt about it.

Elizabeth let out a breath as she put the phone to her ear. "Hello. Mom?"

"Elizabeth." Her throat tightened at the sound of her mother's voice. "How are you, honey?"

Elizabeth fought to keep the shakiness out of her voice. "I'm fine, Mom. I'm good." She glanced up to find Kerra watching her with caution. "I'm really good."

"That's good to hear." Her mother's voice broke, and Elizabeth could hear the sniffle of her tears. "I miss you, Beth."

Elizabeth wiped at the tears collecting in her own eyes. "I miss you too, Mom."

"Beth, I'm sorry that I put us here." Her mother's breath shook across the line. "I just want my little girl back. I want my best friend back."

"Mom." She couldn't control the sea of water that poured from her and the sobs that escaped her throat. "Mom, I—"

"Can we have dinner? Bring your roommate. Let me try again. You were right. You're an adult. You can make your own decisions."

The suggestion shocked her out of her emotional crumble. She needed to tell her. "Mom, Kerra's not..." She let out a breath, rethinking her words. *Not over the phone.* "Dinner sounds fine...but we should do it here. At our place." Elizabeth's mind was running in circles as she played out in her head how the conversation would go. Her mother certainly wouldn't welcome the news with open arms, and she wanted to be on her own playing field when she told her about Kerra.

"Okay."

"Okay, Mom. I'll send you the address. Come over around seven." Her heart was racing in her chest, and she purposely ignored the glare she could feel coming off Kerra.

"Okay, honey. I love you."

"I love you too, Mom."

Elizabeth hung up the phone and wiped her face with the tail of her sheet. She took a deep breath before she turned to face Kerra, who stared at her expectantly.

Elizabeth racked her brain as she tried to find the words to explain herself. "Umm... My mom is going to come over for dinner tonight." It wasn't much of an explanation, but the pressure of Kerra's stare forced her to say something.

Kerra nodded. "Yeah, I got that part. It's the why and the how that's concerning me."

Elizabeth took a step forward to rest her palm on the counter. "She apologized and said she wants to fix things and I—"

"Didn't tell her that we're..." Kerra trailed off, not needing to finish the thought.

"No. But I will. I just didn't want to over the phone."

"It won't go over better face-to-face, Lizzie."

"I know, but I need to do it this way. And I want to see her. She's my mom."

Kerra let out a sigh and moved toward her, stopping in front of her to rest a hand on her cheek. "I love you, and if this is what you need, then I guess I'll deal with it."

Elizabeth's lips pulled into a smile, and she wrapped her arms around Kerra. "Does that mean you'll cook?"

Kerra nodded and returned her smile. "I will but not for free."

Elizabeth's grin widened as a familiar look wandered into Kerra's eyes. "Oh. And what, might I ask, will be the payment?"

Kerra moved her hands to her waist, pulling her in closer. "Well, I think a kiss to start." She leaned in to place a kiss on Elizabeth's lips.

Elizabeth delighted in the taste of her, eager to hear what the rest of her tab would entail. "And then what?"

Kerra loosed her grip on Elizabeth's waist, to pull at her sheet. She licked her lips in seduction as she watched the sheet cascade off her body. "And then..." She placed a kiss on Elizabeth's neck, traveling down to her shoulder and back up to her lips.

Elizabeth let out a moan, letting herself enjoy the touch of Kerra's mouth on her before stepping out of her reach. "I think I should see the product before I pay," she taunted.

Kerra beamed down at her, taking pleasure in her teasing as her eyes rolled hungrily up her exposed body. She shook her head. "I require a deposit."

☆☆☆

Elizabeth strolled into work, still giddy from her morning delight with Kerra. Her mother was speaking to her again, and she was head over heels in love. It seemed all things were coming up Elizabeth.

"Well, aren't you chipper?" Krissy greeted her as she made her way behind the counter to set up for opening hours.

"Hey, what are you still doing here? I thought you were leaving yesterday?" Elizabeth's already bright mood brightened even more at the sight of her. She had been moderately dreading spending the day at the café alone with Lola.

"I had some last-minute details to take care of, but I am leaving tonight," Krissy informed her with a smile.

Elizabeth felt a tinge of sadness that she would only have Krissy around for the day.

Krissy's expression changed, and her gaze fell to the ground. "Umm, so I heard about your mom."

Elizabeth stared at her in surprise. "Wow. That was fast." She had known the information would get to Krissy eventually, but this kind of turnaround was almost unbelievable.

Krissy gave her a sad shrug. "Kerra's worried. She calls quickly when she's worried."

The surprise stayed on Elizabeth's face as she absorbed what Krissy was saying. "Kerra's worried?" Elizabeth played back the morning's events in her head. She had seen a flicker of apprehension in Kerra's eyes as she spoke to her mother, but she thought it had passed. "Why wouldn't she tell me that she's worried?"

Krissy smiled at her, a smile of understanding and empathy. "Kerra's funny that way. She treats everything she loves like glass. As if even the slightest shift in handling will shatter us all into a million pieces. She didn't tell you because she loves you and that's how she loves."

Elizabeth processed Krissy's words, taking in how true they rang for what she knew of Kerra. "She can't protect me from everything, all of the time."

"That won't stop her from trying." Krissy reached out for her, placing a comforting hand on her shoulder.

Elizabeth's emotions began to well in her chest, and she bit back a sob. "Krissy, I..." Tears stung her eyes. She willed herself not to cry. She had been a bad enough employee as it was; she didn't need to add "emotionally unstable" to her list of reasons to be fired.

Krissy sensed her turmoil and pulled her into her arms, squeezing the emotions right out her. "It's okay, honey." She stroked Elizabeth's head as she began to sob.

"Krissy, I don't know what to do." She sniffed, bringing her arm up to wipe her tears. "She's my mom."

Krissy hugged her tighter, pulling her in closer as if she could shield her from the hurt that she was feeling. "Honey, you're going through a lot of changes right now. Everything in your life is new, and it doesn't make you a bad person to want to reconnect with your one constant."

Krissy leaned back to look in her eyes, and Elizabeth's body rocked with more sobs. "But—but she's not going to be okay. She won't be okay with Kerra and I..." She wiped in vain at more tears cascading down her cheeks.

"And that's okay too. It doesn't mean that you love Kerra any less for wanting to see her." Krissy swiped at a loose braid that had found its way into Elizabeth's face.

Elizabeth pulled Krissy back into an embrace, leaning into her for stability. "Thank you, Krissy," she whispered through the tightness in her throat.

"No problem, honey."

Krissy held her, letting her cry herself out until she was ready to let go before sending her home. Elizabeth vowed to herself to one day be the employee that the Bean Spot deserved as she untied her apron and made her way out to her car.

She slid in behind the wheel and let out a breath as she sunk herself into the seat. It was only hours ago that she was living in a blissful bubble of glee as she celebrated in triumph the call from her mother. She banged her palm against the steering wheel in frustration as she considered what Krissy had told her. Maybe Kerra was right to treat her like glass. Now that she knew Kerra was worried her own waves of terror seemed to take over her mind.

She had felt strong and powerful when she hung up the phone with her mother, as if standing up to her and making her see reason would somehow lead to a dialogue about what was happening with her now. But she was being naive, and now that she had a moment alone to dwell on it, she knew how unrealistic it all was. Her mother wouldn't just be upset by the news and forgive her later. This was different. This shook the fundamental core of everything that her mother held in absolution.

She would disown her. *Am I really ready for that?* Elizabeth shook the question out of her head, scolding herself for asking questions she didn't want to know the answer to.

She took a deep breath and tried to clear her mind. She turned the knob of the radio up as high as it would go to drown out her thoughts as she drove the distance home.

She parked reluctantly in the parking lot, not ready to release herself from the mindless numbing of the pop songs spilling from her speakers. She tried to hang on to a meaningless song lyric as she made her way up the stairs, repeating it to herself in distraction as she made it to the door of her apartment.

She pushed open the door, expecting to see Kerra busying herself behind the stove, but the kitchen sat empty and quiet. She couldn't help the trace of disappointment that ran through her. Kerra cooking was a sight she had grown accustomed to. It was something she welcomed, and she missed it when it wasn't there.

"Kerra? Are you home?" she called out through the apartment, taking note that it was a weird time in the afternoon and Kerra had not been expecting her to get the evening off. She resolved to herself that maybe Kerra was out.

Just as a pout climbed to her lips at the thought of being alone, Kerra came stumbling out of her room. "Hey." Kerra stared at her in surprise. "Did employee of the year get another day off?" she joked.

Elizabeth gave her a halfhearted laugh in response. "You okay, love?" Kerra moved toward her, reaching out for her hands.

Elizabeth opened her mouth to quell her concern and tell her that she was just distracted thinking about her mother, but she changed her mind. "Are *you* okay?"

Kerra nodded her head in confusion. "Yeah, I'm fine. Why wouldn't I be?"

Elizabeth let out a sigh, taking her hand and leading her to the sofa. She sat down, pulling Kerra into the spot next to her to meet her eyes. "Kerra, are you really okay? Because we didn't really talk about my mother coming over or how you feel about that. We just sort of..."

"Had great sex," Kerra interrupted her with a smile.

Elizabeth shook her head, not returning her grin. "Kerra, I'm serious. Talk to me." Elizabeth stared at her, pleading with her to open up.

Kerra let out a breath, dropping her gaze to her lap and avoiding Elizabeth's eyes. "Lizzie, I'm fine."

"Kerra. At least look at me when you lie to me," Elizabeth huffed.

Kerra ran a hand through her hair, trailing it down to her neck as she opened her mouth to speak. "I'm not lying, Lizzie." She eyed Elizabeth out of the corner of her vision and let out a sigh. "Look, am I crazy about having a homophobe that hates me over for dinner? No. But I get it. She's your mom, and you want to tell her in person."

"And you're okay with that?" Elizabeth reached out to smooth down a hair that Kerra left askew.

Kerra shrugged, placing a kiss to her wrist as her fingers played at her hair. "Yeah. I'm okay."

Elizabeth brought her hand down to rest on Kerra's cheek as she stared into her shiny blue eyes. "I love you."

Kerra leaned in to kiss her gently. "I love you too." Kerra's lips set in a straight line. "But if she brings that dick ex of yours, his face is going to meet my right hook."

Elizabeth let out a laugh. "If she brings RJ, his face will meet *my* right hook." She stopped laughing as the very real possibility crept into the back of her mind. "Oh my God, you don't think she'd bring RJ, do you?" She was suddenly horrified at the night's possibilities.

Kerra reached out to rub her arms in calming circles. "I was just kidding. She's waving the white flag. I'm sure she's going to come alone."

Elizabeth nodded, wanting to believe Kerra's words. "Yeah, you're right. I'm just nervous, I think."

Kerra clutched at her hand. "Don't be. I'll stay by your side."

"Promise?"

Kerra nodded, and Elizabeth could see in her eyes that she meant it, probably more than she realized.

Kerra climbed to her feet, breaking up the intensity of the moment. "So, what should I cook for dinner?"

Elizabeth took her phone out of her pocket to double-check the time. "It's three in the afternoon. You haven't figured out what to cook yet?"

Kerra shook her head with a grin.

Elizabeth let out a giggle and rolled her eyes. "I knew I shouldn't have paid you first."

☆☆☆

Elizabeth smiled as she deeply inhaled the delicious smells emanating from the kitchen. She checked herself in the mirror again, overly concerned with her appearance for the night. As if wearing the right dress might convince her mother to accept her newfound love with Kerra. Elizabeth snorted at the sentiment. *Yeah, right.* She was attacked with another bout of sadness as she remembered that she might be preparing for her last conversation with her mother. She had been experiencing the grief in waves, and that particular surf broke hard over her head.

"You ready?" Kerra tapped at the door to her room, poking her head in to check on her.

"Yeah." Elizabeth nodded, making her way to her.

Kerra let out a breath. "You look amazing." She ran her eyes up and down her body. "How do you think your mother would feel if I made out with you at the dinner table?" Kerra reached out for her waist.

Elizabeth let Kerra pull her in close as she wrapped her arms around her neck. "Horrified, damned, repulsed. The list goes on."

Kerra let out a groan. "Okay, how would *you* feel if I made out with you at the dinner table?"

Elizabeth tightened her grip on Kerra's neck, moving in closer to press her body against her. "Hmm, giddy, elated, euphoric." She licked seductively at her lips and leaned in to whisper the last word into Kerra's ear. "Wet."

"Oh yeah?" Kerra whispered back in intrigue.

Elizabeth nodded, grinning up at her as she felt Kerra's hands begin to travel south from her waist.

Elizabeth moved her hands to rest at the collar of Kerra's shirt, pulling her in to meet her lips as Kerra's hands cupped their target destination. Elizabeth let out a hum of enjoyment as Kerra pushed her backward toward the bed.

Kerra let out a grunt of irritation as a knock on the door echoed through the apartment. Her shoulders sagged with the weight of the interruption. "No, no, no. She's so early." Kerra announced it as if it would convince Elizabeth to return to what they were doing and leave her mother to wait outside.

Elizabeth giggled at her tantrum, taking a step back to wipe her lips and straighten her dress from the crinkles of Kerra's roaming hands. "She's always early." She reached out to straighten Kerra's outfit, fixing her into the picture of perfection that made her want to lay her across the bed. She let out a breath, forcing herself to stay focused. "Okay." She wiped at the lipstick stains around Kerra's mouth. "Just let me find my moment, okay?"

Kerra nodded. "I'll follow your lead."

Elizabeth inhaled, focusing on her breathing as she left her room and then went to the front door. She reached out with a shaky hand for the knob and pulled it open. "Hey, Mom." Elizabeth waved her inside.

"Oh, Beth. You look beautiful. Are you okay? You're doing well?" Her mother launched into an array of questions as she embraced her. "What about school? Are you..." She trailed off as she caught sight of Kerra.

Elizabeth followed her line of sight to stare at Kerra. She thought she looked a vision in a blue silk button-up shirt that matched the color of her eyes and loosely fitting black jeans. But she knew her mother well enough to know that all she saw was a girl being swallowed in boy's clothing.

Her mother took a deep breath as she took in Kerra, taking a cautious step around Elizabeth toward her. "I owe you an apology. I should have been more welcoming when you visited my home." She extended a hand to Kerra. "I would like to start again."

Kerra stared down at the hand and then to Elizabeth, her eyes begging for guidance, but she stood frozen in shock by the sudden change of heart.

Kerra took the hand, confused as to what else to do. "Uh, don't worry about it. Shit happens," Kerra uttered nervously.

Elizabeth stared at her in horror.

"Sorry, I mean... Yes, let's start again." Kerra fumbled for recovery.

Elizabeth's mother let go of Kerra's hand, her eyes widening at Kerra's stumble. "My, you are colorful."

Elizabeth watched as Kerra made a visible effort not to be offended.

"Mom, would you like to see the place?" Elizabeth jumped to break the tension.

"Yes, that would be lovely." Her mother began making her way around the living room and kitchen without prompting.

"Really? Shit happens?" Elizabeth whispered harshly at Kerra.

Kerra stared at her dumbfounded. "She got inside my head."

Elizabeth rolled her eyes as she took off in the direction of her mother.

"This is actually quite a place you've got here... Forgive me, but what is your name again, dear?" Her mother stared at Kerra from behind the kitchen counter.

"Kerra," Kerra answered flatly.

"Right. Quite a nice place, *Kerra.*" Elizabeth couldn't read her mother's tone to tell whether she was being snide or if it was just her usual lack of self-awareness.

"So, where do you sleep, Beth?"

Elizabeth swallowed hard, sensing her opening. "Actually, Mom, I sleep..." She cleared her throat as the words caught. Her mother seemed to be genuinely making an effort, and it felt wrong to ruin it all before dinner. "I have a room, down the hall and to the right."

Kerra furrowed her eyebrows. She had obviously expected her to take her opening as well.

Elizabeth ignored her confused expression and led her mother down the hallway and into her room, giving her a brief tour before leading her back to the kitchen to sit at the table.

"Mom, Kerra is quite the chef. She made all of the dinner tonight." Elizabeth hoped the compliment worked twofold, easing the tension in Kerra from her procrastination to be honest with her mother and to build Kerra up in her mother's eyes.

"Oh, well, that's nice," her mother commented as she placed her table napkin in her lap.

Elizabeth could see the outline of Kerra's jaw spring forward as she ground her teeth, biting back her commentary. Elizabeth reached out to place a comforting hand on her back as she slid into her chair. Kerra gave her a grateful grin as she stretched across the table to pass Elizabeth the pan of carefully crafted pasta. She took the pan and readied herself to make a plate, her mouth watering from the aroma of the food.

"Beth, your grace," her mother scolded as she forgot the traditional eating prefaces.

"Right, sorry." Elizabeth put down the pan and bowed her head.

She peeked out of the corner of her eye to find Kerra sitting perfectly still, her eyes wide open and staring straight ahead at the wall, as her mother muttered prayers.

Elizabeth could tell it was taking a lot out of Kerra to keep it together while she waited for her to make her move. She felt guilty for making her suffer, but she wasn't ready to burst her mother's bubble yet.

"Amen." Elizabeth absentmindedly agreed as her mother finished her prayers and prepared her plate. The dinner seemed to move in slow motion as she toiled, debating with herself if she really had the strength to come out to her mother.

"So you painted all of these?" Elizabeth was snapped out of her daze by her mother asking Kerra a question.

"Yes. Most of them. A few came from friends," Kerra answered without looking up from her plate.

"Oh, so all of you are artists?"

Kerra cringed, probably trying to bite back the question of what her mother meant by "all of you." "Yes, a lot of my friends work with art."

"And those?" She nodded, her eyes falling along the inked outlines of Kerra's hands. "Did your friends do them?"

Kerra awkwardly removed her hands from the table, uncomfortably rubbing at the back of her neck. "Uh, yeah. A few of them."

"A few? How many of them are there?" Her mother watched Kerra with interest.

"Uh..." Kerra looked to Elizabeth for backup, but she sat frozen in place. "Forty or so, I guess. I don't really remember." Kerra fidgeted uncomfortably as Elizabeth's mother continued to probe.

"My goodness. That's a lot of tattoos."

Elizabeth stared down at her plate, trying not to blush as she remembered how intimately acquainted with each one of Kerra's tattoos she was.

Her mother took note of the silence that lingered across the table, breaking it up with fluid commentary. "Well, you know Elizabeth can't even draw a circle."

Kerra contorted her face into what was almost a smile. "Yeah, well, I didn't make her pass a test before she moved in."

Elizabeth's mother laughed, gazing at her, encouraging her to speak.

Elizabeth's eyes darted back and forth between them. She knew she should interject, that she should end the charade, but she didn't have the strength. All the weakness that she thought she'd overcome came rushing back in. She felt like she was right back at the start, beneath her mother's thumb, only this time with a little freer reign.

Elizabeth sat silently through dinner, hardly taking notice of the scarce and trivial conversation that passed between Kerra and her mother. She could feel the disappointment radiating off Kerra as it became increasingly obvious that she was not going to say anything.

By the time dinner was over and Elizabeth led her mother to the door, every vein in Kerra's neck protruded.

"Good night, Mom."

"I love you, Beth."

Elizabeth lingered in the doorway, giving her mother a smile. "I love you too, Mom." She watched her disappear down the stairs before shutting the door behind her. She let out a breath and turned to face Kerra, who stared at her with no discernable expression.

"You didn't tell her." Kerra said the words slowly and barely above a whisper.

"No, I didn't." Elizabeth wanted to give her an explanation, but the truth was, she didn't have one.

"Why? I thought this was what you wanted." Kerra stared at her, searching her eyes for something.

"It was... It is. I just... I don't know. I got scared." Elizabeth fumbled for the right words. Any words that could explain how much she had wanted to follow through.

Kerra watched her without a word.

"I'm sorry," she offered meekly.

"I sat through an entire dinner with your mother." Kerra spoke softly, enunciating every word.

"I know she was a lot to take, and I'm sorry."

"Lizzie, *she* wasn't the problem." Kerra raised her voice. "You were."

"I know, I know. You're angry with me, and you have every right to be, but—"

Kerra shook her head. "I'm not angry. I just... How long do you plan to keep me as your secret life?"

"What?" Elizabeth was shocked by the accusation. "Kerra, you're not."

"Aren't I?"

Elizabeth's heart shattered, seeing the hurt in her eyes.

"Kerra, I love you, and I am so proud to be with you, it's just... With my mom things are...complicated and—"

Kerra held up a hand to stop her. "Lizzie, it's fine. I get it. Coming out is hard. I just wish you would have said you weren't ready before we did all of this."

"Kerra, I didn't know. I-I'm sorry." It wasn't much, but it was the only thing she could muster up to say.

Kerra undid the top button of her shirt. "I'm just going to go to bed, okay."

"Kerra." There was a desperation in her voice as she called out for her.

"Lizzie, it's fine." She turned to head to her room. "Maybe you should sleep in your own room. I think we just need a little space tonight." Kerra gave her a sad smile as she disappeared into her room.

Elizabeth stared after her, her heart sinking into her stomach. She felt nauseated at the thought of putting space between them. She didn't want Kerra to go to sleep angry with her, even if she wouldn't admit it.

She debated going after her and pleading her case, but she had nothing else to say. No logical stream of words to make Kerra feel better. She collected herself and headed to her room, not sure what else was left to do.

She plopped herself down across her bed, having every intention to cry herself to sleep, but Krissy's words echoed in her head. *Kerra treats everything she loves like glass. As if even the slightest shift in handling will shatter us into a million pieces.* The words awoke some latent determination inside her.

She climbed out of the bed and barreled down the hallway to Kerra's room. Knocking softly, she gathered her thoughts. When she received no answer, she gave up courtesy and poked her head inside. She stared at Kerra as she laid sprawled across her bed, staring up at the ceiling.

"You still mad at me?"

Kerra didn't acknowledge her, keeping her gaze pointed upward. "I told you. I'm not mad."

Elizabeth crossed the room to kneel by her bed. "Well, you should be."

Kerra turned her head to glance at her, her expression unreadable.

"Kerra, I lied to you. I told you I was going to do something, and I didn't do it. You had to sit through a dinner *with my mother* with no backup. You stood tall by my side, and I left you hanging. You *should* be angry. No, you should be pissed with me."

Kerra turned her gaze back to the ceiling. "Well, I'm not," she insisted flatly.

"Kerra," Elizabeth pleaded.

"What, Lizzie?" Kerra sat up on the bed. "What? You want me to say I'm pissed? Fine, I'm pissed. I hated every minute of that dinner. I hate..." Kerra paused, running her hands down her face in frustration. "I hate that you didn't tell her."

Elizabeth bit down on her lip, fighting to hold back her tears as Kerra turned to her, that same sadness still glowing in her eyes. "I just hate that you didn't tell her, Lizzie. And I'm scared."

"You're scared?" Elizabeth failed to keep the tremor out of her voice.

"Yeah. I'm scared. I'm scared about what that means. That you didn't tell her because this isn't forever for you. Because when all of this is done, you plan to go back home and chalk this all up as your gay phase." Kerra dropped her head into her hands. "And I love you so much that I wouldn't even be mad." Kerra lifted her head, wiping away tears in an attempt to stop Elizabeth seeing them. "Lizzie, I love you to a point that I can't come back from, and when you didn't tell your mom...I just feel like I'm going to lose you."

Elizabeth wiped at a never-ending stream of tears that spilled down her cheeks. She reached out for Kerra's hand, lacing her fingers with her own. "Kerra, you're not going to lose me. Me not telling my mother about us had nothing to do with me and you and everything to do with who she is." Elizabeth let go of her hand, shifting her weight to straddle Kerra between her legs. She placed her hands on the sides of her face as she spoke. "Kerra, I never meant to make you feel like I didn't think this was forever. And I hate that I made you think, for even a second, that I don't love you every bit as much as you love me." Her voice gave out as her body was attacked with a wave of emotion. "You are more to me than you can possibly know."

Elizabeth brought her face down to meet Kerra's, kissing her with everything that she had. She could taste the saltiness of tears on her lips. She didn't know if they were hers or Kerra's, but she savored it. There was honesty and love in the taste of those tears, and she never wanted to forget them.

Kerra pulled her in closer, wrapping her arms tightly around Elizabeth as she kissed her back with just as much ferocity. Elizabeth pulled at the buttons on Kerra's shirt, nearly ripping it off her. There was so much love and passion generating between them that she wanted to feel that connection with Kerra everywhere. She wanted every part of Kerra to experience how much she loved her, and she could feel that same need coming off Kerra in droves. Kerra needed her just as much.

She gasped as Kerra flipped her over, to lay on her back across the bed. She placed kisses at her neck and down her body, to sneak beneath her dress. Elizabeth let out a happy sigh and closed her eyes as she experienced the all-consuming depths of making love.

CHAPTER TWENTY

Elizabeth was growing accustomed to her morning routine: waking up in Kerra's arms, sharing breakfast, and preparing herself for an earnest day of making coffee. It was all so exuberantly mundane, and she loved every minute of it. She smiled to herself as she watched Kerra butter a piece of toast across the table. She wondered how Kerra could manage to make the most monotonous of tasks seem sexy and hypnotic.

"What? Why are you looking at me like that?" Kerra caught her eye as she took a bite into her breakfast.

Elizabeth shrugged, wearing a grin wide enough to bridge universes. "Because I love you."

"I love you too, but it's starting to get weird." Kerra smiled through a mouthful of toast.

Elizabeth stuck her tongue out at her as she continued her goofy fixation. She loved the sight of Kerra before she went off to work. Her hair was gelled back neatly above her ears, and she was dressed in her idea of artist casual: fitted T-shirts with quirky logos painted across the front.

This morning's borderline inappropriate tee read *"liquor in the front"* with the picture of a pair of lips poking its tongue into the hole of a liquor bottle. Elizabeth didn't need to see the back of the shirt to know that *"poker in the back"* was scrawled across Kerra's shoulder blades with some other obscene picture of humor. Elizabeth rolled her eyes at the vulgarity of her work ensemble, even though she had to admit that she found it incredibly sexy how adamant Kerra was about displaying her sexuality despite her horrendous excuse for a boss.

Kerra swallowed her toast, letting out a chuckle as Elizabeth's eyes still lingered on her. "Uh, do you remember that trip that Lola mentioned?" Elizabeth nodded as she watched Kerra wipe at the crumbs sticking to her lips. "Well, we leave this weekend, and I was wondering if...you know...if you'd maybe want to go?"

Elizabeth pondered the invite. She hadn't been expecting it, but a weekend away with Kerra didn't sound like the worst idea. "I thought it was a family trip?"

Kerra looked down at her food, tearing up pieces of toast and pushing them around her plate. "It is, but...I was talking to Krissy about it, and she wants you to come."

"Oh." Elizabeth couldn't help the disappointment that crept into her tone.

Kerra must have heard it. She looked up from her plate and met Elizabeth's gaze. "*I* want you to come."

"Oh." Elizabeth brightened up, her morning smile returning.

"Yeah, I was thinking maybe we could go up early and hang out. Maybe christen the cabin." Kerra winked at her.

"Oh." The word had taken on a singsong rhythm.

"So, what do you think? You want to go away with me?"

"I'd love to."

"Good." Kerra stood up with her plate and then took it the sink. "I should get to work. I'll see you tonight." She dumped her breakfast and headed for the door, placing a quick kiss to Elizabeth's cheek on her way.

Elizabeth stared after her, giddy with the thought of an impending weekend away. She didn't even let herself dwell on the fact that she only had an hour before she had to head off to work. Not even the terrifying prospect of being stuck alone in the coffee shop with Lola could dampen her mood.

She finished her breakfast slowly, daydreaming about what a vacation away with Kerra would be like. She had crafted about a hundred different scenarios by the time she finally made it to work. All of them came crashing down as she saw Lola standing behind the counter, her usual scowl across her face as she prepared for opening.

"Hi, Lola." She made her way to the back to prepare her station.

"Lizzie," Lola responded with a curt nod. Elizabeth waited for an aggressive assault of her character, but it never came. She let herself believe that the day might not be so bad.

"So, I hear you might be tagging along on our trip to the cabins this year." Lola turned to watch her shift around coffee mugs.

"Uh, yeah. I think I am. Kerra and I talked about it this morning." Elizabeth kept herself busy organizing the glasses, hoping that if she refused to turn around it would disengage Lola.

"Hmm...interesting." Lola hummed.

Elizabeth wrestled against her instinct to turn around and ask her to elaborate. *Don't engage. Don't engage. Do not engage.* She coached herself to no avail as her curiosity won out. "How so?" She turned to meet Lola's burning gaze.

"Well, it just doesn't seem like your thing. The mountains are full of bigots and racists. Most years we just go to piss off the locals. It's not really a trip for the weak-willed." Lola smiled in condescension as she prattled on.

Elizabeth gritted her teeth hard enough that her jaw began to ache. She'd had her fill of Lola's thinly veiled passive aggression. She took a step forward, leaning in to be closer to Lola's face. "Listen, Lola, you can tell me that we'll be rooming with Jeffrey Dahmer and I'm still going on this trip. So, you do whatever it is you have to do to wrap your head around that."

Lola kept a blank expression on her face as the two of them remained locked in a battle-of-wills stare down. Elizabeth's blood began to boil with determination; her feet remained planted firmly in place as she mentally challenged Lola to fire back.

Lola placed her arms across her chest, mirroring Elizabeth's ferocity. The familiar tune of the bakery phone cut through Lola's aggression. She looked away to stare at the little black device emanating the sound that stole her focus.

"You should get that," Elizabeth told her smugly, feeling as if she'd won some small battle.

Elizabeth watched her as she let out a grunt, turning her back on her to answer the phone.

"What?" Lola huffed at whoever was on the other end. "Wait, slow down. What happened?"

Elizabeth leaned in as she heard Lola's tone change. She strained to hear the voice on the other end of the line, but all she could make out were muffled cries of panic.

"Okay, okay. Calm down. Which hospital?" Lola's voice took on a frighteningly calm air. "Okay, we're on our way." Lola turned to face Elizabeth as she hung up the phone, and the look on her face sent Elizabeth's heart sinking into her belly.

"Who's in the hospital, Lola?" Elizabeth's heartbeat raced loudly in her ears as images of Kerra in a hospital bed flashed through her mind.

"Just umm, put everything back. We're closing up shop for the day." Lola spoke in calm, low tones, but her eyes betrayed her. Her entire body was rigid with panic as she pushed things to the side of the counter.

"Lola." Elizabeth made no moves to follow orders. She was frozen in place by fear. "What's going on? Is Kerra okay?"

Lola stopped and braced her palms against the counter as she took several deep breaths. Elizabeth forced her feet to move forward as she reached out to place a hand on her shoulder. "Lola, is Kerra okay?" She gave Lola's shoulder a supportive squeeze, even though her own nerve endings felt like they were on fire as she waited for an answer.

"It's not Kerra." Lola turned to her, giving her a grateful smile for reaching out. "It's Angela. She ran into some trouble on the Southside, and she's in the hospital."

Elizabeth breathed a sigh of relief and immediately felt guilty for it. Angela had been kind to her and given her a helping hand when she was in need. She should have been more troubled by the news that she was in the hospital, not relieved that it wasn't Kerra.

Lola gathered herself and stood up straight. "Come on. We have to go." She wiggled out from underneath Elizabeth's grasp and headed for the front door. Elizabeth scrambled behind her even though she wasn't sure why she should tag along instead of keeping the shop open, but she knew that it wasn't the appropriate moment to ask.

Elizabeth followed Lola to the end of the curb where a boxy, bright pink car sat parked and waiting. Elizabeth stared in disbelief at the vehicle. "This is your car?" The bright and cheerful, eco-friendly vehicle didn't seem to fit with what Elizabeth had come to know as Lola's personality.

"Yeah, it is. Now get in," Lola snapped as she slid in behind the wheel.

Elizabeth jumped to obey, sensing the urgency in her tone. She climbed inside and was met by more surprises. Colorful decorations dangled from the sticker-covered light fixtures inside, and Elizabeth was mystified by the fuzzy seat covers that tickled the backs of her arms. "Wow." She hadn't meant to say the word out loud, but her lips betrayed her.

"Wow what?" Lola huffed as she flew down the road at what Elizabeth could only guess was twice the speed limit.

"Nothing. The car. It just doesn't seem like you." Elizabeth flicked at a dangling teddy-bear-shaped pendant hanging from the mirror.

"Yeah, well it is." Lola reached out to still the swinging teddy bear. "Please, don't touch things."

Elizabeth held her hands up in apology before placing them in her lap. She sat awkwardly still while softly humming to herself until she breathed a sigh of relief as they pulled into a hospital parking lot. She wasn't sure she could take much longer being stuck in the small space with Lola.

"Lizzie." Lola turned to her as she parked the car in an empty spot. Her tone seemed urgent and sad. Elizabeth bit down on her lip as she waited expectantly for whatever it was she was going to say. Lola's expression worried her for reasons she didn't understand.

Lola met her eyes as she tried to find her words. "Listen, Kerra's not really good at this kind of thing. We've known Angela for a long time, and she and Kerra kind of..."

"Had a thing," Elizabeth finished for her. "Yeah, I know."

"You do, but..." Lola let out a sigh. "Kerra feels responsible for everybody, and when she feels like she failed at the impossible task of taking care of everyone, she goes to kind of a dark place." Lola let her eyes drop to the floor as she took in a deep breath. "I've watched Kerra backslide before, and it's not pretty. So, if you're not ready for that other side of her, maybe you should wait out here." There was earnestness in Lola's words. The sharp-tongued, pain-in-the-ass Lola seemed to fade away. Suddenly, Elizabeth could see what Krissy had been trying to tell her. The Lola warning her of Kerra's darkness was simply a girl trying to protect her sister from herself.

Elizabeth reached out for her, taking her hand and feeling as if she finally understood her. "I meant it when I said I wasn't going anywhere. Whatever Kerra is going through, I want to be next to her while she goes through it." She meant every word. Her heart wanted to shatter into a million pieces at the thought of Kerra without that bright light inside her that made Elizabeth's knees go weak, but Kerra deserved a partner who would stand by her through thick and thin. If Kerra needed to borrow some of Elizabeth's light, then she would be there to give it to her.

Lola must have read the sincerity in her eyes because she gave her a warming smile. "Okay then. Let's go."

Elizabeth climbed out of the car behind Lola with less apprehension than she thought she would. Somehow the thought that she needed to be strong for Kerra gave her more strength than she ever thought she had.

"We're here. Where are you guys?" Elizabeth trailed behind Lola as she placed her phone to her ear. "Okay, we're coming up. Heading to the elevator now."

Elizabeth nodded in agreement even though Lola wasn't paying her any attention as she pushed the button for the elevator.

Elizabeth stepped inside when it arrived and was surprised when Lola didn't step in behind her. "Lola?" She stepped out of the elevator as Lola propped herself against the wall, her eyes watering over without actually spilling any tears.

"I just need a minute, Lizzie."

Elizabeth nodded. She stood awkwardly by her side, letting other people onto the elevator and waving them off when they tried to wait for them. She had never even considered that Lola had any sort of feelings at all. In her mind Lola had been some sort of high-tech robot out to make her feel inadequate. Seeing her in her current state seemed wrong somehow. She was shocked by how much she preferred the snarky, condescending version of Lola.

"Lola." Elizabeth gently urged her.

Lola stood up straight, wiping at the corners of her eyes even though she hadn't fully let herself cry. "Okay. I'm fine. I just didn't want to fall apart up there." She pressed the button for the elevator again.

Elizabeth hid the smile that spread across her face at the comment. The more she learned of Lola, the more she reminded her of Kerra.

They rode up three floors in the elevator, Lola taking in slow, deep breaths as Elizabeth fidgeted nervously until the doors bounced open on a room full of turquoise-colored chairs.

Elizabeth moved forward out of the sliding doors, and her breath caught in her throat as Kerra came into sight, her head bowed forward into her hands while Krissy rubbed her back. Krissy caught sight of them coming out of the elevator and whispered something to Kerra before heading toward them.

"Did you put a sign up in the shop?" Krissy asked as she wrapped Lola in a hug.

"Yeah, yeah, I did. What's going on? How's Angela?" The vulnerable Lola from downstairs had disappeared, and the Lola before her was all business.

"Hi, Lizzie. I'm glad you're here. Kerra will be happy to see you." Krissy reached out to embrace her, but Lola stepped between them. "Mom, how is Angela?" she asked again impatiently.

Krissy wringed her hands together and let out a sigh. "We don't know. The last thing we heard was something about head trauma and that they needed to do a scan. I don't remember the specifics, but it all boils down to us playing the waiting game."

"What happened?" Lola kept her voice hushed as she probed for more information.

"She was helping Azul prep for the Southside opening, and some guys broke in. Azul says they just wanted to scare them, smash a few glasses and shout just to hear themselves roar. But you know Angela, she—"

"Fought back," Lola finished for her, nodding in understanding.

"Yeah. Azul took a bottle to the back of the head, and Angela took whatever else they had in them." Krissy held her lips tightly in a straight line, forcing them not to quiver.

"God, that's such a horrible location for a gay bar." Lola shook her head in disapproval. "Where's Azul?"

"He's okay. He's in with the doctors. He's the only one they'll talk to since he's family."

"Shit." Lola grunted the word to no one in particular. "How's she doing?" Lola nodded toward Kerra, and Elizabeth unconsciously leaned in to hear the answer.

Krissy shrugged her shoulders. "She's Kerra. You never know what's going on with her until it's too late."

"Shit," Lola repeated, bringing her thumb to her lips to chew on her nail. She opened her mouth to say something else, but Elizabeth zoned out. Her feet moved her forward without any word from her brain as she crossed the room to sit next to Kerra. She draped herself across her, making a resting place for her head at the spot between her shoulders.

Kerra lifted her face from her hands, startled by the sudden full-body contact. "Hey," she greeted her in surprise, probably shocked to see that she wasn't Krissy.

"Hey." Elizabeth repositioned herself to rest her chin on Kerra's shoulder.

"What are you doing here?" Kerra's attempt to sound lighthearted failed her. Elizabeth could hear the struggle in her tone.

"Wondering how you're doing?"

Kerra gave her an unenthusiastic smile without actually meeting her eyes. "I'm good."

"At least look at me when you lie to me."

Kerra let out a sigh and met her eyes. "I'm *trying* to be good. But the doctors won't talk to us, and Krissy keeps hovering over me like I'm going to do a line off of a bedpan, and I'm...frustrated, I guess... But I'm okay."

Elizabeth kept her gaze. "Do you feel like doing a line off of a bedpan?"

Kerra's expression changed. Elizabeth could see in her eyes that it was a question she was trying to avoid asking herself. Elizabeth placed a hand to Kerra's cheek as she pushed back her hair with her free hand. "Kerra, whatever it is you're thinking or feeling, it's okay to put that on me. We're partners and, baby, if you're hurting, I want you to know that you can share some of that hurt with me. You don't have to be in this alone. I'm not going to break or run or whatever it is you're afraid is going to happen. Okay?" Kerra had always been the one to know exactly what to say to pull her from the edge, and she hoped that maybe, just this once, she could do it too.

Kerra nodded, her eyes welling as she wiped at them. "Okay." The word was barely above a whisper, but Elizabeth could see her shoulders relax with the promise. The tension in her body seemed to ease as the idea of sharing her burdens nested in her brain.

Elizabeth brought her in closer, wrapping her arms around her as she continued to stroke her hair. She glanced across the room to find Krissy and Lola watching her in awe, as if she'd accomplished some special task.

Elizabeth filled the silence as Kerra nuzzled against her. "Do you know the first real conversation I had with Angela, she told me that she was sleeping with you, accused me of being a psycho stalker, and basically told me to go get a grip on reality."

Kerra let out a soft laugh against her chest. "That sounds like her. What did you say?"

Elizabeth smiled as she remembered the day that she walked into the Nipple Slip looking for Kerra Silvers. Never in a million years would she have guessed she'd be recounting the tale with Kerra nestled against her. "Well, I remember being insanely jealous at first and then just thinking, God, I wish I had even half of this woman's strength and confidence. I bet she's never met a wall that she couldn't knock down."

Kerra smiled up at her before her expression faded back into sadness. "I need her to be okay."

Elizabeth met her eyes. "I know." She wished she could promise her that everything was going to be fine and Angela would pull through, but she couldn't bring herself to give her a hope that she couldn't trust.

Krissy and Lola made their way over, taking seats next to them as they stayed in their cuddled position on a two-seater waiting sofa. Krissy and Lola went back and forth making idle chatter as they waited for what seemed like hours for news.

Krissy climbed to her feet as a tiny man with a bandage wrapped around his head made his way toward them. "Azul, how is she? What did they say?" Krissy reached out for him, holding his hands in hers.

Kerra sat up straight, waiting expectantly for him to give them news.

"She's fine. She's going to be on the mend for a while, and they want to keep her overnight for observation, but she's awake, and she seems to be herself," Azul told them with a smile. "The doctor says I can bring you back to speak with her but only two at a time."

Kerra and Lola both climbed to their feet, and Krissy gestured them forward. "Go ahead. I'll wait here with Lizzie."

Elizabeth waited until they were out of sight before she let herself breathe a sigh of relief. She let her head fall forward into her hands as her body relaxed with the news that Angela was going to be okay.

"You did good."

She lifted her head and glanced over to find Krissy watching her intently. "Thanks." Elizabeth accepted the compliment even though she wasn't sure what it was for.

"No, I mean it." Krissy took the open spot next to her and reached out for her hand. "I knew that you would be good for her, but seeing it just puts a whole new perspective on it."

Elizabeth let herself smile at Krissy's awe. "Truth is, Krissy, I think it's *her* that's good for me. Before I let Kerra in, I'd have run. I'd have run as fast as I could from all of this at the first sign of trouble and now... Now, all I want to do is be here, through it all... I just want to be by her side."

Krissy mulled over her words, smiling to herself at some distant memory. "I've known Azul for nearly forty years. We grew up together. On the Southside, if you can believe it."

Elizabeth leaned in to listen to her. She really couldn't believe it. Krissy's brand of eccentric didn't match up with the rough and tough image of the Southside.

"Azul really fed into the Southside mentality. He hated being different. Nothing really caught in his craw the way that being on the outside looking in did. Naturally, we drifted apart. I'm as different as they come, and I wasn't changing for the sake of the Southside." Krissy smiled as she caught Elizabeth stifling a giggle. "When I moved away, we lost touch for about fifteen years until Azul's sister, Marie, died. We weren't close in the end, but as children we were inseparable, the three of us. So, I went home for the funeral."

Krissy never failed to captivate her when she spoke. Elizabeth listened in intrigue, not knowing where Krissy's story was taking her.

"After the funeral, Azul learned that Marie had left her daughter to him."

"Angela." Elizabeth whispered the name, putting pieces of the story together.

Krissy gave her a nod as she continued. "I stayed home to help Azul with Angela, and even though he drove me absolutely insane, I'd never seen anyone love anything as much as he loved his niece. He was like an entirely different person around her. And when Angela was eighteen she came out to Azul. And even now, the Southside isn't really a gay-friendly place, but back then, it was a really dangerous time to be out. Nobody expected Azul to be able to come to terms with Angela after that. Even she had her bags packed, ready to be kicked out onto the street."

Elizabeth's breath caught in her throat. She was completely engrossed in Krissy's tale. "What happened?"

"Six months later he was living in the city, opening the front doors to his bar that Angela so cleverly named the Nipple Slip," Krissy told her with a smile.

"What? I had no idea." Elizabeth laughed to herself.

"I think that's when I first fell in love with him. Seeing him give up everything to show his support for her, it really threw my head over my heels."

Elizabeth's eyes widened at the information. "Wait. You and Azul?"

Krissy put a finger to her lips and gave her a wink. It felt significant that Krissy would share her secrets with her, and a happy tingle spread through her body, shortly replaced by a sour grimace as she tried to picture the two of them entwined. Elizabeth struggled with the image, trying to figure out how Krissy didn't snap the tiny man she'd just met in half.

Krissy chuckled as she watched her try to process the information.

"Sorry, I just..." Elizabeth flushed beneath her gaze.

"You're trying to picture it. I get it. We're an odd pair," Krissy assured her through giggles.

"Do they know?" Elizabeth pointed in the direction that Kerra and Lola had disappeared into.

Krissy shook her head. "Business trips and a house outside of the city prevented us from ever having to talk about it."

Elizabeth couldn't help the goofy grin on her face as she stared in shock and awe at her. Krissy had always been someone she admired, but somehow the scandalous secret made her seem like kind of a badass.

"My point, Lizzie, is that loving someone changes who we are. It makes us capable of everything we didn't think we were capable of. And I like to think that it makes us into who we are supposed to be. It gives us a reason to be better. I'm really happy that Kerra found her reason in you." Krissy leaned over to place a kiss on her forehead.

"Thanks, Krissy," Elizabeth whispered as she wiped at an escaped tear sliding down her cheek.

Elizabeth straightened in her seat as Kerra and Lola reappeared through a set of double doors. Both of them seemed to have let go of the burdens they were carrying before they disappeared.

"Mom, you're up." Lola tossed the words at Krissy as she took a seat.

"Lizzie, would you like to...?" Krissy held out a hand to help her up as she extended the offer.

"Umm... Yeah, okay." Elizabeth accepted the hand skeptically, feeling strange about going to visit her girlfriend's ex–sex buddy. She glanced at Kerra, who gave her a reassuring smile as she followed behind Azul through double doors to Angela's hospital room. She fought the urge to snicker as she eyed him, still trying to picture him with Krissy.

Krissy nudged her playfully as they entered the room, obviously reading her face.

"Krissy." Angela croaked out her name as they stepped inside the brightly illuminated room. She propped herself up in her bed, struggling with the lines of what seemed to be a hundred different machines hooked into her.

"Hey, sweetheart. How are you holding up?" Krissy rushed to her side and engulfed her in a gentle hug.

"I'm okay," she assured her. She watched in confusion as Elizabeth lingered awkwardly by the door. "Lizzie?"

"Hey." Elizabeth waved uncomfortably.

"Hey, come here." Angela waved her over, holding her arms out for a hug.

Elizabeth felt guilty for not remembering that Angela was actually more than just Kerra's old flame. She was her friend. She bent down to give her a hug. "I'm glad you're okay," she whispered to her.

Angela gave her a soft smile. "Thanks." Her smile widened as a thought occurred to her. "I hear you bewitched the bewitcher."

Elizabeth let out a laugh as she recalled Angela's crafty nickname for Kerra.

Angela reached out and gave her hand a squeeze. "I'm glad for you. It's good to see Kerra happy."

Elizabeth smiled, feeling all the awkwardness melt from the room with Angela's words.

"Oh, Krissy." Angela turned her attention away from her to Krissy. "Uncle is going back to the bar to clean up in the morning. Would you mind going with him? I just don't want him there alone, you know?"

Krissy gave her a nod. "Of course. Although, *his* fight-or-flight instincts aren't the ones that are broken."

Angela rolled her eyes at Krissy. "Yeah, I know. In hindsight, I probably could have handled that better."

"I'll go too," Elizabeth offered without really thinking about it. The impulse to help in some way had simply overtaken her.

"You will?" Angela stared at her in surprise.

"Yeah, safety in numbers and all that." Elizabeth shirked off her surprise. "I mean, that is, if I can get the day off of work," she added with a smile in Krissy's direction.

Krissy gave her a grin. "Consider it done."

CHAPTER TWENTY-ONE

Elizabeth listened intently to the raindrops gently tapping against the window frame as she watched Kerra sleep. Her mind kept whirling with thoughts as she watched Kerra's chest rise and fall, each breath ushering in a new terrifying consideration. She closed her eyes, trying to stop herself from worrying and welcome in the sweet release of sleep, but it only led to even more worrisome images flashing like a movie projected against her eyelids. She gave up on the notion of sleep and kept her eyes searching Kerra, listening to the rain intermingle with her breaths.

"Are you going to watch me all night?" Kerra asked, keeping her eyes closed.

Elizabeth knew better than to be surprised. She'd had a hunch Kerra had been awake with her since the moment she'd awakened from her nightmare.

"Probably," Elizabeth answered honestly, seeing no point in lying.

Kerra let out a sigh and opened her eyes. "Lizzie, I'm fine. Angela's fine. Everything is...fine. Just get some sleep."

Elizabeth nodded, knowing that she should take the suggestion and let go of all the doubts rolling around in her head, but it was easier said than done. "But what if it wasn't... Fine, I mean." Elizabeth bit down on her lip, hesitantly posing the question. "What if everything wasn't fine?"

Kerra let out a grunt as she propped herself up on her elbow. "What are you talking about? It *is* fine."

"But if it wasn't? Then what?"

"Then we'd deal with it," Kerra answered nonchalantly.

"Then we'd deal with it?" Elizabeth tried unsuccessfully to keep the frustration out of her tone.

Kerra gave her a shrug, as if there was nothing more to be said on the matter.

"That simple, huh?" Elizabeth rolled her eyes, sitting up to tug at a braid of her hair.

"Yeah, Lizzie. That simple." Kerra let out a groan to match Elizabeth's frustration. "What are you trying to ask me, Lizzie?"

"I'm trying to ask how worried I should be."

"How worried you should be?" Kerra lifted an eyebrow at her.

"Yeah, how unstable are you?"

"Unstable?" Kerra's other eyebrow shot up to match the first.

Elizabeth sighed, regretting her word choice. "Not unstable. Just..." She tried to recollect her frantic thoughts. "I just want to know what I'm in for here. I'm here for you, no matter what. But I need to know. The next time something happens, am I going to have to go search a meth house for you or lock up the medicine cabinet or...?" Elizabeth took a deep breath. She could feel herself growing out of control. "This is new territory for me, Kerra, and I just need to know."

Kerra sat up and reached out for her, rubbing her arms to soothe her. "Okay, none of that. You shouldn't even be worried about this. I'm fine, and I'm not going to relapse because I had a bad day."

Elizabeth waved her off. She usually found Kerra's nonchalance charming, but she needed her to at least consider what she was saying. "Okay, but when does that stop being true? When does a bad day turn into a day that you can't handle?"

"It doesn't," Kerra answered without hesitation.

"It doesn't?" Elizabeth challenged.

"No."

"Because Lola seemed pretty terrified of how she might find you when we went into that hospital."

Kerra's calm confidence flashed with uncertainty. "Yeah, well, Lola's dramatic."

"Is she? Because she said she watched you backslide and—"

"So you and Lola sit around and talk about my sobriety now?" Kerra interrupted her defensively.

"No. She was trying to prepare me, and if *Lola* is warning me about your darkness, it's cause for concern, I think."

Kerra ran a frustrated hand down her face. "My darkness? Jesus

Christ." She took a deep breath as she tangled her fingers in her own hair. "Listen, I'm fine. I'm going to be fine. Lola exaggerates." She let out her breath as she slid back underneath the covers to lie down, turning her back to Elizabeth. "You can stay up and watch me be fine all night if you want, but I'm going to get some sleep."

Elizabeth frowned down at her, unsatisfied with where the conversation had gone but not willing to pick the fight any longer. She stewed in frustration before she let herself consider that maybe Kerra was right. Maybe she was worried about something that didn't matter. Maybe Lola was being dramatic. *Or maybe she wasn't.* She shook off the thought as another occurred to her. If Kerra was changing her, maybe she was changing Kerra too. *Love makes us into who we are supposed to be. It gives us a reason to be better.* Krissy's words swirled in her head. Was she enough to keep away Kerra's darkness? Elizabeth slid back down into bed and wrapped her arm around Kerra.

"Kerra?"

She didn't answer, but Elizabeth knew she was awake. If she was awake, so was Kerra. She placed a kiss to the back of her shoulder. "I love you." She whispered the words into her skin.

"I love you too." Elizabeth felt the warmth of Kerra's hand cover hers. She smiled at her touch and closed her eyes, letting go of her worries and dread. She let herself trust that if Kerra was enough to make her better, then she was enough to do the same.

"I trust you." She muttered the words into Kerra's shoulder as she drifted off to sleep.

☆☆☆

Elizabeth woke to the gentle nudging of Kerra rocking the bed as she slipped on her shoes. "What time is it?" She groaned against the sunlight as she peeled her eyes open.

"Eleven." Kerra leaned across the bed to place a kiss on her head.

Elizabeth scrambled out of the bed, realizing she'd overslept. Krissy was picking her up at noon, and she hadn't even begun to prepare herself. She moved around the room in a hurried frenzy, putting together her outfit for the day, when she felt Kerra's eyes on her.

"Shouldn't you be at work?" It suddenly occurred to Elizabeth how off their morning routine was.

Kerra nodded. "Yep. I overslept." She shrugged her shoulders indifferently.

Elizabeth rolled her eyes. Kerra was the picture-perfect idea of an artist, amazingly talented and vastly unconcerned with punctuality.

Kerra climbed to her feet. "We only have two exhibitions today. I'll probably get off a little early and come by the coffee shop," Kerra told her as she slipped on a red-and-black checkered overshirt without buttoning it.

Elizabeth nodded in response on instinct before she remembered that she wasn't going to the Bean Spot. "Oh, wait. No. I won't be at the shop today. Krissy's picking me up to go help Azul clean up at the bar."

Kerra stopped in her tracks, turning to stare at her. "What?"

Elizabeth was startled by her reaction. The way she stared at her seemed overly cautious. "Azul is going to the bar today to clean up, and we're going to go help him." She spoke slowly, her confusion mounting as Kerra's expression held.

"The bar on the Southside?"

Elizabeth let out an uncomfortable chuckle. "Uh, yeah. Well, the one here didn't get trashed yesterday, so...no cleanup crew necessary."

Kerra narrowed her eyes at her. "No." She spoke firmly, as if there were no more room for discussion.

"Excuse me?" Elizabeth watched her in confusion. A part of her wasn't even sure what Kerra was saying no to.

"You're not going to the Southside, to a gay bar that half the town wants to see go up in flames. I don't know what Angela and Azul are trying to prove by putting it there, but you don't need to get involved, okay." Kerra placed a kiss on her cheek before heading to the door.

Elizabeth stared after her, wide-eyed and dumbstruck by Kerra's proclamation, before barreling down the hallway after her. She watched her silently as Kerra moved in the kitchen, preparing herself a piece of toast. Elizabeth ground her teeth together, trying desperately to collect her thoughts and keep her cool. "Kerra, I'm going to the bar with Krissy today. You don't get to tell me what to do, and maybe that's exactly what

Angela and Azul are trying to tell the Southside."

Kerra's lips pressed into a straight line as she watched her. She said nothing as she removed her toast from the toaster and onto a napkin. She moved toward Elizabeth, eyeing her before nodding her head. "Okay, fine. I'll go with you."

"Kerra, you have to go to work," Elizabeth told her unamused.

Kerra gave her a shrug as she bit into her toast. "I'll take the day off."

"No, Kerra. That's not how this is going to work. You're not going to tag along and babysit me every time I do something you don't agree with. I told you last night that I trust you, but you have to trust me too."

Kerra moved in closer to her. "Lizzie, this isn't an issue of trust, it's—"

"Yes, it is. It is because I'm making it one. Now, you either trust me or you don't." Elizabeth stepped out of reach of her outstretched hand.

"Lizzie."

"Kerra, I'm going to the Southside today. I'm going to help Azul clean, and I'm going to be fine. Do you believe me or don't you?" Elizabeth planted her feet, keeping her glare on Kerra.

Kerra let out a sigh of defeat as she nodded her head. "Yeah."

"Okay then." Elizabeth tugged awkwardly at a braid. All the fire had gone out of her now that she'd won the battle, and she wasn't sure what to do next. "Have a good day at work," she offered weakly.

Kerra let out a grunt in reply, and Elizabeth rolled her eyes at her pouting. "I love you."

"I love you too," Kerra mumbled with lackluster enthusiasm, as if to put a point on the fact that she might have to let her go to the Southside, but she didn't have to be happy about it.

Elizabeth watched her make her huffy, dramatic exit before catching a glimpse of the clock. She groaned at the time, realizing that she wouldn't have time to fix herself up as she'd planned. She hated the idea of heading into the devil's den not looking her best, but the clock was unrelenting. She let out a sigh as she headed for the shower. She hoped to the heavens that the Southside wasn't all it had been painted as. She'd promised Kerra that she would be fine, and she hoped like hell that she could keep her word.

☆☆☆

Elizabeth had barely finished her shower when she heard Krissy's knock on the door echo through the apartment. "Just a minute," she shouted toward the door as she scrambled to slide on a pair of jeans. Three more sharp knocks met her in reply. "I'm coming," she shouted again as she slipped on an oversized tank top and ran for the door.

"Ready?" Krissy's anxious face met her as she swung the door open.

"Yeah, just let me grab something, and we can go." Elizabeth gestured for her to step inside, but Krissy continued to linger impatiently in the doorway. Elizabeth watched her peevishly tap her fingers along the lining of the doorway, and a grin tugged at her lips. She could only hope that one day, twenty years down the road, she was still as excited to rendezvous with Kerra the way that Krissy was to meet Azul.

Elizabeth stopped in her tracks as she realized the thought that she'd just had. She had let herself think fleetingly of a future with Kerra, but it had been nothing more than distant fantasy. But in her current thoughts she could see a life with Kerra. She saw herself in Krissy's shoes, adamantly rushing someone along so that she could meet up with the love of her life, and she loved the vision. Her heart soared at the thought of loving Kerra as much as she did forever.

"Lizzie." Krissy sharply urged her onward, breaking through her daydreams and making her legs move forward again.

"I know, I know. Keep your pants on. I'm coming," she shouted over her shoulder as she made her way into Kerra's bedroom to grab a bra to slip on under her shirt in the car. She could almost hear Kerra's voice in her ears telling her to leave the bra behind and *free boob* it. She smiled, rolling her eyes at the make-believe voice. She wasn't a *free boob* kind of girl. Even if she had the chest to go braless, it just wasn't her thing. She'd never pull it off the way Kerra could. Elizabeth shook off the thought, fighting against the urge to think about Kerra's unholstered chest. Krissy was already anxious; she didn't have time for Elizabeth to get carried away in a sexual fantasy.

"A bra?" Krissy eyed the purple patterned fabric in her hand as she made her way back down the hallway.

Elizabeth couldn't stop her gaze as it dropped to Krissy's chest. "What is it with you guys and your anti-bra stance?" she muttered as she followed behind Krissy down the stairs.

Krissy was practically bouncing as she led her to the car, her face lit up like a Christmas candle.

"Do you always get this excited to see him?" Elizabeth asked as she slid into the passenger seat. She was amused by Krissy's enchantment. Her enthusiasm reminded Elizabeth of an excited child preparing to see Disney World.

Krissy wagged a finger at her as she pulled out of the parking lot. "Now, now. Don't you go judging. You can barely manage to hold a coffee mug without breaking it with just the mention of Kerra's name."

Elizabeth let out a laugh as she maneuvered herself to discreetly slip on her undergarment. "Fair enough," she agreed, wincing at how true the statement was. "So, why haven't you told them? Kerra and Lola, I mean. About Azul?" Elizabeth snapped the back of her bra into place and breathed a sigh of relief at the newfound support. She didn't care what Krissy and Kerra believed; she loved her bras.

Krissy let out a thoughtful hum as she considered her response. "My girls need to believe that they are the center of my universe. It's good for them. It keeps them only competing with each other for my attention."

Elizabeth nodded in agreement, even though she didn't completely understand. She'd never had children, and she certainly didn't have any experience in taking on ones that were troubled.

"What about you? Why haven't you told your people back home about Kerra?" Krissy made an effort to look at her, before shifting her gaze back to the road.

Elizabeth bit down on the inside of her lip as her mind turned over the answer to the question. She watched at least a hundred trees fly by through the window before she finally let out a sigh. "I don't know." She shook her head at herself. "A part of me is afraid of what they might say, and another just feels like the girl that they know is so far removed from who I am now that it doesn't matter. Maybe I never have to tell them, and it'll never make any difference." Elizabeth turned to Krissy, waiting for her to react to her confession, but she kept her eyes on the road. She seemed to hold no judgments either way, and Elizabeth appreciated her for that.

"I can understand that." Krissy finally spoke. "But you'll always have a shaky future if you don't square up with your past."

Elizabeth grunted at the advice. "Yeah, and I'll have one pissed-off girlfriend if I don't figure it out soon."

Krissy shook her head and tapped steering wheel. "Don't let Kerra make that decision for you. Kerra's coming out and yours, even though they may seem similar, are different. You are a calculating person. You think things over a hundred times before you act. I can't imagine how terrifying it must be in your shoes to even consider coming out. You must be living the moment over and over again, mapping out each scenario as it occurs to you. It's a big move, and you should take your time with it. Kerra's always pissed off about something. She'll just have to add that to the list."

Elizabeth grinned wider than she had intended. Krissy seemed to understand her better than anyone she'd ever met in her life. "Thanks, Krissy."

Krissy reached out to give her shoulder a squeeze. "All right, enough heavy-duty conversation for now. Kerra tells me you're going back to school next month. Are you excited? What is your major?"

Elizabeth let out a forced laugh. Krissy thought she was switching topics to an easier conversation, but really the questions she posed were just as complicated. "I actually don't know. I'm starting to think maybe school was a part of that old Elizabeth that just did everything her mother told her to do."

Krissy snorted in disagreement. "No, no, no. School is good. You just have to find your niche."

"And how am I supposed to do that?"

Krissy gave her a shrug. "I don't know. What were you going to school for in Edenfield?"

Elizabeth returned her shrug. "Nothing, really. I changed my major every year since I started."

"Did you try psychology?" Krissy pressed her.

Elizabeth laughed. "No. I can't really see myself as any sort of counselor or anything."

"I could."

"You could?" Elizabeth stared at the side of her head in surprise.

"Yeah. With all that you've been through in the last few months, why shouldn't you be a counselor? They're starting construction on an LGBT center downtown, now that the state is deciding to recognize everyone on the spectrum as actual people and not hidden mistakes. I'm sure I'll know people. I could see if you could shadow someone and see if it's right for you. If there had been more centers like that before I quit counseling, I'm sure that would have been right up my alley."

Elizabeth let herself chew on the thought. She liked the idea of helping some scared kid figure out what she had to figure out on her own. If she had met a younger version of herself, she would have jumped at the opportunity to tell her how much happiness lay on the other side of accepting who she was, and that there were others, outside the small-minded walls of Edenfield, who would accept her too. "I think I'd like that." Elizabeth nodded as her smile widened at the prospect. "School will definitely feel like less of a waste with an end game." It was true. She'd consistently felt like she was just biding her time, running up the tab at her current university.

"Good. I like the idea of another counselor in the family." Krissy flashed her a smile, and Elizabeth's heart fluttered in her chest at being considered part of "the family." "I tried to get the girls to go back to school, but you know, just getting Kerra to get her GED was like pulling teeth, so I took my win where I could. And Lola…" She let out a laugh. "Lola is just not a classroom individual. She's still working on impulse control."

Elizabeth couldn't suppress the snivel that escaped her. Krissy raised an eyebrow in surprise at her.

"Sorry. I'm just very well acquainted with Lola's impulse control issues," Elizabeth offered.

"Sorry about that." Krissy gave her an apologetic frown.

Elizabeth gave her a shrug as she turned her gaze back to the window. She could tell they were getting closer. The festive shops and colorful array of people had begun to dissipate, and the scenery outside took on a darker tone. Buildings with their windows barred for extra protection began to pop up with frequency, along with spray-painted signs and trash bins that read anything from a gang name to a foul slogan.

As Krissy slowed to a stoplight, a group of young and angry boys glared at Elizabeth from the sidewalk, through the window. The largest boy of the group gave her a wink and flashed a gold-plated toothy grin at her. She fought the urge to cringe in response.

"You grew up out here?" Elizabeth kept her eyes on the boy. He made no moves toward the car, but his stare sent a warning her way. The look in his eyes made her grateful there was the distance of the intersection between them.

"Yep." Krissy pulled forward as the light turned green, leaving the menacing boy in the rearview mirror.

"How?" Elizabeth whispered the word without meaning to.

"How, what? How did I make it out without ending up as a strung-out hooker?" Krissy asked flatly.

"Oh no. I didn't mean—" Elizabeth tried to scramble for recovery.

"Yes, you did. And it's fine. I ask myself the same thing every day. The truth is, I have no idea. My mother wasn't a role model. My brother was determined to follow in his alcoholic father's footsteps, and the only positive role models I had were Azul's family. And even they thought I was strange. I think I was just meant to make it out and do what I'm doing. It's the only explanation."

"Yeah. I guess so," Elizabeth agreed, giving another look around as Krissy turned a corner. The Southside was in no short supply of strung-out hookers. She could see that already. Half-naked women, along with a few fully naked ones, stood groggily propped up outside nearly every establishment.

"Why does Azul want to open up another Nipple Slip out here?" Elizabeth asked cautiously.

"I don't know. I think he just wants to bring Angela home."

"And you're okay with that?" Elizabeth shuddered as they passed another shady clump of buildings.

Krissy shook her head. "No. It scares the hell out of me, and I know that the Southside isn't ready for this. It's not going to end well."

"Then why let him do it?"

"Because I'm his lover, not his mother, and I love how much he loves his niece. If he needs to do this, it's not my job to stop him. It's my place to stand by him, come what may."

Elizabeth envied her confidence in Azul. She wished Kerra shared Krissy's sensibilities.

"What?" Krissy eyed her from the driver's seat. "What are you thinking that made your face turn that way?"

Elizabeth kicked herself for always being so easy to read. "Nothing. I just…I wish Kerra saw things that way sometimes."

"Kerra's just trying to hold on to everything in her life as tightly as she can. When you start feeling suffocated, you just have to put your foot down," Krissy assured her.

Elizabeth giggled as she remembered their morning argument. "I did. This morning. She didn't want me to come today."

Krissy patted her on the shoulder. "Good for you." She placed her hands back on the wheel as they approached a large group of people spread out across the road.

"What are they doing?" Elizabeth watched them as they congregated. At least fifty people lined the sidewalk. They poured into the road and stood angrily outside the building in front of them, shouting words that Elizabeth couldn't make out.

"That's the bar." Krissy let out a sigh. "They're showing their lack of support."

Elizabeth felt her jaw drop to her chest as she realized how at odds Azul was with making the community accept his vision. She suddenly had a newfound respect for him. He was a modern-day hero, standing up to a bigoted community in the name of his niece and her right to get drunk and pick up girls in any neighborhood she pleased.

Krissy parked the car across the street and linked arms with

Elizabeth before crossing the road and heading straight for the angry crowd. "Hang on to me and don't let go, okay."

Elizabeth nodded as she took a deep breath, latching onto Krissy before heading into the enemy's territory.

CHAPTER TWENTY-TWO

Elizabeth clung tightly to Krissy as they pushed their way through the crowd, shoving past adamant protesters with glares of warning painted on their faces. The disapproval of the crowd was palpable as they made it to the entrance of the building. Krissy rushed her inside as some rowdy members of the mob began to shout at her.

"You okay?" Krissy scanned her for injuries as she shoved her inside and then shut the door behind them.

"Yeah, I'm fine. You?" Elizabeth eyed her, nodding her head in approval as she found no cuts or bruises. Aside from their frazzled appearances they remained unharmed. The crowd was angry but not yet violent. She silently complimented Azul for not installing windows to look out onto the street. The sight of the bar from the outside seemed somehow less provoking than being able to see the interior and its patrons.

Elizabeth gave the bar a once-over and was impressed by the likeness of it to the Nipple Slip in the city. The décor was so simple and chaotic it had never occurred to her that it was purposeful but, looking around now, she could see that eclectically tacky was sort of their style.

"Hey. Why didn't you call? I would have seen you in." Elizabeth turned to find Azul emerging from a back room.

"Well, there were two of us and one of you. It seemed silly to make you come out and get us." Krissy smiled at him as she watched him set down a tray of glasses. He walked excitedly toward them with his arms outstretched for Krissy, but he stopped in his tracks as his face took on a thoughtful expression.

"Right then. Well I'm glad you're here," he told them awkwardly as he crossed his outstretched arms across his chest. "We're having latch-locks installed tomorrow, so for now we'll just keep an eye out for the crowd." Azul fidgeted in place as he worked around his uneasy stance in front of Krissy.

"It's okay. Lizzie knows," Krissy assured him as she threw herself into his arms.

Azul jumped in surprise, catching her weight with a grin. "But I thought we weren't—"

"We aren't. But Lizzie is different." Krissy placed a kiss to his lips, and Elizabeth cast her glance down to her shoes. It was a simple kiss, but there was an intimacy in it that felt wrong to gawk at.

She cleared her throat as the two of them remained in each other's arms, whispering to one another. "So, what do you need me to do?" Elizabeth chimed in uncomfortably.

"Oh, right." Azul let go of Krissy and straightened himself up, realizing that he'd forgotten Elizabeth was even there. "I've got all of the glass cleaned up, now I'm just relining the walls with the new glasses in the back."

"Right. I'll go get those." Elizabeth was grateful for the excuse to get out of their way and let them whisper sweet nothings to one another without her having to watch.

"Actually, Lizzie isn't the best with glassware. Is there another job for her?" Krissy piped in, memories of all the coffee shop's broken mugs probably flashing through her mind.

Elizabeth pursed her lips in a pout. "It's okay. I'll be extra careful."

Azul was already distracted by the thought of a moment alone with Krissy. "Yeah, she'll be fine." He waved her off to the back room to meddle with the inventory.

Elizabeth smiled to herself as she gave them one last glance before disappearing into the back room. There was so much love between the two of them that she wondered how Kerra and Lola could be so out of the loop and not see it.

The thought of Kerra flattened out her smile. She wasn't one hundred percent happy with the way that they left things, and if she was being completely honest with herself, the crowd outside set her a little on edge. She wouldn't have minded having Kerra by her side to brave pushing through it again.

She slipped her phone out of her back pocket and rolled it in her hands, preparing herself to eat her words as she pressed down the one on her speed dial.

"Hey." The lack of a pet name as Kerra answered the phone reassured Elizabeth that she was still miffed about their morning argument.

"Hey," Elizabeth responded, contemplating how she wanted to approach the subject matter. "Umm, are you busy?"

"Well I'm at work."

"Oh, okay." Elizabeth made no efforts to hide the disappointment in her tone. She could almost hear the wheels in Kerra's head turning as she heard it.

"I can take a minute," Kerra offered begrudgingly.

"Where are you going?" Elizabeth could hear the faint background noise of a female voice.

"I'll be right back. It's my girlfriend." Elizabeth's body tingled at hearing Kerra refer to her as her "girlfriend." It somehow gave her comfort to know that even though Kerra spent her days between the legs of beautiful women with a stencil and a paintbrush, Elizabeth could still make her claim known. She made a mental note to give Kerra a prominent hickey later just to reiterate that she was taken.

"Okay. What's up?" Kerra was sticking to her short, abrupt communications.

"Nothing. I was just thinking, if you're still getting off early and want to come by...we could use the extra pair of hands."

"Oh." Kerra's tone brightened. "So you want me to come by now?"

Elizabeth let out a grunt. Kerra was obviously not going to make this easy for her. "Yes...if you can," she offered, not wanting to seem too eager.

"To lend a hand?" she reaffirmed suggestively.

"Yes."

"Uh-huh."

Elizabeth groaned. "And maybe I want you here."

"Uh-huh."

"There's a mob of people outside of the bar and, I don't know, I guess they just make me nervous, and I'd feel better if you were here," Elizabeth admitted reluctantly.

"Are you sure? I wouldn't want you to think I didn't trust you to handle it on your own." There was a smugness in Kerra's tone that annoyed her.

"I *can* handle it on my own, Kerra. I just want you here because I miss you, and if you're off of work I want to spend the day with you."

Kerra let out a sigh as the guilt trip landed. "Yeah, okay. I'll be there. I've got to finish up with Trisha, but I'll be there in an hour or two."

"Okay."

"Okay."

Elizabeth hung up the phone, joy surging through her at the thought of seeing her woman. It was true; the crowd did make her nervous, but she also really wanted to see Kerra. The two of them had been arguing so much lately, she wanted to just spend the afternoon in love with no complications, and the quiet safety of a windowless bar seemed to be a fitting atmosphere.

She slipped her phone back into her pocket, a smile making its way across her face as she did, and positioned herself to lift the box of glasses in front of her.

She busied herself with lining the walls with neat rows of various sized glasses while she anxiously waited for Kerra. Her mind wandered in and out of thought as she moved around, carefully organizing things to pass the time.

"Wow, it looks great." She jumped at the sound of Krissy approaching her from behind. "I can't believe you did all of this without breaking a single thing. Maybe you should consider bartending. Coffee doesn't suit you."

Elizabeth laughed at her candor. She was right; the coffee shop made her clumsy and awkward for reasons she couldn't explain. "Are you trying to fire me, Krissy?"

"Oh sweetheart, if I was ever going to fire you, I'd have done it by now." Krissy gave her a playful push as she settled in next to her to dust at the cardboard particles coating the bar.

Elizabeth gave her a smile. "Where's Azul?" She realized if Krissy was talking to her that meant she wasn't wrapped up in Azul any longer.

"He went to check the temperature of the crazies." Krissy tried to appear indifferent, but Elizabeth could see the concern written on her face.

"God, I can't believe they're allowed to just be out there like that. Isn't there something Azul can do? Call the police or something?" Elizabeth's blood boiled at the thought of being forced to deal with the whims of obvious lunatics.

"The same police that have been burying me in red tape since the moment they found out what kind of bar this was?" Azul stumbled through the door of the bar, more disheveled than usual.

Elizabeth frowned at his answer. Her own encounter with the city police force reiterated how truly useless they were.

"They have to do something undeniably violent before the police will involve themselves," Krissy offered.

Elizabeth shook her head in irritation. "That's so messed up."

"That's just how it is." Azul gave her a sad shrug as he made his way behind the bar to wrap his arms around Krissy.

Elizabeth let out a groan. It was nonstop with the two of them, and she had to admit she was a little jealous that her own partner hadn't shown up yet. She glanced down eagerly at her phone sitting undisturbed on top of the bar. As if on cue, it began to buzz across the counter.

She didn't even take a moment to check the caller ID before putting the phone to her ear. "Kerra?"

"Hey, we're outside." Kerra shouted through the phone, but she could still hardly hear her through all the background noise.

"We?"

"I brought Lola." Elizabeth felt herself deflate a little. Kerra didn't know it, but this was meant to be a couples' day, and Lola knew exactly how to kill every romantic vibe in the room.

"Okay." *Kerra and Lola. Outside.* She mouthed the words to Krissy, and both she and Azul jumped a foot away from one another. "We're coming to get you."

"Who's watching the shop?" Krissy posed the question as she headed for the door.

Elizabeth shrugged before asking the question into the phone.

"Ralph," Kerra informed her.

"Ralph," Elizabeth repeated to Krissy and watched as her face contorted in annoyance.

"I take it you don't like Ralph?" Elizabeth had no idea who Ralph was, but he didn't seem to be Krissy's favorite person.

"If I wanted Ralph to look after the shop, I wouldn't have fired her," Krissy told her sharply.

Elizabeth wasn't sure what shocked her more; that Ralph was a girl's name or Krissy's sharp tone. "Okay then." Elizabeth backed away from her, and Krissy shot her a look of apology.

"Let's just go get them." Azul stepped in front of them to lead the way out of the door.

The crowd outside had doubled, and Elizabeth could feel the hostility growing in the air. The angry horde of ignorance stood firm outside the bar, and Elizabeth could barely make out Kerra and Lola as they crossed the street to meet it head on.

A small group of policemen had shown up for the event, lingering on the outside of the crowd, and Elizabeth felt uneasy about their presence. If they weren't breaking up the crowd, chances were they were part of the agenda. She tried to ignore the sinking feeling in the pit of her stomach and move herself forward, linking arms with Krissy and Azul as they protectively sandwiched her between them.

"Do you see them?" Azul called out to her as he held out his hands to fend off the aggressive wave of people that shouted for them to "get out of their neighborhood" and "return to the fags in the city." Elizabeth rolled her eyes at the trivial insults and lackluster jeers. Every single one of them needed a swift reality check and a day job.

"Do you know what they want to do with this place?" A scraggly haired old woman with a hard-set face stepped in her path, addressing her with judgment and conviction.

Azul and Krissy pushed Elizabeth forward, ignoring the woman on their mission to retrieve Lola and Kerra.

"There. I see them." Krissy shouted over the crowd to them, pointing in the direction of Kerra and Lola as they slowly made their way through the masses. "We should hurry. Lola doesn't do well in crowds."

Azul nodded, pushing his way more forcefully through the people.

"You're such a pretty girl. You don't belong out here, beautiful." Another angry bystander approached her. A young man this time, planting his feet and refusing to let them through. A small crew of his followers backed him, agreeing in unison that she was too pretty to be associated with lesbians.

Azul attempted to lead them around the group of boys, but they blocked their path, leaving just enough distance between them to not be considered physically threatening.

"Move." Azul's voice deepened, and his tone warned that he was not to be trifled with.

The leader of the young men held up his hands to assure them that he was not a threat. "I'm just talking to the lady here," he said condescendingly. "You don't mind that I talk to you for a bit, do you, gorgeous?"

"I said, move." Azul warned again, but Elizabeth had had enough. She released Azul and held up a hand to signal for him to back down. She narrowed her eyes on the boy, taking him in. He was well built, and his tight-fitting tank top showed that he was chiseled in all the right places. He was just the type to be threatened by women who preferred other women over his pretty-boy looks.

"What's your name?" Elizabeth planted her feet as Krissy tried to move her along, but she refused. She was going to give this guy a piece of her mind if it was the last thing she did.

"Camron, but I let all of the pretty girls call me Cam." The young man winked at her, and his crew of Neanderthals erupted in cheers.

"Listen, *Camron*. I absolutely belong here, which is more than I can say for you. Why don't you and your pathetic ring of followers go grab a hooker? In case you haven't noticed, there's one on every corner. Your neighborhood's got bigger problems than gays." Elizabeth could feel anger and triumph pumping through her body in unison. Her vision was nearly bleeding red with fury at the audacity of the crowd before her to pass judgment on who she decided to love when their entire block was whimsy to the pitfalls of debauchery on every street.

Camron stared at her openmouthed, searching for a response. His cool confidence melted away as words abandoned him. He settled on an impassioned profanity before moving his crew out of their path.

"Wow." Krissy gazed at her in pride and surprise, and Elizabeth shrugged in response. In honesty, a part of her was surprised with herself as well. She parted her lips to say something, but a series of shouts from the center of the crowd distracted her. Her feet were nearly swept out from underneath her as the crowd moved in the direction of the shouts, surrounding a small group of individuals who had come to blows.

"Oh, shit." Krissy sprang forward toward the swarm of people who had crowded around the tussling collection of men and woman, and Elizabeth followed close on her heels. She elbowed her way through a tightly packed circle of people until she could see the two girls violently thrashing against a set of oncoming enemies. Elizabeth's heart dropped into her stomach as she watched Kerra and Lola take on at least four different adversaries. A stream of blood trickled down Lola's face, pouring from a cut prominently collecting dirt across her eyebrow.

Elizabeth jumped to make her way into the inner circle as Kerra caught a kick to her side from one of her attackers. She could see Krissy fighting to make her way into the ring of cheering and shouting people rooting against them.

Elizabeth shouldered her weight into the onslaught of people that blocked her path, desperate to get into the circle to provide her friends with backup. She was exhausted by the time she finally made it through the last person, but she clenched her fists, bringing them up into what felt like the appropriate fighting stance. She was ready to take on anyone who came her way, but nobody made a move toward her.

She'd been so consumed with making her way into the circle she hadn't noticed the slow-moving task force of policemen doing the same. She gasped in shock as two large policemen tackled Kerra to the ground beside her, pushing her hard into the pavement as she shouted and rocked against them.

"Kerra, stop!" Elizabeth fell to her knees, shouting at her to quit resisting. Her eyes watered over as the sound of handcuffs being slapped across Kerra's wrists echoed in her ears. She glanced over to see Krissy coaching Lola through the arrest process as she flopped and resisted on the other side of the circle.

Elizabeth felt like the world moved in slow motion around her as she watched the officers drag the two of them off, throwing them with more force than necessary into the back of two squad cars before tearing off down the road. She climbed to her feet, spinning in a circle and looking around at the bruised knuckles and bloody noses surrounding her. She couldn't help but feel angry that none of them were being dragged away in handcuffs along with Kerra and Lola.

"You should all be going with them," she shouted into the crowd.

Krissy ran over to her, Azul trailing behind her. "Calm down. It's okay. They're going to holding in Davinson County. We'll go get them and post bail. I have a few friends that will help us out." Krissy rubbed at her shoulders, soothing her as she trembled at the edge of her sanity.

Elizabeth nodded at Krissy's words, following her toward the car. She couldn't find her voice to speak. She tried to mimic Krissy's calmness, but she felt like she was losing her mind.

"I'm going to hang back here and keep an eye on the bar. Call me if you need me." Azul placed a kiss on Krissy's cheek, and she nodded as she slipped into the car. Elizabeth slid into the passenger seat and watched as Azul disappeared back into the crowd.

"It's okay. Everything is going to be okay," Krissy said aloud, probably more to assure herself than to calm Elizabeth, but she nodded in response anyway as they took off down the road toward Davinson County.

CHAPTER TWENTY-THREE

Elizabeth nervously paced across the hard cement floor. They had been at the county jailer's office for hours, and she hadn't seen even a glimpse of Kerra or Lola. Krissy had managed to talk to every person in the building, bartering trades for their release and getting closer with each promise. She had more pull than Elizabeth had anticipated, but the process was still slow going. With each passing hour a new horrible thought entered her head about what atrocities Kerra must be facing in the confines of a jail cell.

Krissy had attempted to assure her that the two of them were fine, that being kept in holding and the horrific landscape of the prison system she was imagining were two completely different things, but her comfort was to no avail. Elizabeth had worked herself up into a frenzy, and no amount of logic was going to bring her down. She needed to see Kerra, or speak to her, or anything.

She tugged furiously at the ends of her hair as she continued to pace. "How much longer do you think it'll be?" Elizabeth asked Krissy for possibly the millionth time.

"Lizzie, I still don't know. Just take a seat, okay. Julius promised me they were on their way to process out. It's a *process*. You have to be patient." Krissy was the perfect picture of tranquility. Elizabeth studied her, looking for a crack in her unruffled armor, but she found none.

"How are you so calm?" While Elizabeth was nearly crawling out of her skin, Krissy was acting as if she were waiting for her order at the drive-thru window.

Krissy gave her a shrug and gestured for her to sit in the seat next to her. Elizabeth eyed the seat, the pale-gray leather of the chair making it all the more unenticing. The building had too much gray. The absence of color was making her even crazier than the waiting. Krissy let out a sigh as Elizabeth shook her head at the offer to sit down. "Lizzie, this isn't Kerra's first stint in a holding cell, and it certainly isn't Lola's. They're fine."

Elizabeth stopped pacing and let the thought soak in. Kerra did have a rather sordid past, and as Elizabeth let herself think on it, she was certain Kerra had probably seen much worse. She let out a breath of relief and plopped herself down in the chair next to Krissy. Dropping her head into her hands, she let herself believe that everything would be fine if she could just be patient.

Krissy laughed as she rubbed a hand in circles across Elizabeth's back. "There you go, honey. Just let it all go."

Elizabeth did as she said, sobbing into her hands without reprieve. She didn't even know why she was crying, but she felt like she had been holding it in for ages. She struggled to gain control of herself, but Krissy kept rubbing her back, urging her to let everything loose. She handed Elizabeth a tissue, which she accepted without asking where it had come from. She wiped at her eyes with it, feeling some of the crying spell dissipate. She gave Krissy a grateful smile. "Thanks."

Krissy gave her a nod in reply before bursting into laughter. Elizabeth joined her, giggling along through sniffles.

"God, I thought dating the bad girl was supposed to be fun," Elizabeth told her with a chuckle.

"They leave out the part where you wait and worry for six hours while she's being processed," Krissy joked.

Elizabeth caught her gaze, stilling her laughter. "I'd be a basket case if you weren't here."

"Honey, you *are* a basket case." Krissy grinned as she raised an eyebrow at her.

"Well, I'd be even more of a basket case, then. I'd be insane asylum–ready."

Krissy kept grinning at her. "You really love her, huh?"

Elizabeth met her eyes. "Yeah, I do."

"Good. She really needs that."

"I really need her," Elizabeth assured her, keeping her eyes steady on Krissy's.

Elizabeth's eye contact was interrupted as she saw Lola emerged from steel-plated double doors across the room. She shot to her feet and nearly stumbled through the room to her. She could hear Krissy scrambling to follow her.

Elizabeth reached out to embrace her, the overwhelming drama of the night making her forget that she didn't particularly enjoy Lola as a person. Lola jolted in obvious surprise at the show of affection but returned the hug.

"Where's Kerra?" Elizabeth let her go, glancing over her shoulder for Kerra, but no one else emerged from the locked doors.

"She's coming. She had to reclaim her watch." Lola stepped out of her path to hug Krissy, who clutched her until she winced in pain.

Elizabeth nodded, biting down on her lip until she drew blood in anticipation as she watched the steel doors, waiting for Kerra to emerge. She nearly collapsed in relief when Kerra finally made her way grumpily through the doors, holding up a choice finger to an unseen foe behind her.

"Assholes," Kerra grumbled as she let the door slam behind her. "Hey, love," she called out to Elizabeth as she came into view.

Elizabeth threw herself into Kerra's arms, holding her as if she was life itself. Kerra placed a kiss to the top of her head, returning her embrace before letting out a slow breath of air. "I'm glad you missed me, love, but I took a pretty killer blow to the side, and this kind of hurts."

"Oh." Elizabeth recalled watching her take a kick to her torso and quickly released her. "Sorry. Are you okay?"

Kerra nodded, leaning forward in obvious agony as she clutched at her side. "I'm fine. Definitely worth it." Kerra gave her a wink as she straightened up.

Elizabeth moved to help her, propping Kerra's arm around her shoulder for extra leverage. Krissy must have seen the struggle because she flanked Kerra's other side, supporting her as they moved toward the door of the building.

Lola led the way to the parking lot, chattering on about the subpar quality of the facility as they went. She slid into the passenger seat of the car without hesitation as she continued to prattle on, and Elizabeth rolled her eyes at her unwarranted sense of entitlement as she eased Kerra into the back seat.

"You okay?" Elizabeth questioned as she noticed Kerra grimace.

"Yeah, I'm fine. I can sit in the car, Lizzie," Kerra snapped, evidently over the extra attention being showered onto her.

Elizabeth held up her hands in surrender. "Okay. Sorry." Elizabeth closed the door and then rounded the car to slip into the backseat next to her. Krissy followed behind her, lingering at the driver's-side door.

"Hey, you did good today." Krissy offered her the compliment with a nod.

Elizabeth smiled in return. "Thanks. Let's hope we don't have to do it again."

Krissy nodded in agreement before opening her door and sliding in. Elizabeth followed her lead, lowering herself into the backseat. She wanted to scoot across the seat and snuggle up next to Kerra but, even if she wouldn't admit it, Elizabeth could see that she was in a noticeable amount of pain. She settled for reaching out to entwine their fingers. Kerra gave her hand a grateful squeeze as she met her eyes with a smile.

Krissy started the car but didn't pull out of the parking lot. She let out a sigh and turned to face Lola, sweeping her glare from Lola to Kerra. "So, tell me now. What happened?"

Kerra and Lola shook their heads as they echoed one another. "Nothing."

Krissy nodded, a sarcastic nod that Elizabeth hadn't thought she was capable of. "Okay, so now I'm going to ask again, and you're going to pretend like I'm not the biggest idiot on the planet."

Elizabeth stared at Krissy in surprise. She was in full mom mode, and it was terrifying and absorbing all at once.

Elizabeth glanced at Kerra and Lola, watching them as they contemplated a response. It was entrancing the way that Krissy could reduce them both to children with just a change of tone.

Kerra was the first to break. "There was a guy in the crowd. He said some stuff and grabbed Lola and then..." Kerra trailed off, timidly glancing at Lola for a sign of what to say next.

Lola let out a sigh of annoyance. "And I hit him. Right in the face.

Typical Lola, always throwing the first punch."

"Lola, I thought we were past this." Krissy kept her tone even, compassionate, and reprimanding at the same time.

"I am." Lola's voice cracked, and Elizabeth finally saw some glimpse of the human beneath Lola's rock-hard outer shell. "Everything just got away from me a little too fast." She shook her head as she wiped at a phantom tear that she hadn't let herself actually cry. "I'm sorry." Elizabeth could see how hard it was for her to apologize, and a part of her felt sorry for Lola.

"And you? How did you get involved in this?" Krissy turned her gaze on Kerra.

Kerra stared back at her in amazement, as if the answer was obvious. "He hit her back, so I—"

"You made her problems your problems," Krissy interrupted her knowingly.

"Yeah." Kerra was less remorseful than Lola, obviously feeling completely justified for her actions.

"Kerra."

"What, Krissy? What was I supposed to do?"

"Not escalate the situation," Krissy scolded.

Kerra sunk into her seat, giving Krissy a petulant shrug in response.

"You both took two steps backwards today," Krissy told them in disappointment as she turned her gaze to the road and pulled out of the parking lot.

"Yeah, well, those homophobes deserved a lot more than we gave them," Lola griped, and Krissy shot her a pointed glare. "But that doesn't justify our actions," she offered in repentance.

Kerra rolled her eyes, still pouting in her own corner of the car. Elizabeth squeezed her hand in support. She wanted to say something, but she wasn't sure what there was to say. She could see that Krissy's disappointment troubled Kerra more than she was letting on, but Elizabeth couldn't help but agree with Krissy. There was a better course of action, and Kerra chose the wrong one.

"Hey, RFTL for life, huh?" Lola turned in her seat with a grin, extending her fist to Kerra who chuckled in response, easing out of her sulky tantrum.

"RFTL," Kerra agreed, bumping Lola's fist with her own. "It's a nickname Krissy gave to us," Kerra explained, catching Elizabeth's questioning glare.

Krissy let out an exasperated sigh as she shook her head. "One that was never meant to be a term of endearment."

Elizabeth shook her head in confusion. "What does it mean?"

"React first. Think later," Lola told her with just a little too much pride. "It's kind of our modus operandi."

Kerra giggled as Lola beamed with pride over the term.

"And you're proud of this?" Elizabeth tried to keep the judgment out of her tone and failed as she stared expectantly at Kerra.

Kerra's grin began to fade as she caught the look of concern in Elizabeth's eyes. "Well, yeah. I mean, you're either ashamed of it or you own it."

"Or you fix it," Elizabeth insisted. She gave Kerra's hand a squeeze and lowered her voice to a gentler tone. "I'd actually like to see you do a little more thinking and a little less reacting."

Kerra dropped her gaze to stare at their laced fingers. "Yeah, I know."

"I just want you to be safe and a little less reckless, maybe," Elizabeth suggested.

"Yeah, I'll try," Kerra agreed, meeting her eyes.

Lola stared at them, a frown of disapproval on her face. "Whooshp." Lola mimicked the sound of a lashing whip at Kerra.

"Shut up, Lola," Kerra warned.

"What? I just didn't think you'd be the one to go soft on me," Lola teased without letting up.

"Shut up, Lola." Kerra raised her voice, practically growling the words at her.

Elizabeth ignored her, keeping her eyes trained on Kerra. "I love you, and I just want you to stay in one piece."

Kerra nodded, wincing as she leaned forward to meet Elizabeth halfway for a soft kiss.

Lola scrunched her face in disgust. "Oh, gross. Come on, Ker. Are you really going to let Yoko break up the band?"

"Lola, I'm going to kill you if you don't shut up." Kerra whirled on her, reaching into the front seat to shove Lola's shoulder.

Lola stuck her tongue out and contorted her face in a tease at Kerra.

"Krissy," Kerra called out for intervention.

Elizabeth giggled at them. It was the first time she'd seen them interact in a way that reminded her that the two of them had been sisters for a long time. She was thoroughly annoyed with the both of them, but it somehow felt like family to watch them go back and forth. She felt at peace as she listened to them argue, with Krissy stepping in to intervene every so often on their drive home.

Elizabeth brought Kerra's knuckles to her lips and placed a soft kiss on them as she watched her face pull into a snarl at something Lola said.

Meeting Krissy's eyes in the rearview mirror, she gave her a smile that Krissy returned. Elizabeth felt at peace, drifting off to sleep in the backseat of the car, content to be a part of their dysfunctional family forever.

☆☆☆

Elizabeth woke to Kerra gently nudging her as Krissy parked in front of their apartment complex. She groggily made her way out of the car and rushed to try and help Kerra out, but Kerra beat her to the punch, climbing her way out of the car without assistance. Elizabeth dashed to her side to prop her up and support her going up the stairs.

"We're okay." Elizabeth waved off Krissy as she climbed out of the car.

"You sure?" Krissy offered as she lingered in the door.

"Yeah, we've got it. Thanks, Krissy." Elizabeth gave her a nod of thanks, hoping she understood that she was thanking her for more than just the offer to help.

Elizabeth shouldered Kerra's weight as they struggled up the stairs, stopping every few steps to catch their breath. By the time they made it to their apartment, Elizabeth's shoulders and thighs ached like she'd run a marathon.

She fumbled with the keys on her keychain, trying to find the right one without letting go of Kerra. Kerra shook her head at her. "I got it," she offered, pulling a ring of only two keys out of her pocket and then shoving the right one into the lock.

"How do you only have two keys?" Elizabeth watched in amazement as she pushed the door open.

Kerra lifted an eyebrow at her. "Why do you have so many? I have an apartment and a car. Two things, equals two keys."

Elizabeth shuffled her inside the apartment, moving her carefully across the threshold. "Yeah but I have keys to other people's things. The Bean Spot, my mother's house, RJ..." She stopped, not wanting to tick off any more places that she had unrestricted access to. "You know what? You're right. I should probably get rid of some of these." She frowned at the key ring.

She led Kerra down the hall and to her bedroom. She gently placed her across the bed before heading to the kitchen to get Kerra some ice for her bruises.

She gathered up a towel full of ice cubes and made her way back to Kerra, stopping in the doorway of the room as she caught sight of her, exhausted and uncomfortably sprawled across the bed. She had her eyes closed as she clutched at her side, an expression of pain contorting her features.

"You really took a beating today, huh?" Elizabeth crossed the room to her. She made her way carefully onto the bed, so as not jostle Kerra as she agonized.

"Pft, you should see the other guy." Kerra tried to grin, but it came out as a grimace instead.

"Here." Elizabeth tentatively leaned forward to place the ice onto Kerra's side. She watched as Kerra sucked in a breath, adjusting to the cold.

"Thanks." Kerra whispered the word as she slid closer to Elizabeth to rest her head against her leg.

"No problem." Elizabeth smiled down at her, lifting her free hand to run her fingers through Kerra's hair.

Kerra closed her eyes, letting out a tranquil sigh as she rested against Elizabeth, clearly savoring their quiet moment together after a day of chaos.

Kerra's eyes popped open, and she groaned in annoyance as Elizabeth's phone began to chime in her pocket.

"Shh, it's just a text," Elizabeth assured her as she shifted her weight to finagle her phone out of her pocket. "It's Krissy," she announced as she scrolled through the short message. "She said don't forget that you and Lola have court dates scheduled for after the trip."

"Okay," Kerra answered irritably as she reached up for Elizabeth's hand and then returned it to her head.

Elizabeth let out a giggle as she let her phone fall onto the bed and returned to stroking Kerra's hair. She let the silence engulf them, enjoying it for the peaceful moment that it was. "Kerra?"

"Mhmm?" Kerra answered her without moving.

Elizabeth smiled down at her, her heart physically aching with how much love there was in it for the woman in her lap. "I think I want to tell my mom...about us."

Kerra's eyes shot open as she stayed frozen in place. "You think?"

Elizabeth shook her head. "I *know*. I'm *going* to tell her. Tomorrow."

Kerra's eyebrows jumped into her hairline, and she struggled to sit up and face Elizabeth on eye level. Elizabeth held out her hands to steady her.

"Lizzie." Kerra let out a sigh as she dropped her makeshift ice pack onto the bed. "I don't want to do this dance again. You're going to invite her over, and then when you see her—"

"No." Elizabeth shook her head, cutting her off. "She's not coming over, and I'm not changing my mind. I'd call her right now if I thought she was awake."

Kerra frowned at her, the expression on her face a tell-all that she didn't believe a word of Elizabeth's promises.

"Kerra." Elizabeth reached out for her hand and met her eyes. "I watched you get the shit kicked out of you today because a bunch of assholes think that we shouldn't be together. Assholes that don't know anything about you or me, think that they have the right to tell us we shouldn't love each other." She looked away from Kerra, trying to contain the tears that threatened to spill from her eyes. She cleared her throat against the sobs building up in it. "Kerra, my mom is one of those assholes." Her shoulders slumped forward as one of the sobs broke free. Kerra reached out for her, bringing her into her arms with a wince.

"Hey, it's okay, love. It's okay." Kerra attempted to comfort her, but Elizabeth shook her off, shaking her head against her words.

"It's not okay. It's the furthest thing from okay. This false truce that we have between us is bullshit, and I don't want her in my life if..." She stopped, trying to collect herself and control the emotional overload that her senses were experiencing. She reached out to lace her fingers with Kerra's. "Look at us. We're good together."

"We're great together," Kerra agreed, placing a kiss to the back of her hand.

Elizabeth smiled at her through the tears. "I don't want anyone in my life that doesn't see that. I won't let anyone make me feel wrong for loving you."

Kerra let go of her hand, bracing herself as she shakily leaned forward to place a kiss on Elizabeth's lips before collapsing back onto the bed. She let her head fall back into its resting place in Elizabeth's lap. "I love you too," she offered breathlessly as she grabbed at her ice pack to return it to her side. "And if I didn't feel like my rib cage was about to explode we'd be doing something your mother could really disapprove of right now."

Elizabeth let out a giggle as she returned her fingers to Kerra's head. "Promises, promises."

Chapter Twenty-Four

Elizabeth awoke in an uncomfortable sitting position with Kerra comfortably propped in her lap, a pool of melted ice making a wet spot down her torso. Elizabeth attempted to slip quietly out from underneath Kerra's resting head, but her attempts not to stir her failed.

"Where are you going?" Kerra groaned at her.

"Nowhere," Elizabeth assured her. "I'm just going to get a little packing done before work."

"Packing? What are you packing for?" Kerra reached out for her empty spot on the bed.

"For the trip. We leave in twenty-four hours, and I won't have time to do it later today because I have to work," Elizabeth informed her as she shuffled through drawers for things that she might want to wear for the weekend.

"So pack tomorrow. It's three days. It'll take you two minutes to pack a bag. Come back to bed." Kerra patted her hand against the empty space beside her.

"No, Kerra. It'll take *you* two minutes to pack. I need time to think and to organize." Elizabeth pulled a dark-blue tank top out of the open drawer and held it up to her chest. "Is it cold in the mountains?" She asked the question out loud to herself, folding the tank top before placing it back into the drawer. She decided to play it safe and pack for moderate weather.

Kerra let out another exasperated groan. "Can you please just come back to bed until you have to go to work?"

"No, Kerra. I just told you—"

"Yeah, I know. You have to organize for a three-day trip." Kerra rolled over onto her back, opening her eyes for the first time.

"You know, you don't have to be awake just because I am," Elizabeth told her with a little more sharpness than she meant to. She didn't know if it was the lack of sleep or the uncomfortable pain in her back from sitting in such an awkward position all night, but she was unusually cranky with Kerra.

"Actually, I do. Especially when you're walking back and forth opening and closing drawers all morning," Kerra snapped back, obviously feeling her own bit of morning crankiness. She sat up and inhaled sharply at the pain in her side.

Elizabeth whirled on her, ready to pick the fight, but changed her mind as she saw her wince. She let out a sigh as she crossed the room to take a seat at the foot of the bed. "I'm sorry." She reached out to place a hand on Kerra's leg. "How's your side?"

Kerra gave her a half smile. "Better. Before it was like an excruciating, mind-numbing pain, and now it's like a dull excruciating, mind-numbing pain."

Elizabeth rolled her eyes at her attempt at humor. "I'll get you more ice," she told her as she climbed to her feet and headed to the kitchen. She placed a few more ice cubes into a new towel and then rummaged around in the kitchen drawers until she found a bottle of Advil. She filled a glass halfway with water before heading back to Kerra, extending her morning gifts to her.

"Thanks." Kerra accepted the items with a smile.

Elizabeth watched her as she swallowed a handful of the pills, a much higher dose than she was sure was safe. "Should you really take that many?" she asked cautiously.

Kerra let out a grunt when she caught her expression. "It's Advil, not crank, Lizzie."

Elizabeth held up her hands in surrender. "Fine." Elizabeth watched her expectantly, waiting for an apology for her snippy attitude, but it never came. "Fine." She climbed from the bed and returned to her task of packing. She took extra concern to close each drawer with just a little more force than required, as if to make a point. *If she wants to be on the outs today, then so be it.*

Kerra's lips pressed into a straight line as she watched Elizabeth parade around the room, slamming drawers and tossing items in an unorganized fashion into a bag.

"So are you going to be pissed off with me all day or just for the morning?" Kerra asked as her eyes followed Elizabeth back and forth.

"I'm not pissed off," Elizabeth argued, contradicting herself as she pitched another shirt into her bag with excessive force.

"Sure you aren't," Kerra agreed, antagonizing her.

"I'm not." Elizabeth continued to shove things into the bag. Some of the clothes she gathered she was sure didn't belong to her. "You want to be awake with me at four in the morning, that's up to you. You want to down a bottle of Advil, go right ahead." She tossed a single shoe into the bag without its matching counterpart. "It's your world, Kerra, I'm just living in it," she finished as she added a hairbrush to the collection of chaos.

"Okay, okay, okay." Kerra climbed slowly out of the bed. She held the pack of ice to her injuries as she made her way over to Elizabeth, who continued to frantically toss the contents of Kerra's room into the bag. She reached out for Elizabeth's arm, aiming to stop her frenzy.

"What, Kerra?" Elizabeth snapped at her, throwing the bag to the ground and making a greater mess of its already spilling-out insides.

"Okay, so we're off today."

Elizabeth rolled her eyes at the understatement. "You think?"

Kerra nodded, sliding her hand up Elizabeth's arm to rest on her shoulder. "Look, I know you've got a lot on your plate today, and I know you want to pack just to have one less thing to think about, but I really think you should sleep."

"Kerra, I—"

"Hear me out." Kerra cut her off. "Leave this—" Kerra kicked over the messy pile of clothes on the floor "—here for now, and tomorrow I'll do whatever you need me to do to help you pack, okay?"

Elizabeth put a hand to her head. She really was exhausted, mentally and physically drained. "Okay."

"All right." Kerra led her to the bed and then lay down with her. She maneuvered herself to rest on her ice pack and wrap her arms around Elizabeth. "Let's go to sleep and try this day again in a few hours." Kerra kissed the back of her head as she lightly squeezed her.

"Okay," Elizabeth agreed softly as she drifted off to sleep without encouragement.

☆☆☆

Elizabeth woke up, peeved to find Kerra's arms no longer wrapped around her. "Kerra?" she called out to her, realizing she wasn't even in the room any longer.

"Yeah?" Kerra popped her head into the door frame with a toothbrush hanging from her mouth.

Elizabeth eyed her suspiciously. "You got dressed?"

Kerra cocked her head at her. "Yeah."

"Why?"

Kerra disappeared to the bathroom, likely to spit into the sink. "Because I usually do that before work," she answered without returning to the doorway.

Elizabeth climbed out of the bed, trying her best to ignore the sloppy pile of clothing still on the floor as she made her way to the bathroom. "You're going to work?" she asked accusingly.

Kerra stared at her, confused by her tone. "Yes."

"What about your side?"

Kerra shrugged. "I'm feeling better, a little worse for the wear, but I'll live. I've been worse off."

"Right, of course you have," Elizabeth huffed. Dating the bad girl with the questionable past was beginning to wear pretty thin for her.

"Do you not want me to go to work?" Kerra fished for whatever was bothering her. "Because you know I have to take tomorrow off, so I really should go in today."

Elizabeth let out a sigh. "No, I know. I want you to go to work."

"So...Why are you mad at me?" Kerra put her toothbrush away to meet her eyes.

"I'm not, I'm just... Lola told me that the mountains are full of small-town racists and bigots. Is that true?"

Kerra blinked at her as she scrambled to find her words. "Uh, yeah, but we don't have to leave the cabin if you don't want to. We'll never have to see any of them."

Elizabeth shook her head. "No, I'm not worried about me."

Kerra's face set into a line of understanding. "You're worried about me." Kerra closed her eyes and propped herself against the sink. "Lizzie, I've been going to the mountains with Krissy and Lola for years. You don't need to worry about it."

"It's different."

"How is it different?" Kerra opened her eyes to stare at her.

"Because they aren't your black girlfriend."

Kerra's lips set into a frown as she let her words sink in. "Okay, so what do you want me to do? Do you not want to go?"

"Of course I want to go. I just want you to be aware that this trip may be a little different." Elizabeth approached her cautiously.

Kerra watched her as she slowly maneuvered into the bathroom to close the distance between them. "Okay. Noted."

"And I want you to promise me that you'll think." Elizabeth reached out to place a hand to her chest.

"Okay." Kerra answered her without meeting her eyes.

"Promise me," Elizabeth urged her.

"I promise." Kerra met her eyes. "Can I go to work now?"

"Can I have a kiss first?" Elizabeth smiled up at her. They were having a rocky morning, and she didn't want to end it that way.

Kerra beamed down at her as she closed a hand around Elizabeth's. She held it tighter to her chest as she brought her lips down to meet Elizabeth's. "I'll be home tonight to call your mom with you," she promised as their lips parted.

"Okay," Elizabeth whispered after her, watching her disappear down the hallway and through the front door. She knew that the promise she'd just made Kerra make would be a hard one for her to keep. She was well versed in the nastiness that came with small-town racism, and she wasn't sure Kerra was built to watch it be directed at her.

She spent the morning trying to keep herself from thinking about the possible trouble Kerra might have in the mountains and to keep her mind on one thing at a time. She was coming out to her mother in a few hours. It was sure to be a fireworks show, even through the telephone. She debated if she would hang up when her mother began to spew some hateful, revamped version of a Bible verse or if she would take the abuse in hopes that it would lead to some chance of future acceptance. Would she ever be able to repair their relationship after this?

She toiled over every possible scenario, playing each one in her head as she drove to work, recklessly swerving in and out of her lane as she let her mind wander too far away from her.

She strolled absentmindedly through the doors of the café and then made her way through the assortment of tables and chairs to the counter, without noticing Krissy at the register behind it.

"Hello?" Krissy dragged the word out, waving her hands in front of Elizabeth's face to get her attention.

Elizabeth snapped out of her own head, finally acknowledging her. "Oh, hey, Krissy."

Krissy cocked her head in concern as she watched Elizabeth move slowly behind the counter to organize a tray of coffee mugs. "You okay, honey?"

Elizabeth nodded, not wanting to get into a conversation about her mother with Krissy first thing in the morning. "Yeah, I'm fine. I was just thinking about this weekend," she lied, hoping Krissy would bite the deflection.

Krissy narrowed her eyes, grumbling under her breath as she debated how much she believed her. "All right then," she finally settled. She turned away from her, returning to her task at the register. "Oh." Krissy turned to her, putting a finger in the air as she suddenly remembered something. "By the way, I know you aren't scheduled but could you work tomorrow? I have a bit of business to see to, and I don't want to leave Lola to hold down the fort alone."

"Oh, sorry. I can't, Krissy. Kerra and I..." Elizabeth paused, thinking twice about telling Krissy that she planned to run off to the mountains a day early for a twenty-four-hour sex-a-thon with her daughter. "Umm...are going shopping." She instantly wanted to kick herself for not being a better liar.

"Shopping? With Kerra?" Krissy furrowed her eyebrows at her, trying to process the statement.

Elizabeth cleared her throat, giving herself time to think. "Uh, yeah.

We got into a fight this morning, and she offered to shop with me tomorrow to shut me up."

"Oh, I see." Krissy nodded, believing her more when she painted it as an obligatory shopping trip.

Elizabeth smiled, a little proud of herself for her deception.

"Wait, a fight? Are you guys okay?" Krissy's expression suddenly changed to one of alarm.

Elizabeth waved her off. "Yeah, we're fine. It was a stupid fight, nothing worth rehashing." Elizabeth surprised herself with how true her lie was becoming. *The best fibs are founded in truth.* She shook her head to herself.

"Oh, so we didn't scare you off last night?" Krissy let out a stiff laugh, her attempt at not sounding panicked failing her.

Elizabeth met her eyes. "Of course not, Krissy. I have been very aware for a long time that things with Kerra won't always be smooth sailing."

Krissy reached out for her, placing a hand on each of her shoulders. "You are one tough cookie, Lizzie." She brought her in for a hug, and Elizabeth jumped in surprise. She wasn't expecting it, but after a moment she gave in, wrapping her arms around Krissy to return the embrace. "I'm so happy you're here," Krissy whispered into her hair, holding her tighter and longer than she probably realized.

"Can I ask you something, Krissy?"

Krissy let her go, giving her a nod. "Always."

"Lola said the mountains are full of bigots and racists, and I was wondering—"

"Why we go?" Krissy finished her thought for her.

"Yeah. I mean, it just seems like more trouble than it's worth." Elizabeth imagined how difficult it must be for Krissy if the mountains were as full of prejudice as Lola had said. Even without Lola and Kerra's tempers, Krissy's caramel-colored skin must have put her on the receiving end of a few hateful comments.

Krissy nodded as she leaned back to rest her weight against the counter. "It would seem that way, wouldn't it?" She paused for a moment, her face creasing in thought. "If we never leap a hurdle, we will never know how high we can jump."

Elizabeth stared at her in confusion, and Krissy let out a sigh. "I appreciate the opportunity to thrive in the face of adversity. And as for my girls, when they see that they can overcome in an isolated environment like the cabin, it helps them to realize they can overcome everywhere else as well."

Elizabeth moved her head up and down in rhythm with Krissy's words, seeing their trip in a new light. "So, it's kind of like a test run for them."

Krissy smiled at her. "Kind of." Her eyes clouded as the corners of her smile turned down. "I'm always worried for them. They don't think. I love them for how guttural and honest they are but—"

"You wish they could choose their moments," Elizabeth offered, knowing exactly what she meant.

Krissy's clouds cleared a bit as she met Elizabeth's eyes. "Exactly." Her smile returned as she shook her head. "You know, I've always felt so alone in my fear for them. Azul doesn't really understand. He's always matching Angela's crazy, pound for pound, and I just...ugh, I don't know. It's nice to have you to worry with me."

Elizabeth matched her smile and reached out for her hand. "You're not alone anymore."

☆☆☆

Elizabeth and Krissy spent the rest of the day going back and forth, sharing their thoughts and concerns with one another between orders, until it was finally time to close up shop. She felt closer to Krissy than ever, but she was saddened by the thought that it was closer to a mother-daughter relationship than she'd ever had with her own mother.

"Hey, go ahead and head out. Azul is on his way over. He'll lock up with me," Krissy shouted at her from behind the counter as she wiped down tables.

"Are you sure?" Elizabeth asked the question, but she was already removing her apron, ready to hightail it out of the shop.

"Yeah, positive. Go ahead. Get out of here." Krissy threw her a smile as she headed for the door.

"Good night, Krissy."

"Good night, Lizzie."

Elizabeth reached her car. She jumped inside at the speed of light and then barreled off down the road to her apartment. She was buzzing from her day with Krissy, and she didn't want to lose that momentum. She was ready to square things off with her mother. She wanted the relationship that Krissy had with Kerra and Lola. She wanted a mother who accepted her for her differences and loved her through her trials. If her mother wasn't ready to offer her that, then she no longer wanted to have her in her life, no matter how distantly.

Elizabeth could still feel the fire rumbling in her belly, ready to launch every word at her mother with Kerra by her side. She nearly tripped on the stairs as she hurried herself up them to the front door of the apartment. She called out for Kerra as she threw herself inside, heading straight for her bedroom.

"Kerra?" Her heartbeat began to slow as she searched the apartment for her. "Kerra?" she called out again, but she could tell by the quiet that Kerra wasn't home yet.

She returned to the living room and plopped herself down on the couch, feeling the fire she had only moments ago beginning to extinguish. She shook her head at herself, rallying her nerves back up. She needed to do this now, before she lost her resolve. She couldn't wait for Kerra. It was now or never and never wasn't an option.

She took her phone out with trembling fingers and then dialed her mother's number. She was no longer privy to the prestige of being on Elizabeth's speed dial.

"Hello?" Her mother's voice through the phone made her heart kick up speed again. "Hello? Elizabeth?"

"Hi, Mom." Elizabeth finally found her voice to respond.

"How are you, sweetheart?" Her voice was as sweet as honey, honoring their delicate reconciliation.

"I'm okay. How are you?" She was stalling, and she hated herself for it, but she couldn't bring herself to just drop the bomb on her mother without at least giving her the decency of some friendly pretext.

"I'm wonderful. I was actually just talking about you." The overly sugary nature of her mother's tone suddenly became clear. She wasn't treading carefully. She was in the presence of company. Elizabeth waited in silence, feeling a blow to her chest as she slowly realized her mother's intentions.

"Elizabeth?" She fussed at her, still using her nectar-enriched tone. "Don't you want to know who I was talking to?"

"No, Mom. I don't," Elizabeth answered flatly.

"Oh, of course you do." Her mother completely ignored her as she continued on. "I was just sitting here with RJ and Lindsey Cantell, when you called. How crazy is that?" She let out a fluttering laugh. "I was telling them how well you are doing in the city. Getting ready to go back to school and exploring your passion. It's actually kind of fate that you called."

Elizabeth rolled her eyes. Her mother was completely delusional. "Mom, you can't be serious."

"What do you mean, Beth? Of course I am. I always boast of your accomplishments."

Elizabeth searched her tone for some indication, any sign that her mother wasn't completely insane. That she knew on some level that she was lying to herself and everyone around her. She let out a groan of irritation as she found no such sign. "Are you even going to ask how Kerra is doing?" She hoped that maybe bringing up Kerra's name would bring her mother back down to reality.

"Oh, right." She could hear the strain in her mother's voice as she tried to keep the bitterness from intermingling with her diabetic tone. *Good, at least I know she hasn't completely suppressed the memory of Kerra.* "How is the roommate?"

Elizabeth gritted her teeth. She knew what her mother was doing. Calling Kerra "the roommate" as if she was undeserving of the human entitlement of a name. Elizabeth could feel the fire reigniting inside her. "Do you really hate her so much that you can't call her by her name?" There was a viciousness in her tone that she had never directed at her mother before. She'd hardly directed it at anyone before.

"Elizabeth." Her mother lowered her voice to a whisper. Elizabeth could envision her, whispering into the phone and trying to scurry away from her guests to have a less-than-pleasant conversation. "I don't hate your roommate. I just recognize her for what she is."

"And what exactly is that?" Elizabeth was practically yelling into the phone as she climbed to her feet. The energy building in her body had grown too ferocious for her to continue sitting.

"A distraction. A latent teenage rebellion. And when you're done punishing me for whatever it is that I've done to you, I, being the forgiving woman that I am, have made sure to keep your life intact for you for whenever you decide that this phase is over." Her mother's tone had lost all its phoniness, and Elizabeth knew she must have excused herself to another room.

She put a hand to her forehead, her skin burning hot from the rage inside her. "A distraction? A latent teenage rebellion?" She huffed into the phone, her breathing coming in ragged from the emotion building in her chest. "You forgot one, Mom. She's also my girlfriend," Elizabeth snapped at her. It wasn't the confession that she had planned, but her mother was bringing out the most vicious side of her with her insults at Kerra.

"Yes, I know. She's your friend, for now, and I'm willing to let you—"

"No, Mom." She was no longer interested in playing the delusion game with her mother. "She's my *girlfriend;* hand-holding, makeout sessions, gay-pride girlfriend, Mom." She finished her impassioned declaration and waited for her mother to react, but she said nothing.

Two minutes of silence passed before she began to think maybe her mother had thrown the phone into the yard. "Mom?"

"Is this your idea of a joke, Elizabeth?"

"No, Mom. It's not a joke." Her anger and ferocity had dissipated in the moments of silence, and she was suddenly feeling guilty for the way that it had all transpired.

She could hear her mother sniffle through the phone. "I just don't know what I've done to you, Beth."

She sat back down on the couch, her heart sinking to her stomach. "Nothing, Mom. You haven't done anything. This isn't about you. I love Kerra, and I—"

"Oh, don't you give me that." Her mother's voice dropped to a growl. "I don't know why you're doing this, but you've crossed the line,

Elizabeth Bridges, and I'm done. I don't know who you are anymore."

"Mom, I'm still me. I just—" She tried to console her, but her mother didn't want to hear it.

"No. You are not the daughter that I raised. And you are not any sort of daughter that I want."

"Mom." There was an intricate mix of hurt and disbelief culminating inside her.

"Good-bye, Elizabeth." There was a finality in the words that said good-bye to more than just the end of the phone call.

Elizabeth listened to the silence of the disconnected line as she sank deeper into the cushions of the couch. She had fully expected to be disowned, but it was a completely different kind of heartbreak expecting it than actually experiencing it.

She pulled her legs in close to her chest and rested her chin on her knees. Hot streaks of tears made their way down her face as she lost the will to move. Her mind felt blank and dark as the feeling of being unwanted and unloved by her own mother sank in.

"Lizzie?"

She wasn't sure how long she had been sitting in the same spot before she heard Kerra's voice call out to her, but the neck of her shirt was soaked through with tears, and the bottom of her chin tingled with the numbness of being propped on her knees too long.

She blinked her eyes clear, finding Kerra at her side and reaching out to cradle her in her arms. She had no idea when Kerra had come in or how she managed to make it so close to her without her noticing, but she was grateful to have her home.

"What's going on, love?" Kerra wiped at the tears on her face.

"I told my mom." Elizabeth fought against the sob that threatened to escape from her throat. "She—she…" Her shoulders heaved as she lost her battle against the building fit.

"Hey, hey. It's okay." Kerra brought her into her arms, rubbing at her back to calm her. "It's okay," she repeated, waiting for Elizabeth to regain control of herself. "I thought you were going to wait for me." Kerra finally spoke again as Elizabeth's sobs ceased.

"I was. I wanted to…but I couldn't wait. I had to…" She stopped as another crying spell hit, and Kerra hugged her in tighter.

Elizabeth managed to compose herself, and she leaned away from Kerra to look at her. "I'm sorry," she sniffed, wiping at her eyes. "How was work? How is your side?"

Kerra laughed, sliding in closer to her. "Work was fine. I'm fine. I think your day may have been a little bigger than mine."

Elizabeth shook her head. "No, I don't want to talk about it anymore."

Kerra met her eyes. "Are you sure?"

Elizabeth nodded, maneuvering Kerra's arms to wrap back around her as she rested her head on her chest. "Yeah, I just want to go away with you tomorrow and be away from everything that isn't you."

Kerra nodded as she placed a kiss on the top of her head. "I love you, Lizzie."

Elizabeth closed her eyes, letting the words fill her up with warmth as she lay in Kerra's embrace. The world couldn't get to her inside those arms, and she felt undeniably safe in the comfort of Kerra's love.

CHAPTER TWENTY-FIVE

Elizabeth woke up spread out across the tan couch alone. She rubbed at her eyes in disappointment at the absence of Kerra. She hadn't expected her to sit on the sofa all night with her sleeping in her arms but she would have liked a nudge that she was going to bed.

Elizabeth made her way clumsily off the couch, squinting against the sunlight that beamed in, and then headed down the hall to Kerra's room.

"Wh-what are you doing?" She had expected to find Kerra nestled against her pillow, sleeping the morning away, but the sight before her eyes baffled her. Kerra stood over four neatly stacked piles of clothes laid out across the bed next to her travel bag.

She finished folding a shirt and turned toward Elizabeth. "I told you I'd help you pack." She added the shirt to one of the piles before reaching out for Elizabeth. She grabbed her hand and pulled her toward the bed. "Shirts. Tanks. Jackets. Jeans." Kerra pointed to each pile as she listed them off.

Elizabeth watched her in awe. "You organized for me?" She was impressed. Kerra's own pile of clothes was an assortment of random items, unsurprisingly so, as it was the way that she kept all her drawers.

"Of course I did." Kerra answered her as if she should have expected as much.

Elizabeth wrapped her arms around her and placed a kiss on her cheek. "I love you, Kerra Silvers."

Kerra smiled down at her, completely unaware of the heart-melting sweetness in her gesture. "Okay." Kerra returned her embrace, still baffled. "I love you too."

Elizabeth let her go, the smile on her face refusing to leave.

"I told Angela we'd stop by this morning before we left, to check up on her," Kerra informed her as she stacked the clothes into Elizabeth's bag.

Elizabeth watched, still amazed that Kerra had packed for her.

"We should get going pretty soon so that we can beat the traffic heading out of the city and..." Kerra stopped speaking, noticing Elizabeth still staring at her in amazement. "What?"

Elizabeth debated tempting her to break her schedule. She knew it wouldn't take much to convince Kerra to throw timeliness to the wind, but she really didn't want to spend the day stuck in traffic. She'd have to save her appreciation for Kerra's thoughtfulness for the cabin.

"Nothing." She shook her head, still unable to wipe the grin from her face. "Sounds like a plan. I'm going to shower." She bit her tongue, fighting the impulse to invite Kerra to join her.

She showered and dressed in nearly record time, ready to be snuggled up in the mountains in a cabin with her woman.

"Here." Elizabeth tossed Kerra her keys on the way out of the door. "We should take my car. It's better on gas." Kerra scrunched her face in disapproval. She hated Elizabeth's tiny, eco-savvy car. The last time Kerra had expressed her thoughts on it, she'd deemed the car too "dainty," whatever that was supposed to mean.

"You expect me to drive your car into the mountains?" Kerra asked snidely as she led her down the stairs of the apartment.

"Yes. I looked it up. It's better to take a small car."

"You looked it up?" Kerra groaned at her efficiency.

Elizabeth rolled her eyes at her. "I can drive if it makes you feel better?"

Kerra shook her head as she headed for Elizabeth's car. "No, no, no. I got it." Along with not approving of Elizabeth's style of car, Kerra also didn't think much of her driving skills.

Elizabeth frowned at Kerra's passive jab at her driving as she tossed her bag into the backseat of the car. By the time she slid into the passenger seat her smile had returned. Her excitement bubbled in her belly at the trip to come.

"All right. Here we go." Kerra started up the car. She reached for Elizabeth's hand as she pulled out of the parking lot. Elizabeth gave it a squeeze as they headed for the bar.

She was even excited to see Angela, having grown quite fond of her since visiting her in the hospital. She was a woman of steel. Only a few days out of the hospital and she was back on her feet, refusing to be kept down by hate and ignorance. Elizabeth admired her. In fact, she was even a little inspired by her.

She clutched at Kerra's hand, giving it a squeeze as she stared at the side of her head. She hoped that one day she could be as brave and courageous as Angela, if for no other reason than for Kerra. She leaned over to place a kiss on Kerra's cheek as she reached out to tuck a stray strand of black hair back behind her ear.

Elizabeth spent the drive to the Nipple Slip feeling utterly and hopelessly blissful. By the time they pulled up in front of the bar, she was nearly bursting at the seams with affection for Kerra. She found every reason to touch her, never wanting to lose the sensation of her skin on hers.

Kerra reciprocated her affection, grinning at her with every touch and returning it with one of her own. They stumbled through the doors of the bar, intertwined in each other's arms.

"Hey." Angela greeted them from behind the bar as they entered, her face lighting up at the sight of them.

"Hey, Angela." Kerra and Elizabeth echoed one another, giving them yet another reason to deliver sickly sweet kisses to one another.

"Wow, okay. So, I take it you two are doing well," Angela noted as she approached them, scrunching her face up at their public displays of affection.

"How are you doing?" Elizabeth reluctantly let go of Kerra to wrap her arms around Angela.

"I'm okay. I'm great, actually. We're opening on the Southside next month, come hell or high water." Angela let go of her and beamed at them, the bruised circles around her eyes not concealing her excitement.

"That's great, Angie." Kerra reached out to embrace her, and Elizabeth tried not to flinch at the irrational jealousy that built in her chest.

"Oh, I've got something for you, Lizzie." Angela bounced off back behind the bar as she searched the counter for something. She remerged in front of them holding an expensive-looking bottle of liquid with a language Elizabeth didn't understand on the label.

"Wow. What is it?" Elizabeth stared wide-eyed at the bottle. She was impressed with it, whatever it was.

"It's vodka. My uncle buys it in bulk when he visits my grandmother in Poland." Angela handed her the bottle. "It's sort of a thank-you for helping my uncle out when I couldn't."

Elizabeth accepted the gift with a smile. She'd never had anyone specially gift her with imported liquor. "Thank you, Angela."

Angela gave her a nod. She stepped back, letting her eyes shift from her to Kerra. "Though, I don't think you'll need much alcohol for the two of you to have a good time this weekend."

Elizabeth's cheeks heated in embarrassment as Angela's meaning registered with her. Kerra was having the opposite reaction, her hands slipping around Elizabeth's waist in pride, as she nuzzled her chin into the crook of her neck.

"It's a family trip," Elizabeth blurted, feeling the need to justify herself.

Angela nodded knowingly. "Sure it is." She turned her back to them as she headed back to the bar. "All right, lovebirds. Go on your *family* trip. I have to do some work here." She put her hand up in the air and waved them out of the bar.

Elizabeth's breath caught in her throat as they turned to leave and nearly slammed into Sierra as she entered the bar, her flawless bronze legs shimmering against the sunlight as it hit her. She was a vision in a short skirt and shirt that fit her in all the right places. Even the wind seemed to desperately want to be part of her outfit as it kissed against her, blowing her hair back in a complimentary gust.

"S-s-sorry." Elizabeth stumbled over her apology as she scrambled to collect her thoughts. Kerra hugged her in tighter, almost protectively, as Sierra turned down her nose to peer at Elizabeth over the top of her sunglasses.

"Don't worry about it, sugar." The words rolled off her tongue almost hypnotically, and Elizabeth found herself swooning despite herself. "You can make it up to me by giving me that phone call you owe me." Sierra pursed her lips, kissing at the air in her direction.

"Oh." Elizabeth jumped in surprise at the offer. Sierra was hitting on her as she was wrapped in Kerra's protective grasp. She wasn't sure what the appropriate reaction was supposed to be.

"Phone call?" Kerra loosened her grip to stare at her.

"Umm, yeah. I-I-I met Sierra a while ago and—" Elizabeth tripped over herself trying to explain, while at the same time trying not be distracted by Sierra's disrupting presence.

"And we hit it off, but you never called me." Sierra pushed her lips into a pout.

Kerra's hands fell from Elizabeth's waist as she stared at her accusingly. "What?"

Elizabeth shook her head. "No, not like that. We just talked." She shot Sierra a hard look for making things seem like more than they were.

"Aww, come on, Kerra. What do you care? As I recall, you were never one for playing house." Sierra took a step forward, stepping between Elizabeth and Kerra. "Don't you remember all of the wild fun we had?" Sierra trailed a finger beneath Kerra's chin. "I miss the fun we have." She whispered the last bit into Kerra's ear before Kerra jerked away from her, out of her reach.

"Stop it, Sierra," Kerra warned her.

"Yeah, stop it, Sierra." Elizabeth stared in anger and disbelief at Sierra's boldness. She perched a hand on her hip as her temper began to flare.

Sierra gave her a once-over before returning her gaze to Kerra. "Fine. Whenever you're done with—" She glanced back at Elizabeth. "—whatever this is. Give me a call. I don't even mind if you bring her." Sierra gave Elizabeth a wink. "Remember, there's nothing like your first love," she whispered, placing a kiss on her fingers and tapping them against Kerra's lips before she made her way to the bar.

Elizabeth's body was nearly shaking with rage as she ground her teeth together and stared after Sierra. She wasn't prepared to watch someone shamelessly flirt with Kerra right in front of her, and she certainly wasn't ready to hear Kerra's first love proclaim that she missed her. Elizabeth shifted her gaze to Kerra who stared back like a deer caught in the headlights.

"I-I..." Kerra scrambled for something to say as Elizabeth's lips set in a hard line, and her eyes narrowed. "Okay. Listen. I..."

"Ugh." Elizabeth let out a furious grunt as Kerra continued to fumble. She turned on her heels and stormed out of the bar, making a straight path to the passenger door of the car. She pulled at the handle relentlessly as if she could unlock it with sheer force of will.

"Lizzie." Kerra ran after her.

"I don't want to talk to you right now." Elizabeth crossed her arms in a defiant gesture of will. "Open the door."

"Come on, love. I just want to—"

"No. No *loves* and no Kerra-charm witchcraft. I don't want to talk to you. So, please. Open the door," Elizabeth huffed, not wanting to be swayed into letting it go.

Kerra made her way around the car to stand in front of her. "Sierra was a long time ago," she explained, reaching out for her.

Elizabeth pulled out of her grasp. "But you didn't tell me."

"I didn't think I needed to."

Elizabeth shrugged antagonistically. "Good. Great. I'm glad we got that settled. Open the door."

"Lizzie, come on." Kerra breathed an exasperated sigh. "I'm sorry that I didn't tell you about Sierra, but it's not like you didn't know I was with a lot of women before us."

Elizabeth narrowed her eyes at her. "Is that really what you want to say to me right now?"

Kerra shook her head. "No. It's definitely not. I'm sorry. That's what I want to say. I'm sorry, I'm sorry, I'm sorry." Kerra reached for her again, resting her hands on her shoulders.

Elizabeth didn't pull away, but she didn't give Kerra any inkling that she accepted her apology either.

"Okay, there may have been other girls playing the game, but you're the one that won me over," Kerra offered. She frowned as she took in Elizabeth's growing expression of disappointment.

"Really, Kerra?" Elizabeth shook her head, anger continually building inside her.

"Okay, no. Again, I immediately regretted that as I said it. I just... Shit." Sighing, Kerra unlocked the door and watched as Elizabeth climbed in without looking at her. She slammed the door behind herself and returned her arms to cross over her chest in a huff.

She watched Kerra round the car to slide into the driver's seat without a word. She turned to Elizabeth, opening her mouth to say something but instead shifted her gaze back to the road and started up the car.

Elizabeth fumed as she considered how quickly their romantic trip away had turned into hell fire.

☆☆☆

Elizabeth continued to silently fume on her side of the car, refusing to look at or speak to Kerra, who fidgeted relentlessly in the silence.

"Lizzie, I'm sorry," Kerra announced for the hundredth time in the hour that they had been driving. She let out a groan as she received no reply for the hundredth time.

Elizabeth knew she shouldn't be as angry with Kerra as she was, but she couldn't help herself. She was perpetually being dwarfed by gorgeous women who had had Kerra before her, and it made her feel inadequate. And angry, apparently.

"Sierra wasn't good for me." Kerra spoke softly, keeping her eyes on the road. "You're good for me, Lizzie."

Elizabeth kept her form, keeping her anger apparent. She didn't want to be the good-girl choice. She wanted to be sexy and seductive like Sierra. Or ferocious and gorgeous like Angela. She didn't want to be the "good for you" girl.

Kerra let out a sigh. "Okay, how about we play a game?"

Elizabeth gave her nothing in response. She remained perfectly still in her corner of the car with her arms closed tightly across her chest.

"All right," Kerra continued, unrelenting. "This game is called *What I Love About You*." Kerra smiled at her hopefully, but Elizabeth gave no reaction.

"Okay, sure. I'll go first." Kerra cleared her throat. "I love how kind you are. You're the most forgiving person I know."

Elizabeth gave her a pointed glare.

"Usually," she added. "Okay, now you go."

Elizabeth gave her an unamused grunt. She was being unreasonable, but her ego was bruised. She appreciated Kerra's effort, but her own self-image fueled the fire of her anger.

"Or, I'll go again," Kerra resolved. She hummed under her breath as she thought. She stopped at a red light and let her gaze fall to Elizabeth. Kerra's eyes rolled up and down her body before she spoke again. "Okay. I love it when you eat breakfast with me wearing nothing but my sheet."

Elizabeth dropped her arms from her chest and turned to meet Kerra's eyes. "You do?"

Kerra nodded as she bit down on her lip. "Yeah, I think it's sexy as hell."

Elizabeth fought in vain against the smile that forced its way onto her lips. She toyed at one of her loose braids as she caught Kerra grinning in satisfaction at her.

"The light's green," Elizabeth warned, not wanting Kerra to see how completely thrilled she was to hear that Kerra found her *sexy*.

Kerra turned her gaze back to the road as she drove forward.

"Okay. I love your smile." Elizabeth gave in, feeling her bruised ego heal.

"Yeah?"

"Yeah. It's like one half of your face is really, really happy, while the other side is just kind of happy." Kerra let out a laugh at her description, and Elizabeth joined her. It felt good to not be angry.

"Okay, okay. Your go," Elizabeth urged her, suddenly a fan of the game.

"All right." Kerra drummed her fingers along the steering wheel. "I love the sound you make when I kiss you."

Elizabeth reached out to softly shove her. "Shut up. No, I don't."

Kerra laughed as she proceeded to tease her. "Yeah, you do. It's cute though."

Elizabeth swatted at her again, and Kerra caught her wrist. She let her hand slide down to cup Elizabeth's.

"I love everything about you, Lizzie." Kerra clutched her hand without taking her eyes off the road.

Elizabeth gave her a squeeze back in response. "No more surprises, Kerra."

Kerra shook her head. "None. I swear."

Elizabeth let out a sigh. "God, you make me into a crazy person."

"But you love me anyways?" Kerra glanced at her out of the corner of her eye.

"Pull over." Elizabeth let go of Kerra's hand as she shuffled around the car, rummaging through the glove compartment.

"Right now?" Kerra asked the question, but she was already weaving her way through traffic to park at the side of the road.

Elizabeth waited until she put the car in park and turned to stare at her expectantly. She took a deep breath before she spoke. "I have something I want to give you."

Kerra suggestively raised an eyebrow at her. "Oh yeah?"

Elizabeth rolled her eyes. "No, not that. I have a present."

"Oh."

Elizabeth tried not to be upset by the tinge of disappointment in her tone.

"Here." She handed her the item that she pulled from the glove compartment.

Kerra took it tentatively, furrowing her eyebrows at the crumpled item in her hand. "A dirty napkin. You shouldn't have," she said flatly.

"It's not just..." Elizabeth let out a sigh. "You know the mural you painted after we met?"

Kerra gave her a slow nod.

"Well, this is my mural," Elizabeth told her, holding up the napkin.

Kerra squinted at her in confusion. "I'm not following, Lizzie."

Elizabeth groaned in frustration, as she placed the napkin back in Kerra's hands. "Just read it."

Kerra carefully unrumpled the paper and scanned its contents. "It's a bunch of addresses." She shrugged in indifference.

Elizabeth leaned in closer to her. "The day that I met you at the bar, I searched for you."

"You searched for me?"

"Yeah. On the Internet. Before I went to the bar, I looked up your name and found these addresses."

Kerra smiled at her, staring back down at the napkin with a new perspective. "But my address isn't on here."

Elizabeth nodded. "Well, yeah. It turns out you aren't listed, but that's not the point."

"It's not?"

"No. It's not. The point is that even before I knew that I loved you, *a part of me knew that I loved you.*"

Kerra stared at her without speaking before returning her gaze to the napkin.

"If I could draw, I would have sketched you," Elizabeth offered, breaking the silence.

Kerra shook her head. "No, this is better."

Elizabeth beamed at her and reached out for her hands. "Everything in my life before you was something that someone else wanted for me. You are the first thing in my life that I've ever chosen. And you will always be my first choice. I'm always going to love you, Kerra Silvers, no matter how crazy you make me."

Kerra let go of her hands, reaching out to cup the sides of Elizabeth's face as she stared into her eyes. Her gaze reached every part of Elizabeth, consuming her mind, body, and soul. Kerra leaned forward, bringing her lips to kiss Elizabeth's in a slow rhythmic caress. Elizabeth knew that she would never stop melting at the touch of Kerra's lips on hers.

"You sure I can't interest you in a car quickie?" Kerra offered against her mouth.

Elizabeth licked the taste of her off her lips. "I could be convinced."

CHAPTER TWENTY-SIX

Elizabeth stared out of the window at the blur of passing trees. She had begun to see more of them in the last hour of their drive as they moved in closer to the mountains. Nature had begun to overtake the building-infested style of the city, and a tranquil peace took over. The trees grew taller with every mile, and the air smelled like a soft kiss of pine wafting through her nose. She pressed her arms against the seal of the window to let the wind play at her hair as she took it all in. She unhooked her seat belt to lean farther out of the window, wanting to feel the cool, crisp air engulf her.

"Hey, you're going to fall out of the car if you keep doing that," Kerra told her through a chuckle.

Elizabeth lowered her body back into the car. "No, I won't, and you'll catch me if I do."

Kerra shook her head as she kept her eyes on the road. "I appreciate your confidence in me, but I'm not Superman, Lizzie."

Elizabeth stared at her in seriousness. "Of course you're not. Superman had a morality complex. You're more like Catwoman. Sexy and dangerous. Kitty-Cat Kerra." Elizabeth giggled to herself, amused by her own joke. She slid across her seat to lightly press herself against Kerra. "Come on, Kitty-Cat, purr for me," she whispered as she burst into a fit of laughter.

"Okay, so this is obviously too much fresh air for you," Kerra noted, biting back her own giggles.

"No, it's the perfect amount." She placed a kiss on Kerra's cheek before sliding back into her seat. "Hey, why are we stopping?" Elizabeth stared in confusion as Kerra pulled over, parking on the shoulder of the road in front of a sign that read *Welcome to Bellowsview*. She glanced around at the surrounding trees and highway. "I don't think there are any cabins out here."

Kerra turned off the car and grabbed a backpack out of the backseat. She slipped it onto her shoulder as she turned to Elizabeth. "The cabin is about ten minutes from here, but there's something I want to show you first." Kerra's face took on a serious expression as she met her eyes.

Elizabeth nodded, afraid to speak. She didn't know what was happening, but it felt significant.

She climbed out of the car and then followed behind Kerra as she led her into a throng of trees. Elizabeth wanted to complain; she had never been a fan of nature, and a stroll into the forest wasn't particularly on her bucket list, but there was a serious determination in Kerra that kept her silent.

Kerra stopped in front of a tall, skinny tree that seemed to tower so high it met the skyline. She shrugged the backpack off her shoulders and set it down to rest at the base of the tree. Elizabeth watched her from a distance, wondering what in the world they were doing. *What could she possibly have to show me out here?*

"Come here." Kerra motioned for her to move closer, and Elizabeth timidly obeyed. She watched Kerra shuffle through the backpack for a moment before pulling out a bright yellow string of ribbon. "Here, hold this." Kerra handed the string to her as she continued to rummage through the bag for a pair of scissors. "Okay." She held the scissors up in triumph.

"Are we going to gift wrap the tree?" Elizabeth joked, watching her in amusement.

Kerra shook her head at her and pointed up to a low-hanging branch with several brightly colored ribbons tied along the length of it. "Wow." Elizabeth was still confused, but she was getting that this was some sort of tradition that Kerra was letting her in on. "What are they for?" Elizabeth asked, taking in each ribbon.

"They're for me."

Elizabeth lowered her gaze from the tree to stare at Kerra as she continued.

"After I was arrested, I got clean because I was in JDC, but once they let me out..." Kerra met her eyes and gave her a sad shrug.

Elizabeth moved closer, reaching out to place a hand on the back of her neck. She gave Kerra a nod of understanding.

"Uh, so, once they let me out, I kind of went off the rails. I missed all of my appointments with Krissy, and I never checked into my group home. I was pretty much a delinquent digging my own grave."

Elizabeth gave Kerra's neck a reassuring squeeze as she watched her relive her mistakes.

"And then one day, I don't know if I was reaching out or if I was just too high to think straight, but I showed up in Krissy's office. I barreled through the door during her lunch hour and scared the hell out of her. I have no idea why she didn't call the cops on me." Kerra smiled as she recalled Krissy's act of valor. "Instead she brought me up here. She dried me out in her cabin and never left my side. Lola too. She was just a kid, but she wanted to help so bad. She'd bring me a dozen popsicles a day every time I got the sweats."

Elizabeth tried to picture a young and sweet Lola, but the image eluded her.

"After about a week, Krissy brought me here. Right to this spot, and made me tie a ribbon to that branch." Kerra pointed up at the hanging ribbons. "She told me that every year I could make a choice; I could come up here with her and Lola and add another ribbon to this tree or I could go back to living the way that I was."

Elizabeth returned her gaze to the tree, looking up at the branch with new eyes. She squinted up at it in confusion as she counted the ribbons again. "Wait, you were sixteen, right?"

Kerra gave her a silent nod.

"But there are only eight ribbons." Elizabeth returned her gaze to Kerra, who frowned in shame.

"One year, I made the wrong choice," she answered sadly.

Words that Elizabeth couldn't push out of her head rang in her ears. *She wasn't good for me, Lizzie. You are good for me.*

"Sierra?" Elizabeth asked the question before she could give herself a moment to reflect on it.

Kerra nodded. "Four years of sobriety down the tubes."

Elizabeth took a moment, processing all the information placed on her. She moved to position herself in front of Kerra as she wrapped her arms around her neck. "You're amazing, you know that?" She leaned in to press a quick kiss to her lips. "Now, walk me through how I'm supposed to get you up there to tie this ribbon."

☆☆☆

Elizabeth was nearly bouncing in her seat as they pulled up in front of the cabin. She jumped out of the car before Kerra even had a chance to put it in park. She took in the simplistic beauty of the quaint hut, tucked away in the woods. She ran her hands along the wooden railing outlining the porch and let each crack and crevice dance along her fingertips, before making her way to the front door.

She waited impatiently, bouncing on her heels as Kerra took her time trailing behind her. "So, I guess I'll get the bags?" Kerra shouted as she lugged two heavy bags out of the backseat before making her way to the porch of the cabin.

Elizabeth pursed her lips in a pout. "There was a time when you would have loved to get my bags for me."

"That was before you put out." Kerra stuck her tongue out as she teased her.

Elizabeth laughed as she playfully pushed her shoulder. "Well, don't expect any more of that with that attitude."

"Ouch." Kerra placed a hand to her heart in mock pain as she moved around her to unlock the door.

Elizabeth pushed it open, unable to contain herself as she skipped inside. She gasped in excitement as she took in the interior. It was everything she thought it would be. There was the delicate touch of Krissy's eccentricities intermingled with the artistic touch of Kerra and Lola. Dark furniture decorated the living room that sprouted off to connect with a bright and lively kitchen that seemed out of place with the rest of the space.

"Our room is down the hall," Kerra told her as she followed her inside.

Elizabeth nodded. She wasn't ready to see the bedroom yet. She

250

wanted to take her time admiring each piece of the place that had helped shape Kerra.

Kerra dropped the bags and watched her as she stared in awe at the walls. "What are you doing?" she asked curiously.

"I'm just admiring the place," Elizabeth answered, turning to stare back at her.

"It's just a cabin." Kerra shrugged.

Elizabeth shook her head. "It's so much more than that."

Kerra furrowed her eyebrows in confusion but didn't ask for clarification. She took a step closer to Elizabeth, a smile playing on her lips. "Well, we're here. So what do you want to do?"

Elizabeth moved forward, closing the distance between them. "First, I want you to kiss me," she informed her as she reached out for Kerra's collar, pulling her in for a kiss. It was a long and slow kiss that she could feel heating up her body as a precursor to something more intricate.

Kerra released her mouth, giving her lip a soft bite as she rested her forehead against Elizabeth's. "Is that all?"

Elizabeth shook her head, licking her lips to taste the lingering remnants of Kerra. She took Kerra's wrist and placed her palm beneath her shirt. "Now, I want you to touch me," she told her as she guided her hand upward to cup at her chest.

She smiled as Kerra's breathing picked up pace with her own, and her hand began to obey her commands. Kerra leaned forward to kiss her again, this time deeper. Her lips pushed into Elizabeth's with a new ferocity.

"And then what?" Kerra whispered the question breathlessly against her lips.

Elizabeth clutched at her wrist again, guiding her hand down to dip into the waistband of her shorts. "And then I want you to slip your fingers into my—"

"Dear Christ, please don't finish that sentence."

Elizabeth jumped, ripping Kerra's hand from her pants so quickly she was afraid she may have hurt her.

"Lola." Elizabeth cleared her throat, maneuvering her outfit back into place before turning to stare at a smug-faced Lola. "What are you doing here?"

"I could ask you the same question," Lola retorted. She raised an eyebrow at Elizabeth as she blushed in embarrassment. "Though, I think I already know the answer."

"Good. If you already know the answer then get out," Kerra grumbled at Lola. She reached out for Elizabeth, but she pulled out of her grasp.

"Actually, I was just about to do that." Lola's cool expression turned worrisome. "I was just waiting for a friend."

Kerra peered at her in suspicion. "A friend? What friend?"

Lola opened her mouth to respond, but the knock on the door caused her to shut it. She stared at Kerra for only a moment before she leaped forward for the door. Kerra caught her around the waist and held her in place.

"No, I'll get it," Kerra told her knowingly as she moved to the door. She opened it to a tiny girl in a baseball cap and an oversized jumper. The girl's eyes widened when they landed on Kerra standing menacingly in the doorway.

She took a step back. "Oh, uh. Hey, Kerra."

"What the hell are you doing here, Ralph?" Kerra made no attempts at pleasantries.

"I-I came for Lola." Ralph stumbled over her words, nervous in Kerra's shadow.

Kerra shot Lola a disapproving glare that Elizabeth felt, even though it wasn't directed at her. Kerra turned her glare back to Ralph. "Get out of here, Ralph," she commanded with no room for compromise.

"Kerra, you can't—" Lola stepped forward to protest.

Kerra whirled on her. "Yes, I can, Lola, and you know Krissy would say the same thing."

Lola stared down at her shoes, like a small child being told no to ice cream. Elizabeth watched the scene in front of her in amazement.

"Don't come back here again, Ralph," Kerra finished, turning to slam the door on the tiny girl.

Kerra turned back to Lola, anger written in her eyes as she marched closer to her. "Is that why you're here right now? To hang out with that loser?" Elizabeth had never heard Kerra yell before, and she wasn't a fan of it.

"Kerra, I'm an adult. You can't tell me who I can and can't hang out with." Lola brought her gaze up from her shoes to yell back at Kerra. Elizabeth had wondered how long a suggestible Lola would last before the fiery, defiant girl that she knew resurfaced.

Kerra nodded a viciously antagonistic nod as she ran a hand through her hair. "Okay. If I see her here again, I'll kick her ass and then yours. How's that for telling you what to do?"

Lola's eyes burned with fury as she stared back at Kerra. "You can be a real grade-A asshole, you know that."

"And you can be really naive and immature." Kerra threw the words at her before storming off to a room at the end of the hallway.

Elizabeth stared after her, shocked by her outburst. She turned her gaze to Lola, who stood angrily propped up against the wall, her arms folded protectively across her chest as she sniffed in the corner.

"You okay?" Elizabeth wasn't sure what else to say. She'd only caught very few glimpses of a vulnerable Lola.

Lola blew a stray piece of hair out of her face. "Yeah, I'm fine. I honestly don't know how you put up with her." She stared in the direction of the door Kerra had disappeared into and rolled her eyes.

"Yeah, well, she approves of who I date," Elizabeth joked awkwardly.

Lola met her eyes. "I'm not dating Ralph." She dropped her gaze to the floor and uncrossed her arms. "I mean, I want to, but..." Lola let out a groan as she lifted her eyes again to stare at Elizabeth. "She only hates her because she's just like her."

Elizabeth nodded, a part of her understanding what had just taken place. "I'll go talk to her, okay?" She reached out and gave her shoulder a squeeze, a gesture she never thought she'd extend to Lola.

"Thanks, Lizzie." Lola gave her a smile before Elizabeth turned to make her way to Kerra. "Oh, and Lizzie?" Elizabeth turned to face her again. "I'm really glad that you came." She whispered the words so low that Elizabeth barely caught them, like they were some sort of shameful confession.

Elizabeth nodded, not sure if she was supposed to acknowledge them or not. She turned and made her way to the room at the end of the hallway, where she found Kerra laying across a lumberjack comforter staring at a large drawing of a dragon taped across the ceiling.

"Yours?" Elizabeth pointed up at the drawing, and Kerra gave her a nod.

Elizabeth made her way to lie next to her. "So, umm...that whole thing with Lola?"

Kerra sat up with a grunt. "Yeah, she can be a brat sometimes."

Elizabeth sat up to meet her eyes. "Yeah, sure. But...you weren't all that easy to deal with either."

Kerra frowned at her. "You don't know Lola. You've got be that way with her or she'll just—"

"I think you hurt her feelings. Which is saying something because I didn't even think that Lola had any feelings." Elizabeth blurted out the words in a rushed stream of consciousness.

Kerra paused for a moment before she shook her head. She maneuvered herself to hover over Elizabeth. "I don't want to talk about Lola anymore." She dipped her head to lock her lips with Elizabeth's.

Elizabeth gave into the kiss, letting their mouths intermingle as Kerra leaned her backwards to lie flat against the comforter.

"It's just I think she really cares about what you think about her." Elizabeth inserted one more thought as Kerra's mouth left hers.

Kerra shook her head again. "I said I don't want to talk about Lola." Her eyes burned with hunger as she stared down at Elizabeth. She moved her lips down to place a soft kiss on her neck, and Elizabeth let out a sigh as she forgot what point she was trying to make. Kerra's kisses made their way down her neck to her shoulder, and she could feel Kerra's hands beginning their dance across her body.

"Kerra." Elizabeth tried to gather her thoughts as Kerra trailed her lips down her belly. "Kerra, she's right next door."

Kerra glanced up at her from her lip work on Elizabeth's torso. "So?"

"So, I don't want her listening to us have sex."

"So, we'll be quiet," Kerra assured her as she placed a kiss over her belly button.

"You know I can't do that," Elizabeth protested flatly.

Kerra smiled up at her, a cocky and arrogant grin plastering her lips. "I know." She propped herself up on her palms and leaned forward to return her kisses to Elizabeth's lips.

"Kerra, please don't tempt me." She had been craving Kerra's touch all day, and it wouldn't take much for her to give in to her allure. "Lola and I are finally on okay terms, and I'd just like to tread carefully."

Kerra met her eyes, noting the sincerity in them. She let out a grunt and rolled onto her back. "So, now what?"

CHAPTER TWENTY-SEVEN

Elizabeth stared holes into the side of Kerra's head as she distantly admired the drawings on the ceiling. She let out a sigh. "I'm going to go check on Lola," she announced, having had her fill of watching Kerra pout. Lola was avoiding their room like the plague, and Kerra was refusing to extend an olive branch. Elizabeth, out of sheer boredom, decided to elect herself the peacekeeper.

Kerra nodded, barely acknowledging her as she excused herself down the hallway. Lola's room was only about five paces away, giving Elizabeth no actual time to gather up what she intended to say, but she knocked on the closed door in front of her anyway.

"What?" Lola's tone held no friendliness as it raged over the hard riff of rock music coming from inside her room.

"It's Lizzie. I just wanted to talk, I guess." Elizabeth was quickly regretting her decision to cross the picket line. A pouty Kerra was much less threatening than a moody Lola.

The door swung open on Lola holding a tiny metal contraption in one hand and a grapefruit in the other. "Oh sorry, Lizzie. I thought you were *her*." Lola scrunched up her face, putting emphasis on her distaste for the "her" in question.

"Oh, no. Just me," Elizabeth told her nervously.

"Well, come in." Lola waved her inside, and she took a timid step forward. Lola's room was dark and haunting. The walls were painted a dark blue and sheer black curtains hung from the window, letting in only a scarce amount of sunlight. The whole thing reminded Elizabeth of what she imagined a torture chamber looked like. She gasped as she caught sight of a big black chair with several mechanisms connected to it in the corner. A bright light shone down on the chair, making it the only illuminated item in the room. *Oh, my God, it is a torture chamber.*

Elizabeth noted the mystery device in Lola's hand. *A torture item, no doubt.*

"So, what are you doing in here, Lola?" Elizabeth asked cautiously, her heart thudding in her chest.

Lola shrugged her shoulders. "Practicing."

Elizabeth eyes grew wide at her indifference. "For?"

Lola made her way across the room and placed the grapefruit in her hand on the arm of the chair. She sat down on a tiny, nearly hidden stool next to it and connected her torture device to a wire in the wall before setting it down next to the ball of fruit. "Every year I give Kerra and my mom a tattoo. It's sort of tradition," Lola informed her.

Elizabeth let out a sigh as she looked at the chair again with new understanding. "Oh, it's a tattoo chair."

Lola furrowed her eyebrows. "Of course it is. What did you think it was?"

Elizabeth shook her head. "That's not important."

Lola eyed her curiously before accepting the answer. "Okay."

"So, tattoos huh?" Elizabeth took a seat on the edge of a black comforter covering the bed.

Lola nodded. "Yeah. When Mom took me in, I had a few anger issues."

Elizabeth let out a snort at the ginormous misuse of the word "few."

Lola gave her a hard look before continuing. "Anyways, she thought it would help if I had a hobby. Something that required a lot of focus and the responsibility of people's trust."

"So she taught you how to tattoo?"

Lola shook her head. "Well, no. I was ten when she took me in, and I was in sort of a butch-lesbian phase. I thought there was nothing cooler than a short haircut, a motorcycle, and a tattoo sleeve."

Elizabeth squinted at Lola before bursting into laughter. Lola wasn't what she would call "butch" at all. After a baffled moment, Lola joined her in her laughter.

"I was ten, okay." She defended herself through chuckles.

"Okay, okay, okay." Elizabeth wiped at the corners of her eyes. "So, you wanted to be a butch lesbian and then?"

"I started hanging out at whatever tattoo parlors would let me in, and everything just sort of came together from there."

Elizabeth stared at her in amazement. "Wow. You're no butch, but that's pretty freaking cool." She reached out and nudged Lola's shoulder.

"Thanks."

"So you did all of Kerra's tattoos?"

"Hell no." Elizabeth nearly jumped out of her skin at the unexpected voice lingering in the doorway. She turned around, staring in shock as Kerra propped herself up against the archway of the door. "She gets one a year. That's it," Kerra finished.

Elizabeth froze in place, waiting for a nuclear war to start, but it never came. Lola stared at Kerra with an expression that Elizabeth couldn't read. Kerra reacted to the look with one of her own. It was as if the two of there were sharing a private conversation that Elizabeth wasn't privy to. She watched the exchange, dumbfounded by what was happening as the two of them smiled at each other, as if they hadn't spent the last hour and a half wishing the other nothing but misery.

"Whatever." Lola finally broke the silence. "With all of the stupid shit that you've put on your body, you should be begging me to do all of your tattoos, if for nothing else than a second opinion."

Kerra made her way into the room, moving closer to the corner where the two of them sat watching her. "All of my tattoos are special to me, and every single one means something," she said defensively, moving closer to close the gap between them.

"Oh, yeah?" Lola reached out for her, pulling her in and flipping her arm over to be inspected beneath the bright light. "Then what does—" Lola searched over her ink-covered arm before pointing to a tattoo written in a language that Elizabeth couldn't even be sure was a language. "—that one mean?"

Kerra squinted down at the skin work, moving her arm to catch different angles on it. "It means 'too much tequila,' you little prick." Kerra ran her fingers upwards through Lola's hair, making a mess of the golden strands before placing a kiss on top of her head.

Elizabeth let her eyes dart back and forth between them as Kerra took a seat on the bed beside her. She had no idea how they had let a fight rage on for so long and then made up with no words in the span of five seconds. She wanted to ask, but she definitely didn't want to relive the tension of their anger.

"Okay then." Elizabeth accepted the peace treaty without questioning it. "So what's the—?"

She was cut off by the sound of two voices spilling into the cabin. Kerra jumped up first, protectively stepping forward to put Lola and Elizabeth behind her.

"Who the hell?" Lola stood up from her stool, staring questioningly at her door before taking a step forward.

"No, Lola. Just wait here." Kerra held up a hand to her, not giving her a moment to protest before she went flouncing off into the hallway.

Lola ignored her commands, following after her with Elizabeth jumping up to trail on her heels.

"Krissy?" Kerra stood staring at Krissy as she made her way into the cabin with Azul stumbling in behind her.

Krissy dropped the bag in her hand and froze in place, staring back at all of them lined up along the hallway, looking at her in confusion.

"What's Azul doing here?" Lola questioned.

Krissy cleared her throat as she composed herself, thinking on her toes and turning the tables on Lola. "I think the better question is what are *you* doing here? Who's watching the shop?"

Lola stared down at her feet, avoiding Krissy's gaze. "I closed." She popped her head up and rushed to explain. "I mean, we were going to be closed for the weekend anyways. What was one more day?"

Krissy shook her head in disappointment. "Were you even going to tell me that you closed the shop?"

Lola's face contorted in guilt. "I was if you found out."

Krissy let out a sigh. "Lola." She picked her bag back up off the floor. "Why would you do that?"

Lola looked to Kerra, her eyes begging her for secrecy.

"She came up with us," Kerra offered upon seeing Lola's distress. "Lizzie and I were coming up early, and Lola asked to tag along. She wanted to show Lizzie around."

Krissy stared at her, her lips pursed in disbelief. "Uh-huh. Well, when you ladies are ready to tell me the truth, I'll be in my bedroom." Krissy moved forward to a door off the main room.

"With Azul?" Kerra questioned. Her tone held a secret knowledge beyond her words.

"He's here to fix the sink in my bathroom," Krissy answered without missing a beat. Elizabeth was impressed. She could have never thought of a coherent lie that quickly.

"Where are his tools?" Kerra smirked, crossing her arms across her chest in smugness as she waited for an answer. Lola snickered at Kerra's blatancy.

"I have tools in the bathroom," Krissy nearly growled at her, clearly done with entertaining her questionnaire.

Azul stared wide-eyed back and forth, keeping silent and making an effort not to been seen. He followed behind Krissy through the door and into a room that Elizabeth hadn't noticed before. The door shut behind them, and Lola and Kerra burst into laughter.

"Wait. Do you know?" Elizabeth took a step forward and turned to face them.

"What? Azul and Krissy? Of course we know. We're not idiots," Lola informed her through laughter.

"We just don't talk about it." Kerra slung an arm around her.

Elizabeth laced her fingers through Kerra's hand, which dangled off her shoulder. "So, it looks like everyone's romantic getaway was ruined, huh?"

☆☆☆

Elizabeth let out a laugh as Kerra and Lola went back and forth bickering their newest nonsensical topic. She was enjoying her time curled up in Kerra's lap, listening to her fight with her sister like two children vying for mommy's attention.

"Oh, shh." Kerra shushed Lola as Krissy emerged from her room, leading Azul to the door and pretending to thank him for his sink-fixing services.

Elizabeth bit back a laugh as Kerra and Lola snickered and made faces at them.

Krissy let Azul out and closed the door behind him before joining them in the living room.

"Where's he going?" Kerra asked snidely.

"Azul is staying at the inn farther down the mountain," Krissy answered.

Kerra rolled her eyes. "Krissy, he can stay here. We don't mind." Lola gave a nod to back her up, but Krissy shook her head.

"No, no, no. This is our weekend." Krissy made her way behind the couch to place her hands on Lola's shoulders. "How about we go get a drink to welcome Lizzie to the family."

Elizabeth jumped in surprise as they all turned to look at her expectantly, waiting for her to answer some unasked question.

"Oh, umm... Yeah, let's go." Elizabeth hoped that was the right answer.

"All right, let's go," Lola echoed her, climbing to her feet and gesturing for them to do the same.

Elizabeth reluctantly made her way out of Kerra's lap and extended her hand to pull Kerra up behind her.

They followed behind Lola as she led them outside. "Lola, where's your car?" Elizabeth asked when she realized her car was the only one parked outside.

"Oh, I took the train here," Lola informed her without thinking.

"I thought you all rode here together?" Krissy gave Kerra a sharp glare.

"Oh, uh...hmm... We should get to that bar now. I'll drive." Kerra held out her hand for Elizabeth's keys, which she handed over without a fuss. She wasn't very confident driving in the mountains, and Kerra's insistence that she was a bad driver was starting to make her question her skills.

Krissy grunted at Kerra's avoidance of her question but didn't press her further. She slid into the backseat of Elizabeth's car after Lola without making a scene.

Breathing a sigh of relief, Kerra plopped down behind the steering wheel. She probably wasn't ready to make up an excuse for lying about Lola's intentions for the day. Whatever Ralph had done to them, she was a hot-button issue.

Kerra started up the car and took off down the road, driving them in silence to a bar on the edge of town. Elizabeth admired the rustic theme of the exterior of the bar. Everything in the area was simply built and beautiful in its own right.

Kerra led them through heavy, wood-lined glass doors to a table toward the back of the smoky bar. The atmosphere of the room seemed to stall as they entered it. The two men playing pool stopped to stare at them, watching without shame until they took their seats. The woman behind the bar made a conscious effort to not acknowledge them. They were the obvious pariahs of the establishment.

"Ugh, every year," Lola grunted as she snapped her fingers in the air to get the woman's attention. "Hey, miss, we'd love it if you could come take an order or two. You know, and maybe do your job."

"Lola," Krissy warned her. "The point of this is to *not* be antagonistic."

Lola rolled her eyes at Krissy, but she closed her mouth to saying anything more to the frazzled bartender who looked to the two men in the bar for instructions.

The tallest of the two men nodded, seemingly giving her permission to wait on them.

Lola let out a groan as she watched the exchange. "And she officially just set all women back fifty years."

Elizabeth bit back a smile as she caught Krissy's warning glare to Lola. "No more," Krissy warned again, all of her motherly authority backing up the warning.

Lola ran an imaginary zipper across her lips, nodding at Krissy in compliance.

"Hi, what can I get y'all?" The bartender made her way to their table, holding a pen and pad in her hands as she waited for their order. She still refused to look at them, talking into the air as she asked the question.

Kerra took the reins, ordering everyone's drink for them with confidence. The bartender fidgeted uncomfortably as she took down Kerra's words, her eyes fluttering around the room to sneak glances at

Kerra as she wrote.

"Okay, comin' right up." She turned on her heels and nearly ran back to her post.

"I guess she's still carrying that torch for you." Krissy watched the bartender scramble back to the bar as she spoke across the table to Kerra.

Kerra gave her an indifferent shrug in response.

"Wait. That bartender has a thing for you?" Elizabeth turned back to look at the bartender again, taking her in. She was a tiny, petite blonde with hair just a little too big to be all her own. She was certainly attractive, in a girl-next-door sort of way, but Elizabeth couldn't see her with Kerra in any way.

Kerra smiled at her. "Does that surprise you?"

"Not at all. You seem to attract all sorts." Elizabeth hadn't meant for it to sound as bitter as it came out. "Wait. Did you and her...?" Elizabeth stopped herself, wondering if she really wanted to know, but Kerra answered anyway.

"No. Never."

"But she offered though," Lola interjected. "You remember that, Kerra?"

Kerra glared at Lola. She had spilled a detail Kerra obviously hadn't intended to disclose. "Yeah, Lola. I remember," she growled through gritted teeth.

"So, she offered, and you didn't..." Elizabeth couldn't help but be surprised. She loved Kerra, but she knew firsthand that she was an insatiable lover of the female form.

Kerra narrowed her eyes, taking offense to her shock. "No, I didn't. Contrary to popular belief, I have my standards."

"Plus, sleeping with girls that deep in the closet out here will get you six to the chest, no questions asked," Lola added.

"What?" Elizabeth stared at her, not sure if she was joking or not. She took a look around the bar, and all eyes were on them, watching and waiting for them to get uncomfortable enough to leave. Elizabeth had a sneaking suspicion that Lola was not exaggerating.

"Yeah, out here they think being gay is like being a witch or something.

Like, you can hex their women into sleeping with you," Lola started.

"Because God forbid they're actually gay and did it on their own volition," Kerra finished for her.

"Exactly," Lola agreed.

The bartender returned with a tray of drinks that she slid across the table as she stole another glance at Kerra. "Here ya go." She pulled a piece of paper from her pocket. "And here's the check," she said, placing the ticket onto the table. Elizabeth watched her, wincing at how uncomfortable she was. She didn't feel threatened by her at all; she just felt sorry for her.

"Thanks," Elizabeth offered.

Lola shot her a look of reprimand. Apparently, it was supposed to be them against the mountain people. Thanking any one of them was a breach of war terms.

The tiny blonde nodded an acknowledgement to her thanks without speaking another word before fleeing the table.

Krissy held up her glass and proposed a toast to Lizzie, breaking the awkward silence as they watched the bartender.

"Cheers." They all echoed one another as they clinked glasses together.

Kerra leaned over to slip her arm around Elizabeth, and she unconsciously leaned into her grip, the mechanical impulse to rest in Kerra's warmth overtaking her.

"P-D-A," Lola noted as she sat back in her chair and crossed her arms. "Won't be long now."

The two men in the bar grimaced at them, their faces contorting in abhorrence before they started toward their table.

"Keep your cool," Krissy warned under her breath as the men approached them.

They stopped in front of their table, hovering without a word. They used their size to command attention, casting their shadows over the table of women.

"Yes?" Krissy looked up from her glass, staring the tallest of the two directly in the eye, her indifference to their intimidating stance evident in her gaze.

He shook his head at her. "Nothing. Joe and I here," he started, tapping his friend against the belly with the back of his hand. "We was just wondering when you plan to stop bringing your little faggot up here to ruin everybody's weekend."

Kerra sucked at her teeth, making a visible effort not to react further as their eyes fell on her.

Krissy didn't move. She continued to stare him in the eye. It was Lola who reacted.

"Probably around the same time you start leaving your ignorance at home," Lola sneered.

Krissy broke her eye contact with the man to turn on Lola, giving her a look of reprimand.

"We ain't ignorant." The man gave Lola a glare before turning his gaze back to Kerra. He propped his hand against the table and leaned down to look Kerra in the eye. "We just can't figure out what this little twinkie is. Are you a girl or a boy, fruit fly?"

Kerra dropped her arm from around Elizabeth's shoulder as she balled her hands into fists. The rest of her body remained perfectly still as she kept her eyes on the man leaning in just a little too close to her.

"Seriously?" Elizabeth hadn't meant to interject, but wondering if Kerra was male or female was just about the dumbest thing she'd ever heard.

The man's eyes flickered from Kerra to Elizabeth. He attempted to make his way around the table to her, but Kerra slid her chair out to block his path, her eyes burning with a warning that was borderline threatening.

"Breathe, Kerra," Krissy whispered across the table, clearly seeing the same aggression flare in her that Elizabeth did.

Elizabeth mentally kicked herself for bringing attention to herself. Kerra wasn't ready to keep her cool for what was coming, and Elizabeth already knew that.

"Well, look at that," the man mused, letting out a laugh with his counterpart as his eyes burned into Elizabeth. "The beaner's faggot got a girlfriend." The man looked to Kerra and gave her a wink. "She's a pretty little nigger too."

Kerra shot to her feet, her fists balled at her sides, and her chest rising and falling at an accelerated rate. "What did you just say?"

Elizabeth stumbled to her feet, placing her hands on Kerra's shoulders. "Kerra, it's okay," she assured her, but Kerra shrugged her off.

Krissy and Lola tentatively climbed out of their seats, watching and waiting for their cue. Lola stood on the balls of her feet, ready to attack at any moment, while Krissy posed herself to subdue.

"What? You gonna fight me, you little he-she?" The man laughed, grabbing his partner's shoulder to bellow with him. "Well come on then. I'd love to kick the rainbow right out of you."

Kerra moved to take him up on his offer, and Elizabeth caught her arm. "You promised me you'd think." Elizabeth met her eyes, watching the fury in them inflame and die down.

Kerra dropped her hands to her sides before enclosing them around the back of her head in frustration. She let out a growl before running a hand through her hair, her breathing still coming in heavy.

"I've got to get the hell out of here," Kerra grumbled as she turned to leave the bar without giving any of them an opportunity to interject. Elizabeth followed on her heels. She could hear Krissy and Lola shuffling to pay the bill and follow their lead.

"Kerra," Elizabeth called after her.

Kerra whirled on her. "Lizzie, I can't right now. I just...can't." It was all she said before throwing herself into the driver's seat of Elizabeth's car and slamming the door behind her. Elizabeth watched from the outside as she banged her hand against the steering wheel in a solitary fit.

"Just, give her a bit." Krissy approached her from behind, giving her shoulders a light squeeze before she slipped into the backseat of the car with Lola following behind her.

Elizabeth wiped at her cheeks. She wasn't sure when she had started crying, but the wet paths down her face assured her that she had. She slipped silently into the car and rode without uttering a word back to the cabin. There was a quiet tension building between the four of them, and none of them ventured to break it.

By the time they made it back to the cabin, Elizabeth was nearly vibrating with emotion. She followed behind Kerra as she stormed through the cabin to their room.

Kerra whirled on her. "Look, Lizzie. I know. I know I should have handled that better. I know I shouldn't have stormed out. But what am I supposed to do? I just got—"

Elizabeth cut her off, throwing herself into her and pressing her lips into Kerra's. Her hands entwined themselves around the back of Kerra's head as she brought her in closer, deepening the kiss as her emotions grew hotter. "I'm not mad." Elizabeth finally released her lips, to assure her that anger was the furthest thing from her mind.

"You're not?" Kerra looked down at her skeptically, and Elizabeth shook her head. "But I thought—"

"Well you were wrong." Elizabeth pushed their mouths together again, letting her hand sneak its way up Kerra's shirt as their lips intermingled.

"But what about Krissy and Lola?" Kerra asked breathlessly.

Elizabeth shrugged, bringing her lips to Kerra's ear to whisper. "What about them?"

CHAPTER TWENTY-EIGHT

Elizabeth rolled over onto her side, working to catch her breath. She'd never understand how she managed to live her life without the euphoric pleasures that Kerra gave her.

"If I had known I'd get these kind of rewards for not hitting people, I'd have probably gotten in less fights in my youth." Kerra reached out to brush a stray braid away from her face.

Elizabeth let out a giggle as she leaned forward to place a peck on her lips. "I'll never get tired of this," she declared, letting out a sigh of sheer contentment.

"Never?"

Elizabeth shook her head. "Never," she repeated.

"Never is a pretty long time." Kerra wrapped an arm around her waist and pulled her in closer.

"I know." She reached out to stroke Kerra's cheek before resting her hand in her hair. "Every time I think about my life five years from now, or ten years from now, or even fifty years from now, you're always there."

"Yeah?" Kerra's smile widened.

"Yeah." Elizabeth closed the tiny gap between them, pushing her body against Kerra's. "I want to be with you forever."

Kerra licked her lips before placing them on Elizabeth's. "Did you just propose to me?" she asked with a smile pressed against Elizabeth's lips.

Elizabeth giggled, pushing her away and onto her back. "No."

"Are you sure because it sounded kind of like a proposal." Kerra chuckled.

"If I was, would you say yes?" Elizabeth probed.

Kerra raised an eyebrow at her. "Are you?"

"No." Elizabeth shook her head.

"Hmph." Kerra moved closer to her, returning their bodies to a touching position. "Probably for the best. I should do the proposing, since I'm the one that can afford the ring."

Elizabeth let out a squeal. "So, you're saying no to me because I don't have a ring?" She set her lips in a pout.

Kerra let out a laugh. "So, you are proposing."

"No," Elizabeth protested again. She leaned in to press a kiss to Kerra's collarbone, but the knock at the door stopped her.

"Hey, if you guys are done in there, Krissy's ready to get inked," Lola's voice teased through the wood.

Elizabeth's face heated up as she sank beneath the covers. "Oh my God, I forgot that they could hear."

Kerra uncovered her. "Trust me, love, they knew we were having sex long before today."

Elizabeth eyed her, debating if she wanted to ask for further elaboration and deciding against it. "Fair enough." She climbed out of the bed and then started picking up her carelessly discarded items of clothing strewn around the room. "So, what are you getting?" she asked, slipping on her shorts.

Kerra fastened the buttons down her shirt as she thought it over. "Uh, I don't know. Whatever Lola's in the mood for, I guess."

Elizabeth smirked at her. "Good to see you take something so permanent so seriously."

Kerra gave her a shrug. "If I go to my grave covered in Lola's therapeutic artwork, I'll call it a win."

Elizabeth stopped straightening her shirt to stare at Kerra. "That's actually kind of sweet."

Kerra smiled at her. "I have my moments."

Elizabeth crossed the room to wrap her arms around her. "Yeah, you do," she agreed as she placed a kiss to her lips, reigniting a fire that she should have let simmer.

Lola banged on the door again, interrupting their kindling. "Come on," she insisted through the door.

Elizabeth released Kerra. She let out a laugh as she pulled the handle, swinging the door open. She led them down the hallway to Lola's room.

"Finally," Lola grunted at them from her chair in the corner.

Krissy flashed Elizabeth an all-knowing smile that made her ears burn red.

"All right, you're up, Mom." Lola tapped at the seat of her tattoo chair, gesturing for Krissy to take it.

Krissy plopped down on the chair, turning her back to Lola. "No swearing, no obscenity, and nothing rude," Krissy warned as she tied her hair into a messy bun on top of her head.

"Yeah, Mom, I know. Only rainbows and sunshine on this canvas." Lola rolled her eyes as she wiped at the skin across Krissy's back.

"You don't tell her what to do either?" Elizabeth was completely mystified by the immensity of trust they put in Lola's hands.

Krissy shook her head at her in response, and Elizabeth took another look around the dungeon-like room, wondering how they could be so completely out of their minds to trust someone so erratic.

Elizabeth watched on in awe as Lola worked with Krissy's skin. It was almost as absorbing as watching Kerra work. Lola took careful steps putting together each piece of the tiny, intricate artwork that she placed between Krissy's shoulder blades.

The room had fallen into silence as Lola worked. The only sound penetrating the air was the tiny buzzing of her tattoo gun as she glided in across her canvas.

"It's beautiful." Elizabeth finally spoke. She had no idea what she was looking at, but the intricate web of shapes and colors really suited the eccentricity of Krissy.

"Thank you." Lola beamed at her as she wiped at her finished product and handed Krissy a tiny mirror.

Krissy nodded at the reflection of her tattoo in approval. "Another job well done." She reached out to pat Lola's shoulder as Lola wrapped her new artwork in a plastic cover.

"All right, you're up." Lola motioned for Kerra to come forward, but Elizabeth stopped her, climbing to her feet and moving to the chair.

"Hey, do you mind if I get one?"

Lola stared at her, blinking in shock and silence. Elizabeth looked to Kerra who was also staring at her in surprise. She didn't need to glance at Krissy to know that she was probably doing the same.

"What? I can't want a tattoo?" Elizabeth felt insulted by their surprise.

"Of course you can, love. It's just..." Kerra tried to find the words.

"Well, it just doesn't seem like your thing," Lola finished for her.

Elizabeth let out a sigh of indignation. "Well, I'm full of surprises."

Lola cocked her head at her. "Are you though?"

Elizabeth let out a grunt. "Yes. I am."

Kerra reached out for her. "I don't know that this is a good idea, Lizzie."

"Well it's probably a good thing that I wasn't asking you then," Elizabeth retorted, turning her gaze back to Lola. "Please, Lola."

Lola shrugged. "Sure. Why the hell not? Have a seat." She smiled at her, ignoring the glare she received from Kerra. "So...what do you want?"

Elizabeth took a seat and pursed her lips. "I don't know." She decided she must have caught the insanity too. "Do what you feel," she suggested, surprising herself and Lola too, as her eyebrows shot into her hair.

"Okay. Where do you want it?"

Elizabeth gave her another shrug. She really hadn't thought things through. "Maybe...here?" She pointed at a spot near her clavicle.

"Okay. Are you sure?" Lola asked again, staring into her eyes for any hints of doubt. Elizabeth nodded. She wasn't entirely sure, but it was too late to back out.

Lola moved around quickly, doing things to the front of her shoulder that she didn't see a point to. Kerra moved to her side, clutching her hand and placing a kiss to her cheek, her will to protest obviously gone.

"This is actually kind of badass," Kerra whispered into her ear before kissing the side of her head.

"I know." Elizabeth couldn't help the cocky grin that spread across her face. She waited for what seemed like an eternity for Lola to draw out what she planned to permanently place onto Elizabeth's body.

"Do you want to see it first?" Lola asked her as she loitered over her with a square sheet of paper.

Elizabeth shook her head. "No, just do it." She didn't want any extra reasons to doubt herself. She only wanted to see it when it was too late to do anything but like it.

Lola nodded in understanding and prepped her tools in silence.

Elizabeth closed her eyes as she waited for the buzz of the gun to ring in her ears, but she opened them again when it didn't come. She let out a sigh as Lola laid the outline against her skin. She rolled her eyes at all the prep work. The anticipation was killing her. She was ready for it all to be over.

Just as the thought occurred to her Lola picked up her gun. "Okay, here we go," she warned before pressing it to her skin.

"Oww, son of a..." Elizabeth bit back the profanity, grinding her teeth against the eye-watering pain in her shoulder.

"Hurts, huh?" Kerra laughed alongside Lola and Krissy who stared down at her in amusement.

Elizabeth fought the urge to cry out again, clutching at Kerra's hand tight enough that she was sure she was going to break it.

☆☆☆

"Okay. You're good." Lola finally finished her dance of pain across Elizabeth's skin. She handed her the tiny mirror to check out her new lifetime ink.

Elizabeth stared at the tattoo in silence, taking it in with awe. The intricate design of a tiny heart-shaped lock with an "L" decorating it sat staring back at her. "It's perfect." She meant it, even though if it wasn't, it was forever. She loved every bit of Lola's creation, and though Lola wasn't aware, it represented everything in her life that she had come to hold sacred. The cursive "L" across the lock seemed to smile at her. The new body decoration reaffirmed that she was now and forever Lizzie.

CHAPTER TWENTY-NINE

Elizabeth woke with a smile on her lips that quickly gave way to a grimace as the soreness in her shoulder attacked her. "Ow," she called out, sitting up in horror as she immediately went into panic mode. *Pain equals infection.*

"Kerra?" she called out, realizing in a huff that she wasn't lying beside her any longer. She climbed out of the bed to search for her, and a piece of paper came floating out of the bed with her.

Went for beer with Krissy.

Elizabeth stared down at the words on the note. "Great. I'm dying, and you're out getting beer," she grumbled, realizing that her dramatic side was beginning to flare. She took a deep breath and looked at the note again, a realization hitting her as she did.

"Lola?" She climbed out of the bed and then slipped on an oversized shirt to cover herself as she bolted down the hallway to knock on Lola's door. "Lola?" she called out again, her heart sinking as she realized Lola might be gone too.

She jumped back in surprise when Lola swung the door open. A scowl painted her face as she stared daggers at Elizabeth for disrupting her sleep. "What, Lizzie?"

"Oh, I—uh...I think I have an infection."

Lola's squint quickly disappeared as her eyes popped wide open. "I don't think I'm qualified to help you with that, Lizzie."

Elizabeth shook her head at her. "What? What are you talking about? The tattoo. I think the tattoo is infected."

Lola's face softened in understanding. "Oh." She nodded as she propped herself against her door frame. "Okay. First-time paranoia. I get it." She pressed a hand to her mouth as she yawned. "Does it burn or sting?"

Elizabeth took a moment, trying to pinpoint the type of pain she was feeling. "No. It just kind of hurts."

"Hurts like a hundred needles inserted ink into your skin over and over again?" Lola raised an eyebrow at her, and she flushed with embarrassment.

"Yeah," Elizabeth answered, looking at her feet.

"Yeah, well that's sort of to be expected, Lizzie. It'll feel like that for a day or two. Just take care of it like I told you to, and you'll be fine, all right." Lola reached out and squeezed her arms in support.

"Yeah, all right." Elizabeth suddenly felt like the dumbest person on the planet as she turned on her heels to head back to her room.

"Hey, Lizzie," Lola called out, stopping her in her tracks.

"Yeah?"

"Can I ask you for a favor?" Lola's tone took on a soft edge that Elizabeth had never heard from her before.

"Uh, yeah. Sure." Elizabeth returned to linger in her doorway with her.

"Can you, maybe, keep Kerra occupied tonight?"

Elizabeth stared at her skeptically.

"It's just, Ralph is still around, and I wanted to maybe see her, just for a little bit tonight before she has to go back into exile," Lola explained.

Elizabeth nodded. "I see." She toyed at a loose braid. "Is there a reason that Kerra hates her so much?" She wanted more information before she agreed to a deal that would make her public enemy number one in Kerra's eyes. She was sure to receive some sort of probation for even entertaining the idea.

Lola let out a sigh, seeming to sink farther into the frame of the door as she did. "Ralph didn't always treat me very kindly, and Kerra can be a bit overbearing, as you may have noticed."

Elizabeth let out a chuckle. "Oh, you mean kind of like you?"

Lola stared at her in disbelief and denial. "Me?"

"You didn't exactly welcome me with open arms, Lola."

"Oh, that." Lola waved her off. "That was just a little friendly initiation. Kerra is downright cruel."

Elizabeth shrugged, not wanting to push the fact that Lola exhibited her own set of cruelties.

"Will you keep her busy?"

"I don't know, Lola. This Ralph girl sounds like bad news." She didn't approve of Kerra's methods for keeping them apart, but she had to admit, the chips were stacking up to paint Ralph in a pretty negative light.

"And I'll admit that she was, but she's trying to change, Lizzie." Lola stared down at her feet. "And where would Kerra be if she hadn't been given a second chance? Or a third? Or a fourth?"

"Okay, okay. I get it. I get it." Elizabeth mulled over the pros and cons, debating if she would ever be able to make Kerra see that Lola was an adult capable of making her own choices. "Maybe we can just talk to Kerra together and—" Elizabeth started, but Lola cut her off.

"Come on, Lizzie. You know Kerra better than that. She's never going to see me as anything more than the little kid that clung to her leg, yearning for her approval. She can't even help herself." As Lola met her eyes, Elizabeth knew she was right. Lola would always be the little girl who brought her popsicles, and Kerra would never approve of her taking a risk on someone that was likely to hurt her, no matter how much she wanted it.

"All right, I'll keep her occupied," Elizabeth agreed reluctantly.

Lola wrapped her arms around her neck with a squeal. "Thank you."

Elizabeth returned the embrace. "Just, know your worth okay? Don't let Ralph mistreat you."

Lola took a step back to meet her eyes before giving her a silent nod of understanding.

Elizabeth tucked a strand of golden hair behind Lola's ear before leaving her doorway to return to her room with an odd mix of feelings. Without her realizing it, it seemed she and Lola had somehow become friends.

☆☆☆

Elizabeth managed to get dressed and make lunch for herself and Lola before her irritation with Kerra set in. She and Krissy had been gone for hours, and Elizabeth couldn't help but feel slighted by the lack of a phone call. "Geez, how much beer did they go to get?" She pouted distantly to Lola.

Lola sat cross-legged on the dark sofa in front of her as she shrugged her shoulders. "Who knows. Krissy and Kerra can drink all day and then some."

Elizabeth considered how much alcohol she had watched Kerra consume in the past and nodded in agreement as she tapped her foot against her chair. She was getting impatient. The sun had begun to dip below the horizon, and she missed the comfort of Kerra's arms.

Lola nervously clicked her fingers against the fabric of the sofa. Her timeline to meet up with Ralph hadn't accounted for Kerra being missing in action all night. "Where the hell are—?"

Before Lola could finish the thought, Krissy and Kerra came stumbling through the door, sharing an overly boisterous laugh with one another.

"Where were you guys?" Lola huffed in annoyance at them.

"We went for drinks and then a walk…" Krissy stumbled over her words.

"And then more drinks," Kerra giggled.

Lola crossed her arms as she looked on at them in disapproval. Krissy rolled her eyes before turning to leave the cabin again.

"Wait, where are you going?" Lola probed.

"Azul is outside. We're going to go sightseeing."

Kerra wiggled her eyebrows at Lola, and she let out a giggle through her anger.

"Fine. Go." Lola practically pushed her out of the door once she composed herself.

"You guys don't want to come?" Krissy offered, still tripping over herself as she slurred.

"Nope. All of the sights I want to see are here," Kerra answered as she made her way across the room to scoop up Elizabeth.

Elizabeth let out a laugh as Kerra wrapped her arms around her, pushing her backwards toward their room. She had intended to make a fuss about Kerra's disappearing act, but all the anger floated out of her as Kerra's hands clutched her waist.

"Great. Everyone's got plans. I'll just hang out here," Lola shouted after them, throwing Elizabeth a thumbs-up.

Elizabeth rolled her eyes at her. She wasn't purposely luring Kerra to the bedroom for Lola's rendezvous, but Lola clearly thought it was for her benefit.

Elizabeth let out a gasp as her legs flew out from under her and her back met the soft plush of the mattress. Kerra delivered a soft kiss to her lips as she tumbled down to the bed with her.

"Hey." Elizabeth pulled their lips apart, feeling the urgent need to express herself. "I really missed you today." Kerra met her eyes, and she pushed a strand of dark hair from her face.

"I really missed you too, love."

Elizabeth narrowed her eyes at her. "No, you didn't."

Kerra let out a giggle. "Yeah, I really did. I had fun with Krissy, but I still missed you."

Elizabeth kept her gaze on her, a smile creeping at the corner of her lips. "Do you want to drink some more?" She wormed her way out from under Kerra and scurried over to her bag in the corner to retrieve the bottle of mystery vodka Angela had gifted her.

"Yeah, I could probably up my buzz." Kerra smiled as she pulled the bottle out, modeling it like a lavish car.

A pair of bright headlights flashed into the window, temporarily blinding them both. "Who the hell?" Kerra climbed off the bed to her feet and headed toward the window, but Elizabeth blocked her path, pushing her back to the bed. She made a mental note to skewer Lola for not telling Ralph to be more incognito about her arrival.

"How about we play a game?" Elizabeth deflected the question, catching Kerra's attention.

"Okay." Kerra plopped back onto the edge of the bed, forgetting about the distracting headlights.

"This game is called...questions." Elizabeth moved forward, placing her legs on either side of Kerra to straddle her at the foot of the bed.

Kerra's grin widened. "Okay. Yeah." She nodded. "I think I may have played this one once or twice."

Elizabeth wagged her bottle of vodka. "No, you haven't played this one. This is my own special game of questions."

Kerra lifted an eyebrow at her. "I see. Well, how do you play?"

Elizabeth let a smile dance on her lips. "Well, I'll ask a yes or no question, and if you answer yes—" Elizabeth unscrewed the top of the vodka bottle. "—you have to drink. And if you answer no…" Elizabeth took a sip of the burning liquid. "Ugh." She let out a cough, shocked by the strength of the liquor. "I have to drink," she finished.

Kerra giggled at her reaction to the alcohol. "Do I get to ask questions?"

Elizabeth shook her head.

"Well, that doesn't seem fair."

Elizabeth shrugged her shoulders before she let out a sigh. "Okay, you can have a question for every three of mine."

"All right," Kerra agreed.

Elizabeth placed her arms to rest on Kerra's shoulders, continuing to keep her in place between her legs. "Okay, first question." She waved the bottle around as she debated what to ask. "Have you ever kissed a boy?"

Kerra let out a fit of laughter. "You know if you took your pants off this would be exactly like a fantasy I used to have in middle school."

"Oh yeah?" Elizabeth pursed her lips in thought before she climbed off the bed to slip her shorts down the length of her legs. She kicked them across the room. "Happy vacation, middle-school-Kerra," she shouted with a grin before returning to her position to straddle Kerra.

Kerra licked at her lips, taking in the thin barricade of panty between them. She reached out to grip Elizabeth's waist, slipping her hands down the small of her back to find their way to a private destination.

"Hey, no." Elizabeth returned her hands to her waist. "You have to answer the question."

Kerra let out a grunt before the smile returned to her lips. "Okay. Umm…yes." She took the bottle from Elizabeth's hand and prepared herself to drink.

"What? Really? Nu-uh. When?" Elizabeth stared at her in disbelief.

Kerra bit down on her lip, thinking to herself. "When I was eleven. One of my brother's friends kind of cornered me, and I wasn't sure what else to do."

Elizabeth stared down at her. She shook her head and took the bottle from her hands before taking a drink. She laced her fingers into Kerra's hair. "No, baby. Some kid taking advantage doesn't count." She placed a kiss onto Kerra's lips and felt her smile.

Elizabeth let her go, meeting her eyes and feeling her chest explode with familiar affection.

"Okay, next question." Kerra dropped her hands from Elizabeth's waist to lean back and prop herself up onto her palms.

"Okay. Umm...have you ever blamed Lola for something you did?" Elizabeth sat back as she waited for the answer.

"Nope. Drink," Kerra commanded.

"Never?" Elizabeth questioned.

"Never. Lola's blamed me for a ton of shit though."

Elizabeth laughed before she sucked in a deep breath, holding it as she downed another swig from the bottle.

Kerra laughed at her. "How are you losing at your own game?"

Elizabeth let out an exasperated gasp of indignation. "I'm not losing. I'm just not winning."

Kerra sat up. She leaned in to kiss Elizabeth, pulling her in closer for a moment before releasing her again. "It's okay. I still love you."

"Did you love her?" *Sierra*. She couldn't bring herself to say her name out loud. She let the question roll off her tongue before she had a moment to think it over.

Kerra stared at her in silence. Neither of them ventured to make a sound. Kerra finally cut through the quiet, breaking their locked gaze as she turned her eyes away from her. "I thought I did."

Elizabeth swallowed, not sure if she was ready to hear any part of what was coming. She took a drink from the bottle, even though she wasn't sure she had lost.

"Before you, I thought that's what love felt like. I thought that she accepted me for all of my flaws and that loving me was being willing to be in the trenches with me."

"And now?" Her lips trembled as she asked the question.

"And now, I know better. Real love is not following someone down the rabbit hole. It's giving them a reason to want to climb out of the darkness." Kerra returned her eyes to meet Elizabeth's. "That's what you do for me. Every day, you give me a reason." She ran her thumb across Elizabeth's cheek as her eyes stayed trained on hers.

The air caught in Elizabeth's throat, and she melted beneath that stare. She leaned forward, suddenly needing every part of Kerra. She placed her lips against hers, pushing herself in closer to her body and making her hunger evident.

Kerra's hand automatically went up to cup her face, while the other roamed her body, clutching at her in areas that matched her needs.

"It's your question," Elizabeth said breathlessly into Kerra's kiss.

Kerra licked her lips, resting her forehead against Elizabeth's. "What are you thinking right now?" Her breathing was just as ragged as Elizabeth's as she posed the question.

Elizabeth gently shook her head as it rested against Kerra's. "That's not a yes or no question."

Kerra leaned in to kiss her again, but Elizabeth pulled back, enjoying the tease.

Kerra let out a sigh. "Are you thinking what I'm thinking?"

Elizabeth smiled, taking a long sip from the bottle before returning her lips to Kerra's. She pushed her backwards, leaning into her until her back met the mattress, and Elizabeth lorded over her, bottle in hand.

She held her hand to Kerra's chest, pinning her in place, as she delivered a kiss to her chin and then to her collarbone. "Do you like it when I kiss you here?" Elizabeth placed a slow, long kiss to Kerra's neck.

Kerra let out a soft sigh as she nodded. Elizabeth sat up to meet her eyes. She handed her the bottle. "Drink."

Kerra smiled at her, never taking her eyes off her as she sat up to take a smooth sip of liquid.

Elizabeth kissed her lips again, and a smile spread across her face as she posed her next question. "Are you wet for me?"

Kerra returned the bottle to her lips, and Elizabeth's grin grew. She unbuttoned Kerra's jeans to slip her hand inside and check Kerra's answer.

Kerra let out a choked sound as Elizabeth touched her, circling her as her lips traveled back to her neck. Kerra lifted her hips into her hand and let out a soft moan that was music to Elizabeth's ears. She loved to make her moan; it was a sound she never got tired of hearing.

Elizabeth dropped her lips to toy at Kerra's chest through the thin fabric of her T-shirt. She was thankful for Kerra's anti-bra stance as a shiver went through Kerra's body at the close contact of Elizabeth's lips against her breast.

"Mmm...no, Lizzie, don't stop. It feels good," Kerra encouraged her, but Elizabeth's hand had stopped its circles, and her lips had ceased their motion.

She removed her hand from Kerra's pants and then rolled off her to sit up straight.

"Love?" Kerra sat up with her, disheveled and confused.

"Kerra, I don't..." She stopped talking as the room began to swim, and every drop of alcohol began to catch up with her. She scrambled off the bed and bolted to the bathroom, barely making it over the toilet as the contents of her belly emptied themselves.

Kerra followed after her, scrunching up her face as she stood in the doorway watching Elizabeth puke into the toilet bowl. She let out a sigh as she rebuttoned her pants. "This is why I don't sleep with drunk girls," she grumbled to herself before crouching down to rub at Elizabeth's back. "You okay, love?"

Elizabeth waved her off. "Yeah, it's okay. I just need to get it all out, and then we can finish." She held up a finger as another wave of vomit attacked her throat.

Kerra held her hair, shaking her head and frowning down at her. "I think the mood is sufficiently dead, love. Maybe tomorrow." She handed Elizabeth a towel from the sink. Elizabeth wiped her mouth with it.

"I'm sorry, baby."

"It's okay." Kerra let out a soft giggle before wrapping her arm around her shoulders and lifting her to her feet. "Come on, let's get some water in you and get you to bed."

Kerra shouldered her weight, gently laying her down across the bed before scurrying away to place a waste bin next to her.

"I think...I think I'm okay now," Elizabeth muttered deliriously. She closed her eyes to the spinning room in front of her.

"Kerra?" She frowned into the darkness behind her eyelids as she received no response. "Kerra?" she called out again.

"Yeah, love. I'm here." She could hear Kerra moving around the room, but her eyelids refused to open. "Here." Elizabeth felt her head being moved by Kerra's soft hands as she propped her up. "Take this and drink this." She opened her eyes as Kerra placed a small pill in her hand and shoved a water glass into her face.

Elizabeth shook her head in defiance. "I don't want to."

Kerra frowned at her. "You'll regret it in the morning."

Elizabeth pursed her lips in a pout as she stared down at the pill. "No."

Kerra let out a grunt. "Christ, Lizzie." Kerra crouched to meet her eyes. "Please?"

Elizabeth stared back at several pairs of blue eyes that all seemed to blend together in a dancing blur. She popped the pill into her mouth and then swallowed reluctantly. "Okay."

Kerra brought the glass of water to her lips and waited for her to drink. Elizabeth cautiously took sips from the glass before the weight of her head began to be too much for her neck. She slumped forward, the drunkenness overwhelming her limbs as it inched through every part of her.

"Okay, okay." Kerra tensed as Elizabeth's body became dead weight in her arms. She laid her back down flat across the bed. "All right, get some sleep."

"Kerra?" Elizabeth's lips seemed to move of their own volition.

"Yeah?"

"I do want to marry you."

Kerra placed a kiss to her heated forehead. "I know, love. I'll make it happen."

☆☆☆

Elizabeth woke up with her arms wrapped around a waste bin and the threatening feeling of nausea in her gut. She let out a groan as she sat up to prop herself against the headboard. She waited for the headache to hit, but it never came. *Well, at least there's that.* She silently thanked the universe for not punishing her as severely as she certainly deserved. "I'm never drinking again," she announced out loud to no one in particular.

"Yeah, I've heard that one before." Kerra sleepily rolled over to face her.

Elizabeth didn't acknowledge her. She stared down at her waste bin, clutching her torso and preparing to throw up whatever was left in her body. Instead, she was attacked with a series of dry heaves, giving her no actual release from the growing queasiness in her belly.

"No, I mean it," she affirmed after she finished gagging over the trash can. Kerra leaned over to place a kiss on her arm before she climbed out of bed and headed for the bedroom door.

"Where are you...?" Elizabeth never finished the question as a vodka-drenched burp stuck in her throat. The taste in her mouth was enough to bring on the vomiting.

Elizabeth closed her eyes to the puddle of sick sloshing at the bottom of the bin in her lap as she patiently waited over it for any aftershocks. "Never again," she reaffirmed as she gagged over the makeshift bucket.

"Here."

She opened her eyes to see Kerra had returned and was thrusting a glass of water at her. "Thank you," she noted as she gratefully accepted the glass.

"And I'll go burn this," Kerra joked as she removed the bin from Elizabeth's clutches before disappearing down the hallway with a grimace.

Elizabeth downed the water, feeling better as it flooded her empty stomach. She breathed in deep, feeling some of the nausea subside after her last vomiting session. Her fingers shook unrelentingly against the glass from a combination of dehydration and the shock to her body from spewing everything inside it in the last twenty-four hours, but overall she felt fairly functional. She began to reconsider her proclamation to never drink again. Never was an awful long time.

"I think I feel better," Elizabeth announced as Kerra reentered the room with a new, clean trash can.

Kerra crashed down onto the bed next to her. "Good, because after getting rid of that, I think now *I'm* hungover."

Elizabeth rolled her eyes at her in response.

"Hey, you remember when I told you you could make anything sexy?" Kerra asked through giggles. She had obviously found a way to humor herself through Elizabeth's pain.

Elizabeth narrowed her eyes at her. "You should *really* think about what you plan to say next before you say it," she warned.

Kerra nodded, a smile still playing at her lips. "Got it. Too soon."

Elizabeth gave her one last eye roll. "I think I need food...and a toothbrush. Probably not in that order."

Kerra sat up, placing a kiss on her cheek before shuffling off the bed. "I'll get on the breakfast part. I'll leave the tooth-brushing business to you."

Elizabeth watched after her as she disappeared down the hallway. She had no idea how Kerra could manage to be so functioning in the mornings after drinking as much as she did. She slowly made her way out of bed and dragged her feet across the hallway to the bathroom. Lazily, she prepared her toothbrush to get rid of the disgusting taste in her mouth.

She halfheartedly ran the brush across her teeth and jumped in surprise as Lola's face hovered above her in the bathroom mirror.

"Hey," Lola greeted her as she met the reflection of her eyes.

"Hey," Elizabeth grumbled around a mouth full of toothbrush.

"Thanks for last night." Lola gave her a smile as she shrugged in nonchalant gratitude.

Elizabeth nodded in response before remembering that she was upset with Lola. She spat a cheek full of toothpaste into the sink before she whirled on her. "Hey, so the next time you ask me to cover for you, how about you use a little discretion?"

Lola stared at her in confusion. "What?"

"Yeah. The bright headlights shining into our window just about blew everything to hell."

Lola's face clouded over with more confusion. "I have no idea what you're talking about, Lizzie. Ralph walked here last night." She held up two fingers in a promise. "I swear. Whatever lights you saw, they weren't ours."

"Oh." Elizabeth suddenly felt guilty for her assault on Lola's character. "Okay then."

"Okay."

The two of them stood awkwardly staring at one another, both uncertain of what to do next.

"Did you have fun?" Elizabeth groaned at herself. She sounded like an old mom trying too hard to connect.

Lola gave her a slow nod, sensing the awkward pit that they were slipping into. "Okay, I'm going to go see if Krissy came back last night." She excused herself, and Elizabeth breathed a sigh of relief. She was still too weak to navigate the waters of conversation with Lola.

Elizabeth returned her toothbrush to her mouth and let her mind roam around what Kerra might be whipping up for breakfast. She desperately hoped it was something that would stay down. She was feeling better, but she was wary. Her body had suddenly caught the chills, even though the air around her was warm. It was a sign that the hangover was not done with her.

"Kerra?" She placed her toothbrush back into its casing. She made her way to the kitchen. "Kerra?"

"Yeah, love?" Kerra shouted back at her, no doubt whisking away at some dish that Elizabeth couldn't make in a million years.

"Did you pack any jackets?" Elizabeth stepped into the kitchen, smiling at the sight of Kerra over the stove. If she hadn't been freezing, she'd have stayed to watch the show.

"I think there's one in the car," Kerra informed her, without taking her eyes off her meal in progress.

Elizabeth nodded, giving Kerra one last once-over before heading for the front door. She sucked in a breath as she gripped the handle, preparing herself for the cool air of the outdoors.

She swung the door open, shivering at the expected gust of wind that smacked her in the face before the air caught in her throat. She took three timid steps forward, bringing the full view of her car into focus before she sank down to the ground. She inched herself forward to rest against the railing of the porch as she stared out at the hateful slurs scrawled in paint across her car.

Elizabeth stared on in silence. She'd experienced hate before, and she'd experienced vandalism, but something about the sight in front of her struck a painful chord. She could feel the nausea in her stomach build up again, and this time she knew it wasn't from the hangover. She could feel tears burning at the back of her eyes, but she stopped herself from letting them fall. She wouldn't give whoever had done this the satisfaction. She wished she could find the strength to pull herself off the ground, but her limbs had given up on her, forcing her to keep staring at the atrocity in front of her without reprieve. She had no idea how long she sat there before Lola's arms engulfed her.

"Oh my God." Lola embraced her, dropping to her knees to bring her into her chest. "Kerra!" Elizabeth could hear her shouting Kerra's name, but she couldn't quite process what was happening. She flopped back and forth in Lola's arms, swaying with her movements. "Kerra," Lola shouted again.

Kerra was nearly tripping over herself as she spilled out of the house with a spatula still in her hand. "What?" she sneered before catching sight of the two of them crumpled on the ground. Her annoyed facial expression was immediately replaced with concern. "Woah, hey love. What's going on?" She crouched down to meet them at eye level.

Elizabeth still couldn't find the will to move herself, and Lola took the lead, pointing Kerra's line of sight in the direction of her car.

Kerra found the destruction, hastily painted across all ends of her car, and fury set in her features. "What the—"

"It's those assholes, Sam and Joe." Lola climbed to her feet, letting go of Elizabeth to face Kerra. "Every year they harass us, and every year we let it slide, but *this*..." Lola shook her head in outrage. "This is crossing the line, Kerra."

Kerra nodded, emphatically bouncing on the balls of her feet like a bull that had been caged too long. "You're right," she agreed. She disappeared into the cabin and returned a moment later with two long wooden bats in her hands. She handed one to Lola, which she accepted without a word. She followed on her heels as Kerra led them down the steps of the porch.

"Where are you going?" Elizabeth finally found her voice.

Kerra rested her bat across her shoulders. "I'm going to go teach those dicks a lesson."

"Kerra." Elizabeth climbed to her feet and then shakily walked herself down the steps. "What are you doing?"

"I just told you," Kerra insisted, shrugging off her tone.

"Kerra." Elizabeth couldn't mask the disappointment in her voice.

"Lizzie, I know. I promised I'd think. But I *am* thinking. We can't just let—"

Elizabeth shook her head, backing away from Kerra as she reached out for her. "You're not listening, Kerra. How can you not get this?" Every tear that Elizabeth had managed to hold back came spilling from her eyes.

"Lizzie." Kerra let her bat fall off her shoulders to rest at her side as she reached out for her again. "I-I don't..." Kerra searched her eyes, trying to find some sort of answers.

Elizabeth wiped at her cheeks with her fingertips. She closed her eyes to Kerra and the monstrous sight behind her, trying to compose herself. "Kerra." She opened her eyes, feeling a sob choke at the back of her throat as the images of hate flooded her vision again. "Look at this." She stomped to her car, gesturing at it as an indescribable hurt and anger built in her chest. "People that don't even know me did this. The most hateful words, delivered to me in the most hateful way. Do you think that I'm not angry? That I'm not hurt?" Tears sprayed from her eyes in an uncontrollable stream.

"Lizzie, I—" Kerra started, but Elizabeth cut her off.

"I don't need vengeance, Kerra. I don't need you to jet off into the night with your sidekick to avenge my honor. I just need..." Elizabeth's voice gave out on her as the building emotions attacked her. The tears in her eyes blinded her to everything but the blurry outline of Kerra in front of her. "I just want my girlfriend to hold me and tell me everything is going to be okay." Elizabeth finally got the words out before her legs gave out from underneath her.

"Hey, hey, hey, I got you." Kerra's arms caught her as she went down. "It is going to be okay." Kerra wrapped her arms around her, holding her in against her chest. "I promise. It's all going to be okay." Kerra held her in tighter, resting her chin against the top of her head. "I'm sorry," she whispered, as she stroked her hand against Elizabeth's hair. "It's all going to be okay," she repeated again as Elizabeth sobbed in her arms.

CHAPTER THIRTY

Elizabeth woke up to the soft sounds of someone sleeping next to her. She frowned in disappointment when she realized it wasn't Kerra.

"Krissy?" She softly nudged Krissy awake.

Krissy wiped at her eyes with her fingertips and shot straight up in the bed. "Oh sorry, honey. I guess I fell asleep for a bit."

"No, it's okay." Elizabeth sat up, scratching at her head in confusion. "Hey, umm...why are you in our bed?" She attempted to pose the question as gently as she could manage.

"Oh, you fell asleep, and Kerra assigned me to keep an eye over you," Krissy answered with a yawn.

Elizabeth let out a sigh. "And where is Kerra?" She knew there was no answer that wouldn't make her angry.

Krissy slid to the edge of the bed, putting distance between them. She must have seen the spark of fury ignite in Elizabeth. "She's outside with Lola and Azul trying to get the paint off. They've been out there for a few hours."

Elizabeth dropped her head into her hands and resisted the urge to cry into them. Tears of frustration burned at the back of her eyes, threatening to break her resolve.

"What's the problem, honey?" Krissy reached out for her, placing a hand on her back.

Elizabeth kept her head in her hands, knowing that if she met Krissy's eyes the tears would fall. "It's like talking to a wall, Krissy. I say 'be here for me' and all she hears is 'fix it for me.' I just..." Elizabeth hugged her knees into her body. "I don't know." The urge to cry had turned into the urge to scream.

Krissy slid closer, placing her free hand on her leg to cradle her. "Kerra is a fixer. She can't even help herself. To her, being there for you *is* fixing it."

Elizabeth curled into her, appreciating her warmth. She let out a sigh against her. "God, she drives me insane. On every level. I don't think I've ever had anyone love me the way that Kerra does."

Krissy stroked at her hair, offering her a motherly comfort. "Don't I know it. Lola and Kerra are ferocious individuals. Everything they do comes with intensity. But with that extreme love comes a hundred other extremes. Passion always comes with consequences."

Elizabeth nodded in her arms. "And I'll take them. Every time."

Krissy held her closer, grateful for her answer.

"But she still makes me want to rip my own hair out," Elizabeth added.

Krissy chuckled into her hair. "I know, honey. I know."

Elizabeth let Krissy hold her for a long time before they heard Lola and Kerra stumble through the door of the cabin with Azul.

Elizabeth climbed off the bed with Krissy. The two of them trudged down the hallway to meet their counterparts. Krissy leaped to Azul's side, discreetly touching him and speaking to him in whispered tones.

Lola rolled her eyes at them before making her way to Elizabeth. She placed her hands on Elizabeth's shoulders and stared into her eyes. She sucked in a breath, preparing to say something, but then appeared to lose the words.

Elizabeth gave her a gentle smile, understanding the words that she didn't say. She brought Lola into her arms for a hug and sighed contentedly when she felt her return it. Lola let go and gave her a grateful nod before making her way farther down the hall to her room.

Elizabeth stared after her until she disappeared behind her door before returning her gaze back to the living room. She stared at Kerra. Her sleeves were a damped and darker blue than the rest of her shirt, rolled up to her forearms. Flecks of dried paint were splattered across Kerra's face and jeans and hidden in the strands of her dark hair. She stared back at Elizabeth, a thousand different emotions flaring in the lakes of her eyes.

"How are you doing?" Kerra finally spoke, but Elizabeth kept the intensity of her stare on her, studying her. She took in every part of the effort Kerra had put in to make sure that she didn't have to see any more of the hate that had so vehemently shaken her to her core. She examined the dirt stains that had been ground deeply into Kerra's jeans as she scrubbed on her knees at every letter painted across her car. Elizabeth noted her wrinkled and cracked knuckles from several hours of being worked and dipped into a bucket of soapy water. She let her eyes dance along every colorful stain of dry paint caked across her arms and fingertips. They had taken Kerra's tool—her paint, her art—and used it against her. And she had unrelentingly worked to undo it to protect Elizabeth. Every frustration Elizabeth had felt for Kerra melted away at the sight of her.

"Love?" Kerra took a step toward her as her eyes watered over with emotion.

Elizabeth moved forward the rest of the way, closing the distance between them. She cupped Kerra's face in her hands and felt a lump build in her throat as she caught her eyes.

"We got as much of it off as we could, but—"

Elizabeth tightened her hands around her face and brought her lips down to entwine with hers. "Thank you," she whispered against her mouth.

Kerra stared down at her, a hint of surprise in her features. She had obviously been unsure of what Elizabeth's reaction might be. Even Elizabeth herself hadn't anticipated being so overcome with affection.

Elizabeth brought her down into another kiss. A breathless, passionate kiss that caused Kerra's hands to roam up her body.

"Wow, I guess we should excuse ourselves," Krissy noted, grabbing Azul's arm and guiding him awkwardly to her bedroom door.

Elizabeth barely acknowledged them as she pulled Kerra in deeper to her mouth.

"Wait, wait, wait." Kerra brought her hands up to clasp her fingers around Elizabeth's wrists as she pulled away from her.

Elizabeth stared at her in surprise. "Wait?"

"Ah, shit. Yeah. We have to go somewhere." Kerra winced in pain as she stepped away from Elizabeth, turning down the offer of impromptu sex.

"We have to go somewhere that can't wait?" Elizabeth stepped forward, closing the distance that Kerra had put between them and pressing her chest forward.

Kerra's stare zeroed in on Elizabeth's pressed-forward bosom, and indecision flashed in her eyes as she licked her lips. "Umm..."

"No. It can't wait," Lola interrupted with a huff at Kerra. She stomped across the room to shove her. "Were you really about to blow me off to have sex with your girlfriend? Hello, she's yours, you can have sex with her anytime you want. This—" Lola held up a bag she had strapped across her chest "—we only get once a year. Tradition trumps your libido, you ass."

Kerra rubbed at her shoulder where Lola shoved her. "I wasn't going to blow it off," she shouted defensively.

"Liar. I saw you thinking about it," Lola challenged, meeting her eyes.

Kerra dropped her gaze to the ground and rubbed at the back of her neck. "All right, okay. I thought about it. But I'm not now. So can we go?"

Lola narrowed her gaze and grumbled something under her breath. Her eyes traveled to Elizabeth who jumped to attention. She wasn't sure what was happening, but she was painfully aware that she was a hindrance to whatever it was. "So, I guess you're coming with us then?" Lola asked.

"Umm..." Elizabeth looked to Kerra for help.

"Yes, Lola. She's coming," Kerra answered for her.

"I am?" Elizabeth felt like an intruder already, and she wasn't even sure what they were going to do.

"Yeah, I guess you are. Which is fine, just don't kill the vibe, okay?" Lola stared at her, waiting for a response.

"Yeah, okay," Elizabeth agreed.

Lola nodded at her agreement and moved to the door. She led them outside and to her car.

Elizabeth gasped as her car came into sight. Another wave of love for Kerra hit her as she saw the work they'd put into getting all the paint off it. You could hardly tell anything had ever even been there. She'd have to file an insurance claim for a paint job, for sure, but she wouldn't have to drive around town with the atrocities decorating her doors until the claim came through, and for that she was grateful.

She reached out for Kerra's hand and held it, squeezing it as she smiled up at her.

"Here, Lola. You drive." Kerra tossed Lola the keys and slipped into the backseat with Elizabeth, not wanting to let go of her hand any more than Elizabeth did. Elizabeth didn't even protest that Lola was a worse driver than she was. She was just so grateful to keep holding on to Kerra.

Lola smiled as she slid into the driver's seat. She'd probably been itching for her opportunity to drive recklessly in the mountains, where speed limits were mere suggestions.

Elizabeth rested her head on Kerra's shoulder, nearly melting into her when she brought her arm to wrap around her waist and pull her in closer. "I love you." Elizabeth whispered the words into her side as she wrapped herself in Kerra's arms.

She rested her chin on Elizabeth's head and let her nestle against her for the duration of the drive. Elizabeth wasn't sure how long they had been driving, but when Lola brought the car to a stop, they were parked in a desolate lot with no light or cars or any forms of other life around. Elizabeth could hardly make out the outline of her hand in front of her face.

"Where are we?" She vocalized her concern as she lifted her head away from Kerra's comforting shoulder.

"We are at the Christening Court," Lola announced, bouncing out of the car and flashing a tiny flashlight around the area.

Kerra climbed out after her and then reached back to help Elizabeth out of the car.

"The what?" Elizabeth asked flatly as she took Kerra's hand and struggled out of the backseat. She still couldn't see anything, but Lola walked confidently across the darkness with the tiny beam of light in her hands to guide her.

"The Christening Court," Kerra answered her. "It's where I gave Lola all of her firsts."

"*All* of her firsts?" Elizabeth stared up at Kerra questioningly even though she couldn't see it in the darkness.

"*Most* of her firsts," Kerra corrected, hearing the insinuation in Elizabeth's tone.

Elizabeth jumped as the buzzing sound of the streetlight above her head echoed through the quiet. The dim light flicked on and moderately lit up the area. She saw Lola standing triumphantly next to it, obviously having been the one to turn it on.

Elizabeth let her eyes adjust to the light before taking in the newly lit area where she stood. She let out a laugh as she finally understood the title that the little spot had been given. "A basketball court." She laughed harder. "How very nineties of you guys."

"Hey, don't shade the Christening Court. It's a privilege to be here," Lola reprimanded.

Elizabeth held up her hands in apology. "You're right. I'm sorry." She bit back another laugh.

Kerra wrapped an arm around her shoulders and guided her to an old bench and table at the edge of the court. Lola happily skipped over to them.

"Time?" Lola commanded.

"Seven fifty-eight," Kerra called back.

"Okay, a few more minutes." Lola reached into her bag and pulled out two cans of beer. She placed them both on the table and stared apologetically at Elizabeth. "Sorry, I forgot to bring you one."

Elizabeth shrugged in indifference, still not sure what they were doing at the Christening Court. "That's okay," she assured Lola as she watched her pull more things out of the bag.

Lola placed an open pack of cigarettes and a lighter onto the table, and Elizabeth stared at it skeptically. "You smoke?" Elizabeth had never seen Lola smoke before, and she found it odd that she'd have the habit without it being obvious.

Lola shook her head. "No. But Kerra did. And she gave me my first cigarette, along with my first beer, right here on these very benches when I was fourteen."

Elizabeth turned her gaze onto Kerra. "You smoked?"

Kerra grimaced. "Kind of. Not as a habit or anything but occasionally, yeah, I did."

"Gross." Elizabeth frowned, and Kerra shrugged in response.

Elizabeth turned her gaze back to Lola and the magical bag as she retrieved more items. She pulled out a tin container and set it on the table.

"And what is that?" Elizabeth inquired as she stared down at the tiny container.

"This, my dear Lizzie, happens to be one of my favorite firsts of the Christening Court." Lola popped open the top of the tin to reveal what appeared to be more thinly wrapped cigarettes at first glance, but as Elizabeth inspected further she gasped in surprise.

"Lola, no. Kerra can't..." Elizabeth whirled on Kerra. "Kerra, you can't."

Kerra held up her hands and placed them on Elizabeth's shoulders. "Okay, okay. Calm down. It's weed not heroin. It's not that serious."

"Kerra," Elizabeth protested.

Kerra held up a hand to silence her. "But, I know it's a slippery slope, and I'm not going to risk it. I'm just an observer. I'm not smoking it," she promised.

"We are," Lola interjected, passing Elizabeth one of the tightly packed joints.

"We are?" Elizabeth looked down at the rolled paper between her fingertips.

"Yep," Lola assured her.

Elizabeth shook her head. "No. I-I'm not... No."

Lola put a hand on her hip and sighed in annoyance. "Oh, Lizzie. Come on. Can you for once show me even a glimmer of hope that you might be cool enough to date my sister?"

Elizabeth frowned at her. "So what? This is some after-school special on peer pressure now?"

Lola continued to stare at her. A pleading pooled into the brown irises as they bored into her. Elizabeth let out a sigh. "All right, fine. So, we drink the beer, we smoke the cigarettes, we get high and then what?"

"And then we bask in the tradition," Lola informed her with a dramatic sweep of her hands.

Elizabeth rolled her eyes. "Fine."

"Great."

Elizabeth put the joint to her lips.

"Wait, wait. Not yet," Lola cautioned. "Time?" She called out to Kerra.

"Two minutes after," Kerra answered.

"Okay, it's time." Lola reached into the bag again and pulled out a tiny set of speakers hooked into an iPod. She took a deep breath and handed Elizabeth a lighter before gripping a beer can in her hand. Kerra grabbed the other and readied herself to open it. Elizabeth took her cue and held the lighter closer to the end of the joint hanging from her lips.

"Okay." Lola let out a squeal before pressing the play button on her iPod. "Let the tradition continue," she shouted as she raised her can into the air in time to the sounds of the music.

Kerra mimicked her movements and popped the tab on her can before bringing it to her lips. Elizabeth buried the urge to roll her eyes again as she lit the end of her joint and inhaled. She was immediately assaulted by an uncontrollable coughing fit as the smoke entered her lungs. Kerra and Lola erupted in giggles.

"Wow. That does not feel good at all," Elizabeth spit out through coughs, triggering more laughter.

"Give it a minute," Kerra assured her as she patted at her back and placed her beer in her hands.

Elizabeth took a sip from it, and the intermingling taste of smoke and beer in her mouth just made her feel sick to her stomach. "Oh God, being cool sucks," she pouted, handing the joint to Lola and giving Kerra her beer back.

She sat quietly on the bench and listened to the music flow while she caught her breath. A lyric that mentioned "proceeding recklessly after eight" sounded in her ears, and she suddenly understood Lola's preoccupation with their timetable. Every aspect of their tradition seemed to be planned out perfectly and set in stone. She looked up to see the glow in Kerra's eyes as she sipped her beer, smiling and nodding along to the music, a happiness radiating from her that matched the level of Lola's excitement as she pulled in a drag from the joint in her hand.

Elizabeth reached for it. Lola smiled at her in surprise as she tried it again, this time holding in the smoke a tiny bit longer before she fell into another coughing spell. She smiled along with the laughter this time, suddenly understanding the importance of the tradition. She was being christened. It was no small gesture for them to include her in the ceremony. She was appreciative of them for that, and if she had to cough up a lung to prove it, that's what she would do.

They sat for nearly an hour, listening to the same song on a loop and smoking and drinking until Elizabeth was green with nausea. She had begun to sway without realizing it, and Kerra reached out to still her against her side. "All right, I think you are sufficiently baked, love. We should probably head out, Lola."

Lola nodded slowly, her own path to "sufficiently baked" very clearly approaching. She put out the cigarette in her hand and made a wavy path to the car.

"Uh, I think maybe I should drive," Kerra insisted, holding out her hand for the keys.

"If you insist," Lola shrugged, sliding into the backseat beside Elizabeth. Elizabeth let out a series of giggles for reasons she wasn't entirely sure of, but something about the sight of Lola in the backseat with her suddenly seemed hilarious. Lola glanced at her skeptically before she joined her laughter, falling into her own fit of giggles.

Kerra turned to stare at them and rolled her eyes, letting out a sigh. "Do you guys even know what you're laughing at?"

Elizabeth and Lola turned to stare at each other, both shaking their head in unison, which made them spiral into more laughter.

"All right then. Glad we got that cleared up." Kerra smiled at them before turning her gaze to the front of the car and starting it up.

She pulled out of the Christening Court, and Elizabeth waved good-bye to the empty old court. "Good-bye C.C.," she whispered at the rearview window.

Lola's eyes went wide, and she gasped in awe. "That's what we should call it, Kerra." Lola scooted forward in her seat to speak directly into Kerra's ear, even though she was already shouting. "Kerra, that's what we should call it. C.C."

Kerra covered her ear with her hand and leaned away from her. "Yeah. Got it, Lola. Can you sit back in your seat, please?" Kerra kept her eyes on the road and used one hand to reach back and shoo Lola back into her seat.

"Boo, you're no fun," Lola insisted as she sank back into her seat.

Elizabeth giggled more at the exchange, and Lola turned her gaze on her. "Lizzie. See, Lizzie is fun," Lola insisted at Kerra.

Elizabeth's mouth dropped open in shock, and she caught Kerra's eyes in the rearview mirror. "Baby, I'm fun," she exclaimed, proud of herself for earning the title.

"So I heard," Kerra assured her with a smile.

The edges of Elizabeth's high were beginning to dull, but she was enjoying the fuzz while it lasted.

"Hey, wait. Stop." Lola sat up straight in her seat and commanded that Kerra pull over.

Kerra ignored her, continuing to drive forward.

"No, Kerra, really. Stop," Lola insisted.

"Why?" Kerra asked flatly without slowing down.

"Because that's Joe's truck." Lola pointed out of the window at a big truck parked along the road.

Kerra stayed silent without slowing the speed of the car. She finally answered Lola. "So what?"

"So what?" Lola sat up in outrage. "So what? So what, we know that asshole is responsible for the hours we spent scrubbing this car. We should go give him a taste of his own medicine."

Kerra pulled the car to the side of the road, and Elizabeth sat up in her seat.

"No. No, we shouldn't." Elizabeth felt all of her high float away from her as she caught sight of Kerra's expression in the mirror.

Kerra met her eyes as she drummed her fingers along the wheel of the car, a flash of indecision in her eyes before she pulled the car away from the curve and turned to head back in the opposite direction.

"Kerra. No." Elizabeth unbuckled her seat belt, her fingers trembling as she went.

Lola placed her arm across Elizabeth. "Lizzie, we have to do this. Just chill. "

Kerra avoided her eyes in the mirror as she continued to speed toward the parked truck.

Elizabeth's heart thudded loudly in her chest as she racked her brain for ways to convince Kerra out of her current decision.

Kerra stopped the car in front of the truck, and Elizabeth pleaded with her. "Kerra, think. You promised me," she shouted after her as she climbed out of the car, but Kerra had already blocked her out.

She attempted to climb out of the car after her, but Lola pushed her back into her seat. She shut the door on Elizabeth to slow her down, then followed behind Kerra to back her up.

Kerra rummaged around in the trunk before pulling out a heavy black tire iron. She barreled toward the truck with it, Lola on her heels.

Elizabeth watched in horror as Kerra smashed through the truck's front window, the sound of shattering glass echoing through her ears.

"Kerra, stop it," she shouted helplessly after her, but she knew that it was pointless. Kerra had made her decision, and all the shouting in the world wasn't going to slow her down. She smashed out another window, and Lola cursed in glee as she stabbed at the tires with something glinting in her hands.

Lola stepped back to admire her handiwork as the car sunk down a level and sagged unevenly. "Paint that, Joe," she muttered triumphantly.

"Hey!" someone shouted at them, and Elizabeth's heart jumped into her throat. Kerra and Lola shared a glance before they bolted for the car.

Kerra shoved Elizabeth inside before sliding in behind the wheel. She tore off down the road, back to the safety of the cabin.

Kerra parked in front of the cabin. She climbed out, sharing a high five with Lola.

"That was awesome." A smile was plastered on Lola's face as she stumbled out of the car.

Elizabeth slowly and quietly made her way out of the car, nearly seething with rage.

Kerra caught her expression, and the smile she wore turned down at the corners.

"Hey, I know you're pissed, but..." Kerra reached out for her, and Elizabeth held up a hand to her.

"Don't," she warned, pulling out of her grasp.

"Come on, Lizzie. The guy had it coming."

Elizabeth nodded, not trusting herself to speak. She walked past Kerra and started toward the cabin, no longer wanting to look at her.

"Lizzie."

Elizabeth ignored her and kept moving forward. She went into the cabin and made her way to their room with Kerra on her heels.

"Lizzie," Kerra called again as she settled into the bed and tucked herself under the covers.

"Lizzie, come on. So, you're just not going to talk to me now?"

Elizabeth closed her eyes in answer.

"Lizzie, what was I supposed to do? The guy messed with us. I just messed with him back. What's the big deal?"

Elizabeth grunted, opening her eyes. "The big deal is I asked you not to." She sat up to face Kerra. "I don't want to live my life quid pro quo. I don't want to set up my future living by some primitive, 'eye for an eye' quota, Kerra, and it's becoming really clear to me that you do."

Kerra took a step back, her lips setting into a straight line. "So, I'm primitive now because I don't want to be a doormat?"

Elizabeth crossed her arms over her chest. "You know what, Kerra. Yeah. Yeah, tonight, you were really freaking primitive, and it's not an attractive quality on you."

Kerra sucked at her teeth before turning to leave the room.

"Where are you going?" Elizabeth called after her.

"The primate needs a walk," Kerra called back without turning to look at her.

Lola stood in the doorway of her room, watching them. She flashed Elizabeth an apologetic look and followed after Kerra.

Elizabeth listened in anger as she heard the cabin door close behind them. Tears of anger and frustration clouded her vision. She didn't even see Krissy as she approached.

"Well, that was quite the showdown." Krissy placed herself next to Elizabeth and squeezed her shoulders.

Elizabeth shook her head. "It's like it's the two of them against the world and nobody else is allowed on their team."

Krissy squeezed her tighter, letting her bawl into her side. "I know, honey. Trust me, I know."

CHAPTER THIRTY-ONE

Elizabeth sat with her knees pulled into her chest on her bed. Krissy had long since left her to go to sleep, but Elizabeth couldn't rest knowing she and Kerra were still fighting. She heard the sounds of Kerra and Lola approaching outside and shuffled herself to the sofa in the living room to be the first thing Kerra saw when she reentered the cabin.

Elizabeth wiped at her eyes, hoping they weren't as puffy and gaudy as she knew they were. She held her breath as the door creaked open. Lola tiptoed across the threshold until she caught sight of Elizabeth.

"Oh, you're awake," Lola uttered in surprise. She threw a look over her shoulder at Kerra who followed behind her.

Kerra caught Elizabeth's eyes and held them, both of them staring at one another but neither venturing to speak.

"I-I'm going to go to bed," Lola stammered, feeling the tension that vibrated through the air like a bolt of lightning. She gently hugged Kerra and then reached out to give Elizabeth's knee a squeeze before scrambling down the hallway to the safety of her room.

Elizabeth smiled after her but never took her gaze off Kerra. She let out a sigh when she heard Lola's door close her into the room.

Kerra let out a long, slow breath as she moved to her and then took a seat on the couch with her. "Lizzie, we need to talk."

Elizabeth sucked in a breath, bringing her legs in closer to herself. No conversation that started with *we need to talk* ended well, but Kerra was right. They did need to talk. They had issues that seemed to keep resurfacing, differences that always seemed to stand in their way.

"I know," Elizabeth agreed quietly. She slid backwards across the couch to put distance between them but then changed her mind. She moved closer to Kerra, stretching her legs out and taking her hand.

Kerra clutched it to her chest before letting it go to run a hand anxiously through her hair.

"Lizzie, this person... This passive, thoughtful person that you want me to be... That's never going to be me." Kerra's eyes gleamed as they pierced into her. "I'm never going to be able to watch someone hurt you or anyone that I love and not retaliate. It's who I am, Lizzie. And I can't change it. Not even for you." Kerra's voice cracked as she finished, her eyes watching Elizabeth for any trace of what she was thinking. "Lizzie, if you can't handle that..." She didn't finish the thought. She didn't have to. Elizabeth already knew. If she couldn't handle this particular facet of Kerra's intensity, then she wouldn't get any of it.

She was silent for a long moment as she let herself envision the rest of her life. She was still there. Kerra was still there, in every scenario. Kerra was her constant, even if she was an erratic one.

Elizabeth reached out and placed her hand to Kerra's cheek, running her thumb over the soft skin as she stared into the captivating pools of blue that had so effortlessly swept her off her feet time and time again.

"I can handle it," she whispered, letting her fingers make a path down to Kerra's chin.

Kerra gripped her wrist, closing her eyes for a moment at her touch. "Are you sure?"

Elizabeth nodded, watching Kerra's shoulders relax in relief. "I love you. I think that you are reckless and impulsive, and sometimes you just outright scare me, but..." She lifted herself off the couch to swing her leg over Kerra, straddling her and pinning her to the cushions. She wanted there to be no space between them. She pressed her body into Kerra's, relishing her touch as her arms wrapped around her.

"But?" Kerra inquired, a half smile making its way to her face.

Elizabeth kissed her softly, tenderly taking her lips into her mouth. A surge of warmth ran through her as she savored the familiar flavor of Kerra. "But I love you," she finally answered breathlessly against her lips. "It's that simple and that complicated all at once. Whatever your faults are, I'll take them tenfold over not having your love." Elizabeth's heart swelled and ached in her chest with her words. She let out a flutter of laughter at herself. She literally loved this woman so much that it hurt.

Kerra tightened her grip around Elizabeth, pulling her in closer. "You have my love. Always." Kerra lifted her head to capture her in another kiss, her hands traveling up Elizabeth's body to cup her face.

Elizabeth let herself be devoured in the warm embrace of Kerra's tongue. She could feel herself slipping past the threshold of love and affection to white-hot lust.

"We should go to our room," Elizabeth suggested, her chest rising and falling with the rapid pace of her heartbeat. She climbed off Kerra, gripping onto her hand to pull her along behind her. She was suddenly burning with need for her.

"Wait." Kerra stopped her, pulling against her hand to still her movements.

Elizabeth stuck her hip out and placed the hand that wasn't holding Kerra's to her hip. "Wait? Again? I don't know that my ego can handle you turning me down again."

Kerra shook her head, her cheeks flaring red as she did. Elizabeth nearly gasped at the sight. She'd never seen Kerra blush before. "No, I'm not turning you down. I just, umm... I have something... I, uh...shit." Kerra's cheeks flared a crimson color that spread across her face.

Elizabeth kneeled down to rest in front of her as she sat rigid against the sofa. "Kerra?" Elizabeth generally loved the few and far between moments when she caught a glimpse of a flustered Kerra, but she had long surpassed flustered. She was nearly exploding with nerves, and Elizabeth's concern had peaked. "You okay?" She met her eyes, and Kerra let out a long, low breath before nodding her head.

"Yeah, I'm fine." She let go of Elizabeth's hand and set it in her lap, probably hoping to hide the fact that her fingers were trembling, but she was unsuccessful. Elizabeth eyed her shaking hands skeptically before Kerra demanded her gaze once more. "I need you to stand up," Kerra insisted, gesturing for her to stop kneeling and climb to her feet.

"Okay." Elizabeth let the word out slowly, suspiciously making her way to her feet. "All right, I'm standing. Now what?"

Kerra licked at her lips as she drew in a slow breath. "Okay. I, uh...I got you something. It's not official or anything, and I plan to get you a new one when we get back to the city, but..." Kerra let out a sigh and climbed to her feet, meeting Elizabeth at eye level as she reached into her pocket and handed her a tiny velvet box. "I love you, Lizzie. And I told you months ago that there was no going back for me. So, if you don't want to give up on this and you want to stick this out with me, I want to be with you forever."

"I-I love you too," Elizabeth stammered, clutching the box in her hands, afraid to open it. It was too soon for the box to contain what she thought... No. What she *hoped* was inside.

"Open it." Kerra nodded at her, waiting anxiously as she stared down at the box with her.

Elizabeth turned the box in her palm, her fingers trembling as violently as Kerra's. Her heart thudded loud enough that she was sure Kerra could hear. Hell, she was sure the entire mountain could hear her heart rapidly running rampant in her chest. She steadied her hands long enough to lift open the top of the box and gasped as the shiny, glinting silver ring stared back at her.

"Oh my God. Kerra." Elizabeth put an unsteady hand to her mouth as it gaped open at the sight of the ring. She tore her eyes away from the glint of the silver to meet Kerra's eyes, but they were no longer in front of her. She dropped her gaze to find Kerra kneeling in front of her, her cheeks still scarlet with nerves as she asked the question that Elizabeth already knew the answer to.

"Lizzie, will you marry me?"

CHAPTER THIRTY-TWO

Elizabeth sighed contentedly as she let her head fall back against Kerra's shoulder. She hadn't been able to tear her eyes off her new most prized possession. Even as she and Kerra had an intimate celebration of their engaged status, she was sure to keep her left hand within her line of sight, her lips curving against Kerra with every glint of the silver. It was probably the most distracted sex she'd ever had, but she couldn't help herself. She was completely mesmerized.

"You know that's not the actual ring, right, love? I'm getting you a new one when we get home." Kerra wrapped her arms around her, pulling her in closer across the bed as she continued to examine her ring.

Elizabeth shook her head as she wiggled her ring finger. "No, this is the ring. It's on, and I'm never taking it off."

Kerra let out a grunt as she nestled a kiss into the crook of her neck. "It's just a band, love. Engagement rings have stones."

Elizabeth shook her head again. "This is the ring you proposed with. This is the ring I will wear," she insisted. She lifted her unringed hand to stroke Kerra's cheek before placing a quick kiss to it.

Kerra let out a laugh. "Lizzie."

"Hey, if you wanted me to wear a different ring, you should have waited to propose."

Kerra let out a sigh of defeat as she trailed her fingers down Elizabeth's arm to rest at her hand. She clutched it and brought it to her lips to deliver a kiss to the ring. "I couldn't wait."

Elizabeth's heart fluttered at the sight of Kerra's lips on her newly decorated finger. "And I can't take this ring off."

Kerra nodded, smiling at her as she did. "All right, compromise. How do you feel about two rings?"

Elizabeth giggled, grinning in approval. "I could get behind that."

"Yeah, I thought you might like that one." Kerra placed a kiss on her shoulder, trailing her fingers down her back and sending a shiver through Elizabeth's spine.

Elizabeth turned in Kerra's lap to face her, propping herself up to position Kerra between her legs.

Kerra moved her grip to rest at Elizabeth's bottom as she leaned forward to bury her head in her chest.

Elizabeth leaned back out of reach with a giggle. "Kerra, I'm not trying to have sex with you. I just want to look at you."

Kerra arched an eyebrow at her. "Are you sure? Because you're naked, and you just trapped me between your legs. If you don't have sex with me, that kind of makes you a tease."

Elizabeth rolled her eyes and wrapped her arms around Kerra's neck. "You should probably get used to it because I'm officially your tease, forever."

Kerra narrowed her gaze on her. "I don't know if I like the sound of that."

Elizabeth nodded at her. "You do."

"I do?"

"Yep."

Kerra let out a dramatic sigh. "Not even my wife yet and you're already telling me what to do."

Elizabeth giggled. "Yep, and next I'm going to decorate your couch with throw pillows and change your wardrobe," she teased.

"You are?"

"No. I like your couch...and your clothes."

Kerra leaned in, taking Elizabeth's breath away with an intimate kiss that slowly made its way from her mouth to her neck to her shoulder.

"Kerra." Elizabeth tried to regather her thoughts, but Kerra's hands, placed at the crevice of her bottom as her kisses traveled down her body, provided her with enormous distraction. "Kerra, stop." She was unconvincing in her protest, but Kerra ceased her kisses to meet her eyes.

"I, umm..." She cleared her throat to collect herself. She hadn't actually expected Kerra to stop, but now that she had, she figured she should have some follow-up. "I want to tell Krissy and Lola."

"Oh, okay." Kerra smiled and delivered more kisses to her body before meeting her eyes. "Oh, you mean right now?"

"Well, I think if we don't do it now, we'll end up in bed all day." Elizabeth tapped at the hand gripping her butt.

"Right, good point." She let out a groan as she rolled Elizabeth off her, climbing out of the bed to look for clothes. Elizabeth watched her in regret. The gorgeous, half-dressed woman in front of her made her wish she had let Kerra continue her assault of kisses to her body.

"Are you going to get dressed?" Kerra stopped putting on her clothes to gaze at her. "Because if you keep watching me like that with no clothes on, we're never getting out of this room."

Elizabeth debated tempting her further before letting out a sigh and climbing off the bed to slip on her clothes. She really wanted to tell Krissy and Lola before they all had to leave and go back to the city.

"Oh, hey. Umm, Lola might already know." Kerra buttoned up the last button on her shirt.

"What?" Elizabeth's shoulders drooped in disappointment. She had been so looking forward to watching their initial reactions.

"Yeah, well, she knew I had the ring and..." Kerra shrugged in apology at Elizabeth's frown.

"Does Krissy know?"

Kerra shook her head. "No... I mean, I didn't tell her, but you know Krissy."

Elizabeth nodded, knowing exactly what she meant. Krissy probably knew before Kerra did.

Elizabeth let out a breath as she fell back onto the edge of the bed. "So everyone already knows."

"I doubt Azul knows."

Elizabeth gave a small shrug. "I guess."

Kerra took a seat next to her and reached out for her hand. "How about we go to lunch with Krissy, Azul, and Lola, and I propose again. We can make a big, huge scene about it and make everyone around us uncomfortable."

Elizabeth lit up, a wide smile gracing her face. "I really want to do that," she confessed.

"Consider it done." Kerra placed a kiss to the back of her hand and helped her to her feet.

Kerra led her down the hallway to Lola's room. She knocked softly on the door and was immediately met face-to-face with a wide-eyed and grinning Lola. Lola's eyes immediately shot to Elizabeth's hand, and she let out a squeal, throwing her arms around her.

Elizabeth could feel the air being crushed out of her. "Ow, Lola."

Lola loosened her grip. "Sorry," she apologized as she released her and then set a hug on Kerra.

Elizabeth smiled at them and slowly left them hugging in the doorway while Lola fired off a series of inappropriate questions. She made her way to Krissy's door and knocked softly against the wood. Krissy swung the door open. With one look, her eyes watered over, and she scooped Elizabeth into her arms. Elizabeth's chest tightened. She felt so overwhelmingly happy in Krissy's arms and in her family, but there was a brick of guilt sitting heavily in her stomach.

Krissy let go of her and caught her expression. "What's wrong, honey?"

"My mom," Elizabeth confessed, knowing it was useless to lie to Krissy. She would see right through her anyway. "I should tell my mom."

"So tell her." Krissy gave her arms a gentle squeeze.

"I don't want to let her ruin it."

"So don't. She doesn't have to accept it, but if you need to tell her, you tell her for yourself, and then you leave it up to her what she does with it."

Elizabeth nodded and ventured a look down the hallway to find Kerra and Lola still hugging and laughing together. "Tell Kerra I went outside for a minute."

Krissy nodded in understanding.

She slipped out of the cabin and paced along the porch, palming her phone in her hand. She needed to make the call; of that much she was sure. Even if her mother spewed her venom it wouldn't weigh nearly as heavily as the guilt on her conscience of getting married without telling her mother it was coming.

She stepped off the stairs of the porch, hoping the fresh air would help steady her resolve. She wandered aimlessly in a circle around her car as she slowly punched in her mother's number and held her breath as she brought the phone to her ear.

She waited, silently and breathlessly, as the phone rang in her ears, each ring seeming louder than the previous one.

"Hi, you've reached Cynthia Bridges. At the current time I am not available to answer your call, but please leave a message and I will gladly get back to you. Have a nice day and God bless."

Elizabeth let out a sigh at her mother's answering machine. She debated hanging up, knowing that her mother was screening her calls, but she had things she wanted to say, and a message was just as good as talking to her. *Probably better,* she thought with a scoff.

Beep. The soft beep of the answering machine, signaling for her to record, sounded in her ear, and she stumbled over herself for words.

"Umm, hey, Mom. I uh, I was just calling to...to say hi, I guess, and that...that I'm getting married." She blinked back the tears collecting in her vision. "I know that you don't approve, and it seems like I hate you, but I don't. You're my mom. And I love you. And I miss you...and...I guess, I just wanted you to know." She kicked at the mossy grass beneath her feet. "So...that's all that I wanted to say. I love you, Mom."

She hung up the phone, and an unexpected relief washed through her. She hadn't spoken to her mother, but she still felt like a weight had been taken from her shoulders. She let out a breath and started back toward the cabin, having fulfilled her daughterly urge, but she stopped in her tracks at the sound of the approaching car behind her.

Her heart fluttered in excitement as she turned on her heels, expecting to see Azul pulling into the driveway. *Finally, someone that doesn't already know.* But the thought was crushed as her eyes fell on the patrol car that parked just a little too close to where she was standing.

"Elizabeth Bridges?" The grizzled-looking sheriff stepped out of his car with more authority than should probably have been granted to him.

"Yes." Elizabeth rolled her eyes at him. "Sheriff Willis, we've met before."

He ignored her, barreling in on her and shoving her onto the hood of his patrol car.

"Ow, what the hell?" Elizabeth winced as he pinned her wrists aggressively behind her back, the pressure of his fingers unconcerned with gentleness.

"You're under arrest for destruction of private property."

Elizabeth let out a tense scoff. "Destruction of private...are you kidding me?"

"No, ma'am. I am not. And this is not a joking matter."

"Interesting, because when you came here after my property had been vandalized you weren't as adamant about kicking in doors and making arrests."

Her comment earned her another hard shove into the cold steel of the hood.

"Hey, what the hell is going on?"

Elizabeth turned her glance to Kerra as she stepped off the porch, a scowl on her face as she approached them. Elizabeth tried to sit up and meet Kerra's eyes before she made the situation worse, but the sheriff shoved her back down, ignoring Kerra's presence and readying himself to secure cuffs on Elizabeth's wrists.

He fastened the cuffs and pulled her up, then shoved her toward the back of the patrol car.

"Hey, whoa, Lizzie. What's going on?" Kerra's voice was more adamant as she got closer to the sheriff.

"She's being arrested. Your friend destroyed a truck last night."

Kerra rolled her eyes at the word "friend."

He shoved her again, and Kerra held up her hands to stop him. "Hey, buddy, chill. She didn't do it. It was me. I did it."

"You did it?" The sheriff looked at her, indecision on his face as his eyes bounced back and forth between Kerra and Elizabeth. He scowled as he reluctantly released Elizabeth from the cuffs and pushed Kerra against the car.

Elizabeth rubbed at her wrists and watched as he arrested Kerra, aggressively slapping the metal restraints to her wrists. Kerra gave him nothing, huffing in annoyance as if his arrest were only a minor inconvenience to her day.

Elizabeth could see him growing agitated with her lack of respect for his authority.

"Kerra." Elizabeth's voice was sharp, reprimanding her for being a smug pain in the ass.

"It's okay, Lizzie. Just tell Krissy to meet us at the station." Kerra consoled her, jerking out of the sheriff's grasp to place a peck on her lips. "Just go get Krissy."

The sheriff yanked her backwards, his face scarlet with fury. "No, don't you move," he warned Elizabeth, the agitation written in his features. "You dykes think that you can do anything you want."

Elizabeth's eyes widened, and her mouth dropped to her chest at his blatant display of bigotry. She was suddenly uneasy about watching him drive away with her future wife handcuffed and helpless in the backseat of his patrol car.

Kerra let out a choice reply that only escalated the situation, earning her a sharp blow to the side of her face from the sheriff's elbow. Kerra spat out a mouthful of blood, and he drew back again to give her another solid hit to her side.

"Hey," Elizabeth cried out and lunged forward on instinct. The impulse to intervene propelled her forward before she could give it a second thought.

The sheriff whipped out his holstered weapon, aiming it at her chin to stop her in her tracks. Elizabeth held up her hands, freezing in place as her stomach sank, making her head swim in nausea.

"Hey, hey. It's all good. I did it. We're cool. Let's just go." Kerra's voice lost its antagonistic edge. The sight of a gun on Elizabeth was clearly enough for her to lose her arrogant exterior.

The words seemed to calm him down as he lowered his gun to his side and shoved Kerra forward again.

"Kerra. No." Elizabeth shook her head. She didn't move. She couldn't move anything but her shaking head. She had no plan and no way to stop the scene in front of her, but everything in her urged her not to let Kerra get into the car with the sheriff on a power trip.

"It's okay, Lizzie," Kerra promised her as she let him propel her forward. He shoved her into the back of the police car with little regard for her comfort or safety.

☆☆☆

Elizabeth watched after them, a sinking pit filling her belly as the lights of the patrol car faded into the distance. Her nerves coiled inside her, and she nearly jumped out of her skin as a hand grazed her shoulder.

"Whoa, Lizzie, chill out. Where's Kerra?" Lola stared at her expectantly, obviously having expected her to be with her.

"Sh-she, umm..." A sob stuck in Elizabeth's throat as she tried to pull herself together. "We have to get Krissy. Kerra's been arrested."

Lola frowned at her. "Without me?"

Elizabeth let loose the sob that had choked her, and Lola moved in to wrap her arms around her in stiff reassurance. "It's all right, Lizzie. We get arrested a lot in this family. We'll go get her."

Elizabeth nodded, her shoulders still heaving with emotion. She wanted to tell Lola what had happened, to explain to her the hate-filled look in the eyes of the man who had just stolen Kerra away, but she couldn't find the words. And what good would it do to worry her?

"I'm going to go get Krissy, okay." Lola let her go, hurrying off into the cabin. She emerged mere moments later with Krissy on her heels and keys in her hand.

Elizabeth silently slipped into the backseat of her car, trying her best to think positively.

She didn't know what she expected to happen, but all the possibilities worried her. Hate drove people to dangerous places, and Kerra wasn't one to play the passive card. The sheriff had already threatened them with his authority once; what would he do when left alone with Kerra and her obsessive need to be out and loud? She suddenly wished Kerra weren't so proud to be gay, and she hated herself for the thought. She hated the world for making her think it.

"Lizzie, breathe, honey. She'll be fine."

Elizabeth glanced up, catching Krissy's eyes in the rearview mirror. She hadn't realized she was holding her breath until she inhaled a fresh lungful of air. She nodded a thanks to Krissy and caught the flash of concern in her eyes as well. Krissy knew these people. She'd probably lived with their adverse opinions of her background her entire life. The weight of the situation wasn't lost on her.

Elizabeth felt the pressure in her chest lighten. It somehow felt better to be in the worried trenches with a partner.

Lola seemed to be the only one taking the situation lightly. She sat in the passenger seat still pouting that her sister had left her behind as she embarked on her next great run-in with the law. Elizabeth envied her naïveté. Her long blonde hair and bright green eyes were like a free pass for her to melt into any crowd she desired. She was only met with aversion and hostility when she chose to be, and it was a privilege that she seemed completely unaware of.

Elizabeth was pulled from her thoughts as Krissy pulled the car to a stop in front of a rustic-looking building that seemed to match the décor of all the others in the mountains. She shot out of the car, hardly waiting for Krissy to turn off the ignition as she flew towards the building with no plan as to how she planned to get to Kerra or even get information as to how she was doing or where she was.

Krissy followed behind her, hustling to match her pace. She caught her elbow in the doorway of the building, pulling her backwards to stop her in her tracks. "First, you need to tell me what happened. I can't get her out of here until I have some details." Krissy placed her hands delicately on Elizabeth's shoulders, meeting her eyes as she waited for her to speak.

Elizabeth fought through the sobs that seemed to forever plague her as she recounted the events of the night and the morning, leaving no detail buried.

"He pulled a gun on you?"

Elizabeth nodded her head, trying her best not to acknowledge the flash of worry that flickered in Krissy's eyes.

"Okay, just stay calm. I can fix this. Trust me, okay."

Elizabeth nodded again. She did trust Krissy, and she knew she had nearly inexplicable powers when it came to finagling her children out of trouble. Elizabeth took a deep breath, letting her trust in Krissy prevail and keep her momentarily sane.

Krissy gave her shoulder a reassuring squeeze as she led her back to the doors and inside the building, waving along a still-irritated Lola as she went. Elizabeth followed behind her until they were met by two officers frowning at them from behind a large desk.

"I'm here for Kerra Silvers," Krissy announced confidently.

"Hmm...Silvers. I don't believe we have a Silvers today, ma'am. Try back tomorrow," one of the surly, frowning officers taunted her, giving the other officer a playful punch as he giggled at his own arrogance.

Elizabeth felt the pit in her belly sink lower. These guys weren't to be taken lightly. Hateful and arrogant were a malicious combination.

Krissy seemed less rattled. In fact, Elizabeth could have sworn she almost saw her grin with satisfaction. She leaned into the counter, her shoulders high with confidence as she whispered at the two men. "Interesting, because the perimeter cameras I had installed around my cabin say that your chief officer arrested her at gunpoint. My lawyer says that she should be here unharmed, unbooked, and ready to leave this place in about five minutes."

Krissy stared daggers at the two men, her confidence seemingly unshakable as they frowned back at her. The officer closest to her stood up to meet her eye level, attempting to use his size as intimidation, but Krissy stood firm.

"Just give us a minute, all right?" The still-sitting officer rose to his feet. He pulled his counterpart along behind him as they disappeared into an office.

Krissy stared after them, a fierce expression on her face. Elizabeth watched her in awe, impressed by the bluff and the ferocity in which she sold it.

The two men returned, and Krissy beamed at them smugly.

"Sheriff Willis will be right out with your thing," one of the officers grunted at her.

Elizabeth couldn't help her wince at the word "thing," as if Kerra wasn't human in their eyes. She forced herself not to think about what they might have done to her if Krissy wasn't so brilliant at thinking on her toes.

Elizabeth paced the floor as she clenched and unclenched her fists, waiting impatiently for her fiancée. Lola watched her in obvious amusement, still not feeling the gravity of it all.

"She said five minutes, right?" Elizabeth asked no one in particular.

"Lizzie, it's been like twenty seconds." Lola grinned at her, tickled by her paranoia.

"Right, of course." Elizabeth twirled at her braids, feeling nervous jitters ransack her body. Her knees nearly collapsed out from underneath her when she saw Kerra emerge from the back of the police station. Sheriff Willis held her roughly under her arms, half dragging her across the room. She looked nearly purple with the intermingling colors of dirt and bruises that covered her face and arms. Her eyes seemed barely open as he shoved her forward into Krissy's arms.

"Take her," he said gruffly as he took an indifferent seat next to the desk.

"What the hell did you do to her?" Elizabeth cried out, moving delicately toward Kerra. She was too afraid to touch her. She'd never seen Kerra so fragile looking. She seemed barely alive.

"Nothing. She fell, and I helped her up. Now, get her out of here." He barely acknowledged her as he said the words, doing his best to showcase how unfazed he was with her condition.

Kerra grumbled something, but the words were muffled in her swollen mouth.

"We need to get to a hospital." Krissy gently maneuvered herself under Kerra's arm, and Lola lost her indifferent bravado as she rushed to get Kerra's other side. Her earlier amusement had dissipated, and she finally understood just how real things had gotten.

Elizabeth followed behind them as they slowly guided Kerra out and to the car. Kerra groaned in pain with every movement, and the sound sent Elizabeth's heart sinking. She crouched on the floor of the backseat of the car, propping herself uncomfortably against the door as they stretched Kerra across the soft leather backseat.

"It's okay. Remember, you told me it's okay." Elizabeth placed her fingertips to Kerra's hair, gently stroking the wild mass on top of her head.

Kerra struggled to say something, but the words were lost.

"Shh, it's okay," Elizabeth repeated.

Kerra groaned as the car jerked forward, Krissy nearly gunning the tiny vehicle down the road. Elizabeth was lost in terror. The only thing she could manage to do was repeat the words over and over again. She was a broken record of "It's okay" as she did her best to keep Kerra steady and awake. She was terrified that if she let her close her eyes, she'd never see them open again.

She flushed with relief when Krissy pulled up in front of the emergency room, laying into the high-pitched horn of Elizabeth's car as doctors and nurses hurried out to them. Krissy took the lead, rushing to tell them what happened as they carefully extricated her from the car and onto a gurney. Elizabeth followed after them, nearly tripping over herself as she attempted to make her way out of the car.

"We'll take it from here." A woman in a nurse's uniform held up a hand to stop her as she approached the emergency entrance of the hospital.

"I'm her family," Krissy announced, taking a step forward to push past the nurse.

"I'm sorry, I can't let you back." The nurse straightened, her voice lowering with authority. "Check in with the front desk, and we'll let you know everything as soon as we know something." She turned on her heels to make her way through the double doors, leaving no room for argument.

Elizabeth turned her focus to Krissy, at a loss for what to do. She felt utterly helpless.

"Okay, let's check in." Krissy grabbed a hold of Lola, carrying her forward as she came apart at the seams. Elizabeth avoided looking at her, afraid that if she watched Lola unravel it wouldn't be long before she crumbled behind her. She needed to keep her head. The second she let herself go down that path, she'd never come back from it. *Everything will be fine* was the only option.

Elizabeth followed behind Krissy into the fluorescent-lit waiting room. She focused on her breathing, tuning out everything around her as she took a seat in an empty chair across from Krissy and Lola.

Krissy busied herself filling out a clipboard full of paperwork as Lola buried her face in her knees, not tasking herself with burden of being strong for anyone.

Elizabeth could feel her heartbeat as it pulsed through her temples on the verge of beating out of her chest. She sucked in a deep breath, forcing herself to calm. She let it out, listening as her heart slowed with the exhale. The calm was short-lived as Krissy rose from her seat to deliver her filled-out paperwork to a perky blonde nurse at a desk. The two of them whispered back and forth, and Elizabeth's stomach somersaulted.

"What did she say?" Elizabeth asked hurriedly as Krissy returned to her seat.

"Nothing new. I was just making sure that they knew about Kerra's addiction before they performed any surgery."

Elizabeth bit down on her lip, her mind whirring as a brand new set of worries settled onto her shoulders. She hadn't even considered the effect that any of this would have on Kerra's sobriety. What if they pumped her full of something that she couldn't stop taking?

"Stop, Lizzie." Krissy gave her a sharp glare.

"What?" Elizabeth met her gaze with confusion.

"Whatever you're thinking right now. Just stop, okay. There's no use tying yourself into knots over something that doesn't matter yet."

Elizabeth nodded. Krissy was right, but it didn't stop the frenzied panic her thoughts had swirled into. She shut her eyes, trying to block them out, and popped them back open as her pocket vibrated at her.

She fumbled her phone out of her pocket, letting out an irritated sigh as she saw her mother's number flash across the screen. She punched the ignore button. She had enough problems without adding her mother to the mix.

"Who is it?" Krissy had watched her angry tussle with her phone.

"My mother," Elizabeth grunted.

"You should call her back."

Elizabeth stared at her crossly, not on board with the suggestion in the least.

"Lizzie, you need something else to focus on. We could be here for

319

a while. A distraction will keep you from driving yourself crazy," Krissy insisted.

Elizabeth frowned down at her phone. Krissy was right; she was on the precipice of going to a wild place worrying about the possibilities with Kerra. But would calling her mother really provide her with a distraction that put her somewhere that wasn't Crazy Land?

She let out a long breath, resolving to heed Krissy's advice. Her mother couldn't possibly put her in a worse place than she already was.

"I'll be right back," she told Krissy, excusing herself from the waiting room. Whatever discussion she was about to have she didn't want to have it in front of an audience.

She parked herself outside the hospital, settling herself onto a wooden bench and shivering against the cool breeze that brushed her skin. She clutched her phone, mentally preparing herself before she hit the return-call button. She waited, listening as the phone rang once, and then twice before her mother's voice echoed across the line.

"Beth?"

She wanted to respond, but her throat closed around any and all words.

"Beth, honey. Are you there?"

She let out a choked sound that was almost some variation of the word yes.

"Beth." Her mother paused, letting the silence hang in the air between them. "I don't know what I'm supposed to say to you. What am I supposed to tell people? You're painting me into a corner here, Elizabeth, and I don't know what you want from me."

"Tell people that I'm happy." She found her voice surprisingly steady as the words came out. "Say that you're happy I found someone that makes me happy. That's all I want, Mom."

She waited in silence for her mother to respond, an endless stretch of quiet as they waited for words that expressed what each of them was feeling.

"I can't do that, Beth." It was less antagonistic than Elizabeth had expected. There was almost the tone of regret in her mother's voice.

"I know, Mom." She let out a sigh, as she accepted that she and her mother may never be on good terms again. "I hope that one day you will."

"Beth, I just..." Both of them knew there was no ending to the thought that would make either of them feel better.

"Bye, Mom." Ending the call, she swiped at the tears that had relentlessly burned at her eyes as she held them back. She pulled her legs into herself, letting her body heave with the weight of her sobs. She let herself cry until she felt like she didn't have anything left. The few people who passed her going into the hospital cast concerned glances in her direction, but none stopped to interrupt her. She was thankful for that. She hadn't realized how badly she'd needed to just let everything out, but she felt better when she stood up, dusting at her pants as she left the bench.

She knew she probably looked like a train wreck as she headed back to Krissy and Lola, but neither of them mentioned it as she settled back into her seat. Krissy shot her a warming smile and even Lola gave her a supportive nod.

She settled back into her chair, nodding in and out of consciousness as she waited for news on Kerra. Her dreams of cream-colored dresses and soft piano melodies as she walked down the aisle were a sharp contrast to her waking thoughts of Kerra fighting for life in a hospital bed. She tried her best to keep the dark thoughts from seeping into her dreams, but it wasn't long before she found herself at the altar facing Kerra's tombstone.

She jumped from her seat, snapping out of the dream with tears streaming down her cheeks as Lola's hands squeezed her shoulders.

"Hey calm down, Lizzie. You were just having a nightmare."

Elizabeth leaned forward, placing her hands on her knees as she caught her breath. "A nightmare?" She still felt hazy and delirious.

"Yeah." Lola waited for her to recollect, helping her to straighten herself as she came to. "Kerra's out of surgery. She's in the ICU, but they say she's stable. We can go see her. She'll probably be under for another hour or so, but we can wait in the room with her." Lola spoke in soft, hushed tones that Elizabeth had never considered she'd be capable of.

Elizabeth nodded her head, her chest tightening as the words settled onto her. Kerra was stable. Stable, stable, stable. The world rattled around in her head until it lost all meaning. She followed behind Krissy and Lola as a woman in a white coat led them through double doors to a room at the end of the hallway.

Kerra lay unconscious on a tiny white bed with metal railings, hooked up to an infinite amount of machinery. It was such an unsettling sight. Kerra was always so fiercely indestructible it felt wrong to see her like this. Bruised and bandaged from head to toe, subject to the whims of nature.

"Kerra." Elizabeth whispered her name as she rushed to her side. She was out cold, and the call warranted no reaction, but Elizabeth reached for her hand anyway. "Kerra, I'm here."

Lola settled in beside her, placing long, pale fingers over hers. The two of them stood there, watching her and waiting as the minutes seemed to tick by slower and slower.

Krissy paced across the floor, her concrete demeanor beginning to show cracks. She stopped in her tracks as a pained moan escaped Kerra's lips.

Krissy rushed to her side, positioning herself opposite Elizabeth and Lola. "Ker-Bear?"

Kerra's eyes cracked open, sleepily taking a sweep of the room. She shifted in the bed as she attempted to move, letting out another moan as her face registered the pain of the attempt.

"Shh, don't try to move. You've got a lot of internal bruising and broken bones. Just stay still," Elizabeth soothed.

Kerra's lips twitched as she prepared to speak, and a pained groan escaped her.

"Sweetheart, your jaw was dislocated. They had to wire it shut. Try not to talk either." Krissy spoke softly, leaning in to gently stroke at Kerra's hair.

"Right, because you're usually such a chatterbox," Lola mocked, a grin a mile wide across her face. The emotional wreck from hours before seemed to have disappeared completely.

Kerra shot her a glare that conveyed more than words ever could.

"Ouch. I guess you don't need words to curse at me, though." Lola laughed, catching Kerra's glower.

Elizabeth chuckled, feeling lighter just touching Kerra.

Kerra shifted her gaze to her, her fingers slowly moving to entwine in Elizabeth's. Her eyes softened, and Elizabeth's heart melted at the sincerity in the crystal-blue pools that stared up at her. It was a silent gesture of affection but one that consumed her.

She placed a soft kiss to her cheek, taking extra care to move slowly and not rattle her. "I love you," Elizabeth whispered into her ear. Kerra gave her fingers a gentle squeeze, a wordless reminder that she loved her too.

Elizabeth looked to Lola who grinned beside her like a little girl on Christmas morning as she toyed with the gadgets on Kerra's bed. It brought a smile to her own lips as she watched her, her confidence in her sister's invincibility restored.

She shifted her line of sight to Krissy, who stroked Kerra's hair adoringly as she stared down at her, the epitome of a doting mother.

Elizabeth breathed a sigh of happy contentment. She stared down at her ring before taking another look around the room. She smiled as she took them in. They were her family, her perfect, indestructible family.

CHAPTER THIRTY-THREE

Elizabeth frowned at Kerra as she hunched over, panting as she lowered herself onto the bed. She winced in pain with the effort as she slowly settled into the mattress.

"If you let me help you, you won't—"

"Lizzie, I can get in and out of bed all on my own. I don't need help." Kerra cut her off, her breathing coming in sharp bursts as if she'd run a marathon.

Elizabeth rolled her eyes. "One week out of the hospital and you're Superwoman then, huh?"

"I'm always Superwoman, love." Kerra threw her a wink, and Elizabeth resisted the urge to smile. Even through the hissing lisp of her wired-shut mouth, Kerra managed to make her melt like a popsicle.

She crossed her arms over her chest in feigned indignation. "I'm not taking you to the hospital when you rip your stitches open again."

Kerra pushed her lips out in an exaggerated pout, forcing Elizabeth to reconsider.

She blew out a sigh, letting her folded arms fall to her sides. "Fine, I'd take you to the hospital, but I wouldn't be happy about it."

Kerra's lips turned up in an undeniably pleased grin. "Come lay with me?" She patted the spot next to her, beckoning for Elizabeth to join her on the bed.

"I can't, Kerra. Lola will be here any minute to switch out with me. I have to at least pretend like I'm still working at the coffee house."

Kerra's grin dimmed. "You know, you guys don't have to watch me all day."

Elizabeth took a seat on the bed to slip on her shoes. "You won't sit still, you won't take your pain meds, and you left the hospital against doctor's orders. You're the epitome of a patient that needs around-the-clock surveillance." She finished securing her second shoe and cast a glance over her shoulder. "Oh, no. Don't look at me like that."

Kerra's eyes focused in on her, a stare she was all too familiar with.

"Just lay with me for a minute," Kerra pleaded.

"I told Lola I'd meet her downstairs to help carry her stuff up." Even as she said the words, she knew she would lose this battle. Kerra was on a mission to get her way.

"So, she'll carry her own stuff," she insisted.

"And she'll be pissed about it."

"And she'll get over it."

Elizabeth met her gaze with a pointed one of her own.

"Please?" Kerra pouted. "I hurt."

Elizabeth rolled her eyes as she settled into Kerra's arms. It seemed the only moments she admitted to pain were the ones in which she wanted something.

She let Kerra's arms encircle her, closing her eyes at the warmth that embraced her. She let out a breath, opening her eyes to stare up at Kerra who stared adoringly back at her.

"I spoil you, you know." Elizabeth wagged a finger at her.

"Oh, I know," Kerra agreed.

She placed a soft kiss against her lips, and Elizabeth relished the contact. She wanted the taste of her on her tongue, to get lost in the full embrace of Kerra's mouth against hers, but she had another five weeks before Kerra would even be able to open her mouth wide enough for a yawn.

"What's wrong, love?"

Elizabeth bit down on her lip. She hadn't realized how she'd let her disappointment seep into her own features.

"Nothing."

Kerra gave her a flat stare, reminding her that she knew her better than that.

"I'm just... I'm so pissed with those cops," she started.

Kerra let out a sigh. "I thought we weren't going to let them take up anymore of our time."

Elizabeth nodded her head. "I know, I know, but I can't just... I feel powerless and hateful and—"

Kerra shushed her, sensing how worked up she was getting. "Hey, hey, hey. You're not powerless, and their time will come. But you and me..." She pressed her forehead against Elizabeth's. "We've got everything. We win."

Elizabeth smiled, lacing her fingers through Kerra's as the words settled over her. "We do win," she agreed, feeling peace wash through her.

Kerra pulled her in closer, wincing in pain from the effort. "All right, so finish telling me about our wedding."

Elizabeth wanted to comment on her pain, tell her once more that it was safe to take her medications, but the inclination to talk more about the wedding was too strong to ignore. She'd tell her to take her meds later. "Okay," she agreed. "I forgot to tell you last night that I think it's best if we both wear dresses."

Kerra glowered at her.

"Kidding," she admitted through chuckles. She stopped her giggling, her face taking on a serious expression. "But Lola's wearing a dress...with lots of tulle."

Kerra's eyes widened with intrigue. "Oh, my fiancée has horns."

"I think Lola can get anyone to whip out their pitchfork."

Kerra nodded. "Fair enough." She laughed.

Elizabeth swiped at a stray piece of dark hair settling onto Kerra's cheek. "I like peach and white for our colors. What do you think?"

"Sounds good," she agreed.

"Or purple and grey."

"That works too."

Elizabeth frowned. "Oh, well, you're super helpful."

"Hey, I just want to marry you. The rest is details." Kerra shrugged.

Elizabeth couldn't help herself as she lit up at the comment. "Always so smooth."

Kerra gave her a smug grin as she placed a kiss to the top of her head.

Elizabeth let out a disappointed sigh as an angry knock at the door interrupted all wedding talk. She climbed out of the bed to make her way to the door, dragging her feet as she went.

She opened the door, and a visibly pissed-off Lola, her arms overloaded with items, stormed past her to dump her things onto the sofa. "I thought you were going to help me with all of this," Lola grunted.

"Sorry, I was on my way down."

Lola narrowed her gaze on her. "No, you weren't."

Elizabeth shrugged in indifference. "No, I wasn't," she agreed.

Lola blew out an exasperated breath. "Whatever. How is she?"

"Good. She's Kerra, so—"

"She's not doing anything she's supposed to?" Lola finished for her.

"Basically," Elizabeth confirmed, making her way back to Kerra's room. Lola followed behind her, lingering in the door as she waited for them to say good-bye.

"I'm headed out. Do me a favor and stay in bed for Lola, yeah?" Elizabeth leaned over the bed, brushing back wild, untamed locks of Kerra's hair from her forehead.

"I'd rather stay in bed for you," Kerra whispered, suggestively wiggling her eyebrows.

"Ew, I definitely didn't need to hear that." Lola frowned at the two of them from the doorway.

"Okay, before you two start the bickering match, I'm going to work." Elizabeth placed a kiss to Kerra's cheek. "I love you."

"I love you too." Kerra reached out for her and gave her hand a soft squeeze.

"God, enough already. You'll be gone for a few hours tops. Just go," Lola grumbled.

Elizabeth rolled her eyes as Kerra fired off a choice comment back. She placed a quick kiss to Kerra's fingers before excusing herself from their feud. She let herself venture a look back before she left the room and watched as Lola animatedly responded to all of Kerra's remarks.

She chuckled at their antics as she closed the door of the apartment behind herself, catching a glimpse of her ring as she keyed the lock. She twirled it around her finger, basking in how its weight made her feel lighter. She smiled as she made her way down the stairs to her car, an indescribable joy swelling in her chest as she settled in behind the wheel.

Her life was perfect. She was happy.

"Happy." She said the word out loud, the notion of happiness having been so unfamiliar to her for so long that it seemed strange to settle into it so easily. The smile that she wore seemed a permanent fixture to her face. She started the car and brought her ring to her lips before wrapping her fingers around the steering wheel, laughing at nothing as she pulled out of the parking lot. The giddiness of pure euphoria seemed to envelop her, squeezing against her and wrapping her tight in its grasp. She was finally happy, and she'd never let anything steal her joy again.

Author's Note

Thanks so much for reading *Finding Lizzie*. I really hope you enjoyed the book, but you might be left with some questions. You may be asking why Kerra doesn't take any action against the sheriff who beats her so badly she winds up in intensive care. After all, she can take it up with a lawyer, or speak to the ACLU—can't she?

Unfortunately, it's not that easy. What happens to Kerra happens all of the time. In America, we've literally seen authorities murder people right before our eyes and get away with it. And those are just the ones we talk about. There are countless others who face injustice but don't take action, or make noise, because they feel there's no safe place for them to do so. There will be countless more as hostilities rise in America. And in rural areas in places like Alabama or Louisiana or Virginia where all of your county officials and state legislature is designed to make you feel unsafe and intimidate you, most people just try to move on. They thank their lucky stars they didn't get killed and continue with their lives, especially if, like Kerra, they committed a crime that landed them in police custody in the first place.

Maybe Lizzie and Kerra's story will inspire you to think about the changes we can all make, so that one day soon, Kerra and those like her will feel safe to speak out and stand up for their rights.

ABOUT THE AUTHOR

Karma is a wine-enthusiast, feminist, activist, humanitarian, vegetarian and just all around liberal and that often seeps into her writing. She loves any place with white, white sand and blue, blue water and an endless supply of mo-suffix drinks (Moscato, Mojito, etc.).

Twitter: http://www.twitter.com/Karma_Kingsley

Smashwords author page:

https://www.smashwords.com/profile/view/karmakingsley

Email me: KarmaKingsley@gmail.com

NINESTAR PRESS, LLC

www.ninestarpress.com

CPSIA information can be obtained
at www.ICGtesting.com
Printed in the USA
LVOW08s0019200317
527767LV00001B/94/P

9 781945 952166